Jones, Kaylie, 1960-
As soon as it rains

APR 8 1986

DATE			

AS SOON AS IT RAINS

As Soon as It Rains

Kaylie Jones

Doubleday & Company, Inc., Garden City, New York
1986

Copyright © 1986 by Kaylie Jones
ALL RIGHTS RESERVED
PRINTED IN THE UNITED STATES OF AMERICA
FIRST EDITION

Library of Congress Cataloging in Publication Data

Jones, Kaylie, 1960–
    As soon as it rains.

    I. Title.
PS3560.O497A8 1986   813'.54
ISBN 0-385-19474-9
Library of Congress Catalog Card Number 85-4496

Grateful acknowledgment is made to the following for permission to reprint their copyrighted material:

"Message in a Bottle," words and music by "Sting" © 1979 by Virgin Music (Publishers) Ltd. All rights controlled by Virgin Music Inc. Used by permission.

"California" by Joni Mitchell © 1971 by Joni Mitchell Publishing Corp. Used by permission. All rights reserved.

"Planet Claire" by F. Schneider, K. Strickland, Henry Mancini © 1980 by Boofant Tunes, Inc. and Northridge Music Co. (Peter Gunn theme © 1958 by Northridge Music Co.) All rights reserved. Used by permission.

To the memory of my dear friend
CAROL ANDREA BAKER

This book was possible without Tim Tomlinson, however it might not have been this short.

I would also like to thank the following for their indispensable advice and encouragement: John W. Paton, Edmund White, Carolyn Blakemore, David Weild IV, Cecile Bazelon, Holly Woodward, Janet Grillo, Willie Morris, Gloria and Jamie Jones, and Poets & Writers, Inc.

PAIN has an element of blank;
It cannot recollect
When it began, or if there were
A day when it was not.

From "Life" (19)
—E. Dickinson

AS SOON AS IT RAINS

Prologue

Inside the house they were whispering. Chloe could hear them through the screen door. She made the rocking chair creak on the planks, pushing hard with her sneakers to bury their words. She was rocking near the edge of the porch steps that led to the garden. The lilac bushes were as big as trees. Sometimes the lilacs came early, sometimes late, but May and June were the months when they filled the house and garden with their seductive perfume. Chloe thought they were beautiful but sad, because for all their power they did not last.

A mist was settling over the sloping lawn. The sun was gone but across the miles of field, above the horizon of trees the sky was still bleeding. She was chilly in just a T-shirt, but she did not want to go inside.

In the living room someone walked toward the bar. The floor creaked under heavy feet. She heard ice drop into a glass.

"Anyone else?" It was Jack.

The ice tinkled as the bourbon (she knew Jack only drank bourbon) poured from the bottle. She pictured him stirring the ice with a thick finger. Then his pouty lips stooping toward the glass. She knew all these sounds too well.

"But I don't understand," her mother was saying, she was slurring a little. "Just the other day . . . How long ago was it, Jack? That we took him in? It was just the other day . . . he made love to me so wonderfully . . . I didn't know. How could I have known?"

Chloe covered her ears with her palms and rocked. Even when she closed her eyes she could see her mother lying on the couch, the back of one hand covering her forehead and eyes while the other searched for the half-gallon of scotch on the floor. Her mother hadn't moved from the couch since last night.

Until dusk yesterday, some of it had still made sense. There had been a pattern to each day. For her it was school, then visit the hospital, then sleep. Then school . . . Now there was nowhere to go anymore. Nothing to do but sit and wait for nothing and listen to the grown-ups in the living room whispering out their plans.

Until last night it had been a little like a movie. This could happen to other people. It had been fun in a way to walk around carrying this immense tragedy. In school she got away with skipping classes and getting stoned because her teachers felt sorry for her. It had been fun for a while. But now she wanted it to stop.

"Cut this bullshit." She pushed the planks away. "Just cut this bullshit." She was saying this to her mother and to the rest of them, but not loud enough for them to hear.

It's all an act they're putting on for each other, she thought. Because nobody knows what the fuck else to do. She'd been swearing lately. It was becoming a habit.

She rocked back and forth at the edge of the steps. She and the chair could easily topple over. She wondered how long it would take and if it would be painful.

She breathed in the damp air till her lungs ached. The smell of lilacs filled her head and she tried again to remember every word of her last conversation with her father. She wanted to capture and hold that memory but it was like chasing someone who ran faster than she did. And then of course there was the image of him that kept forcing itself into her mind like the unwanted guests in the living room.

She had left school at lunchtime to go see him. He hadn't been expecting her and she'd watched him trying to eat his lunch from the other side of the glass wall. It was like being at a public aquarium. He was trying to force the fork between his uninterested lips, his whole grey torso bent over the sliding table they'd placed in front of him. He looked so old and frail. A hundred years old.

She knocked lightly on the door and he lay back on the pillows exhausted. She put on a face and went in. Groping for something to say, she told him about the lilacs.

"They've never been so huge, Daddy," she said.

"It's a good thing we cut them back last year," he said as though waking from a dream. He was coming from miles away and was forcing himself to concentrate.

"I'll bring you some tomorrow," she said. He shook his head slowly.

"No, don't. I can't stand to see flowers cut."

Her face fell apart. She felt it crumble like a wall. Tears fell from her eyes and soaked her cheeks. He patted the bed by his thigh. She went to him and perched herself on the edge, afraid to touch him.

"I'm sorry, sweetie," he said. "Don't be sad, please. You'll see how everything is going to be fine for you. Gee, I wish I could go to college with you. Everybody'll be smart and you'll have to work hard."

"I'll call you every day." He said nothing.

"When are you going to come home?" She wiped the tears away with the back of her hand.

He looked at her guiltily. "I don't know."

She knew he would not lie. So many times he'd hurt her worse because he would not lie and keep bad things away from her. "This is how bad the world is," he would say, "but don't worry, I'm here to protect you."

"Nobody knows," he said, turning a palm toward the ceiling. "Soon, I hope," he added after a while. "I have to finish my damn play."

The screen door yawned behind her. She heard ice clinking in a glass. She hoped it was Jack.

"My it's fine out here at dusk. Reminds me of the old South." It was Jack. She was relieved because she didn't mind talking to him.

And poor Jack. After that last time she'd talked with her father she'd come downstairs from Cardiac Care to find Jack sitting in the hospital lobby in one of the dirty orange armchairs, writing. Writing furiously in a notebook.

"What are you doing?" she'd asked him.

He started. Looked up with eyes full of tears.

"I'm writing down what he told me. For the end of the play."
She must have looked horrible because Jack added quickly, "Just
in case. He doesn't want his play to be left unfinished." Jack ran a
hand across his cheeks and mouth. "You understand, don't you,
honey? It's just in case. Because all he cares about right now is
finishing the damn play."

AND ME! Chloe thought. He cares about what's going to happen to me.

"He's going to finish it," she said defensively, as though someone
were going to try to convince her otherwise. Jack was writing
again.

"Of course he's going to finish it," he said without looking up.

She stopped rocking and waited to see if Jack would come out
and close the screen door, or go back inside. He was shuffling his
feet.

"Aren't you cold, honey?" he said. "It's getting chilly out here."
She shook her head.

After a while he came over and sat at the edge of the steps, by
her feet. His bourbon was in the hand that was dangling from his
knee. He had a cigarette in the other.

"How're you doing?" he said tentatively, as though he felt he
were prying beyond his right. Chloe looked at him. His skin was
tanned and weatherworn; in the pale light the lines at the corners
of his mouth looked like cracks in baked clay.

"I'm okay. What's going to happen now?" She looked at the
drooping purple lilacs that were fading into the green, turning
slowly into black.

"Well, I'm going to have to finish the play for him," Jack said.
"Exactly as he wanted it. Or as close as I can get, anyhow. I think
he wanted me to do it. He trusted me."

It had been Jack who'd driven Chloe and her mother through
the New England college tour. He'd taken her to her interviews
and explained to administrators that he was her godfather, her
own father being too sick to brave the cold weather. It wasn't just
that her father was sick. Even back then he'd been trying to finish
the play. But Chloe knew that if there hadn't been Jack to take his
place, her father would have gone. Sick or not.

"Now I've got to deal with the problem of explaining what happened to the audience. How am I going to do that?" Jack said.

Chloe had been thinking about herself. And about her brother who still had a year of high school to finish. Somebody had to tell them how to go on now. Last night Eric had locked himself up in the attic, their father's study, and hadn't come down since. She had spent an hour knocking and calling at the door. "Eric, PLEASE! It's me."

"Leave me alone!" he'd shouted finally. "Go away."

Nobody noticed his absence.

"Jack, can I have a cigarette, please?"

He handed her his crumpled pack of Marlboros without giving it a thought. He didn't even look at her. She put the cigarette in her mouth, Jack flicked the lighter, and put the pack and the lighter back in the front pocket of his shirt.

On the first drag she inhaled deeply to show him she knew how to smoke. He was staring off at the garden, thinking about something else. The play, she imagined.

"You could dim the lights and have one character step forward and explain that the playwright was forced to stop at this point," she suggested. But who was she to tell him?

In the living room her mother started talking again.

"Let me go take a walk on the beach. I think it would be better. I'll take a walk on the beach and then swim out into the ocean and . . ."

"Goddamn her. Goddamn her. What about us? What about Eric? He still has a year of school left. Why can't she act like a grown-up?" She made the chair rock again; bending over her lap she clasped her arms around her shins. Jack put the glass down and touched the back of her neck and shoulders.

"She doesn't give a shit. She just doesn't give a shit."

"Now that's not true," Jack said mildly. "You know how much she loved him. How much they loved each other. You know all that Chloe. It's terrible for her. You have to be the strong one now, you . . . Oh, shit, honey, I don't know."

She stared out at the dark. It was an abyss that began at the edge of the steps. She always went to her father in times of distress. She wanted to cry on Jack, have him take her on his lap and hold her

like a child. She hadn't been able to cry since she told her father
about the lilacs. She held her breath and pushed from her guts. No
tears came. It seemed futile, she was not alive inside. She wanted
so much to cry and mourn the way normal people do.

PART I

I

They never used to proof her when she was fifteen. At first she went to the Beechouse Bar with the Sandpiper Players, the theater group her father had persuaded her to try out for when her family had first moved to town. One night after a dress rehearsal she did not wash off her stage makeup because with her face painted she easily passed for twenty-five. She called her father and told him that rehearsal would be running very late, and went out drinking with the rest of the cast.

It was a long time before the bartenders found out she was still in high school, but by then they knew her so well they did not have the heart to ask her for ID.

After her first year of college she was still not eighteen. On the big day, which came in the middle of August, she walked into the Beechouse and went straight to the bartender.

"Give me one free, Mike," she said, "I'm finally eighteen." She thought he would either get angry or laugh. He mixed her a Mount Gay and pineapple juice, slid it to her, and said, winking, "You think you've been fooling us all these years?"

And since then drinking in bars had not been the same.

Another school year had passed since then, and she came home to find that nothing had changed. From her table in the corner she watched the smoky, crowded dance floor, the faces glowing from their first sun. Maybe it's just early in the season, she thought. She recognized the faces from high school and from past summers.

There were always a few new faces but there was nothing new about them.

She considered driving back to her dark house and picking up the phone. She could call Joe Gillan in Connecticut and make up with him. She knew he would accept her apology because now that it was summer and she was home, he was afraid he would not be able to control her as easily. She could invite him down for the weekend. Then she would not be alone. But she hated giving in to him so soon, after she'd made the decision to try to be less dependent.

Liz came up from behind and handed her a fresh Lite beer.

"GodDAMN if that little surfer boy doesn't have the cutest, tightest little ass I've ever seen," Liz said.

In the old days Chloe and Liz liked to pretend they were boys talking about girls. Now, especially because Chloe was depressed, the game seemed stupid to her. Liz sensed this and it made her uncomfortable. Every time Chloe came home from college, they had less to talk about.

"Uh, I'm going over there to talk to him for a while," Liz said. Chloe smiled to show she didn't mind.

She thought of Joe in his father's very big, very clean Headmaster's house. The prep school campus would be dead quiet tonight. Joe would be saying his prayers. Or maybe he would already be sleeping.

She watched with detached curiosity while a drunk she'd known for years tried to move in on a blonde girl in a bright red dress who couldn't have been more than sixteen. The girl was tottering in her heels, laughing at everything the drunk said. She must be flattered, Chloe thought, that he's paying attention to her. Chloe did not think the girl would leave with him. She did not look like the daring type. But who knew? Two years ago it would have been her. She might have left with him. Before that, older men left her alone. In the neighborhood they knew her father and did not want trouble with him.

She wondered what Joe would think of that.

Across the dance floor she noticed a lifeguard named Steve watching ass. She tried to look away but it was too late, he'd seen her looking at him. He zigzagged through the dancers toward her table.

Last summer Steve had saved her life, and he never let it be forgotten.

The day had been dry and windy and the blue flag for caution flapped above the lifeguard stand. The waves rolled in white and crashed on the sand. Far out there were surfers in wetsuits catching the swells before they turned to foam. Liz had on a green sun visor which shaded her whole face except for the end of her nose. She watched the surfers and cheered while Chloe watched the lifeguard's bronze glittering back as he sat on the stand, watching the surfers through binoculars. Steve was built like Achilles and Hector, and was probably just as brutal.

She ran into the ocean and tried to swim out beyond the breakers. They crashed down on her one after the other, and she began to swallow water. The undertow tossed her like a sneaker in a washing machine. She thought, Shit, Joe's coming on the six o'clock ferry, nobody's going to be there to pick him up!

Steve's arm suddenly locked across her chest. Right then she loved him. He gracefully brought her back to the safety of the beach. She lay in the wet sand coughing and sobbing, and thanking him.

"God, why do I do things like that?" she said, looking up at him. She became terribly embarrassed and disliked him for having saved her.

He crouched by her shoulder. "Too bad you didn't pass out. I could've gave you mouth-to-mouth."

She was terrified of Steve because she knew he was the kind of guy who would think she fucked.

She watched him as he approached the table and pictured what he would be like in bed. He was probably the type who strategically slides a forearm under your neck so that he can watch his biceps flex while he's fucking you.

"When're you coming down to the beach for that body-surfing lesson?" he said with a self-confident Ultrabrite smile. He sat down in Liz's chair. "Back for the summer?"

Chloe nodded. "We get out of school pretty early."

"I been here all winter. Boring as hell," Steve said.

They sat in silence. He slid his elbows across the table toward hers; she sat back in her chair and crossed her arms. Liz came back with two fresh beers. She slammed them down in front of Chloe and foam spurted onto the plastic tablecloth.

"Guess who's standing over there by the fan?" Liz's lips retreated exposing gum, like a hissing cat. "Andy Fletcher that shithead. Standing there by himself not talking to anybody like he's just too cool."

Chloe absently wiped a spot of foam on her shirt and stared off across the dance floor in the direction of the fan. He was standing in front of it not looking at anything. His white shirt billowed like a sail each time the fan made its half-circle behind him.

"Please go make peace with him," Chloe said.

"No fucking way!"

"Come on."

"No way!" Liz turned to Steve and began asking him about the waves. "Good waves this summer or what?" she asked him. He seemed to enjoy the fact that his expertise on the subject was being solicited.

"Andy has a good heart," Chloe said. Liz shot her a *shut UP* look without turning her head away from Steve.

Liz was furious at Andy because he'd screwed her when she was drunk, in Chloe's driveway, in the backseat of his brother's Buick convertible. Chloe thought Liz was being ridiculous because she'd spent two months playing hard-to-get with him when it was obvious to everybody, including Andy, that Liz was dying to go to bed with him.

"Well *I*'m not mad at him," Chloe said, getting up. She took her beer with her. Last summer while Liz was playing hard-to-get, Chloe played intermediary, and in a distant way, she and Andy had become friends.

In high school they had never said a word to each other. Once he walked up to her at a black basketball party where none of the white kids were dancing and asked her to dance. Chloe was thrilled. They danced for a long time, but after that he never talked to her again. She was furious for a year and then forgot about it.

She would have loved to have gotten to know him in high school. She'd watched him and his brother Ben play basketball with complete awe and respect (she'd watched Andy more because he was better-looking, though Ben was also very good-looking).

Andy was fair and Ben dark. Andy's hair grew out in three shades, like an Abyssinian cat's. Dark at the roots, reddish in the middle, and gold at the tips. Each strand grew out straight as a silk thread. If Ben had had Andy's hair, he would have looked feminine because he did not have his brother's sturdy, bold lines.

But none of this mattered to them: Together they played basketball as one mechanism, Ben penetrating while Andy hit outside shots from anywhere on the court. It was beautiful to watch. They played as though they did not care what the crowd thought, as though they did not even notice there was a crowd. Andy almost never missed a shot. Ben was a year older and an inch shorter than Andy, and neither of the brothers was over six feet tall. This horrified their opponents and flustered coaches up and down Long Island, because on top of it their father was the coach of the East Whitman High School team.

As she walked over to him Chloe wondered why he was alone. Andy was rarely without a girl and never without his buddies. He was standing comfortably watching the dance floor, shifting his weight from one hip to the other. His square chin jutted out almost parallel to the floor. He seemed content to be wherever he was. She liked that because she was never quite content anywhere.

"Hey, Andy. You picked the right spot. It's hot as hell in here."

He took a step to the left to give her room in front of the fan. The cool air blew her hair back, which made her face feel naked.

"Yo, Clo. How was school this year?" He called her Clo because the *e*, often topped with two dots, made no sense to him at all.

"Two more years," she said, neither happily nor sadly.

"Yeah," Andy said slowly. "I fucked up. I transferred out this year. The hell with Louisiana, man."

"Where are you going now?" she asked, pleased that he was willing to talk, because often he wasn't. And she did not believe as most people did that Andy was vain; she thought he was just plain shy.

"I'm starting Sacred Heart in the fall. You know Sacred Heart?"

Chloe thought.

"It's in Connecticut. There's no reason you should know it; there's so many Sacred Hearts and Holy Trinities in this country you can't tell them apart. I'll be a freshman again next year because of the transfer eligibility rule. I have to sit out a year."

"But they accepted your credits?" He nodded. "So you're okay. You get a whole extra year to fuck off."

"Yeah. That's one way of looking at it. I can blow off classes for a whole year and still be a sophomore in a year, like everybody else. It'll be a pain in the ass watching games two years in a row." He smiled in a bewildered way.

YOU WATCHING games? she wanted to say. No, no, no. If he wants to tell you about it he'll tell you about it.

"How's Joe?" he asked her.

Her throat tightened. Last summer while Andy had been courting Liz, Chloe had asked him if her boyfriend from college could play ball with Andy and his friends when he came down to visit on the weekends. She explained that Joe played varsity on the Cromwell team. He bitched and moaned about not getting enough practice when he came down to visit her.

Andy had said, "What position does he play?"

And Chloe, feeling like a great expert, had gone through Joe's basketball history.

"Sure," Andy had said. Right under the nose of the local gang Andy took Joe under his wing. Her respect for Andy grew and kept growing.

"We kind of broke up," she said, swallowing. This wasn't actually true. If he could have, Joe would have locked her into a chastity belt and taken the key with him to Connecticut.

"Hey," she said, feeling guilty both for lying to Andy and for (lying to?) Joe, "that was so nice of you last summer, letting him play with you guys."

"He's good," Andy said, shrugging it off. "How'd the season go for him?"

"Okay," she said, thinking of the agonizing hours she'd spent listening to Joe rage on the coach, complain about his bad ankles and knees, and find excuses for his lousy outside shot. "The team did well but Joe didn't get to play as much as he wanted to."

"Want a beer?"

"Sure. Want a shot?"

They sat at the bar and he ordered two shots of Wild Turkey and two Becks. She liked the way Andy stared at her impassively with his soft-looking mouth hanging open a little as she downed her shot without making a face.

He said "Damn," drank his, and ordered two more.

She remembered she'd left Liz at the table. "Hang on a second," she said, and slapped his forearm.

She watched from the archway by the bar. Steve and Liz's noses were touching. They seemed deep in conversation. Steve kissed her neck, Liz smiled and looked up at the ceiling. Chloe went back to her seat at the bar.

"She's with that guy Steve," she told Andy.

"He's a jerkoff," Andy said. He tapped his shot glass against hers and watched her drink before he touched his own.

"I don't know why Liz is so pissed off at me," he said.

Chloe frowned at him. "Come on." He stared right into her eyes and she realized he wasn't pulling a line on her.

"She thinks you're a cold-hearted shithead, you know, for fucking her when she was blotto that night in my driveway."

"Shit," he shrugged, "I tried to call her a couple of times after that night. She kept hanging up on me. I told her to go in the house with you. She jumped me." He laughed and his eyes widened as though he couldn't believe it himself.

"You're too much. No one forces you to get it up." The Wild Turkey was beginning to heat up the lower part of her stomach.

"Tell me," he said shyly, trying to cover his front teeth with his upper lip, "if you were a guy and Liz jumped you, wouldn't you get it up?"

She tried to think quickly—What if I jumped you, would you get it up then?—No, no, that would be the Turkey speaking. Don't get carried away, she told herself.

"I asked Liz if you were any good," she said dead seriously, "but she couldn't remember."

She wondered if Andy knew how to really make love. She'd learned so much with Joe in a year and a half, about ways to feel and relax and enjoy a person. She was afraid Joe was her Once In A Lifetime love. What if they did for-good-forever break up?

"I don't imagine I was too good *that* night," Andy said.

"You know I haven't slept with anyone but Joe in such a long time. Sometimes I think I *should*. I—" She watched him, wondering, What the hell could he be thinking? She looked down at her empty shot glass. Andy put it in front of the bartender.

A chill grabbed the back of her neck. She thought for a second she could feel Joe standing behind her, watching Andy slowly beginning to lean toward her. You're going to smash it all to bits! she told herself, you're going to push this too far! She thought of Valentine's Day when Joe had sewn Hershey Kisses of all colors onto strings and made a curtain of them over her door. In her mind there was a big empty hole where everything between them had gone wrong.

"I just don't know what went wrong between us," she mumbled, shaking her head.

"What?"

They looked at each other. At that second Andy seemed a complete stranger.

"It seems so easy for you. You fuck and forget. I've become so afraid of waking up and feeling like scum the next day," she said.

They drank another shot. Andy stared at one spot straight in front of him, thinking hard about something.

"If I slept with you," he said slowly, "I wouldn't make you feel like scum the next day. I'd take you out. Anyways, how do you know guys don't feel like shit too, sometimes, the next day?"

He held up his hands and spread his fingers.

"Look, I got poison ivy all over the place. All over my legs, up my arms. When it clears up—"

"Don't hold your cock when you pee," she said, and started to laugh.

"You're damn straight!" he said. The big wide smile puffed out his cheeks and softened his jawline. He looked like a happy kid. Chloe watched his hand encircle the beer. His fingers were not long, but solid and strong-looking like his wrists. She wanted to pick up his hand and kiss it. Just because he was nice. If she were ever going to sleep with him, it would have to be on a night like this, with the booze as an excuse.

"God it must be so easy for you to get laid. I can't believe it. Just go out to a bar and act normal." Jokingly she said, "If you're going to lay me you're going to have to do it the proper way. Courting and everything. In daylight."

"Tomorrow's my day off," Andy said. "Good thing, too. Sweating like hell in the sun cutting hedges, with poison ivy," he shook his head. "You want to drive out to Montauk Point? Go to the beach or something?"

"I have to be at work at six. I'm waitressing."

"No problem. I'll get you back by six."

"Okay," she said.

And she was all excited, and nervous, and happy that she'd come out after all. She was worried about what to tell Liz. Whether to tell Liz at all. Montauk was twenty-five miles away and they would be alone. It wasn't like a date in a bar or at the movies where you're likely to know everybody. She'd wait.

She kissed him on the cheek. He turned his head and her kiss landed on his lips. He said he'd be by to get her at twelve. Do you know where I live? she was about to say.

She left him at the bar and went to find Liz to see if she needed a ride home.

II

Andy went into Ben's room, which was the garage, and flicked on the light. Ben's clothes were all over the floor, he was tangled up in sheets and blankets, and his Converse All-Stars were in bed with him. Andy didn't know where to start looking for the baggie of Jamaican weed. He picked up one of the All-Stars and flung it at Ben's feet.

"Yo, what the fuck you doing?" Ben sat up and rubbed the side of his head. Andy laughed.

"Sorry. I thought that was your feet. Listen bro, where's the pot? I need a couple of joints."

"Damn, what the hell time is it?" Ben shook his head, opened his eyes wide several times. He ran his fingers through his thin brown hair that was sticking out around his head like the crown on the Statue of Liberty.

"Fucking unbeLIEVable," he said, "you out of your fucking mind waking me up? I just got home!"

"Where's the pot?" Andy said patiently. Ben made a big production out of everything.

"Hell if *I* know," Ben said. He fought off the sheets and blankets and knelt on the bed, fully clothed. He pulled the baggie out of his back pocket and threw it at his brother. "Now, out of here!"

Andy took his time crossing the garage. Behind him Ben muttered, head back in the pillow, "What do you need that for so early in the morning?" which Andy was expecting because Ben liked to know every minor detail of Andy's life, and vice versa. Andy was feeling slightly proud of his date.

"It's not so early in the morning," he said, "it's noon. I'm driving out to Montauk with Clo Raymond and I'm taking the car."

"Yo," Ben said, sitting up. "Ain't she a little nuts?"

That was what they said. But they said a lot of things about Andy and Ben that weren't true, Andy thought. And so what if she was a little nuts? After what she'd been through, she wouldn't be normal if she wasn't a little nuts.

"She ain't nuts," Andy said.

"She fucks like a nut," Ben said.

"Now how the hell would you know that?" Andy said, getting angry now.

"I heard."

"Yeah from guys who wouldn't know where to stick their cocks if someone drew a picture for them on a blackboard."

"What about that tree she was going out with? The one played ball with us last summer? That over?" Ben asked.

Andy shrugged.

"Well I ain't saving *your* ass when he comes looking for you," Ben said.

"When he comes looking I'll tell him he's got the wrong bro." Andy turned and slid open the garage door. Before he'd passed beneath it Ben yelled, "Close that Goddamn door!" Just for that he left it open.

*　*　*

He took his time driving to Chloe's house. He was nervous about having to talk. He'd never spent a day with a girl, though he'd spent enough nights with girls. The serious girlfriend he'd had was the captain of the East Whitman cheerleaders, and Betsy was black. Though everybody knew they were seeing each other they'd had to keep it cool because there were a lot of bigots in town who didn't like salt-and-pepper relationships. So they only spent time alone together at night, in the back of his father's station wagon.

At night it was easier not to have to talk. Today he'd let Chloe do the talking. It was a wonderful thing that she could talk on and on without boring him. Usually girls' talk either embarrassed him or bored him to death.

He wondered how nuts she could possibly be. He'd only seen her act up once, and that had been a while back. When her father died she left school and only came back for the graduation ceremony. She'd lost so much weight her face looked like a skeleton and her eyes had lost all their life. She went crazy that night. She started howling at the sky and at God and punched at trees, and Liz had been forced to take her home.

Andy despised strong emotion and violent scenes. If she started any crazy shit with him, OUT.

She came running out of the house, flowered skirt whirling and her wheat-colored hair flying. She got in his car quickly and slammed the door. Andy figured she didn't want anybody to see him. Out of the corner of his eye he watched her organize herself, push her hair back, fix her skirt, cross her legs and slide her feet up under her ass. He noticed she always wore baggy tops, which was too bad because he would have liked to have seen the shape of her breasts.

"How's the poison ivy?" she asked. She smiled nervously and he swallowed with difficulty. Her thick, dark eyebrows and very straight nose gave her an aristocratic air which made him slightly uncomfortable. He thought she was beautiful and was relieved that she didn't think so.

"Good. Better," he said. "I put that Camomile shit all over myself last night."

"Calomine?"

"Yeah."

When they got past the traffic in the center of town he asked her if she wanted to smoke a joint. She said sure, so he lit one of the joints he'd rolled in the car. She sat back and put her bare feet on the dashboard. Her hair was all over the place—it fell over the back of the seat and whipped into his face, and the wind carried it out the window.

They did not talk much. The sun was bright and the air clear. Andy drove comfortably as she watched the road on all sides. She sang along with the radio in a soft, high voice, and said "oops" when she sang the wrong verse.

"What a day," she said. "I like it in the spring, you know, before the tourists arrive and invade."

The stretch between East Whitman and Montauk was a long, flat sandy area specked with garish motels and fast-food joints that closed down in winter. They were open now but not crowded yet. For the next few months the stretch would look like Florida, and then it would become a dusty ghost town again.

Andy was high but he did not feel paranoid. Sometimes when he was high he loaded every word and move with hidden meaning.

"It looks a little like Florida," he said.

"It does," she said vaguely. "Except there's no palms here."

He parked by the jetty at the mouth of the harbor and they got out. They hadn't talked about what they were going to do but it didn't matter. They walked around Gosman's dock, looking at people, commenting on their faces or their clothes. They went into one of the tourist shops and Chloe browsed through the T-shirts. She pulled an extra-large turquoise shirt off a rack and held it up against her chest.

"What do you think?"

"Too big," he said without thinking about it.

"Too big? No way!"

"Then why did you ask me?"

She bought a large instead.

She told him that she was making so much money waitressing she didn't know what to do with it. "See, I get Social Security checks, but I save those for school. I'd feel guilty spending that money on anything else."

They sat at a table out on the wooden deck next to Gosman's restaurant and ate lobster rolls and deep-fried shrimp. The water slapped against the poles beneath them and the seagulls swooped and cried for food they didn't need. There was a stillness in the air and a closeness between them that made Andy immensely happy. The nervousness he'd felt before he'd picked her up seemed to belong to a whole other time.

Then as though she'd meant to do this all along, she began to explain about Joe.

"I don't want to lie to you," she said. "It's very hard to tell the truth, though. See, I don't know what's going to happen between Joe and me. It's so fucked up."

He stared at her face and waited for her to go on. She stared back at him with wide clear blue eyes as though she were asking him for an answer. He had no answer to give her and this made him uncomfortable.

"It's amazing how strong you are," she said to him. "You don't let anybody fuck with your head. I wish I could be strong like that."

He felt like the blood was being squeezed out of his heart.

"Joe has always wanted me to be what I'm not. He wants to clean me up!" she laughed nervously.

"He's real Catholic, isn't he?"

She nodded.

"Catholics are all kinds of fucked up," Andy said. "I should know, I'm Catholic."

"Oh no, you're Catholic too?"

"I used to be," he said.

She said she thought Catholic was something you couldn't stop being. Like being black or Jewish. This made him laugh for some reason.

Her mood changed and the cloud that seemed to be hanging over her eyes passed. She asked him about his year in Louisiana, but not nosily; just, "Was it weird, down there?"

"I couldn't play down there," he said honestly, because he was not embarrassed about it, "those black boys are just too fucking tall. They're like trees. Some of them are seven feet tall."

"Isn't that funny. Joe plays center at Cromwell and he's only six-three."

"That's Division III. At a Division I school like the one I was at in Louisiana, guards were six-five. There's no way Joe could play center. And he couldn't play guard or point guard because he can't dribble." That was just a plain fact. No competition or vanity involved. But Andy would have given anything in the world, even his soul if someone had offered him a trade, to have Joe's size. Andy was too short, plain fact. It didn't matter worth a damn how well you could shoot the ball or how talented you were if you couldn't physically compete. He thought about this every day of his life.

After they were done eating he took her down a private road he knew led to the cliffs. They clambered down the clay ridge to the rocky beach. There wasn't a soul around for miles, only sea birds perched on rocks, a few of them circling for fish. The reflection of the sun off the water was blinding. Andy noticed that she had good balance and was light on her feet. The rocks were sharp and uneven. He held her hand and they walked in silence by the water.

"The thing is," she finally said, "I've liked you for a long time, Andy. I don't think it would be right for us to get involved."

Who wants to get involved? Andy thought. He certainly didn't want some chick hanging onto his ass day and night, fucking up his basketball.

"I like the way you think," she said simply.

"If you want," he said tentatively, "I'll come by the restaurant tonight, when you get off work. We can go out and have a drink or something."

III

It was four in the morning when they drove up to Chloe's house. Andy turned the engine off and sat back, hands on the steering wheel. Chloe felt a little dizzy. At the Beechouse Bar she'd sat drinking with Liz a long time, trying to explain what she was doing with Andy. Liz was already well on the way to peace and harmony by the time Chloe walked over to her and sat. "I can't believe this shit," Liz kept saying.

"I really like him," Chloe said. At that moment she realized that whatever Liz said wouldn't matter, because she really did like him, and that made up for whatever moral details had been left unresolved.

"Well I'mn fuck Joe next time I see'm," Liz said. Then they both laughed and Chloe knew it would eventually be all right.

"This is where you banged Liz," she said to Andy.

"Yeah," Andy said.

"You want to come in?"

The house was completely dark except for the yellow light outside the kitchen door.

"What about your mother?" Andy said.

"Don't worry about it." She opened the door and got out.

Chloe and her mother had a strange arrangement. After her father died, her mother said, "You kids are on your own. You take care of yourselves, I'll take care of myself. From now on, it's everyone for himself." And the situation had not changed. They were like three tenants with their own little apartments, her brother, her mother, and Chloe. They crossed paths in the kitchen in the morning. They said Good morning and did you have a good time last night, wanting to say more but never getting around to it.

The first weekend Joe came to visit, she put him in her room. Joe was horrified. When Chloe went up to his home his mother put her on the opposite side of the house from him.

"Who runs this ship?" he'd asked, his face displaying real concern.

"We all run it," she'd said. Joe said, "There's no organization here." His tone was judgmental and she was so infuriated she told him to get lost. "If you don't like it, go sleep upstairs with Eric."

Joe's face registered unbalance. There was pussy on one side, propriety on the other. He never did go upstairs. Chloe decided that in the final equation, his desire to fuck outweighed his moral outrage.

Andy sat in the car, tapping the steering wheel with his fingertips. She stuck her head in the driver's window.

"You want to go home?"

"No," he said. He got out and followed her up the brick path to the kitchen door.

In the complete darkness she took his hands and put them on her hips. Following behind her step by step like a blind man, she led him to her bedroom which was on the ground floor. She locked the door and did not turn on the light. In the darkness she felt innocent. They sat down on the edge of the bed in silence. He began to kiss her neck, her mouth. Slowly, as he did everything, he undressed her. He held her throat lightly with one hand and ran the other up her back and unsnapped her bra. It seemed to her like a very heavy and ugly bra. When he unsnapped it her breasts felt weighty. He lifted her shirt over her head and tossed it. His shape was becoming clear. He leaned over the edge of the bed and untied his sneakers. She pulled him down by the shoulder. He lay on his back looking at the ceiling, breathing quietly. She knelt between his legs on the floor and unzipped his jeans, thinking, Why does he wear jeans like everybody else? and ran her lips over the soft hair on his stomach. He took her head in his hands and ran his fingers through her thick curly hair.

She was afraid, a little. She always felt this way. A cock existed apart from the person who owned it. You never knew. She freed his cock from his underwear, which she slid down his legs with his jeans. His cock was like his hands and wrists. It felt clean and smooth in her mouth. She followed the movement of his hips. The way he trembled and sighed excited her, because he dealt with all things in such a predictable and calm way, and he was not being predictable and calm.

After a while he stopped moving and pulled her up to his chest. "Hold it," he said. "Hold it." He turned her over. Her head ended up under the window sill and she could see the pine tree swaying in a sky full of stars. She let him touch her and kiss her, opening her legs to him. As he penetrated he let go of himself in a way she had not expected of him. He became almost insane, enthralled, moving and at the same time feeling all parts of her body as though he had been dying to do this for years. Relaxing and happy because she'd wanted to sleep with him since she was fifteen, she watched the pine tree sway, ran her hands over his smooth back. He lasted a long time. She wondered if he'd go down on her after he came and if he'd do it gently.

She thought of the night Joe had knocked her up, a lay she couldn't remember because she'd been blind drunk. It was her own fault. She would remember the reflection of the window panes on the wall of his room for the rest of her life. Those four squares of yellow light that had nothing to do with anything but for some reason announced to her as she lay there that she'd been knocked up and there was nothing at all she could do about it now.

* * *

Andy opened his eyes. It was light in the room, a breeze was blowing the curtains in and out of the open window. He rolled toward Chloe and put his hand on the dip in her lower back. She had her back to him and was lying on her side. She smelled like him and he smelled like her. Both of them smelled vaguely like damp rawhide. And his pillow smelled of the light perfume she wore. He liked it all and wanted to wake her so they could start again.

He blinked and looked about the room. The bedspread matched the curtains, green stems and pink and blue flowers on a white sea. The rug was grass green, the walls white. He could have been in a

rainbow or a cloud. She turned toward him still asleep and slid her
hand under his armpit. Her face didn't frighten him with the
changes it had undergone during the night. It had puffed out a bit
from the booze and sleep.

Now it seemed ridiculous but in high school he'd been afraid of
her. She hadn't been so pretty when she'd first arrived at school.
But even with her defiant and self-contained look, a new girl was a
New Girl. Then he'd found out she'd lived in France, and in New
York City, and in Other Places, nobody was quite sure where, and
he decided she was probably a terrible snob. Yet he'd asked her to
dance at one of the black postgame parties. No other white kids
were dancing, but Andy, having led the game in points, was high
and in the mood regardless. And the black kids liked him. Chloe
was a "foreigner," asking her to dance at a black party seemed a
safe choice.

She danced so close to him he could smell her hair. She watched
him with reckless, defiant eyes. He suddenly wanted desperately
to sleep with her, and knew he could have if he'd made the slightest move. But that kind of reckless sexuality frightened him. Even
the thought of it hampered his basketball playing.

A week later he asked Betsy out for the first time. He wanted a
girl, and Betsy was a safe, level-headed person.

Then during senior year Chloe bloomed, just like a flower. Her
short, frizzy hair grew out thick and golden. The shape of her face
and ass changed from undefined to shapely and refined. The boys
went nuts but by then she had a boyfriend, and when her father
began to get sick, many boyfriends.

She breathed out a tiny moan and ran her nose through the hair
on his chest.

He heard a phone ringing somewhere in the house. A minute
later there were footsteps coming toward her door. And then
someone knocked. Chloe's hand was in his hair.

"Chloe? Chloe, are you in there?" The doorknob turned. By the
sound of the voice he knew it was her mother.

"Chloe? There's a Mrs. Fletcher on the phone who's looking for
her son."

They sat up and stared at each other.

"What do I do?" Her eyes were wide. "What should I tell her?"
Andy started laughing.

"Chloe?" her mother said, knocking again. "Do you know where
he is?"

Chloe cleared her throat. "He's right here, Mom."

Andy shook his head just a second too late.

"Oh thank God," her mother said, "I was so worried. I thought
you'd been in an accident or some god-awful thing. Well tell him to
come to the phone, his mother's waiting, Chloe."

"Shit," Andy said. Chloe threw back the bedspread and went
into the bathroom.

"I'm sorry," she said. "I didn't know what to say." She giggled
nervously as she slipped on her yellow bathrobe. Andy put on his
jeans and went out to answer the phone without deciding first
what he was going to say.

*　*　*

On the way home Andy was laughing aloud. The dull ache at the
back of his head made him feel giddy and slow, too much booze
and not enough sleep, but the pain didn't really bother him.

Even his mother's snit seemed funny. "What are you *do*ing,
Andrew? Your brother needs the car to get to work. It's nine-
thirty, Andrew. You were supposed to be at work over an hour ago.
Burkowski's called for you three times already and I just don't
know what to say."

"I was sleeping," he said stupidly. Fuck her anyway.

And then walking out into the kitchen with Chloe in the yellow
terrycloth bathrobe that was torn and hanging off her shoulder,
they ran into Mrs. Raymond who was sitting at the head of the long
oak table smoking a cigarette. She looked just like Chloe except
older and a little puffier in the face and waist.

"Mom, this is Andy," Chloe said.

"Good morning, Andy," Mrs. Raymond said in a husky voice
clouded by smoke. "I hope your mother wasn't worried." Andy
felt she was saying two things at once. She was genuinely concerned but also might be highly amused if he got in trouble.

"Nah," Andy said, not knowing what to do with his hands, "she
just needs the car."

He left Chloe standing barefoot on the cement floor of the

vestibule. They were both laughing stupidly. He didn't tell her he'd call, but he figured she knew he would. Mrs. Raymond seemed like a pisser. It was too bad for the kids in the world that more mothers weren't as cool as she was.

IV

For two weeks Andy let their affair run its course without giving it much thought. He wasn't worried about it. He was having more fun than he'd had in years, and Chloe's "I can't afford to get involved" attitude aired the thing of heavy nuances.

He would pick her up between twelve and two at the restaurant. If she wasn't done he'd sit at the bar and have a few beers and chat with the bartender till she was ready. They'd go out to the Beechouse Bar (or to other bars on Employee Nights when they got in free) and drink and dance until they'd spent all their money or until the lights were turned up and they were kicked out.

To Andy's great surprise, Ben liked Chloe, even though he was worried about Andy getting involved. Andy noticed Ben watching him stealthfully, as the three of them sat at the bar, as though as his older brother he felt it was his duty to make sure Andy wasn't getting in over his head. This annoyed Andy but also amused him.

And Chloe amused Ben. She could keep up (almost) with his drinking. She even encouraged him by paying for his shots. A couple of times she got Ben so drunk Andy had to drive him home, drag him into the garage, and dump him on the bed.

"Fucking unbeLIEVable," Ben said.

At work, trimming ten-foot hedges or digging cable ditches with a jackhammer on the side of the highway, Andy forgot where he was and imagined being in bed with her. Even the pounding of the jackhammer did not seem so bad. There was something animal about the way they made love. It was unintentional and when he thought about it in broad daylight, he was a little embarrassed. He did not know how she got him to let loose—everybody was always trying to get him to let loose but she did it without meaning to—she attached herself to him when they made love so that he'd forget they had separate bodies. When she came she cried out so loud he had to cover her face with whatever was available, a pillow, his hand, his chest. Mrs. Raymond and Eric were always in the house at night.

At work he started wearing his T-shirt outside his jeans because he couldn't get rid of his hard-on.

Mrs. Raymond did not seem to sleep. She walked around the house all night. Andy listened to her light footsteps going up and down the stairs, sometimes out to the porch. They made him feel sad, and guilty that he was having such a good time in her house when she was so unhappy herself.

In the morning at seven he'd drag himself out of Chloe's bed. Mrs. Raymond would be sitting at the head of the long kitchen table, smoking cigarettes. In her cloudy voice she'd say, "Good morning, Andy" as he stumbled by.

"Good morning, Mrs. Raymond," he'd answer, as clearly as he could in his stupor state.

One morning as he stumbled through, eyes half closed and head still spinning from liquor fumes, he bumped into the cupboard by the table.

"Good morning, Raggedy Andy," she said, smiling. Immediately he flashed onto his little sister's rag doll and wondered if he really looked that bad. He started to laugh, and as he was laughing, said, "Good morning, Mrs. Raymond" in his usual catatonic way.

The same morning he walked into his house and everybody was giggling except his mother, who looked like she had indigestion. Ben was standing at the kitchen counter gobbling down a couple of hot dogs that spilled from his mouth when he laughed.

"Get some sleep, little bro," he mumbled between mouthfuls, "that crazy chick's wearing you out."

Their mother's face was pinched and greenish and she would not speak to Andy. His little sister stood in a corner, watching it all with her curious round eyes and elf's grin.

Late in the afternoon Andy came home from work and lay down on his bed that hadn't been slept in since the first night he'd stayed at Chloe's, and tried to sleep. He was staring at the ceiling thinking about how good he felt when his father came in.

He pulled up the one chair in the room and sat down next to the bed.

"Listen, Andy," his father said as though he were going to make him a proposition. He leaned on his elbows and crossed his fingers.

"What, Pop?" Andy said.

"Well," his father thought for a second, "it's like this. Your mother doesn't think it's such a good idea, you sleeping over there at Clo's every night. It might give your sister the wrong idea. You know what I mean?"

"Sara's old enough," Andy said.

"Well, that's not the point. Your mother doesn't want her thinking she can start doing that kind of thing too. Your mother—"

"Pop, listen. Don't give me this crap. If you were twenty years old and you could sleep at Clo's house every night, wouldn't you?"

His father got up. "Forget I said anything." He waved his hands around behind him as he walked out of the room.

* * *

"Andy's my good friend," Chloe said to Ben. The three of them were sitting in the middle of the bar in the Beechouse. Behind them people were stomping on the dance floor to jukebox music that seemed very loud. Everything was immersed in a cloud of smoke.

"Everybody needs that type of good friend," Ben said.

Andy was getting tired of her calling him her friend all the time.

"How do you drink so much beer and stay so skinny?" she asked Ben.

"Half an hour running up and down the court, it's gone. Ask him." He looked at Andy. " 'Cept the bro's getting fat and weak in the knees from too much love." Ben reached behind Chloe and slapped Andy's back, resting his arm on her shoulders.

"Hey fuck you," Andy said defensively, "I still kick your ass every time."

"Have you guys ever gotten *really* mad at each other? Like over a girl? When I was twelve in Paris I had two friends that were brothers. They were like you guys, really close in age and very good-looking. The girls loved them both. I got in the middle of them you know and it was a very bad thing. I think it was very hard for them not to hate each other. Have you guys ever slept with the same girl?"

Ben blinked his sham dumb-guy blink. "What, at the same time?"

"No, that's not what I meant."

"Hell if *I* know," Ben said. "Why, do you have something in mind?"

Andy was feeling his chest expanding as though he were being pumped up with hot air.

"What do you think, Andy?" Ben said.

Andy shook his head. "No way!"

Ben shrugged, downed his beer, and got off his stool.

"I'm going to check out the chick situation here." He slapped Andy on the back of the head. Andy wanted to slap him back, a little harder, but decided not to. His head told him that he was being ridiculous. He'd never felt stupid in front of Ben before and it was bothering him.

"I think it's strange that you guys have never slept with the same girl," Chloe said.

"Excuse me," someone behind him said. A long hand tapped Chloe on the shoulder. Andy turned his head slightly and saw a tall dark guy who was wearing the same long-sleeved cotton shirt as he was, except on the guy it looked like a Brooks Brothers and on Andy it didn't.

"Hello-o-o!" he said to her, ignoring Andy. She did not seem thrilled to see him.

"Hi, Jay," she said. "This is my friend Andy. We went to high school together. Jay goes to Cromwell."

Andy and Jay stared at each other like two bulls about to go at it. They didn't say a word to each other. Jay turned back to Chloe.

"What did you do your final paper on for Mariaux? I did mine on *On Ne Badine Pas Avec l'Amour.* Mariaux really dug it."

The guy really thinks he's something else, Andy thought.

"I did mine on filicide in the French theater," Chloe said.

Jay said it was an absolute outrage that they dared, after all the years he'd been summering in East Whitman, to charge him just to get in the door of the bar.

"Five bucks, just to get in the door! And they don't even tack on a free drink." He swung his arm around while he talked, his knee pressing into Chloe's thigh. Andy watched her face harden.

"It don't mean shit how long you've been comin out here," Andy said slowly. "You got to know the guy at the door."

"I know you," Jay said, pointing a long index finger at the center of Andy's chest as though it had suddenly come back to him. "I've seen you play basketball downtown. Speaking of which," he said to Chloe, "what's Joe Gillan doing this summer?" And back to Andy, "Do you know Joe Gillan?"

"He's a good player," Andy said, nodding, his voice and his face displaying no emotion whatsoever though he felt that his chest was about to burst. He looked around for Ben.

He wanted to walk away but didn't want to leave Chloe with Jay. Andy slid his arm around her.

"We're outa here," he said. He pressed past Jay to the dance floor.

On the crowded floor she locked her arms around his neck and hid her face in his shirt. "That guy's gonna get his ass kicked if he doesn't learn to behave himself." Andy was no fighter. The sight of blood made him sick. Right then he felt like killing the guy—what the hell was happening to him?

"I think you're so pure," she said, looking up at him.

Pure? What the fuck was that? His cock started to swell as they pressed against each other.

If you had balls you'd get out of this right now, he told himself.

"Goddamn, you turn me on," he told her.

What should she tell her? That the story went way, way back to the beginning of freshman year? That Chloe didn't know the half of it? No. "You must be honest in this, and talk frankly to Andy about how you feel, and tell him that you're worried. You don't want to hurt him if you can help it. And as for Joe. Well, well, all good things in their own time. Wait and see how it is in the fall."

Annie knew that as soon as school started in the fall, the crap was going to fly. She only wished that Chloe were living with her. But now it was too late to worry about that.

Annie never ceased to be amazed at how different their problems were. Maybe because they had no understanding whatsoever of each other's backgrounds, they could objectively advise each other. It fascinated her that for people like Chloe, going to a private, ivy-covered college was a given. It had never been a question to her parents, it seemed. Chloe took it for granted that it was expected of her. Annie's whole perception of the world was brand new, it had grown out of the fact that one morning she'd been faced with a choice. She had personally (she wasn't quite certain anymore what part God had played in this) decided her fate.

Annie had come home from cheerleading practice and found her grandma sitting at the dining-room table with the open letter in her hand. Her grandma never used the dining room except on holidays like Thanksgiving and Christmas, and Annie knew immediately that she'd been accepted to Cromwell University.

Her grandma's fingers were pressing her lace handkerchief to her eyes. Annie thought she was crying out of old Canadian pride, but now Annie knew the tears had meant much more than that.

"Well, Annie girl," her grandma said, shaking her head. "Now it's between Cromwell and Holy Cross." Annie knew that her grandma knew she would not go to Holy Cross. Because there was no comparison. Holy Cross was just a continuation of high school. Same priest professors, same tunnel vision. Annie loved the priests and had nothing against them, that wasn't it.

"I'm going to lose you," her grandma said.

And the day before Annie left, her grandma gave her a talking to.

"Don't be afraid of those rich people. You know they're going to be a whole new can of worms." When her grandma talked seri-

ously, she used clichés. "Remember, just because your grampa
worked in a factory his whole life it doesn't make you any less than
them. To each his own. And I mean that. Don't be afraid to stick to
your guns. But if speech is silver, silence is golden. You know what
I mean."

When they said good-bye outside Annie's ivy-covered dorm,
grampa scurried back to the van and grandma cried. Annie felt
guilty that she was embarrassed by this show of emotion. And she
felt she'd already betrayed them, because given the chance, she
would not go back to live in her grandparents' house.

Joe lived across the hall from a boy named Freddie Beauchamp,
whom Annie had gone to high school with. Freddie Beauchamp
played hockey. Annie loved hockey. Freddie's end of the hall was
full of jocks. The Housing Office, she supposed, had organized it
that way so these small-town boys wouldn't feel so disoriented at
their new, big, liberal arts school.

Annie spent a good deal of time on Freddie's hall, chatting about
sports and this and that. Within the first week, she fell madly in
love with Joe. Who wouldn't have? Tall, Black-Irish basketball
player with a face to melt your heart. And a good Catholic, at that.
He'd been so sweet to her:

"You know, Annie, me, you, Freddie, we're all the same. We
come from our hometowns to this place." He'd make a wide,
disgusted gesture with his arm. "Here we're a minority. Weirdos
everywhere. We have to stick together."

Yes, yes, we have to stick together, Annie thought. Joe said, "I
went to high school in the ghetto of Springfield, Mass. I learned to
play ball with the black kids in my neighborhood. They treated me
like I was one of them. When I got into Cromwell they were so
proud of me they sent me five dollars to help me out. They took up
a collection, can you imagine? But around here, I'm at a disadvan-
tage because of my lack of education."

So she wrote and typed his papers for him. Oh, Annie. What
schlock! She found out halfway through the semester from a girl
who'd gone to Andover that Joe had gone to Andover too, all four
years, on full scholarship. He'd never been raised in any ghetto.
His father was the headmaster of a junior prep school.

Annie stopped writing his papers but never confronted him

with his lies. She felt used and raped and ridiculously naive. And then of course he found someone else. He found Chloe, who slept with him.

He'd tried but Annie, being a virgin and terrified, would not.

Annie's stomach used to churn like an old butter maker when she thought about Chloe. Keep an open mind, her grandma had said, but it was difficult to keep an open mind when she watched Chloe come in and out of Joe's room at all hours of the day and night, sometimes wearing his robe to go to the bathroom. The nerve! Annie thought. The bitch! The girl walked around with her back straight as a T square, never looking right or left as though she had blinders on. Annie had never felt so paralyzed by hatred, so guilty for feeling hatred, and for feeling that grandma's "to each his own," in this case, could be flushed down the bowl.

Annie's aryan roommate who came from Westchester also said "to each his own," but with a fakely pious, self-adoring look on her face. She could have been saying, "I forgive all these poor degenerates for their lack of self-control." And that was just as unacceptable.

It all had to do with sex, Annie decided. She hadn't figured out just how, yet.

In the spring Annie applied for an au pair job in East Whitman, Long Island, because she'd heard that was the Place To Be in the summertime. She knew Chloe came from there but never mentioned the au pair job to her. Then one night while they were all watching TV in Freddie's room, he mentioned to Chloe that Annie was going to be in East Whitman for the summer. Annie wanted to kill him.

Chloe said, "I'll give you my phone number right now, and we'll get together. I'll show you around. It's a lot more fun if you know someone when you're in a new place."

Annie took the number and thanked her. As soon as Joe and Chloe went off to bed, she ripped it up.

They ran into each other in the East Whitman Gristede's. Chloe was stoned out of her mind. She was buying a bag of cookies and a gallon of ice cream. Annie was horrified that anyone would buy store-made cookies when it was so easy to make them oneself.

Chloe asked her why she hadn't called. Annie said she'd lost the number, and that anyway, she didn't want to disturb her.

"What shit," Chloe said. "Are your bosses home?"

It was the middle of the week, the bosses were in the City. Annie just had the little girl to watch. She told Chloe this.

"Tell me where you live. I'm not working tonight, I'll come by with a bottle of wine. Red or white?"

To her surprise, Annie simply said, "White."

Waiting for Chloe's car to roll and crunch over the pebbled driveway, Annie felt a little like she had as a child sitting in the boxcar about to enter the House of Horrors at the traveling fair.

Chloe arrived with a half-gallon bottle of Folonari. They sat on the plush living-room couch and sipped the wine out of long-stemmed crystal wine glasses. Annie felt quite chic.

"I know you don't like me much," Chloe said, looking straight at Annie with clear, unflinching eyes.

—How many times have you said that to people, Annie thought: *"God, I can't stand that girl"?*

"Oh, no!" Annie said.

Chloe looked down at her glass. Annie felt like a shit.

"Nobody knows this, but I think I've been pretty sick."

"Sick from what?" Annie asked, out of politeness and to keep the conversation going; because she already had an idea. Everybody knew that Chloe's father was John Raymond the playwright. Everybody knew he'd died the spring before Chloe's freshman year.

"I have a hard time getting to know people," Chloe said. "I wish I could be more like you."

Annie didn't know what to say to this. Silence.

Chloe went on. "Joe is very possessive and he makes it even harder for me to get to know people. But I'm afraid to contradict him."

"Don't let him take advantage of you," Annie said quickly. She'd drunk her glassful too fast and her head felt dangerously light.

"I used to fuck anybody who flattered me," Chloe said. "I think that's pretty sick, don't you?" She laughed. "You know, it's all about not wanting to spend nights alone. I'm not sure, but that's what I think."

For Annie this was not reconnoitered territory. She suddenly wanted to ask questions. Lots of questions that had been driving her crazy.

"Why are you telling me this?" Annie asked.

"Because you look like you don't have an ounce of bullshit in you and I need someone to talk to."

Oh how Annie wished she wasn't full of shit.

"I didn't like you," she said, "because you seemed so pulled together. Cosmopolitan or something. Like you've never needed anything in your life."

"Ah!" Chloe placed fists on each side of her face. She laughed, and then started to cry. Annie started to cry. It was inconceivable to her that Chloe would cry because she, Annie, had misunderstood her. Who ever gave a darn about what Annie thought?

"I'm sorry," Annie said. She got up and moved closer to Chloe on the couch. "I didn't give you a chance. I was scared of you."

"You know what it is, looking like I don't need anyone? It's protection, because *I*'m so fucking scared."

"Good Lord," Annie had to laugh then. "That's the darn funniest ironic thing I've ever heard."

Annie told Chloe something she'd never told a soul. As far back as she could remember she'd had no parents, and she did not know why. Her grandparents never talked about it, and she was afraid to ask. She thought God had marked her with an X at birth: *different*. Her grandma said it was a blessing to be different. All she'd ever wanted was to know why. Now she didn't care anymore.

"Finally I realized I was never going to be like everybody else, so I said fine, and I decided to go to Cromwell and 'broaden my perspective.' " She made a circular horizontal gesture in both directions, starting at her eyes. "The priests educated us very well, scholastically speaking. I was pretty well prepared. But the rest." She shrugged.

"You're not a virgin, are you?" Chloe asked, wide-eyed.

Oh yes she was.

"My God, you don't know what you're missing!"

In high school, there was Chris, Annie told her. But they never did it. Chris respected her too much, he said. He was afraid they would both end up in hell.

During the summer Chloe and Annie became good friends. Probably, Annie thought, because Joe was not around much. They talked over their troubles. Chloe missed Joe terribly and Annie missed not having someone to love.

Little Laura peed in her bed and cried all the time, at night. She was only five and could not understand why her parents left her alone with Annie for weeks on end. Several times Chloe brought over children's books that she'd found in town. She read them to Laura to put her to sleep. She told Laura it was okay to pee in her bed and she shouldn't feel guilty about it. Thanks a lot, Annie said later; she was the one who had to change and wash the sheets.

Chloe taught Laura to play backgammon, and pretty soon she was beating both Chloe and Annie.

"I think you're probably a genius," she told Laura, quite seriously. Laura was thrilled to have an older friend.

"You've got to treat them like adults," Chloe told Annie. "They understand everything, don't let them fool you."

Annie said if she started treating the child like an adult, she'd have no control over her and it would be the end of her job.

"Oh you're so old-fashioned," Chloe said. "I know what it's like for her. I was left alone with old-fashioned nannies like you my whole life, too."

All summer Annie thought about doing it and who her first one would be. Less than a month into sophomore year, she found her boy. He was an Irish boy from South Boston who played baseball and lived down the hall from her. It was exciting enough, Annie thought. Just doing it was exciting enough. But they did not really like each other and after four or five clandestine screws, they stopped meeting. At least he never told anyone, and Annie respected him for that. At least they still talked to each other when they crossed paths.

Back at school her friendship with Chloe changed. They did not have any friends in common, and Joe was back on the scene full-time. Chloe and Annie had lunch together once or twice a week. And sometimes they drank wine together in Annie's room when Joe had an away game. Annie never told Chloe about Joe lying. Annie didn't think Chloe would believe her. It didn't matter, Annie decided, because someday she'd find out for herself.

VI

Liz called Chloe at ten o'clock in the morning from a phone booth in town.

"I'm pregnant," she said, and started to cry.

"Shit," Chloe said. "Whose is it?"

"Steve's. But we're not talking. I don't want him to know."

"What do you want to do?"

"Will you drive me up the island? See, I can drive *there*, it's coming back. I'll tell my aunt we're going to Smith Haven Mall. And I'll spend the night at your place. Your mother doesn't give a shit, right? I called Planned Parenthood and they gave this number to call up the island."

"You sure that's what you want to do?" Chloe knew Liz was sure; it was just a question she felt she had to ask.

"What the fuck else do you want me to do?" Liz said.

Chloe traded shifts with one of the other waitresses. She did not want to go into work after spending the day with Liz in the clinic. She was not looking forward to taking her, but it was something she would never walk away from. Liz trusted her, and Liz had no one else. Her parents had been killed in two separate car accidents, two hundred yards from each other on the same road. First her father, when she was ten, and four years later, her mother. Now she lived with an aunt she despised. The aunt didn't approve of or trust Liz, and kept her social security checks. For two years already Liz had been talking about moving out. She had a hard time making decisions. In this case she simply did not have a choice.

As they turned onto the four-lane expressway in South Whitman, Liz lit a cigarette and said, "About Andy. I'm not mad at all. I just wanted to tell you that. I think you guys are good together."

"I'm happy to hear that. Did you eat anything this morning?"

"Yeah, a muffin. Why?"

"They didn't tell you you weren't supposed to eat?"

"No. Why?"

"I thought before an abortion you weren't supposed to eat."

"They didn't say anything."

"Are you having local anaesthesia or are they going to knock you out?" Chloe did not want to sound like an expert. She sensed her tone was overly methodical. Since Chloe had gone off to college, Liz and she felt ill at ease with each other. Chloe resented no longer being accepted among the diehard locals. Liz resented the changes in Chloe's speech, the way she talked about the things she'd learned.

"I don't know. It's costing me over three hundred bucks. I had to borrow from George at work. What a nice guy he is, I swear."

Chloe's had cost one hundred and sixty-three dollars. She'd never forget the price. Novocaine, just like at the dentist's, they'd said.

The wind was warm and the early morning sun poured in through her window. Chills kept chasing each other up and down her back.

"They're going to knock you out," she told Liz in a flat, removed tone. "You won't feel a thing."

"How come you know so much about this shit?" Liz asked.

"I took a friend of mine last year." She wondered why she had said this after the words were already out. Maybe if she had told Liz the truth the tension between them would have eased, at least for a while.

"No shit? You did? What a bummer."

Liz probably would have said the same thing if Chloe had admitted, Yes, it happened to me too. She was suddenly relieved that she had not told her the truth.

"Did you tell Andy about this?" Liz asked.

Chloe did not want to lie again. "Yes," she said. "I was pretty upset about it and pretty drunk when I told him. He said he'd never tell anybody. I trust him."

"That's cool," Liz said.

It was so easy, it seemed, for other people. Joe had made such a big deal about her never telling. He'd made her swear on her honor. Keeping it entirely to herself was one of the ways he'd demanded penance of her.

She had told her mother, but that had come about by pure chance. She'd driven home for the winter break the day before Christmas, the day after the abortion. She had waited till then to have it so it would not interfere with her exams.

When she walked into the kitchen, completely exhausted from the three-and-a-half-hour drive, her mother was standing at the butcher-block island in the center of the room. The honey-colored light from the old copy–Tiffany lamps warmed the wood and shone in her mother's gold hair.

"Chloe!" she said with great relief, "are you all right?" Her tone was oddly shaky. "I've had the craziest feeling all day yesterday and today that something awful was happening to you. I tried to call. I even tried to call Joe. There was no answer."

Chloe put her book bag down on the floor. She felt her stomach somersault and all the bravado and silence and discipline Joe had inflicted on her dropped from her like an enormous coat.

"I had an abortion yesterday." She started to weep.

Her mother came around the butcher block and took her in her arms. Her breast was warm and soft and she smelled vaguely of bath oils and scotch, just as she had when Chloe wept in her arms as a child. "Oh my poor baby," she said softly. "My God, why didn't you tell me?"

Chloe wept as she hadn't in years.

Her mother played mommy and nurse for five days, until the bleeding stopped. For the first time since her father's death, they made peace and loved each other without contempt.

But after five days, they had a fight. They were sitting in the library watching TV. Her brother was there, too, being silently helpful and supportive, because he felt guilty too, about her abortion for some reason.

"Why *didn't* you tell me?" her mother asked, offended this time. Eric started to wriggle uncomfortably in his chair.

"Because, Mom, I wanted to go through it on my own."

Chloe felt bad for wanting to punish her mother for forcing her and Eric to take care of themselves. At the same time she was filled with angry pride, because she *had* been able to go through it on her own.

"You're stupid," her mother said. "I could have gotten you the best doctor in New York City."

"The doctor was fine, Mom. He was from the Yale med school. I had to go through it by myself."

"Don't feed me Joe's Catholic bullshit. I was Catholic too, you know. Jesus Christ, I hope you outgrow this phase."

Eric tried to turn his back to them while still watching the TV. "Come on, you guys," he said.

"I didn't need *you* on my ass being hysterical, judging me, and carrying on. I had exams to take. I had enough shit to deal with."

"JUDGING you? Sweetheart, I had two abortions before they were even legal in this country. I'm just saying that it's stupid and unnecessary to suffer when you don't have to. And you have a stupid, tightassed boyfriend."

The next day Chloe went up to Eric's room to tell him that she was leaving to go back to school. He was sitting quietly, admiring his father's knife collection, which he had laid out in some kind of order of his own on an ancient, flat piece of wood he'd brought home from the beach.

"It looks nice," Chloe said.

"Yeah." He looked up, then away quickly as he picked up one of the knives.

"I'm leaving," she said.

"Are you sure you're okay?"

"Yes. Don't worry about me." She watched him for a while. His shoulders tightened under her gaze. There was so much she wished she could say to him. But he despised comforting and sentimentality. She felt sad for him, he seemed so lonely sitting there among his relics. She knew that she must not infringe on his space. It was unfair to expect him to be emotional simply because she was. Eric was dealing with the whole mess in his own removed way.

As she waited for Liz she sat and watched the clock in the waiting room. It was a big metal clock with a dirty white face. The hands did not seem to be moving. She'd brought Faulkner's *The Bear*, which she'd never read but her godfather Jack had been telling her to read for years, and Fitzgerald's *Great Gatsby*, which she'd read twice already. She couldn't read more than a paragraph at a stretch in either book. She kept looking up at the clock hoping that hours had passed when in fact barely five minutes had passed since the last time she'd looked.

She took a walk around the ground floor of the hospital. The antiseptic smells and sounds made her dizzy. She went back to the waiting room, feeling a pinch of pain low in her stomach. She was in the middle of her cycle and it could not be her period, though that was what it felt like. She went to the pay phone to call Andy. She realized once she'd inserted her dime that he would be at work. She had no one else to call, so she went and sat on the hard, straightbacked couch in the dark waiting room and waited.

When the clock finally made it to noon she took the elevator to the fifth floor, which was the abortion clinic. The pinch of pain low in her stomach had begun to spread like an opening hand, the fingers reaching for entrails to pull down and out through her uterus.

The hall was long, the floor sparkled grey, and she could see her reflection walking on herself as her clogs clunked on the vinyl. At the end of the hall she found the room where the girls lay sprawled on white beds with metal bars surrounding them like cribs. The girls' faces seemed grey against the whiteness of the sheets. She felt blood everywhere, she could smell it. It smelled barbaric.

"Clo, Goddamn, I knew it was you, I could recognize your walk anywhere." Liz put her hand next to Chloe's, on the metal bar on the side of the bed. Even her hand was grey. She started to sit up.

"Don't get up yet," Chloe said quickly. She felt the definite harsh pull in her lower back and belly, and then warm blood staining her underpants.

"Liz, I think I have ESP or something," she laughed stupidly, "I just got my period. It's the totally wrong time."

"Hell, we're connected," Liz smiled. She was so pale her teeth looked yellow. Chloe started to cry.

"Girl, cool out, will you? You look worse than I feel."

On the phone later that afternoon Chloe told Andy she'd gotten her period at the hospital. It had completely shocked her. She told him she was feeling sick and didn't think she could go out. Liz was asleep upstairs in the guest room and Chloe thought she should stay home and keep an eye on her.

"You want me to come over?" Andy asked.

Suddenly it seemed strange to her that she had not thought of that.

"Sure. But I'm not feeling too well, you know?"

Andy brought a bouquet of wild pink roses for Liz.

"I picked them off your neighbor's fence," he said. "Tore the shit out of my hands."

Chloe put them in a slender crystal vase and brought them upstairs. Liz turned over in the bed and looked up at her with feverish eyes. The room was cool and somber, and submerged in quiet violence.

"Look what the shithead brought for you." Chloe put the vase down on the night table.

"Where is he?" Liz said groggily, smiling at the flowers.

"Downstairs."

"Well tell him to come the fuck up here."

Andy sat at the foot of the bed. "What's up, Liz?" he said.

"Not me, that's for sure."

The three of them talked for a while about nothing in particular, then Liz's eyes closed and she fell asleep.

Andy and Chloe sat on the couch in front of the TV in the library. Andy put his arm around her, she cried quietly with her head pressed against his shoulder. She felt bloodless and weak.

"It's horrible," she said. "The shit we put ourselves through."

"I know it is."

"Liz's okay. I guess some people take it worse than others."

"I guess so."

Staring at the TV without seeing it, she said, "I had one too."

"I figured you did."

Andy seemed genuinely sorry for her. He was completely accepting. Probably he thought it was none of his business to judge her or to ask her about it.

VII

Annie's return letter told Chloe to keep calm above all things (she was always worried about Chloe's nerves), and to keep this fling with Andy to herself, at least until she got a good sense of things in the fall. "There's no need to tell Joe about your summer antics. As my grandma would say, 'What he doesn't know won't hurt him.'"

Chloe had not meant to minimize her feelings for Andy in her letter. Or maybe since then her feelings had changed. It was painfully complicated, but she was having a wonderful time with him. They were having a real love affair: kissing in public and grinding on the dance floor. He gave her shivers when he touched her. In the street she liked to walk behind him so she could watch his ass move in his pants. She loved his straight reddish hair and his fine strong back. He seemed to walk through life unmoved. Except in bed she knew she moved him and he knew it too. They were in lust.

Was it possible to be in love with two people at once? At Cromwell she could not make it without Joe.

She had visions of Andy transferring to Cromwell (how many times had he said he could transfer?) and becoming the team's greatest point guard ever. Could he pass the courses? Of course he could if he wanted to. He wouldn't want to.

When she spoke to Joe on the phone the urge to blow the lid off the whole thing was so strong she sometimes felt she was standing at the top of a cliff with the wind blowing her dangerously close to the edge. Could she fly?

She decided to sit down and write Joe a letter. She wanted to clarify how she felt about their past and what she hoped would happen in the fall. Right now she'd be eight months pregnant, and where would they be? She could not be as explicit as that. She was afraid Joe's mother read her letters. She kept it vague. This was not satisfying because she wasn't certain Joe would grasp her innuendos. As soon as she began the letter gloom set in so heavily she could barely think.

My decision had nothing to do with how much I loved you. I know you think I was not being responsible.

Joe believed that people had to pay for their sins, and she was not paying her dues.

We all pay our dues in our own ways, Joe. Don't think I don't spend time thinking about it.

The day she'd told him that her test had come out positive and she was going to make an appointment at Yale-New Haven Hospital, Joe went to the campus chapel. She followed him at a distance and then waited for him outside, sitting on the stone steps. It was a cold grey day. She tried but couldn't get herself to cry. When he came out his eyes were swollen and red. He said, "I'm going to go to Hell for this." And since then he'd been afraid of her.

If we're going to keep seeing each other in the fall, our relationship is going to have to change. You have to understand that I need to have friends too. I've missed that so much. You are much too possessive.

But it was at least half her fault she knew. She'd let him do it. He had tried at first to get her to stop studying so much, but on that topic she stood firm. Studying was her obsession, the way basketball was his. She would not allow him to get in the way of her work. In all other respects, he'd come to command her life, and it was this self-inflicted burden that had finally backfired on him and made him feel she was suffocating him.

A few months into the spring term, when she'd thought they had passed through the worst of it and their life was pretty much back to normal, he began pacing her tiny room in the middle of the night. "Joe, what's the matter?" She was terrified.

"You want too much from me," he told her. "You just ask for too damn much." And it was true. She depended on him for everything.

She found herself completely, miserably alone. The summer came as a needed relief from all of it.

Imagine how you would feel about me now if we'd done what you wanted to do. I would own you, I would be completely dependent on you, and you would want to kill me to get me off your back.

She wondered if that was how he'd intended to pay his dues.

You must know that I still love you. How could I not love you after what we've already been through? You are closer to me than anyone in the world. Please try to forgive me, and yourself, and understand that we can still keep growing together if we just give each other a little room to breathe. Someday I'll make it up to you, I promise.

* * *

In the first week of August, just a few days before her birthday Joe called and said he was coming down to celebrate. Chloe panicked. They had been speaking on the phone much less lately, and hearing his raspy, rather high-pitched voice suddenly made her want to see him. She considered and weighed the possibilities. Liz and Andy had put paycheck money aside to take her out on her birthday.

"I think it's better if you don't come down," she said. She felt a big emptiness in the finality of her statement.

Less rigidly, she said, "It's only a couple of weeks till school starts."

"But I want to see you now," he said. He sounded distressed.

She said, "You see, this summer has been very good for me. I've been trying to figure out who the fuck I am." A thought hit her: He's just horny. He probably hasn't gotten laid all summer. He wants to get laid.

"You don't understand, do you?" she said.

"No, I don't understand. You wanted this 'space' and 'time,'" he said with distaste, "and now *I*'m asking you for something. I want to be with you on your birthday."

"I hate my birthday. It's the hardest Goddamn day of the year for me. I want to get through it without you."

Without him but with someone else. Would it be like this her whole life? she wondered.

Last year she'd gotten into bed and cried all day until dusk, when she'd had to get up for the cocktail party her mother had planned in her honor. Her mother thought cocktail parties were good for birthdays—you got presents but you didn't have to spend the whole evening with your guests. Joe had been with her. He'd sat at the edge of the bed most of the day, trying to comfort her without success.

"You're making me very sad, Chloe," he said softly into the phone. "I don't know what's the matter with you. You sound so weird."

"You really want to come down?"

"Yes. I really want to come down and see you."

She thought maybe he was getting nervous with school so close. He had to find out where he stood and see if it was necessary to reassess.

* * *

She had three glasses of wine at the bar while she waited for Andy to come pick her up.

"Problems?" Frank said. He was standing on the other side of the zinc bartop, wiping up wet spots with a rag.

"Yeah," she said. Frank went on wiping. In the mirror behind him she could see the round bald spot at the back of his head. She liked Frank and the bar of the restaurant, especially after she was finished work and the place had quieted down a bit. After running around all night, sweating and shouting at each other, all the waiters and waitresses gathered at the bar and had a drink on the house, and talked about the night. It was pleasant to sit quietly, counting out your money and cooling down. All of them talked about their problems with husbands or wives or lovers. None of them knew each other outside the restaurant, though within it they were a tight-knit group. And of course everyone had an enemy within the group, but it was never very serious. The rest of them had left to go drinking by now. It had been an early night.

"My boyfriend from college wants to come down," she told Frank.

"Hmmm," Frank said. "Well we won't tell on you."

That was reassuring.

When Andy arrived Frank gave him a beer on the house and they chatted for a few minutes about basketball.

When they got in the car she asked him if he'd mind driving to the beach. She slammed the door hard without meaning to.

Andy pulled up to the edge of the beach where the road came to an abrupt end and the dune sloped down to the flatter stretch of sand which calmed and held back the violent ocean.

He left the car idling in park. Two pale beams lit up the foam on the crests of the waves.

"Joe wants to come down next weekend," she said, ready to fight. Andy said nothing.

"Did you hear me?" In the dark she could barely see the outline of his profile. She could not discern the expression on his face.

"Yeah," he said.

"Well, what do you think?"

"I think you shouldn't let him fuck with your head," he said slowly, in a completely impartial way.

"But you. What do *you* think?"

"It's none of my business. You've been straight with me all along. What do *you* want?" he paused. "If you want to see him you want to see him. You won't see my ass hanging out in any bars you'll be drinking in with him, I promise you that. I'd shit if I saw him and you together."

"But what about Liz, and dinner?"

"Fuck it," he shrugged it off.

"You're mad, aren't you?"

"No, I'm not mad. I got no right to be mad. What if I fuck somebody while he's down here. Will you be mad?"

"No I won't. But don't tell me about it, okay? I don't want to know about it." She felt that crawling tickle of jealousy which ended up as a shiver in her shoulders.

"Let's go out, Andy. I feel like getting wasted."

Andy was seeing two and sometimes four yellow lines in the middle of the road. They kept splitting and coming together. He was driving forty in a fifty-five zone. Chloe was kissing him and sticking her tongue in his ear. She nibbled on his nose, which made concentrating on the lines impossible.

"I think you're so wonderful," she said. "You're the best person I've ever met. People talk such shit in life. The smarter they are the more shit they talk. Except you. You never talk shit and you're smart. This town is FULL OF SHIT."

She started to unzip his pants and kiss his stomach. Gently he squeezed the back of her neck and tried to pull her up.

"If you go down on me here, I'll kill us both."

She reached into his underpants with her cold hand.

"We're almost there," Andy said. "Just hold on, we're almost home."

He took the left off the highway onto her road. Just as they passed the old graveyard with the white picket fence she shot up in the seat and threw her hand out in front of his face. He swerved into the left lane.

"My daddy's there. I bet you didn't know that. Let's go see my daddy."

Andy righted the car and kept going. Not for anything was he going to walk in a graveyard in the middle of the night.

"You don't want to come with me. Liz used to come with me. You don't give a shit. You don't give a real damn about anything."

She went limp and her head rolled down his chest, into his lap.

"Oh my poor daddy." She began to cry like a child. He felt completely numbed, as though he were lying in a bathtub filled with ice.

"I'm always crying in front of you when I get loaded," she said, sitting up and sniffling. "And you think I'm crazy. I wish you loved me. I wish you loved me more than anything else."

"You are crazy. You want everybody to love you and take your bullshit but you don't want to love them back." At the time this seemed awfully profound to him.

"BULLSHIT?!" She shouted.

"Yeah, bullshit. You love Joe anyway, so shut up." Now he was mad, and it was okay with him.

She started wailing this time. Andy let her wail. At the top of the driveway he stopped the car and left it idling. He waited for her to get out or to say something, but she just sat there leaning against the door with her shoulders shaking. Just as he thought he was going to have to say something she got out and slammed the door. He watched her stumble up the brick path. Her head was hanging between her shoulders. He felt terrible. She shut the kitchen door behind her and switched off the pale yellow outside light.

He sat in the dark trying to think. Before he realized it he was out on the road, heading toward the highway and his house.

As a kid, Andy had had problems controlling his temper. His father had worried that he would not make a good basketball player. It was bad for a basketball player to have such tenuous self-control. Andy remembered himself back then, when he'd started playing Biddy League, the way he remembered his first lay; with an embarrassment that did not fade with time. He remembered starting fights, Ben standing behind him screaming, and his father picking him up and carrying him kicking back to the bench. He had a temper like a little demon.

He remembered particularly one time in Biddy League a kid elbowed Ben in the eye when no one was looking. Ben fell face first onto the court and bled a puddle around his head. Andy had tried to kill the kid by strangling him. His father had to yank Andy off of him and drag him away. "You're OUT!" his father yelled. "We have Goddamn rules here!" He and Ben spent the rest of the game on the bench, Andy crying and Ben with an icepack over his eye. Ben kept saying, "Shut up, Andy. Shut up, will you? I'm okay." But it wasn't only over Ben's eye and the injustice that Andy was crying. He thought he would never get to play again.

After the game their father drove to the clinic for Ben's eye. Andy sat in the back of the car watching the dead trees pass. It was cold and grey outside. "I don't wanna go to no clinic," Ben whined. "You're going," their pop said.

They left Ben with the doctor and went out to the parking lot. The cold air stung Andy's tear-streaked face. While his pop talked they walked around in a circle.

"You can't act like that," his pop said. "Having a temper is fine, but you have to learn to channel it in a positive way. When you get mad, instead of screaming and kicking balls, play harder. You get overexcited, and don't you think they know it? You love the game, that's all right, that's good. But you always have to play under control. You are very, very good. You could be one of the best players this town has ever seen. Don't think you're going to get away with that screaming and yelling crap because I'm your father. When you're playing, I'm not your father, I'm your coach. Now I'm telling you as your coach, I don't ever want to see you act up like that again."

All this was so long ago he'd made up for it a thousand times since then. He found great safety in knowing that he'd acquired such self-control that nothing in the world could ever get him to expose himself like that again.

The phone was ringing when he stumbled into his house. The dogs started barking and chasing each other around between his legs. The phone rang three times before he could get to it, and he was sure his entire family would be giving him shit about it in the morning. He did not want to answer the phone but couldn't think of anything else to do. He picked up the receiver.

"Yep," he said angrily.

"It's me."

"No kidding. Who else would it be at four in the morning?"

"I've been thinking," Chloe said. "I've been very bad to you. I don't know what's going to happen when I go back to school but for now he can go fuck himself. I don't want him to come down. I don't want to screw up this time with you, you know, because I haven't been so happy as I've been with you since, I don't know, years. When I'm with you everything's so easy and I don't feel bad. Listen, can you forget about tonight?"

"Sure," he said. His voice was bland. He wanted to say something nice, nicely. "Okay, I'll call you tomorrow. All right?"

"All right," she said. "I wish you'd come back."

"No, I can't. I was seeing double the whole way over here."

"All right," she sighed. They said good night. He hung up.

He rolled around in his single bed that was damp and smelled moldy. He had a bad case of the spins, and putting one foot on the floor as he lay on his back did not help. "Fucking rumor," he mumbled. He got up to get a glass of water. He went into the

kitchen in his underwear. While he was running the tap he considered walking out the door and getting in the car and going back to
her. He could climb in the window, no problem. He stuck his head
under the faucet and let the cold stream shock some sense into
him. He went into the garage to see if Ben was home.

He flicked the light switch by the door. The bare white bulb
burned his eyes. Ben sat up in bed and blinked at him like a blind
person. It was even damper in the garage. Andy sat shivering by
Ben's feet and pulled one of the blankets up to his chest.

"Bro," Ben said, rubbing his eyes and cheeks with the palms of
his hands. "What the fuck's going on?"

Andy stared at him stupidly.

"You had a fight," Ben said. He could have said, I told you this
was going to happen, the chick's nuts. But there was nothing
condescending in his tone.

"I think this is serious," Ben said. "I think you love her."

PART II

I

Chloe carried one of her cardboard boxes filled with sheets out of the storage room and down the path to her car. There were cars parked all along the street, their gaping trunks and doors and hatches disclosing books and lamps and rugs and other student paraphernalia. She loved being a student. It was wonderful to be back.

Just twenty-four hours ago Andy had helped her pack up her car, and now Joe was walking in front of her, his arms like a forklift carrying her rolled rug and a box of books on top of it.

She watched his ass swing from side to side as he cruised down to the car. He had the practiced strut of basketball players, the unmistakable dip in the step and swoop in the shoulder. He had a neck like the trunk of a large, branchless tree and a small head perched on top of it like an osprey nest.

She had forgotten how much Joe looked like a playing card. His shoulders were square and broad, supple and lanky; made to surround a basketball or a girl's small frame. When he turned sideways he was so thin he practically disappeared. All these things she noticed with fresh interest, he seemed so unfamiliar. They had said very little to each other since she'd arrived the night before and she felt she barely knew him.

They carried all her stored belongings from her old dormitory to her new apartment. Her bedroom was not much bigger than her double bed at home. A walk-through kitchen separated her room from the other girl's. Chloe barely knew her roommate. They had met last spring at the housing lottery, and decided to chance putting their names in for an apartment since the odds were better if you entered the lottery in a pair.

Once all the boxes were piled on the floor, she told Joe that Annie Dupuy was living downstairs in a three-man, and she wanted very much to go see her.

Joe said, "I haven't seen you in three months. Can't you wait till tomorrow to see Annie?"

"I haven't seen Annie in a hell of a lot longer than three months," she said. "I didn't see her all last year."

"Oh, man. This again." Joe rolled his eyes. He threw himself onto the cloth-covered wooden armchair that faced the bed. Chloe sat on the bare mattress. The room looked as blank as a prison cell. The night before she'd arrived too late to pick up her keys at the housing office, and had gone straight to Joe's fraternity.

She'd found him sitting in the living room of his four-man suite, which was furnished with assorted beds and couches left behind by previous occupants. He was listening to Dan Fogelberg. When he saw her he did not get up or say a word.

It was a song about a man trying to understand a woman. It made him cry. Right then he wasn't crying, his eyes were flitting about the room, pausing on everything but her face.

The song reminded him of his first love at Andover, he'd told Chloe. He'd subjected her to his emotional moments with the song so long that it had come to mean something between them as well. As she listened she wondered if he was being angry because she had not let him come down to East Whitman for her birthday. She didn't know what to say to him, and stood by the door waiting for the song to end.

"Joe, let's go down to Vito's and have a beer."

He looked straight in front of him. "Nah, I'm kind of tired. Let's go to bed."

She felt close to him again when he touched her. There was an urgency and a passion in the way they made love that had always surprised her, that now she understood. It had to do with his guilt over making love in the first place. Since the sin was so enormous, there was no reason not to push it to its extreme and enjoy it as much as possible before repenting. Which was what, she now realized, had been her case with Andy.

After they made love they did not talk to each other. She wouldn't ask him about his summer because she was afraid he'd ask about hers. She hardly thought of Andy now. She had spent the drive up cloroxing the summer out of her system. She told herself that it had been a fantasy and it was time to can and shelve it. School was her reality. She listened only to cassettes that reminded her of the good times she'd had with Joe. She wondered if Andy would ever look up her number. She didn't think he'd call unless she called him first. She felt guilt only toward Joe.

In her empty room she sat on the edge of the bed and tapped her sneakers on the floor. Joe stared at her angrily. He had bone structure that befitted a Michelangelo. His face was pale and as immovable as marble. Compared to him, though she was fair, she seemed very tan. She was certain this infuriated him because he thought lying in the sun was a completely bourgeois waste of time. A luxury he could hardly afford, he used to say.

Suddenly she thought of her last night at home and burst out laughing. She'd walked into her dark bedroom after having been out till four, and fell headfirst over all the cardboard boxes she'd forgotten she'd packed. Behind her Andy sat down in the hallway he was laughing so much. "I knew that was going to happen. I was just waiting for the BOOM."

"I'm going downstairs." She got up. "Why don't you come with me?"

Joe shook his head.

"Sit down a minute." He spread his legs and leaned forward on his elbows. As she took a step toward the door he grabbed her knee.

"Sit down," he said.

"I just want to go tell Annie I'm here. I want to go through the course catalog with her. I need a gut this semester. I don't want to overload, see, and Annie always knows about good easy courses. Listen, Goddamnit, we've been through this shit over and over again. I'm sick of it and I want to go the fuck downstairs!"

"I know, I know, you've changed. You need your space. You've changed," he said, "but you still swear like a truck driver."

"I have changed," she said quietly, and sat back down on the bed.

His face was flushed pink now. She thought it was a pity that she found him so handsome. There was something really striking about his shock of black hair and his soft dark eyes, which were the only soft thing in his face. She wondered if there was any way he'd ever listen to her. He was not giving her an inch. She knew that if she gave in now she would keep on giving in and the semester would turn into a repeat of last year.

She said, "This summer, I fell in love with someone else."

She stretched out flat on the bed and stared at the asbestos squares on the ceiling.

"Who?" Joe said. She started to panic, and laughed.

"*Who?*" she said, "WHO? Is that all you can say?"

"Who was it?" Joe said calmly, as though he were a cop interrogating a prisoner.

Her heart was pounding. Because she had no control over what would happen in the next second, she felt distanced from it. She realized she could lie, take it back, "I was just kidding." She would not do that. It would be the beginning of a series of lies that would go on forever.

"No one you know." A half-a-lie, she thought.

"Did you fuck him?"

"At first it was fucking, I guess. But then it was making love." She was enjoying this. She was really showing him now.

"You're a whore," he said. She turned her face away from the ceiling and looked at him, trying not to laugh. His lips were pulled back over his teeth.

"You've got balls, calling me that," she said.

"Well it's the truth," he said.

Her face got hot and her eyes began to water. She did not want a big fight. How could he not understand what she was saying? She suddenly had the urge to beg forgiveness. She wanted to say, "Can't you understand that it didn't mean anything?" but that was a terrible lie as well. She'd said she'd fallen in love. She hadn't fallen in love. Or had she? Maybe she was in love with the idea of Andy, or maybe it was the summer she'd fallen in love with. Andy wasn't part of this reality. Her throat tied itself into a knot. She was beginning to believe she'd gone too far and Joe was going to walk out on her. She thought of the long winter nights that were going to come soon. The parties. The basketball games, football games.

The fraternity dining room, where all her friends (friends?) ate. If he walked out, she would not know where to go, how to begin all over again.

"Can't you ever see anything any other way than black and white? Can't you try? Please?" Like a statue he stared at her. She didn't know him anymore. How could such a gap exist between them?

"Was it good?" Joe said. She started to laugh again. He had all the classic responses and he was speaking them like an automaton.

"He was good to me."

It was much too late to patch anything up.

"You know something, Joe? You haven't learned a fucking thing here. Your ideas are exactly the same as they were the day you walked into Cromwell. It's just fine I guess to cheat on exams and papers and then go to confession. It clears your soul, doesn't it? I wanted so much to do things with you, travel and see new things. You know what Annie told me last summer when she was living in East Whitman? When people are in despair they narrow their perspectives down to what they can accept and live with. You're so in despair you don't even know it."

He shot out of the chair and loomed over the bed. His fists were clenched and ready to hit her. She hoped he would hit her, throw her across the room. It would at least force him to deal with her afterwards. He lifted the metal bedframe and flipped it on top of her. Her head hit the floor and the mattress pressed down on her face. He kicked the frame. She heard his sneakers squeak on the vinyl tiles. The bedroom door slammed, then the front door, echoing like a gunshot in the empty apartment.

Then there was a heavy silence. She tried to move the bed. She had no strength and lay beneath the mattress a long time. She wondered what her roommate would say if she walked in and found her like this. Chloe giggled at the thought. A long time passed. She began to crawl out, inch by inch. When she freed her legs she turned onto her back and sat on the rolled rug. She stared at the black bedframe that looked like a dead animal in rigor mortis, its four legs sticking straight up.

With difficulty she flipped the bed and mattress over and lay down. A drowsiness swept over her and she was forced to close her eyes. I'm in shock, she thought. I've been through this before. She fell asleep.

She awoke to Joe standing in the doorframe with his arms raised above his head. "I'm sorry," he said.

"Oh please come and hold me," she said.

"I guess I've been really selfish," he said. He rushed toward her. As he got to the bed his hands reached forward and grasped her neck.

"What I really want to do is kill you," he said between his teeth. He began to squeeze and she couldn't breathe.

She sat up gripping her neck. The room was quiet and still, the door was closed as Joe had left it. She lay down again with her face pressed into the cool wall and waited. For night. She wanted a drink badly but could not face the walk down to the liquor store. Who knew who she might run into. She needed to see Annie, explain her side of it. She waited for night to fall.

II

Once her room was completely dark she snuck downstairs and knocked on Annie's door. It was terribly hot in the apartment building. The windows were large plates of glass that had been built right into the brick; they did not open. Ten years of rancid and now humid air hung in the halls. She wiped sweat from her forehead, feeling slightly faint in the heat and at the thought that Annie might not be home, that the only thing left for her to do would be to go back to her room and lie in the dark without anything to ease her into sleep.

Annie opened the door and air from a fan blew past her into Chloe's face. Annie gasped when she saw her. She took Chloe by the arm and ushered her to a seat at the kitchen table. Annie was sipping white wine on ice from a stemmed glass. She brought another glass out of a cabinet and filled it with ice. She was completely moved in because she'd gotten her key from the Housing Office three days early.

Chloe emptied her glass and Annie refilled it.

"He flipped the bed over on me." Chloe looked at her friend and thought, Every year she gets better-looking. Annie's face was getting stronger, her clear grey eyes were still joyful and curious, as though they hadn't yet been burdened with a knowledge of sad things.

"What did you do to him?" she asked, shaking her head which made her chestnut curls bounce.

"I told him I fell in love."

"That's going a little hard, isn't it?" Annie looked down and twirled the stem of her glass.

Chloe felt sick inside. She didn't think she had a right to lay it on Annie so she figured it was better to just play the game. I'm normal, she thought.

"I wish I was living with you," she said.

"I wanted to live with you," Annie said, "but I didn't want to live with Joe too."

Chloe nodded.

"Chloe, I don't want to tell you this, but I think you should know before someone else tells you."

Chloe bit her thumbnail and took a big sip of the wine.

"Do you want me to tell you or not?" Annie asked, leaning forward. She waited a second and then went on. "Joe's been seeing a girl up here. Martie Stein. He came back a couple of weeks early. She's a resident adviser for the freshmen so she's been here for a while too."

"I don't want to hear about it."

"Okay. I just wanted you to know. Here." Annie slid the bottle across the tabletop, which was sparkling clean. "Pour yourself another glass."

They sat in silence. The fan buzzed quietly on the counter.

"Are you sure?" Chloe asked after a while.

"Yes. She's pre-med. Martie Stein. She's very nice."

"Okay, stop."

"Okay, here, let's toast. I know this is indiscreet, but 'nothing ventured, nothing gained,' right?"

They drank. Chloe thought it would be much better for her if she could cry. She spent the night with Annie, sharing her single bed.

* * *

The next morning was hot and even more humid. The Cromwell campus was spread out on a low hill that sloped to the bank of the Connecticut River. The heat hung motionless, trapped by the surrounding hills.

Chloe went back to her apartment only to change, and left determined to get things settled with Joe, though she was not sure exactly what needed settling. She walked along the uneven dirt paths that ran parallel to York Street, the campus's most busy street, so that she would not have to look at or talk to people. She entered Kappa Phi through the downstairs door, walked through the dining room, and climbed the stairs.

Joe's fraternity brothers stopped and said hello to her and she tried to respond normally. They seemed to turn away just a little too abruptly, as though they were embarrassed, already quite aware of the situation. It was impossible to keep anything a secret in the frat. It was just as impossible to try to get information about a Kappa Phi from another Kappa Phi.

She saw from the living room that Joe's bedroom door was open a crack. She walked through without knocking and pushed the door forward with the tips of her fingers. Sweat dripped into her eyes. She wiped her face with the cotton sleeve of her dress, and stared blankly at the girl lying on Joe's bed with her arms crossed behind her head. He was sitting by her bare feet. Her flipflops had been neatly placed, exactly parallel to each other, at the foot of the bed. The girl's legs shot up before she caught herself and relaxed. Chloe concentrated on relaxing the muscles in her face. She wanted to fling her course catalog at them.

"Martie, this is Chloe," Joe said very seriously, as though he were performing some kind of official duty. Chloe didn't say anything, the girl didn't say anything and stared at her with the eyes of a cornered rat. She was dark-skinned, dark-haired, and not especially pretty. She might have been very pretty, but to Chloe she looked like a cornered rat.

"Can you come over later?" Chloe's voice trembled. She looked out the window at the steaming street. "There's a couple of things we should straighten out."

"After lunch," he said.

"Thanks." Chloe thought, You compassionate motherfucker.

She walked out the front door. It was enough to walk in like a spy. She was not going to leave that way. She felt watched, scrutinized. She knew it could have all been in her head.

Across the street the campus green sloped uphill toward the row of ivy-covered buildings. They were the old campus, built of red stone, the oldest, and most beautiful. She plodded up the green toward the Administration building. Her cotton dress of Indian print was soaked through with sweat. She looked up at her adviser's office window and realized that she couldn't possibly go in and talk to him. She sat under a large oak and pressed the back of her head into the bark. It was clearly a way to get back at her, she thought. He couldn't possibly give a shit about the girl. She wondered what he would tell Martie about her. Lies, probably. He always told big fibs to make himself important. He'd tell her Chloe was completely neurotic, fucked up in the head. "I *tried* to help her all I could, but . . ." he'd shake his head with a no-hope look in his eyes.

She wondered what her adviser would think of all this. Maybe he'd think it would make a good scene in a play. He would look up from behind the top half of his split glasses and ask her what in hell was wrong. And it would take all she had not to break down and cry like a frightened child.

* * *

"What in hell is wrong with you?" Francis Morgan said. "You're as pale as a blank sheet." He leaned back in his swivel chair which gave easily, and crossed his arms. There were loose sheets of paper and manila folders and books piled everywhere. He noticed her looking around. "See, nothing's changed. I said I was going to spend the summer cleaning this place up. Never got around to it. Maybe next summer."

Every year he said the same thing.

"I sat under a tree outside for a half an hour before I could get my shit together to come in here," she said, trying to smile. "I guess it didn't work."

"Anything *I* can do?"

"No, it's bullshit. My boyfriend left me for a cow. Actually she looks like a rat."

Francis laughed. She laughed too but it was a sick, painful laugh.

"Will you help me pick my classes?"

Francis was the same age as her father would have been. They were both veterans of the European Theater, but Francis had been a paratrooper and her father a plain infantryman.

Chloe had gathered from the fragments of information Francis had offered about his life, that he'd run away from home at seventeen to join the U.S. Army. He completely severed himself from his staunchly religious, factory-working Welsh-born parents. His story was oddly reminiscent of her own father's. Chloe had never met anyone on the Raymond side of her family. Her father, in 1939, had escaped from home as Francis had. And now there were no Raymonds left but Eric and her.

It was this strange similarity which had drawn Francis to her, she thought. Francis had taken a personal stake in her future because her father, a playwright without relatives, a veteran whose work on war Francis had been following for years, had suddenly died and left a daughter who had landed on Francis's doorstep at Cromwell University.

"Well," Francis said. "I signed you up for my theater writing workshop."

"I don't want to act," she said defensively. She was defensive as soon as anyone mentioned theater.

Francis looked up from the list he was holding. "You don't listen to anything, do you? I said *writing* workshop. You don't want to act, you don't act. But you have to write if you take this class."

"As long as I don't have to act." Her fear came in a recurring nightmare. She is given the lead role in a play. The moment she must go on stage in front of an audience she remembers nothing. Not a single line. She stands in front of a thousand blank and waiting faces unable to utter a single word.

Her heart began pounding at the thought of it. She had the odd feeling she was running late to catch a very important train. Francis went on.

"And I thought you might be interested in this Tolstoy seminar. Since you're a junior and you still have no idea what in hell you're doing here, you may as well get a well-rounded education."

She appreciated the way he ploughed through her ups and downs and neuroses without ever imposing fatherly advice on her. Too many people had tried to play father to her. It never worked and was only offensive. The only other Great One was Jack. Jack never tried to replace her father. Jack had moved back to Mississippi. He called her every couple of months, late at night, drunk, and read poems to her and told her what books to read. Once in a while he sent her money.

"Okay," she said. "Tolstoy. And I'm teaching French. All I need is a gut. I don't trust your opinion on guts so I'll speak to an expert. Like my friend Annie Dupuy."

They talked for a long while. Francis pretended he had nothing else to do, though the phone kept ringing and people kept stopping by. When she left his office, the heat did not bother her so much, and she felt ready to start back to work.

III

She made a pattern for herself. She went to classes and to the library. When she'd finished her work she went to Annie's and they sat in her kitchen and drank wine. Sometimes Chloe spent whole afternoons talking to Francis Morgan about theater, about her father's work, about her classes. Francis wanted to write plays but admitted himself that he was a much better essayist, and teacher. Francis knew everything about theater. And he thought Chloe's father had written the best psychological plays on the Second World War ever. Especially on the Occupation of France, the end of which they'd both witnessed first-hand.

Both with Francis and Annie she found relief from the tornado that wreaked havoc in her guts day and night. She could not talk to them about it. She didn't want them to think she was crazy, though she herself knew she was definitely in the middle of a breakdown. But as her mother would be quick to point out, as long as you *know* you're having a breakdown, you're okay.

She was shedding pounds daily, but didn't mind this because she liked being too thin better than being too fat. She studied like a fiend; when she worked she did not think about Joe or Martie, or what he could be telling his new disciple. The hardest thing was convincing herself that she'd made the right decision. At night she could not bear being without him. She desperately missed having someone to share her entire soul with.

She avoided running into Joe and Martie by staying away from certain spots; Kappa Phi, the gym, the student center. She also avoided places that brought back memories, like her old dorm, certain trees they'd sat under. She felt like a mouse in an electric maze. Remain clear of obstacles at all costs, everything is likely to hurt.

Often she stayed in the library until it closed. The library was a safe place because Joe never studied, and Martie was pre-med and studied in the Science Library.

One night Chloe was sitting in a cubicle in the library reading students' French papers when someone behind her said her name.

"Ms. Raymond, where the hell have you been?"

She looked up. It was John Falcone, one of Joe's Kappa Phi brothers.

"Hi, Falcon," she said, rubbing her eyes. He slid a book face up onto the desk.

"Here," he said, "I'm returning your book."

"What book?"

He winked at her. She looked down and saw *Hitler: A Study in Tyranny*. There were four lines of cocaine one inch long spread out across Hitler. She slid over in the booth.

"Here, sit down a minute." He handed her a plastic bic pen emptied of cartridge and ballpoint. She stuck the wider end in a nostril and inhaled two of the lines. She handed him the pen.

"Thanks, Falcon."

"No problem," he said. "Now seriously, where've you been hiding? You're not eating at Kappa Phi this year?"

She blinked at him. Her eyes hurt. "Are you kidding?"

"It's Joe. The chick doesn't eat there. What do you care for, anyway? You've been hiding from everybody. Some people even think you took the semester off."

"Don't give me ideas," she said.

He tugged at the sleeve of her sweatshirt. "Come on, let's go down to Vito's and have a beer. Have a few brewskis, huh?"

He handed her the pen again. "Here, do the rest. You look like you need it, Ray."

Falcon was five-eight and weighed around a hundred and sixty-five pounds. None of it was fat. He had dark brown hair and piercing cold blue eyes, a narrow chin and a broken nose. The nose came from playing hockey. They said he used to play like a possessed man. But he'd quit. "I wanted to study," he'd told Chloe. "I had a revelation."

On the way down to Vito's he told her he'd awakened one morning and it hit him. He just couldn't buy the frat shit anymore. As freshmen they were all so dumb and full of themselves.

"Brotherhood my fucking ass," he told her. They were against him now, at Kappa Phi, because he was dealing cocaine. And the hockey players were mad at him for quitting hockey. "There are more important things in life. Like studying because pretty soon we're going to be outa here, and then what? I don't want to move back in with my folks."

She wondered when Falcon studied. She'd never seen him open a book. He was always partying. But they said he was a wiz in economics, top of the class. All his papers and exams came back with big red A's on them. "Shit, I give my papers to the Kappa Phi files, what else do they want?"

Falcon began meeting her in the library every night, and they walked downtown to Vito's for a few drinks. Joe never went out during the week; basketball season had started. As it got colder they began taking her car.

They talked about books, mostly. Falcon liked Pynchon, and Tom Robbins, and spy thrillers. She'd never read Pynchon or Robbins; he told her about them and she told him about *War and Peace*, which was her new passion. She was having a hard time in Francis's playwriting class. Her scenes kept coming out lousy. "My heart's not in it," she told Falcon.

"Write about something that hurts," he said.

"What are you nuts?" she said, thinking that maybe Falcon was in the wrong field.

There was a gang of diehards that hung out in Vito's every night. Falcon sold them a lot of cocaine. Chloe began to get a reputation as a coke head, which didn't bother her at all since she wasn't the least bit interested in cocaine. Unless she was completely exhausted, the high made her feel like she was walking a tightrope, it made her think ugly things. On it she could not sleep. She would much rather get drunk, and sleep.

Falcon never made a pass at her. In the beginning she'd been distant, stepping away when he touched her. Joe had made her paranoid of boys a long time ago. "All the guy wants to do is hose you," he used to say. Chloe never got the sense that Falcon was even remotely interested in her sexually. She had heard that cocaine tended to destroy people's sex drives. Maybe that was true. But she did not want to blame it on the cocaine; she wanted to prove Joe wrong.

They never spoke about Joe. She knew Falcon saw him every day, knew everything about him. She did not want to hear about the new girl; she wanted to believe she meant nothing to Joe. And Falcon did not volunteer any information.

"Some things you shouldn't think about," he told her one night. "Or talk about. It's like picking at scabs. They heal much better if you leave them alone. Even if they itch. And then when they heal, you get this BIG, HARD scar. Then you can start scratching all you want. You can even start writing about it. Get it?"

Every night she waited for Falcon and fretted that he might not show up. At around a quarter to eleven she began watching the clock, her mouth watering at the thought of her first Mount Gay and pineapple juice. She fretted about everything; that she would not wake up in time for class the next morning, would not finish her papers on time, that her car would break down, the heater in her room would break down. It was her nature.

One night Falcon was ten minutes late. Chloe was almost hysterical. She considered calling the Kappa Phi pay phone. What if Joe answered?

When they'd left the library and were alone she said, "Falcon, I'm scared one night you won't show up and I'll freak out."

In the dark she couldn't see his face. "If I can't show up one night, I'll let you know." He gave her arm a good squeeze.

"This is the nicest part of my whole day," she said. "I look forward to this so much."

"I do too. Every Goddamn day there's fewer and fewer people I want to talk to around here," he said angrily. "They gave me hell tonight. About the cocaine. They don't want me dealing out of the frat. But they all buy the shit, right?"

"Why do you want to deal, Falcon?"

He stopped under a streetlight and stared at her as though he were uncertain whether to take her question seriously or not.

With a pained frown he said, "I can't cut it out. I can't get out of bed in the morning without doing a line."

She couldn't imagine cocaine being physically addictive. She thought of cocaine as she thought of Mount Gay and pineapple juice. Without alcohol she could not sleep. It was psychological because her head was fucked up right now. She wondered what could possibly be wrong with Falcon's head. She felt very fragile when she thought Falcon could be leaning on her, because she was leaning on him.

"That's the way I feel about drinking," she said. "I think it's psychological. It's in your head."

He nodded, she thought, to end it rather than because he agreed. They got in her car; Falcon drove.

At the bar he ordered a pitcher of beer and Chloe had her Mount Gay.

"And that fucking Joe," Falcon said, rubbing his face with his palms. He looked at himself and then at her behind the bottles in the mirror. She looked down and ran her feet over the sawdust on the floor, making little piles of it.

"We used to be good friends, even though he always thought I was trying to fuck you. At dinner tonight that asshole Oakwood starts raging about junkies. You know Oakwood, the tackle? Rigor mortis with arms like that?" He encircled his thigh with his hands. "Oakwood says he won't eat his meal with a junkie at the table. Hey, I don't want to eat with you either, buddy, I wanted to say. But fuck him, I'm no junkie.

"Joe's sitting across the table from me, right? We just came downstairs from snorting lines in my room. He's sitting there looking pious and uninvolved. Doesn't he know Pontius Pilate? Good fucking Catholic. *I've* never cheated here. The priests may have been tough, man, but they taught us right.

"I can't count on my two hands the times Joe's come up to my room looking for blow. I never asked him to pay me. He brings that chick Martie up to my room to show off how cool he is, how he's got so many friends that'll do him favors." Falcon stopped as though someone had slapped him in the face. He looked worried. She felt betrayed.

"I'm sorry," he said numbly. She felt like she'd swallowed half a lemon and it was stuck in her throat.

"Goddamnit, I'm sorry. But he's a spineless chickenshit. He bends whatever way the wind's blowing."

Tears streamed down her face. She pulled the cocktail napkin out from under her glass and pressed it to her face. It was icy cold.

"He's a court jester. I'm telling you."

She took a bunch of cocktail napkins from the bartender's pile and pressed a few to her eyes. She folded one around an ice cube from her drink.

"Come on. You've got to get your ass out of this funk," Falcon said. "Find someone new. Come on." He shook her gently by the shoulder.

"I can't stand it. I want to plant a bomb in his room and watch them both come flying out the fucking roof."

"Ah, she's a ninny," Falcon said, "you should see the way he pushes her around," as though that could help.

Chloe had not told a soul that Joe still came over. Once in a while, he stopped by her room in the afternoon. He made it seem like he was checking up on her, making sure she was okay. He'd talk about his aches from basketball practice, looking truly pained but fighting it. She could see that he was a self-indulgent poseur, yet she still loved him and couldn't bring herself to tell him to leave. In her confusion she would sit back and stare at his no longer familiar face and wait for him to decide whether or not he wanted to sleep with her. She never received him in the kitchen, which would have solved that problem. She wanted it. She was powerless.

"Are you sleeping with Falcon?" he'd ask, now a concerned analyst, now fidgeting like a small boy at a dinner table full of grown-ups. Her fury exhausted her so she refused to answer him.

They inevitably ended up in bed. She hated him for not having the strength to refuse her. They made love more violently and passionately than they ever had, because now it was even more forbidden. They did not talk to each other afterwards. He'd sit up immediately and start putting on his clothes. She'd watch his long, flat back head for the door, wanting to scream and throw books at him. He paralyzed her.

It was a weak thrill, and not a very satisfying one, to know that he was fucking around on his new chick.

Falcon was drumming the bar top.

"Isn't it mental with cocaine?" she asked.

"No."

"Well. It can't be that bad yet. Is it?"

"I don't know."

"If you want to stop, I'll try to help you any way I can."

"I don't feel like it. When I feel like it, I guess I'll quit," he said.

IV

She had nightmares about Joe every night. It got to the point where she couldn't remember what was real and what had taken place in her mind.

One night during midterm week, a strange thing happened. She was lying in bed rereading the battle of Austerlitz in *War and Peace.*

There was a knock on the outside door. She put the book down and went to open it. Her father was standing in the hallway wearing a grey tweed jacket. A leather carryall bag like an old postman's satchel was slung over his shoulder. He smiled and stretched his arms out to her. She clung to his neck like a child. He smelled of his spicy English after-shave and of thick smoldering cigars.

"Daddy! What are you doing here?"

"I came to visit you," he said.

"Where have you been? My God, it's been so long."

"I know," he said. "It's been a long time. I had a hard time finding you."

"Why didn't you write to me?"

"There was no mail."

She did not want to get him angry by asking too many questions.

"I heard you had a pretty serious boyfriend."

She shrugged. "It's over now. I don't care much."

"Want to take a walk?"

"Sure," she said. "I have to get dressed. You want to come in for a minute?"

"No," he said. "Just throw your coat on over your nightie. I don't have much time."

She slipped into her boots without putting on socks and grabbed her coat.

Outside it was drizzling. A warm wind was blowing. She unbuttoned her coat. The streetlights made pale glimmering circles on the walkway and the rain fell like gold needles.

She took him to York Street and showed him the Language building, which was only two houses down from Kappa Phi, but she was not afraid tonight. She tried the glass door but it was locked. From the sidewalk she pointed to the window hidden in the ivy where her Tolstoy seminar met on Tuesdays and Thursdays, and to the window below it, which was her French class.

"I'm teaching French, Daddy."

He squinted at the windows and smiled. "Do you like Tolstoy?" he asked.

"I love Tolstoy," she said. "We're reading *War and Peace*."

She looked at his profile, the wrinkles at the corner of his eye. His forehead was long and full of lines, his eyebrow thick and grey. He had not changed at all.

"You look exactly the same," she said.

He smiled. "You look older. But you're too sad."

She led him slowly up one of the paths toward the row of red buildings.

"Isn't it pretty here," he said.

"Daddy? I'm scared."

He said, "You have to grow your own roots now."

"But I don't want to grow my own roots." She wanted to ask him so many questions, tell him everything she'd learned, and make him proud. She wanted to kiss him out of happiness and relief but was afraid of being too forward, not grown up enough. She did not want him to get angry and go away.

She showed him Francis Morgan's window.

"Does he help you pick your classes?" her father asked.

"Yes. He helps me a whole lot. You know, he was in the War too. In France. He's read your plays. He thinks they're great."

He chuckled quietly. "Isn't that funny?" he said.

"Your plays are the best, Daddy."

"Your mother loves you kids more than anything in the world. She's still trying to get over me being gone. But you'll see, she'll get better with time."

"Aren't you going to stay now?"

"For a little while."

She gripped the hard muscle in his upper arm and pulled herself closer to him. They walked down the path, past the Admissions Office and the old theater. When they got to the chapel, he stopped and looked up at the stained-glass window above the door.

"Isn't that beautiful," he said. "I wonder . . ." He took her hand and led her around to the back. The wind blew her coat open and the rain, stronger now, blinded her eyes.

He reached into his leather bag and pulled out an old rusted key.

"There's an entrance here, I think," he said.

He slid the key into a slab of stone and a whole section of the wall opened up. Above the entrance something was written in gothic lettering. She saw "I AM . . ." before he pulled her down a steep stairway into darkness.

At the bottom there was a long lit-up passage of dirty yellow mosaic, like a public bathroom, or a Paris subway station.

"Where are we going, Daddy?" She felt adventurous and not a bit frightened. They walked on.

He stopped in front of a grey door that said "Men" above it.

"I have to go now," he said. He brushed her wet hair away from her face and kissed her forehead. His lips were cold.

"Can't I come with you?"

"No," he said. "My heart hurts again."

She said, "Oh, no, Daddy."

She wanted to take the hurt upon herself. She couldn't stand to see him hurting again, and remembered that this was impossible. She'd seen his blue body stretched out on the hospital bed. He disappeared behind the door. She banged on it till her knuckles bled.

She woke up soaking wet. The window was open. The rain had made a little puddle on top of the radiator. The blankets were on the floor; her nightgown was glued to her. The room was unfamiliar and in the silence it seemed to be breathing. She heard the alarm clock ticking and the wind blowing outside the window.

Shivering uncontrollably she reached for the phone wire and pulled it toward her. She dialed Andy's phone number at Sacred Heart University.

V

They were playing Frisbee in the hall. Andy stood in the doorway of his room ducking back when the Frisbee flew by. The guys got extra points for smacking people in the head. Andy worried that they'd get Chloe when she walked through the swinging glass doors. One of the glass panes was missing. They'd been playing basketball in the hall the first week and the ball had gone right through it. No one had come to fix it yet. Andy noticed for the first time that the hall looked like shit. There was graffiti on the walls, broken glass; it looked like New York City.

He went into his room to flip the Grover Washington, Jr., album. They were shouting and swearing outside his room, then suddenly there was a dead silence and he heard the Frisbee slide all the way down the hall and smack against the far wall. He heard Chloe nervously asking for him, and he walked out of his room.

The whole damn basketball team was standing around staring at her as though she were an apparition. She was wearing a blue pea coat and jeans, but her hair was still that sunny wheat color, and though she seemed awfully thin, she was still beautiful in a delicate way. He went up to her and gave her a small hug. You could have put two of her in the coat. The cold and distant look was in her eyes. It was the look he'd once taken for belligerence, which now he recognized as plain fright. He knew her better than they both thought.

When she'd called the other night he'd been in bed with a girl he sort of liked who was on the gym team. He'd been lying with his face to the wall and the girl's ass against his, which seemed like an extremely personal position, when he'd heard the hall phone ringing. The guy down the hall who stayed up all night bellowed "FLETCHER!" and he knew immediately it had to be Chloe. He threw back the covers and hopped over the girl who was out cold and ran down the hall, zipping his pants up along the way.

She'd never called this late at night. He asked her right off if something was wrong. She said she was having terrible dreams, her voice trembling. "I'm afraid to go to sleep because of these fucking dreams I'm having," she said.

"Do you want me to come up?" He was already figuring out what time he'd have to leave Cromwell to get back in time for practice.

"No, no," she didn't sound sure. "It's the middle of the night. I'm sorry."

He told her to come down for the weekend. She said she had a lot of studying to do. Would he go with her to the library? she asked. Hell no, he said, he wouldn't go to the library, but he didn't mind if she studied because he had basketball practice Friday night and Saturday morning.

"Thank you, Andy," she said.

Now as they stood in his hall he didn't know what to say, whether he should introduce her to the guys or take her straight into his room. He decided on the room.

She dropped her bags on the floor. She had two bags, a little one with clothes in it, and a big heavy arm bag filled with books.

She couldn't sit still for a minute. She sat on the bed, then got up and went to the stereo, put on an album, let one song play, and then went back and changed it. She looked at the pile of dirty clothes he'd kicked into a corner, and at the picture of her he'd taped to the closet door. Andy sat down on the bed.

"You put that up to make me feel good?" she laughed.

"Yeah, I put it up this afternoon, just for you." The picture infuriated every girl he brought to his room.

She went to the pile of clothes and pulled a cranberry-colored sweatshirt out that his sister had given him. She held it up and asked if she could have it.

"Sure. Just don't wear it around my house. My sister'll have a fit. It's dirty," he said.

"Oh I don't care."

"You want to go eat somewhere?"

"Let's party."

"You're too thin," he said. She laughed. She wrapped the sweat-shirt around her shoulders and kneeled in front of him. She looked up, her lips parted a little. He wanted to kiss her. Her face came toward his crotch and kneeling between his legs she held on to him with her head in his lap.

"I missed you," he said, patting her hair, smoothing it.

"I wish things could be different," she said.

They lay facing each other on the bed. He ran his hands over her body nervously. It was like touching a new person. She was much too thin.

"You're too thin," he told her. Her breasts felt deflated, as though the juice had been sucked out of them.

"I miss the summer," she whispered.

"I miss you more than the summer," he said.

"I feel terrible. I can't drag you down in this shit with me."

He didn't know what shit she was talking about.

"Don't worry," he said, "you couldn't drag me into any shit."

"I didn't know if you'd want to see me. I've been really bad about taking time off from school. Once you're there, you know, it seems hard to leave."

He felt strongly that he did not fit into her Cromwell life. She had no space for him there. He didn't like the way it made him feel, but he didn't blame it on her. She couldn't help the way she was.

"Ever since the first day when I told Joe I fell in love with someone else, in my dreams he's been getting me back."

Andy didn't believe she'd really fallen in love with him, though he was sure she loved him. For him it was a terrible new feeling, this caring for someone else. Sex, in the end, had so little to do with it. He looked at her picture and then at her. His throat ached.

"You can come down here weekends if you want to," he said slowly and evenly. "You can stay here with me if it's the place that's driving you crazy. You're reminded of him all the time."

"It's too small," she agreed. "It's like getting divorced and then buying a house on the same block as your ex-husband. It's insane.

Joe's got a chick living with him. My pride is completely destroyed." This made them both laugh.

"Well you can come down here and stay with me."

"Andy, I'm so fucked up. I feel like my whole life is school and I have nothing else in the world." She looked around again. "It's so strange to see you in a strange place!"

He did not know if he should try to make love with her. He was afraid to hurt her she seemed so fragile. They lay on the bed talking until it was time for him to go to practice. He left her propped up, covered with blankets. She was reading *War and Peace*. What would his buddies think of that? Not a single one of them cared a damn about what Sacred Heart had to offer academically. Play your four years and get out with a degree. Andy wanted to go to Australia when he was finished, play semipro ball for a few years.

During practice he imagined her sitting in the bleachers watching him. "Bravo! Bravo!" she'd be shouting. Andy had taken her to a summer league scrimmage once. His father had been coaching. Whenever his father's team scored she shouted, "Bravo!" and Ben, who was sitting on the other side of her, ducked into the collar of his shirt.

He took a shower and went back to his room. She was still reading. Her eyebrows were one black line above her nose.

"How's it going?" he said. She looked up and smiled.

"How was practice? My favorite character in here is called Prince Andrew. You're my Prince Andrew," she said, laughing. "I think of you when I'm reading this, even though he's nothing like you, really. Or maybe he is, a little."

Andy shook his head. He said he couldn't believe anybody would sit down and read a book that size and actually enjoy it. "Maybe if I was in jail I'd enjoy it," he said.

He took her down to the pub. He didn't care if the girls he'd screwed saw them together. He'd decided Chloe was the serious one for him. On the way in she said, "I love making enemies that don't even know me," elbowing him. He liked that she expected nothing from him in the chastity department. Fidelity and chastity, as far as he was concerned, were two very separate and unconnected things.

Andy had never seen her drink so much so fast and it worried him. He stopped counting after she'd had eight screwdrivers. She did not seem to be getting drunk, though her eyes were getting foggy. He asked her to dance to get her away from the bar. She said no. It was the first time she'd ever said no to dancing.

Walking back to the dorm she didn't say a word. He had his arm tightly wrapped around her waist when suddenly her legs gave out and she slipped through his grasp like sand. She threw up all the screwdrivers, crying with her hair falling over her face. Crouching behind her he held her hair back and patted her shoulder blades which felt bony like the wings of a bird. He picked her up and held her tightly. She was crying hot tears against his neck.

"I love you, little girl," he said. He was sure she didn't hear him. It was better that way.

He undressed her slowly, enjoying it. She was limp as a rag doll and did not resist. When he'd tucked her into his bed he undressed himself and pressed in against her.

"Please don't ever go away. Just stay right there," she mumbled. He thought of practice in the morning as they began kissing each other.

Sunday morning he watched her brown Rabbit from his window as it disappeared around the corner of the building. He felt sad. Saturday afternoon, after practice, she'd read *War and Peace* while Andy watched basketball on TV. He'd taken her to Beefsteak Charlie's for dinner and she'd eaten a little bit.

Over Christmas break they would be home and things would be back to normal. Once school was out they would be okay together. Sometimes he had the urge to eject himself out of this whole fucking scene and take her with him. To a place where it would be warm and they wouldn't have to think about a thing.

VI

Prince Andrew is going to die. Chloe couldn't stand it. After he'd gotten wounded in battle she looked ahead and read the chapter summaries. There it was: *Prince Andrew's last days and death*. She didn't want to read on but had to read on because half the final exam would deal with this book. Well, it's only a book, she told herself, and tried to keep thinking that way.

While Prince Andrew is dying he's thinking how sad it is that the people he loves can't see death as he does. He doesn't mind death at all. He just feels sorry for them that they have to suffer while he's feeling at peace for the first time in his life.

A thought clear as a lightning bolt flashed through her head. The person who's dying doesn't give a shit! It's us. WE give a shit.

"How the fuck could he know that?" she said out loud in her cubicle. The dry heat in the library burned her nostrils and eyes.

She fished for a dime at the bottom of her book bag. She wanted to call her professor. She looked at the clock and saw it was already ten-thirty, too late. She thought of calling her mother, but her mother wouldn't know what the hell she was talking about. She decided not to call anybody and paced the area between the elevator and the stairs, waiting for Falcon.

In Vito's, after they'd settled down at the bar, Falcon said, "You're weird tonight," and glanced at her anxiously.

"Falcon, what do you think of this?" She wondered now if she'd made the whole thing much bigger than it was. Maybe it was only important to her because she knew what it was like to watch someone die.

"Can I read you something?" She was excited and Falcon was staring at her strangely.

"Sure, read me something. Let's go sit in the back."

They sat in the last dark booth, far from the pinball machine and the jukebox. Chloe opened the book and held it up to the dim yellow lamp that hung on the wall above the table.

She read him only what was essential: Prince Andrew watching the ones he loves grieve over him, sorry that he can't explain that in the end there is just peace and death is a friend.

They sat in silence. Chloe wiped her wet eyes; Falcon went to the bar and came back with a scotch on the rocks.

He took a deep breath, a long swig, and said, "You know, I've thought about dying a lot. About how they'd feel about it. My family." He made a vague gesture behind his shoulder. "I'm selfish. I like to think of them grieving. They'd go to church, pray for my soul. It would make them feel better to think of me up there." Another vague gesture, this time toward the ceiling.

"We didn't have religion in my family," Chloe said. "Death is death and then you rot. We didn't have anything."

"I think it would help a whole lot to have something else to turn to. Even if it's bullshit."

Chloe shook her head. "I just hope, you know, that this is true." She tapped the cover of the book. "Everybody was screaming and carrying on because my father didn't finish his play. It was a tragedy. A terrible shame for everybody. I hope that at the end he didn't give a shit if he finished his play or not."

It was not possible for her to explain to Falcon either that she had suddenly understood a crucial thing. Her father had tried to tell her without being harsh that he was going to die, but she wouldn't listen to him. She did not want to believe the world could continue without him. The world, she'd come to realize, continued perfectly well without him. Everything continued perfectly well, except her.

She made Falcon drive when they left the bar. Main Street was completely deserted. Falcon did not take a right and head back toward the campus. He cruised through town and then took the road that ran along the bank of the river. He drove fast down the straight road that he knew would soon begin to curve.

He pressed down on the gas pedal.

He wondered if he'd make it to Sci Li tonight. He felt drained of everything but alcohol.

He hated the creeps who went to the library so that people would know they studied hard, who went up to the professors at the end of class, who ratted on cheaters because they felt it was their moral duty. Sci Li late at night was a haven for Falcon. From 2 to 7 A.M. there was nobody but him. At seven in the morning the old Italian janitors came in with their sweepers and wrecked the silence.

"Drive faster," Chloe said.

He was going ninety and the wheel was jiggling furiously in his hands. This was just another way of having sex, he thought. It was definitely sexy. He knew he would keep going faster till she told him to slow down. The road began to curve and the tires screeched. He told himself to play the game fair and right. He had to take the car to its limit without losing control. No point getting reckless. Trees jumped in front of the windshield with their white arms and fingers spread—*BOO!* they said, and then retreated.

Up ahead to the right was a weigh station. Falcon knew there was a hairpin right after it. He asked himself in all seriousness if they could make it around the bend. He didn't think they could. He wanted to try it anyway.

"Go faster," she said.

No more Cromwell or Kappa Phi or Sci Li. Just as they were passing the weigh station he pulled the wheel as hard as he could to the right. The car spun doughnuts in the weigh station parking lot.

He was sweating under his down jacket. Sweating as though he'd run six miles. The car breathed heavily, making its ticking, crackling noises.

As he wiped his forehead he noticed his hand was shaking.

"I know what I'm going to write my Tolstoy paper on," Chloe said. "I'm going to write it on death."

She has no idea how crazy I am, he thought.

* * *

The next morning was a Friday. She had to hand in a written scene for Francis Morgan's Playwriting class by five. She hadn't tried to write anything that week. Every week she became more and more discouraged. Francis liked her but he was not a sap, and maybe especially because he liked her, he was harder on her than on the rest of his students. Maybe because her father had been such a good playwright Francis expected her to have inherited some of the talent. Her talent was acting, and she'd given that up anyway; so WHY was she in this class?

She sat down at her typewriter—her father's IBM Selectric II which she'd appropriated from his study when her mother had started giving his belongings away to all his dear friends—and tried to think of what she could possibly write that would please Francis and get her off the hook. She hated it.

After several tries at bed scenes (Francis seemed to like her bed scenes alright though he'd never had *any* of her writing read aloud in class), she crumpled all her half-written pages and threw them on the floor.

Fuck him, she thought. I'll drop the class. She couldn't drop the class, though. She tried to relax and make her mind a void. Sometimes it helped. She knew it did with acting.

Daughter: The lilacs have never been so huge, Daddy.

Father: It's a good thing we cut them back last year.

She thought for a while, feeling like a very cold person.

Daughter: You should see them. Will you be home in time to see them?

Father: I don't know, honey.

She typed on furiously through the afternoon. In the scene a man is lying in a hospital bed. He can't move his arms very well because he's hooked up to all sorts of tubes and wires. His daughter comes to see him. He tries to tell her that he is going to die, but he won't come right out and say it because he doesn't want to frighten her. She also knows he's probably going to die but she won't admit it. The man is resigned, and his manner is calm and benevolent. The girl, being his daughter, is stubborn and proud.

When Chloe was finished she did not read the scene over. She made a title page—"No Title," it said—and ran the paper over to Francis's office. It was a quarter to five. She hesitated before dropping it in the cardboard box marked Theater 251. She lifted the first few papers in the box and slid hers in underneath.

On Monday she found a note from Francis in her mailbox. "This is your best yet," it said. "I've xeroxed and handed your piece around to the class. We'll do a reading of it on Wednesday—Francis."

She stormed into his office.

"I don't want it read, Francis!" She was almost shouting. Francis sat back in his swivel chair with his hands folded calmly over his little round belly.

"I told you you don't have to act in this class, but as far as the work is concerned, you're just like everybody else. What do you think a play's about? You have to share your work. You're not writing a diary." The diary comment infuriated her.

"I'm *not* writing a diary," she said. She had nothing to say. She turned her back on him and headed for the door. She could feel him smiling behind her. Goddamn him, she thought. Francis was the only other person who'd ever succeeded in making her feel like a total fool for all the right reasons.

The class was held in the old theater. They made a circle of folding chairs in the center of the house, read aloud, and then discussed whatever scene Francis had chosen and handed out to them earlier. Sometimes he picked terrible ones (Chloe was thankful he'd spared her this), which was supposed to teach you what not to do but ended up blocking the poor writer beyond repair.

Chloe was nervous as hell and hoped it didn't show. She had on her cold, taut, distant face, which she could not shake off; it was her involuntary shield.

Francis was being a serious hardass. "Alright let's get started here, we don't have all day. Has everybody read the scene?" ("Yes, yes, yes" mumbles from everybody.) "Okay," he said loudly, "do I have any volunteers?"

Clark Smith said, "I'd like to try reading the father." He was older, he'd been a marine in Vietnam.

Chloe, who'd sat paralyzed in her chair, relaxed. She knew Clark would read the father right. He was a quiet, modest person with deeply sad eyes, and by far the most experienced and most talented writer in the class. Francis had selected them from personal interviews. He had a waiting list forty names long.

"I'd like to read the girl," Isabelle Vincent said in her sweet voice, and Chloe cringed. Isabelle was French-Canadian; a real one, not from descent like Annie. She was a black-haired girl with a pale olive complexion, high, round cheekbones, and shiny dark eyes. She was very pretty. Chloe didn't like her, but it was not because Isabelle was pretty. She was a talented actress, and had already starred in several main-stage productions. Chloe had seen her perform and found that, unlike everybody else, she had problems taking Isabelle's acting seriously. Isabelle did not interact with the other characters. She was absorbed with displaying her talent, regardless of whether her talent, at the moment, served the action of the play. Chloe thought she was not terribly intelligent, which went badly with vanity. Isabelle took herself very seriously.

"Okay, let's go," Francis said.

"The lilacs have never been so huge, Daddy," Isabelle said, barely looking at the xeroxed page. Her voice was a loud whisper, her face already drooping with grief.

"It's a good thing we cut them back last year," Clark said dreamily. Chloe thought he was almost smiling.

"You should see them. Will you be home in time to see them?" Urgency in her voice, a tremble.

"I don't know, honey." Clark seemed uncertain of whether to react to Isabelle's open display of grief, or to continue as he'd begun. He was frowning slightly as they went on. Pretty soon Isabelle was shedding genuine round, sparkling tears.

"But in February you only stayed in three weeks!" she said, panicked.

By the time Isabelle started crying Chloe was livid. Her face was burning and tears were forming in her own eyes. She had the sensation she was being robbed. It was not meant to be read this way. It was not honest and it wasn't true.

"Excuse me," she said. She was surprised by the hardness of her voice. "This scene is not supposed to be read sadly. That's the whole point."

"Well there are no directions here," Isabelle said, "I mean, except for *pause* and *quickly* and so on."

"I didn't think it needed explicit directions. I thought the scene spoke for itself." She looked at Francis, hoping he would say something.

"Would you like to read it?" he said.

She could not look at Isabelle. She could feel Isabelle's dark eyes scrutinizing her. She had never seen Chloe act. Chloe did not want to read it but thought it would be chickenshit to back down now.

"All right," she said.

They started back at the beginning. Her tongue and throat were parched and she wished she had a drink with liquor in it in her hand. It was good, she thought, that she was feeling defensive the way the girl was feeling defensive with her father.

"The lilacs have never been so huge, Daddy." Chloe faked enthusiasm, but only slightly. She kept her voice down. The girl's whole countenance was much too hard and fragile to be truly enthusiastic.

They read on. Clark played the father the way she'd hoped he would. Tired, calm, gentle, without frustration. The father was kind and also stubborn and wanted to avoid lying to his daughter, to prepare her in some way without causing her pain.

"It'll be okay. You'll see. You'll be going away soon. You'll meet all new people. Gee, you're going to love college. I wish I could go with you."

"I'll call you every day, you can help me write my papers over the phone." She wasn't so tough now. She weakened the more her father talked calmly and lightly about a future that might not include him.

Clark paused a long while, not responding to the last line. Then he went on, lightly, to something else. Something that was bothering him.

"You have to promise me to be nice to your mother. I know she's not acting normal with me in here."

Very seriously, she said, *"I'll do anything you say, Daddy."*

They talked about the garden. Which plants bloomed when, and how long the lilacs would last. The father's voice slowed with exhaustion.

"I . . . I'd better go now, Daddy. You're tired. I'll see you tomorrow." This was a question without being one.

"Bye bye," the father winked. *"Go on home now."*

"I'll see you tomorrow," Chloe said again, her voice trembling now.

A long pause. *"Go on home, sweetie."*

When she looked up her eyes were blinded with tears. She wiped them quickly with the tips of her fingers, and saw that Francis's eyes were tearing too. The class sat in silence a long while afterwards. Clark blew his nose. Chloe still could not look at Isabelle. The discussion went very well.

After class Clark came up to her and asked her if she'd like to go for coffee. "I think you should be acting," he said.

"I can't act," she told him.

"I still think you should be acting," he said, as though what she'd said was irrelevant. They walked out the door together.

VII

The next time Chloe went down to see Andy she also came back early Sunday morning. There was nothing for her to do at Sacred Heart and it was difficult for her to study while watching TV. When she got back to Cromwell she went straight to Annie's apartment. She dropped her bags in the corner and sat down at the kitchen table. Annie was baking cranberry bread. The kitchen smelled like a pastry shop. Chloe's stomach ached. Annie sliced a piece off the hot loaf and handed it to her on a napkin, then resumed writing out an application across the table. Annie was always applying for this and that: loans, memberships, jobs.

"What's that?" Chloe asked.

"This?" Annie looked up. "The Cromwell Program in Paris. It's due tomorrow. "As usual, I've been putting this off and putting this off."

"You're applying for the Paris Program?"

"You're an airhead, you know that? I've been telling you about this for months." She shook her head, her chestnut curls bounced. "Ah, my dear. Paris in the spring, imagine that."

"You won't be here next semester. God, what am I going to do?" Chloe said. Annie looked up from the application.

"What are you doing back here so soon?"

"I—I didn't feel very well. I felt like he wanted me to leave. I think I make him nervous."

Annie ran her hand across her forehead.

"Why don't you come to Paris?"

"What, on the Program?" Chloe said.

"Why not? You speak French fluently. You must still know people there. Why don't you? You won't lose any credits. It's not like taking a semester off and sitting on your rear end brooding somewhere."

Chloe could not, if she went back, look up anybody. Her past was her past and she'd spent so much time trying to forget she'd ever lived abroad, what good would it do to dig all that up now?

"God," she said dreamily, thinking of the quais around Notre-Dame in spring. And their old apartment on the Quai aux Fleurs that overlooked the Seine. "You'll be there in the spring."

"You could sit in on Lit courses at the Sorbonne," Annie said. "Listen, this is a selfish request. You'd change the whole thing for me if you went. I don't know a darn thing about the French. You could teach me."

Chloe shook her head. "It's too late. You said the application's due tomorrow."

"So what? You TA'ed for Al Mariaux, he likes you. He won't give you a hard time." Annie's eyes were bright and smiling. "Hell, call him up right now."

Annie dialed campus information and got Al's number. Looking at Chloe, she dialed the phone. Chloe thought if Al didn't answer immediately, she'd forget the whole thing. It was crazy anyway. Annie jumped as she handed her the phone.

"Hi, Al. This is Chloe Raymond."

"What can I do for you?" he said in his deep, calm voice. Al was a hypnotist as well as a French professor.

"I want to apply to the Cromwell Program in Paris," she heard herself say.

"You're a little late," he said.

"I know," she said. She didn't know what kind of excuse to give him. There weren't any.

"I just found out about it from Annie Dupuy," she said.

"Ah, yes," he sighed. "Well, do you have time to stop by my place right now? I think I have a few blank forms lying around here somewhere. If you get it in by tomorrow afternoon, you have a fair chance of making it. Of course, we won't tell the board you made your decision at the very last second simply on an impulse to get away from Cromwell problems, yes?" Al was a hypnotist and also a clairvoyant.

"Thanks so much, Al," she said, and hung up.

Annie was staring at her with her mouth halfway between a smile and O of surprise. "You're nuts! You're going to do it!"

Chloe got up, knocking over her chair. "It was your idea. I'll be right back."

"I'm coming with you," Annie said.

They drank a bottle of Folonari, then Chloe called her mother collect.

"Mom, I'm going to try to go to Paris next semester." She didn't give her mother a chance to respond until she'd explained the whole thing in one slow monologue. Knowing her mother, she expected the worst. Immediate rejection of the idea, fret fret fret, though Chloe knew she wouldn't stop her even if she wanted to.

"Fine," her mother said. "Whatever you think is best."

"I think I have to get away from here."

"What about money? You say it won't cost any more than if you stay at Cromwell?"

As calmly as she could she went through the whole thing again. Her mother would have to advance her six months' worth of Social Security checks.

"Fine," her mother said again. Chloe sensed a twinge of anxiety in her mother's voice. Forever her mother would worry in her quiet way and Chloe would feel guilty because of it.

"Mom? Don't worry about me, okay?"

"No, no. I'm not worried," she said quickly. "I don't care what you do."

When she said she didn't care it only made Chloe feel worse for a whole slew of complicated reasons she didn't quite understand herself.

Tuesday morning she dropped a note in Joe's mailbox. It said, "I'm going to Paris next semester." She didn't sign it. She walked around feeling light-headed and calm for the rest of the week. She was doing the only correct and honorable thing. Leaving Joe serious time to think things over. As long as he knew he could keep coming back to her and getting her to give in he would not think he'd lost her for good. She hoped by the time she got back he *would* have lost her for good. She wanted him to be a part of her past, not her present.

He never responded to her note, and his afternoon visits ceased. She figured it was for the best, though she could not get herself to believe he had truly given up on her.

VIII

Falcon sent Chloe a formal invitation to the Kappa Phi Christmas dance. It was an old-fashioned card with the Kappa Phi crest as a heading and the text printed in delicate script. She received it through campus mail. Falcon scribbled in, "I'm not asking you to be my date, don't get me wrong. I just want you to come because people miss you."

She sent him a note, also through campus mail. "Are you out of your fucking mind?" it said. "But thanks for thinking of me."

He called her at lunchtime. "Don't be ridiculous," he said. "People want to see you before you go away. Who knows, you might never come back. Hell, bring somebody. Bring Annie."

Chloe said she had to think about it.

Annie had received her own invitation from Freddie Beauchamp. She thought it was absurd for Chloe to even consider not going. They discussed it over a bottle of wine in Annie's kitchen.

Annie sat up and arched her back. "Go out with a bang! Show that fool Joe who's boss in your life now." She tugged at a curl and watched it bounce back to her forehead.

"Well?" she said, "what can he do to you?"

"Nothing, I guess." He could do lots of things. He might stand off somewhere in the back of the room and stare at her with a pained look tacked to his face. He was so tall he could hardly be inconspicuous. Or he might come right up and talk to her so all would know what a concerned ex-boyfriend he was—"You shouldn't be so hostile, Chloe. I want to be your friend." Nobody but Chloe knew how completely full of shit he was. She did not want to talk to him. But she could see herself telling the girlfriend that he'd been fucking around on her since the beginning of the semester. First-hand information. Could she be that mean?

"I'll go," she said to Annie. Immediately she began to imagine every possible smart answer, smart move, tactical mind-fuck to leave Joe with something heavy to think about while she'd be gone.

Annie tried to dress her for the party. Chloe had no decent clothes. She had a few summer dresses but they were too bright and flowery for a Christmas dance. Annie pulled Chloe's one beige skirt with blue flowers that was passable for winter out of the closet, and laid it out across the bed. She ran her fingers over the wrinkles. Chloe sat down on the floor.

"I'm not wearing that skirt. I wore it last year. I was sick and miserable and I looked like hell and I'm not going to remind me or anybody else of that night." And she changed her mind about going.

"Fuck it, I'll stay home."

Annie looked down at her, perplexed. She said nothing and waited.

"Annie, I was pregnant last year at the Christmas party."

Annie put the skirt back in the closet. "I'm so sorry for you that you had no one to talk to back then," she said softly.

She suggested they go down to her room and look at the dresses her grandma had made for her. Her grandma made all her clothes from patterns she cut out of fashion magazines.

On the way down the stairs Chloe said, "I should have talked to you. You would have helped so much."

"I'm sure Joe didn't want you to tell me. I understand how bad he must have felt. Christ, Chloe, for him that's a mortal sin."

"Well what would you have done?"

"I don't know."

They left it at that. They drank a bottle of champagne while Chloe tried on dresses. Chloe didn't bother to look at herself in the mirror, she let Annie decide. Annie picked a cream-colored dress with a low round neckline that hung from the shoulders. The sleeves were large and gathered in tight folds at the wrists. "It's rayon," Annie said, "but it looks just like silk, doesn't it?" The only dress Annie didn't give her to try on was the one she was going to wear herself. It had been her grandmother's, a red velvet antique, a genuine fifties party dress. In it Annie looked like a rose.

They drove to Kappa Phi in Chloe's car. They stumbled up the path in their high heels, laughing as the heels caught between the bricks. Falcon was waiting at the front door, gripping a bottle of André champagne in one fist. He waved the bottle at them as they approached. He looked them over, up and down.

"We should have parties like this more often," he said. "Smell this. Guaranteed hangover. Smells like a fart."

Chloe sniffed the champagne. It smelled exactly like a fart.

"I never smelled anything that smelled so much like a fart in my life!" Falcon said. He was already drunk, his eyes were tearing and his face was pink. He was wearing a blue pin-striped suit. He noticed Chloe looking at it.

"Like my suit? It's my interview suit. Bet I'll get sick of it when I gotta wear it every day. What d'you think?"

He took their arms and led them into the living room. The tables and chairs had been moved to the corners and the rug was gone.

"Ridiculous. Absolutely ridiculous!" He waved the bottle of champagne around the room. "In a year we'll all be wearing these clothes for real! Except you, Chloe, you'll never be wearing these clothes for real."

Annie spotted Freddie Beauchamp and left them. Falcon dragged Chloe onto the crowded dance floor. She looked for Annie over her shoulder but she'd disappeared. They passed the André back and forth until it was finished. They went to the bar and drank there a long time.

Annie appeared behind them and asked Falcon to get her a drink.

"How about a little cocaine, ladies?"

He pushed Annie up the stairs and pulled Chloe behind him. He spread lines on the Stop sign he used as a coffee table and demonstrated the California technique, which involved not holding your other nostril while you inhaled the entire line in one sweeping sniff.

"Heavens above," Annie said, "what would grandma say about this? It's all your fault, you're bad influences on my innocence. But what can I say? I love trying new things."

The three of them began talking to each other at the same time. Time became inconsequential.

Later downstairs Billy Mac pressed Chloe into the wall by the dance floor. "I'm insulted, I'm really insulted," he was saying. "You've been avoiding me *and* Kappa Phi like we're a bunch of animals or something." Billy McCarthy was six-two, and weighed about a hundred and ninety pounds. He was blond like Steve the lifeguard at home. His face was pink and his eyes were cold and small.

"I'm crazy Billy Mac, so don't fuck with my head."

"Good Lord I do think you're shitfaced," he said.

He brought his face close to hers. Close up he looked like a piglet. Their noses touched. It frightened her and she moved back and tried to look up at the ceiling. Her head ached. She remembered a talk she'd had with Billy Mac a long, long time ago, at a party like this one where everybody let go. Billy Mac had told her if she ever left Joe he'd take care of her. Treat her right.

"How do you treat your ladies in Boston, Mac? Do you beat them if they don't do what you say?"

"We make love to them," he said hoarsely. She knew he had to be way past his limit because Mac never talked like that.

"You're too big," she heard herself say. "It would be like fucking a refrigerator."

Falcon approached out of nowhere and slid a hand behind her back. He squeezed her hands.

"Come dance with me," he said, looking at Billy Mac.

Then dancing slowly in circles holding each other up he put his mouth against her ear. "Don't fuck him."

"What the hell are you talking about?"

"I can see it coming. Please don't fuck him. You need to get laid? You're blind. Don't act crazy, Ray."

"But I am crazy, see. You don't even know it. I have dreams that I think are real."

"You're *not* crazy, Goddamnit. You want to get laid? I'll lay you. You want to jump off a cliff? You screw Mac it's just like throwing yourself off a cliff."

She pushed him away and squirmed through the crowd. She stood at the bar with a new drink. She couldn't remember why she'd pushed him away but she wanted to cry. Falcon was nowhere though she looked and looked. Billy Mac was there, leaning against the same wall, watching her. He was jiggling something shiny and silver in his hand. She focused on the jiggling silver and recognized her car keys. She walked over to him unsteadily.

"Where'd you get those?"

Billy Mac smiled. "I got them from Annie. I told her you told me to drive you home. You're not driving anywhere in your condition, and Annie's no better either."

Chloe tried to find Annie but all the colors of the dresses faded together.

"She's with Freddie. Don't worry about her."

She closed her eyes. "Falcon'll take me home."

On the other side of the dance floor she saw Joe standing on the food table. He started doing a jig, kicking up his heels and clicking his fingers above his head. She'd forgotten about Joe. She hadn't thought about him all night. Everyone was whooping and clapping. Billy Mac gently took her chin in his hand and turned her head toward him. "Don't watch him," he said. The floor fell away.

"Making me dizzy," she said.

He pressed her face into his chest. She felt good there. It was warm and safe and away from the noise.

Then there was a loud bang and a crash of falling plates. Billy Mac let her go. Across the room they weren't clapping or hollering now. Someone turned the music down. Joe was not on the table. The table was overturned. The crowd was bending over Joe who was spread out on the floor like a bear rug. There was blood on his white shirt and blood all over his face. Three football players lifted Joe and carried him out. The girlfriend followed behind, looking dazed. Billy Mac was laughing.

"Oh my Christ, that's the funniest thing I've ever seen. What a ham, probably broke his nose. Looks like it anyway."

Chloe started to follow the procession to the door. Billy Mac held her arm. She felt manacled to a tree.

"Don't do that," Billy Mac said. "It's not your problem."

She thought for a moment that maybe he really did like her.

"Am I supposed to walk home and pick up my keys tomorrow?"

"I'm driving you home."

He loosened his grip for a split second and she freed herself. She ran toward the stairs heading for Falcon's room.

She was crying though she hadn't the faintest idea why. She found Falcon sitting on the third step bowed over his lap with his head in his hands. He looked like he was crying too though she knew that was absurd.

"Falcon, my darling, you've got to help me. Billy Mac's trying to take me home. He has my keys."

There was a big commotion going on in Joe's suite, across the landing from the stairs.

"Where is that motherfucker?" Falcon shouted. Chloe tried to ignore the commotion.

"Please don't get mad. Just make sure I get home, Falcon."

She sat on the step next to him, right in a puddle of beer. "Annie's dress!" she said.

Joe came out and leaned against his door, holding a towel packed with ice against the bridge of his nose. He watched them in silence, like Zeus watching from Mount Olympus.

Falcon patted her knee. "Chloe, I love you, you're my dear friend. I would like to take you home and try to seduce you myself. Do you think it would affect our friendship?"

"You're drunk!" she laughed. She couldn't help looking at Joe. Falcon was blind. She felt completely unprotected.

"Man, I made a fortune tonight," Falcon said. "Want some more cocaine?"

Now the girlfriend was standing outside Joe's suite as well.

"Let's get out of here," Chloe said. Joe watched in horror and disbelief as she pulled Falcon to his feet and walked him toward the door. The girlfriend was watching Joe to see his reaction to this breach of etiquette.

Blindly making their way down the footpath, arms around each other, Chloe felt a great sisterly love for Falcon. Taking him back to her place was breaking some kind of law.

"I'm afraid my sexual performance will be hindered by the affection I feel for you," Falcon said. "You see, my dear, I don't sleep with girls I like. Never have slept with a girl I liked."

"That's good Falcon, because I don't want to sleep with you."

In the morning they awoke with a start, nose-to-nose in her single bed.

"What am I doing here?" Falcon mumbled. They were still dressed. Falcon even had his shoes on. His jacket lay twisted in a pile on the blue chair.

Chloe felt a terrible drunken emptiness. At Kappa Phi they would be talking. She was worried about Joe. Falcon sat up and crossed his hands behind his head.

"I better get out of here," he said.

"You don't have to go."

They had always thought she was a badass at Kappa Phi. That she would not be the type to spend a drunken night with someone without fucking him. She felt a black bilious hate building up in her guts. What a tiny tiny small-minded crowd she'd gotten herself involved with. She hated herself for not being able to get rid of her guilt.

In the back of her mind the clock had begun to tick. Four days to count down. It would be the first anniversary of the death. She would have called him John Raymond. She was certain it had been a boy. She would have taken all the love she felt for her father and transferred it to his little soul. During her pregnancy, while she'd hated Joe for causing her this pain, she'd loved the little unprotected thing she was carrying, realizing it was instinctual. During the abortion, she begged forgiveness not of Joe nor of God but of her father. Maybe it was herself she had tried to kill. The more she tried to understand it, the less she understood.

IX

They were watching *Airport* on TV in Andy's room. It was snowing outside and Andy watched the flakes dance in the yellow light which lit up the driveway. The movie didn't interest him. Chloe and Liz were sitting on the bed with their eyes glued to the screen. Ben was on the floor in front of them with his shoulder pressing into Chloe's knee. Andy wanted her to move away from Ben's shoulder but what was he supposed to say? The snow kept falling.

Andy didn't want to drive back to Chloe's house. Not after the accident they'd had in her car the week before. He tapped her on the thigh. She didn't look up from the screen but took his hand in hers and squeezed it.

"I have to talk to you," he whispered. She followed him into the hallway. He pulled the door shut behind her. The bathroom light was a pale white streak across her face. She looked tired. Since the accident she'd had a frown on her forehead and circles under her eyes. Neither of them had been hurt, but it was a close call.

Chloe had been driving them home from the movies. A pickup truck coming toward them with its brights on swerved into their lane. Chloe cut the steering wheel hard to the right and lost control. The car flipped over twice. Andy remembered hearing no sound except his heart beating in his head. We're going to die, he thought. The car landed on its roof two feet from a telephone pole. The police came immediately. They wanted to give Chloe a breathalyzer test. Andy calmly told them who they were and that they'd had nothing to drink. She was in shock.

The cops drove them back to her house and she'd had to wake her mother. Her mother shook her head and said, "One of these days you're going to kill yourself. You get self-destructive like this. I don't know what it is. Remember when you fell through the skylight on that barge in Paris? That was a week after you got hit by a car. It's very bad. You should stay home and take it easy. Jesus Christ. How bad is the car?"

"Not so bad," Andy said. The next day they found out there was three thousand dollars' worth of damage.

Chloe trembled all night. He held her pressed to him. By dawn she fell asleep and he sat up, looking out the window at the dark pine tree and the grey oak that seemed lonely and sad without its leaves.

He wanted the summer back. She needed him now but at school she'd had no time for him. They only had a few weeks left before she took her plane to Paris. He thought of leaving her, getting up and hitching home. He'd pick up his stuff and head back up to school early. It would be easier on him.

In the hallway they looked at each other. She leaned against the wall with a hand on his waist. Andy fumbled in his back pocket for the little velvet box.

"Merry late Christmas," he said as he handed it to her. He hadn't bought her a present yet because he'd had no money. Once he'd gotten paid for his work at the Long Island Lighting Company, he'd gone straight to the store and spent the whole damn check. It was money he needed for next semester. It was ridiculous. But he was superstitious and he wanted her to have good luck over there.

"Oh God, Andy!" Her mouth dropped open as she held up the gold chain. There was a little twisted gold heart hanging from it. She put the chain around her neck and kept her finger over the heart. They sat down in the hallway. He wanted to ask her to give up the trip. Come back to school with him till the season was over, and then they could go down to Florida. It was completely unrealistic to think she'd give up her life. He certainly wouldn't give up his life. He remembered a night during the semester when he'd showed up drunk at her apartment and she'd looked at him as if she couldn't remember who he was.

She'd been with a friend called Falcon. They were sitting in her tiny kitchen talking politics, practically yelling at each other. Andy sat there in his dirty lumber jacket staring at nothing, not knowing what to do with himself.

The guy was talking about the hostages in Iran, which was what everybody in the entire country was talking about.

"You can't pretend it's not going *on!*" he yelled at Chloe.

"I don't want to hear about it," she said.

So they talked about Hitler and Julius Caesar and other conquering dictators, about Napoleon and historians' opinions on Napoleon as opposed to Tolstoy's.

"I still think we should defend ourselves," Falcon said, "against those Muslim lunatics."

Andy said if there was going to be some stupid war because of fifty American hostages, he was going to move to Canada. He didn't give that much of a shit about his country's pride. Not to lose his ass over.

Her friend was horrified and she was embarrassed.

Now that they were home again, she needed him and he felt like he was taking care of a wounded bird. When he was little he used to find wounded birds in the yard and he'd bring them in and put them in a box with food. Once he cured one and it flew away. But every other time they'd died. When he looked at Chloe, he was reminded of how he used to cry when the birds died. He was certain Chloe was not going to die. She'd probably grow into some kind of eagle.

He stretched his legs out in the hall and she put her head on his lap. He liked the quiet of his house when his parents went away to visit relatives. He ran his fingers through the thick strands of her hair.

"You want me to take you to the airport?" he asked.

"Yes. Listen, Andy. I don't want to go. But I can't think of what else to do."

"I understand," he said. He was tired of thinking about it.

X

It was raining and the windshield wipers left thick icy streaks on the glass. Andy could hardly see the yellow lines.

"Good fucking thing it's not snowing," he said, more to himself than to Chloe. She'd been very quiet the whole day. He patted her leg. He'd seen a side of her the last few days that he was not likely to forget. Two days before he'd witnessed a fight between Chloe and her mother and it had frozen his blood.

They'd come into the kitchen from the snow and Mrs. Raymond had been sitting at the butcher block drinking a scotch. She watched them with worried eyes but said nothing until Chloe said that they were going out again.

"You have to sit your ass down and start thinking about your trip. You haven't even started to pack yet."

"I'm going to pack later."

"You don't have any decent clothes at all. You look like a bum," her mother said.

Chloe stopped halfway between the butcher block and the door to the living room. She wheeled around and stared at Andy, who was still by the outside door. He wanted to run away.

"What the hell do you care what I look like?" she said to her mother.

"The French are going to care what you look like. You know how they are about clothes. You'll probably be going out."

"I won't be going out," Chloe said. She was furious. Andy didn't think her mother had said anything wrong. She was just concerned about the trip and Chloe's head, especially after the car accident. And Chloe was hysterical about leaving.

"Just leave me alone, okay? I've done all right up to now without your advice." Chloe's voice was so cold and filled with disgust he couldn't believe it was coming from her.

"Who the hell do you think I am?" her mother said. Her lips were parted slightly as she sat there looking more and more indifferent. "You're out of control. You are way out of line, kid. You don't need me; I don't need you." She pulled her pocketbook across the top of the block by its strap and slapped a checkbook onto the wood. "Here, I'm still going to advance you six months' worth of your social security checks. But after this you're on your own. When you get back, I want you to move out of this house completely. How's that?"

"What's new about that?" Chloe said, as though it didn't matter to her a bit either. The whole time they acted as though Andy weren't there. He watched them, two twisted mirror images of each other. Two tears rolled down Mrs. Raymond's expressionless face. "Why are you doing this to me?" she said. Andy felt sick for both of them.

Chloe stood rigid and hard-faced. "Let's get out of here," she said to Andy. She made sure to take the check from the edge of the butcher block, where her mother had left it.

He kept his hand on her thigh.

"I'm scared," she said.

"Don't be scared. You're going to have a good time. Annie's there waiting for you."

She hadn't had a chance to talk to her mother after the fight. Mrs. Raymond left that afternoon for New York City and though Chloe could probably have guessed where her mother had gone, she had not tried to call her.

Andy didn't think he sounded very convincing about Chloe having a good time. It was bad luck for her to leave this way. She didn't seem ready for such a trip.

"Hell," he said, "you'll have such a good time you might never come back."

She shook her head.

When they got to Kennedy airport the neon lights and signs

loomed over them in the icy rain. She squeezed his arm so tightly he was sure she would never get out of the car.

"It's funny." Her voice was shaky. "She thinks I'm too fucked up to take care of myself, and she thought your car would never make it to the airport." Chloe had been talking about her mother continuously since their fight, referring to her as "she."

"This old car could make it to Florida," Andy said.

"What if I decided not to go to Paris?"

He thought she was reading his mind.

"Want to forget it?" he said. It suddenly seemed quite simple. His heart was beating fast and he felt breathless.

"God, I *am* crazy," she said. "I have to go now."

He didn't respond. He parked in the Air France lot and dragged her huge overstuffed duffel bag out of the trunk. She had a pocketbook, an old one of her mother's, slung over her shoulder. It looked awkward because she was not one for high heels and pocketbooks and things like that.

Once they'd checked the duffel bag and the suitcase they went to the bar. They had an hour and a half to kill. They drank screwdrivers. She raised her glass. "I hope Joe falls down and breaks his legs."

Andy didn't drink to that. He was surprised that she was thinking about Joe now. She hadn't mentioned him at all in the past few weeks. Andy had taken that as a good sign.

"As soon as I get there, Annie and I are going to Notre-Dame to light candles. I'll light one for you. You know Notre-Dame?"

"It's a big football school."

"But there's a church in Paris called Notre-Dame too."

"I know that," Andy said. "I was just kidding." Her head was somewhere else, already away from him. She was psyching herself up. Just like he did before a game.

"But I'll light a candle for you, to bring you good luck. I don't believe in God and stuff but it can't hurt."

She stared at him as though she were trying to brand his face into her memory. She smiled and the corners of her mouth twitched. He thought she would burst into tears right there in the bar. He wanted to tell her that she didn't have to go to prove anything. It didn't matter. But he couldn't get a word out.

"I hope my plane doesn't crash."

They were drunk by the time they got to the gate where the
customs officials X-rayed her pocketbook. She walked through the
metal archway, picked up her bag, and stopped to stare at him
from the other side of the ropes. He came and stood a foot from
her. She was swaying a little.

"I don't want to go."

"Climb over."

"But my bags are on the plane already."

"I love you," Andy said. "I think I always have and always will."
He thought he sounded ridiculous. Across the rope he kissed her
mouth and cheeks and tasted her salty tears. He thought of the
ocean and was afraid he'd wait for her and wait for her until she
came back. He'd wait and be miserable and lonely and disgusted
with himself. When all the passengers had passed through the arch
and disappeared down the long corridor he told her to go. She
turned away from him, hit her shoulder on the corner of the wall.
He watched her weave unsteadily toward her gate. He felt sick, as
though someone had just landed a punch low in his gut. It moved
in a wave up to his heart. He ran out of the building into the rain.

He took a random exit in Queens and found a liquor store. He
bought a pint of Jack Daniel's and started taking pulls from the
bottle before he got back in the car. He didn't want to face the
two-hour drive back out to nothing, and headed for Long Island
City instead. He had a friend there from the basketball team at
Sacred Heart. They'd have a good party, at least. He wanted to
party with the guys and have nothing to do with females for a long,
long time.

* * *

Chloe found an Air France postcard in the flap under the folding
table. The picture was of a 747 floating in a deep blue sky above
the clouds. Tears kept falling out of her eyes. She sighed out of her
nose because there was an old man sitting next to her and she was
afraid he would smell her drunken breath.

She couldn't imagine herself in Paris again. It was all a terrible
nightmare and she wanted to wake up in East Whitman with Andy
next to her. She wanted the old summertime back. She loved him
so helplessly. It would never change, though they both would
change and grow further and further apart.

She took a pen out of her pocketbook and wrote on the card. "Dear Andy. I didn't tell you that I love you. I don't know why I didn't tell you when I still had the chance. I'm miserable and I wish I hadn't gone away."

She thought for a minute, and continued. "Please wait for me Andy because next summer will be just like last summer."

She tried to envision next summer. It was like trying to imagine heaven.

She stared at the card a long time. She put it in her pocketbook and looked out the window, at the sea of white cotton clouds. They made her feel she'd lost all control of her life. She wanted to turn the plane around. If she'd been on a train, she'd have gotten off at the next stop.

She sat back and shut her eyes. The plane buzzed in her ears. When it got dark outside she felt better. She hoped Annie would be at the hotel when she got there. Chloe couldn't stand the thought of being alone. When she thought of her mother and remembered the two tears rolling down her face she felt a gaping hole in the center of herself. In her life she'd seen her mother cry once. It had been in their Paris apartment, and she couldn't remember why her mother had cried.

Being around people was just an excuse to avoid loneliness. She thought about this and her desperate fear and without realizing it, took the postcard out of her pocketbook and ripped it in half.

PART III

I

Annie was laughing and out of breath when she handed Chloe the first bad news. They were dragging Chloe's duffel bag up the four flights of stairs to their hotel room. Chloe's brain felt like an alcohol-soaked sponge, and the rest of her felt like a gutted building.

"The dollar hasn't reached four francs this week," Annie said. *"Not* five. Not even four. And the rate of inflation! My dear, Peg and I had a vodka tonic in a café last night: twenty-five francs each. More than six bucks a drink. We're not going to make it. Peg and I figured, back at school we miscalculated by one hundred per-cent."

Annie really thought it all very funny. "To put it simply," she told Chloe, "we're up shit's creek. Without a paddle, I might add."

Chloe couldn't see the humor in this.

She had woken up as the plane was landing at Roissy-Charles de Gaulle. The captain was on the loudspeaker talking about the weather. "Unusually cold," he was saying, and Chloe was sweating icicles. Still woozy from the drinks she'd had with Andy, her mind would not accept that this was it and she was on the other side of the Atlantic. She still saw herself standing on the other side of the customs gate with a choice to make.

From the window of the hotel room they had a view of the Panthéon's dome which stood tall above the slate-grey rooftops. Chloe stared at the Panthéon and at the netted grocery bag that was hanging outside the window from the latch. The bag twisted and struggled like a fish on a hook when the wind caught it.

Without the groceries the view could have been a poster on a Cromwell dorm wall.

Annie told Chloe that Peg was pounding the pavements looking for a place to live. Au pair deals were the best, she said. Annie had already found herself the best of deals, with an American family that lived off Avenue Victor Hugo in the sixteenth.

Chloe wanted to cry. Annie could sense that things weren't right with her friend and softly she said, "Why don't we take a walk? Get you a little used to being here. We can go to Notre-Dame. I haven't been there yet. I waited for you."

In the street Annie slid her arm through Chloe's and guided her as though she were blind. Annie pointed out her favorite courtyards and doorways. She liked the old cobblestone walkways and the large clay flowerpots, the ivy creeping quietly up the courtyard walls. She'd been walking around by herself quite a bit, she told Chloe. "It's the only way to get to know a place."

Chloe paid no attention to the courtyards.

"I wanted us to get an apartment," she said.

"But my darling," Annie said, "how do you suppose we'll pay for an apartment? Of course we could walk the streets. No, really. Don't you think I've been asking around? It's impossible. A studio the size of a bathroom runs from 1,500 to 1,800 francs a month. Both of us put together don't have that to *live* on."

They walked down Boulevard Saint Michel, passing the front gates of the Luxembourg Garden on their left, and farther on, a McDonald's restaurant that Chloe was certain—well, almost certain—hadn't been there when she'd lived in Paris before. She pointed to it.

"That embarrasses me. American fast-foods spreading over Europe like warts." Once you have one, she thought, forget it. As they neared the heart of the Latin Quarter, the sidewalk became crowded with street vendors who beckoned the *piétons* toward their folding tables. Earrings, belts, medallions, strange odds and ends glinted on the square planes of old black felt. Annie wanted to stop but Chloe tugged at her arm. Chloe didn't like the derisive look in the vendors' eyes. As they walked on Annie said, "They say by the end of the week some agreement will be made about the hostages and the dollar will go up. I doubt it'll go over four francs. The situation looks pretty bad for us. It looks like the Iranians (Annie no longer said Eye-rain-ians) aren't going to let the hostages go."

"The hostages!" Chloe cried out. Annie stared at her with a blank face.

Chloe thought: But—my God, what does this have to do with me? That politics were affecting her trip seemed outrageous. Why were they—simple, destitute American students—being blamed?

At school when people talked about the hostage crisis, Chloe walked away. She did not read newspapers. She thought newspapers preyed on disaster and exaggerated for effect. Chloe did not want to know about bad news.

They crossed the Place Saint Michel, and for a moment stood leaning over the rampart that ran from the Seine's lower embankment to the upper quai. They contemplated the green murky water, watched an old bottle bob in the current and disappear under the bridge. On the other side of the bridge was a big police station. Twenty or so black and white paddy wagons were lined up on the quai like dominoes.

As they walked along the river toward Notre-Dame, Annie stopped to browse through the wine-bottle-green bookcases that straddled the rampart. The bouquinistes hovered over their merchandise and watched Annie with suspicious eyes.

"Touchez pas!" they grumbled. "Faut pas toucher." They were as ancient and weathered as the bookcases.

Chloe pulled at the sleeve of Annie's white coat that was already turning grey. Chloe was in a hurry to get to Notre-Dame because she feared that now that she was so close, it would be gone.

Notre-Dame was where it had always been, looming across the river, its reflection shimmering green in the water below. In her memory Notre-Dame was grey and sooty, but now every stone stood out white in the gloomy sky. The two rectangular towers and the spiked steeple appeared and then vanished in the low-flying clouds.

When Chloe had been nine and Eric eight, he had led her to the top of one of the towers. They had done it without permission. He'd taken the incentive for once, pulling her by the hand, up the winding stairwell. She'd felt the cold wind whistling through the stones, and around every turn she was afraid they'd meet the Hunchback who rang the bells.

Notre-Dame had been their neighborhood church. They could see the steeple from their living-room window. Whenever the bells rang, their mother would put up a finger and say, "Listen! The Hunchback is pulling the ropes and making the bells ring."

They did not meet the Hunchback, and at the top of the tower Eric held her by the waist as she peered over the edge with her arms extended, imagining she was a bird. They looked for their building and argued over which roof was the right one.

They'd been friends then. And there had been a home to return to and rules to break.

Chloe remembered their Spanish nanny. Candida was very religious. She told them that if you lit a candle in the church and gave a franc, the franc would go to the orphans and your wish would come true.

Chloe wanted to be friends with Eric again. She longed for a family and she missed her mother and Eric and felt closer to them, looking up at Notre-Dame, than she had since the day their nucleus shattered and left them to fight and survive as three separate cells.

Inside the church Annie went to the marble basin to the right of the center aisle, dipped her hand, and crossed herself. Facing the altar, she touched a knee to the ground. Chloe touched the water and rubbed her fingers.

At the first candle rack Chloe dropped a ten-franc coin in the wooden box. She took one of the longer candles, lit it from another, and placed it in front of the marble saint who smiled down at her with open arms. She thought:

—For my family. For Andy.

She had nothing to say. She turned away and saw Annie standing close behind, her face solemn as a nun's.

"Well what the fuck," Chloe whispered. "It can't hurt."

"You may get to heaven yet," Annie said, her face breaking into a smile.

They walked past Chloe's old home on the Quai aux Fleurs. From across the street she pointed to the four tall French windows of the second floor. These had been the living and dining rooms. There were no lights on inside the apartment, and the flowerpots on the balconies had been removed.

As always, old man Piccard the concierge was out front hosing down the sidewalk. He did not seem to notice that it was about to rain. Chloe remembered him as a mean, hunched man with a red face who hated children and liked to pinch their cheeks whenever he could grab ahold of them. He cultivated the art of idleness, and somehow always managed to look busy, though nothing in the building was ever repaired. Chloe's cheeks suddenly stung with the memory of Piccard's pinches. On a whim, because she felt grown-up now, she crossed the street.

"Bonjour, Monsieur Piccard," she said sweetly, approaching him. He glanced at her suspiciously and continued with his hosing.

"Don't you remember me?" she asked in French, "I'm Monsieur Raymond's little girl."

"Raymond?" he muttered. "Don't remember." He would not look at her. She did not pursue it. With a sunken heart, she crossed back to the other side of the street where Annie stood waiting.

* * *

That evening she tried to write to her brother.

My Dear Eric,

Today I went to Notre-Dame. It's clean and white now. I lit a candle for you and Mom. I put in ten francs and thought about how you always used to give money for the orphans. I feel so lonely. Seeing the towers made me think of you and that time we climbed to the top by ourselves. I'm frightened because maybe something will happen to you or to me before I see you again. I have to find a place to live now, and I have very little money . . .

She did not like the letter. She tore the sheet from the notebook, crumpled and threw it across the room. On the last page of the notebook was her mother's list of people to call in Paris. There was a lawyer, a doctor, an agent of her father's, his French publisher, and Dominique Augier.

Chloe was afraid to live alone in an attic room with no running water and no toilet except for a Turkish hole at the end of a dark hallway. She couldn't see herself anywhere in the city.

She looked at Dominique Augier's phone number and tears fell on the page. She ran downstairs to the pay phone in the lobby of the hotel and called Dominique, who was a pretty wild and unpredictable lady, but the closest thing to family Chloe had living on this side of the Atlantic.

"You don't sound good, darling," Dominique said. Her English was fluent, but she'd never lost the French intonation and pronunciation of words.

"It's hard to be back here," Chloe said, her American sounding coarse to her own ear.

"That's sure," Dominique said. "Old memories around every corner. There are still *quartiers* I can't walk through without thinking of your father." Yoor fazeur.

"Oh I don't remember too much about Paris," Chloe said quickly. "That's not it."

"Where you are staying? You have a place, no?"

"No. Just for now. For a week or so."

"Well. I received a letter from your mother you were coming. I have Stéphane's room if you want. The little shit [leedle sheet] went to live with his father in Italy. What can I do? He likes his father better than me. You come see, anyway. You remember the apartment?"

"No. I really don't remember anything."

"It's okay, really, you know. You can stay here with me. I love your parents. I owe them a lot."

Chloe got out of the subway at Place Saint Sulpice and sat on a park bench in front of the church. The bench was the same wine-bottle green as the bookcases on the quai, which seemed to be the color of all municipal metal and wood objects. Chloe watched the pigeons clucking and pecking at the ground and thought about living with Dominique Augier.

Chloe remembered Dominique pregnant with Stéphane. She remembered the wedding and the party afterwards, Dominique already enormous around the stomach but drinking and dancing just as much as anybody. Chloe had been confused about Dom's stomach and had asked her mother. Wasn't that supposed to happen afterwards? "Well," said her mother. "Not always. You know how Dom does things backwards."

She did do things backwards. One summer when Dom came to stay with them at the beach in Long Island, she had a red bathing suit with straps that crossed in the back. She turned the suit around one morning so that the straps crossed in the middle of her breasts. She made breakfast and set the table and just went along as she did every day. Eric sat at the breakfast table with his mouth hanging open, and their father shed tears from laughing.

Dominique's apartment was clean and sunny and filled with flowers. "I hate plants," she said. "Too much trouble. Flowers, you buy them, put the water, they die. Then you throw it all away, no problem."

In her bedroom, at the head of the double bed the whole wall was papered with a tropical beach, a crescent of yellow sand and a turquoise sea, coconut trees stretching off in the distance. Life-size.

"What can I tell you, in the winter I miss the sun," Dom said when she caught Chloe staring.

"Soon I get a suntan lamp for over the bed. We pretend. But no sand. It's a pain in the ass even on the beach."

Stéphane's room was empty but for a double bed and a desk with shelves above it. A few of his playthings, trucks and cars and comic books, had been left behind on the shelves.

Dom walked her around the rest of the apartment, down the long red hallway to the toilet, which had a closet-sized room of its own, separate from the bathroom which was next to the bedrooms.

"In the night it's cold sometimes and it's far to walk down the hall, I pee-pee in the bidet," Dom said.

She made them a salad and hamburgers for lunch, and set down her rules. Chloe said nothing and nodded her head to everything. No phone calls at night, no phone calls on the weekend. Dom sleeps very, very badly. "Okay," Chloe said.

"You pay me no rent. I just ask you to help with gaz and electricity, and phone if you make calls out."

Chloe watched Dominique talking. Her teeth were slightly

large and there was a space in the middle of the front ones, her nose was wide and rounded at the end, her eyes had a look in them that told you she'd been there and back and almost hadn't made it. All together these features made her strength and beauty. And in a strange way, Dom never aged.

At twenty-five she'd landed herself the lead role in the earliest American production of Chloe's father's first play. She'd become famous playing that part: Ava, a half-Jewish French hustler who survived the Nazi occupation and then the liberation by being smarter than anybody else and fighting only for herself.

"So, okay?" Dom said. "So you move in whenever you want."

II

From where Chloe stood, elbows leaning on the balcony railing, she could see an angle view of the Arc de Triomphe at the end of the avenue. The Arc was illuminated by white lights which made it look frosty in the humid air, like a wedding cake.

Behind her red and blue lights were flashing and the music blared. She was not familiar with the music, which seemed a combination of Jamaican reggae, American bebop, early rock and roll, and sometimes like nothing she'd ever heard.

She'd stood by the table-bar for a while watching people dance. They were doing parodies of the twist. Disconnected movements, limbs ignoring each other. And, strange thing! Everybody was dancing alone.

Chloe would have said something to Annie like "My dear, would you just take a look at these outfits?" had they not been the only two who were completely out of style. The French girls were all skinny-thin and wore tight jeans that cut off above the ankle, like the pedal pushers popular back in the fifties. On top, baggy purple, black, or red T-shirts or sweaters that camouflaged their shapes. They wore low shoes that were pointed both at the heel and toe, and bobby socks.

Chloe had wanted to appear normal and inconspicuous. She looked down at her Frye boots and baggy blue corduroys and wanted to kick herself. You look like a dumb American, which is exactly what you are, she told herself.

So to avoid scrutiny she'd retired to the balcony. Annie was off somewhere in the middle of the crowd, discussing the wonders of being an American student abroad. "The funniest thing!" Chloe had heard her say to the host (a guy Annie had met in a bookstore who after ten minutes invited her to his party), "back home, we have no rez-de-chaussée. Our second floor is your first floor, et cetera. Well, my first night in Paris, in the hotel where my friends and I were staying, I was on the wrong floor and got into bed with a strange man."

Annie could charm her way out of any situation.

Chloe took a large swig of the rum and orange juice she'd brought out to the balcony, and perched the glass on the railing between her hands.

She missed Falcon and the dingy atmosphere of Vito's. The pinball machine and the sawdust on the floor. Pitchers of cheap beer, Mount Gay rum. She wanted to get drunk and swear and carry on and do things she couldn't possibly do here.

Because everyone was so polite and sober, really. She took another big sip. In the back of her mind she was telling herself to slow down.

She knew it was all right to drink too much at a party, when everybody was drinking too much. But not every day, every night, too much. Maybe for a while, one glass of wine with meals would be a good idea . . . But she knew one led to two and so on. Because she liked the way liquor brought her to levels of joy and levels of sadness she could not otherwise reach. These were the extreme emotional levels at which she could deal with the visions that haunted her. And when it went too far, when she could not take it, she could push it further with liquor, and obliterate everything. She could find peace.

But she didn't have a problem yet. She knew this instinctively, just as she knew she had to watch herself.

She considered pouring the rest of the rum and OJ onto the street. Get a glass of water. She'd watch the ice tumble and smash to bits on the pavement.

She felt someone approach from behind.

"If one took all that hair and put it in braids, one at each side of your face, you might just pass for a *Come Visit Colorado* airlines poster. Or some such thing."

Chloe jiggled the ice and tossed off the rest of the drink. The fellow spoke perfect, standard English, slightly heavy on the a's and o's. He stepped onto the balcony and leaned against the railing. He followed her gaze toward the Arc.

"From my studio, I have a full view of the Arc," he said.

Out of the corner of her eyes she saw he was fair-haired and was wearing a sports jacket. She couldn't see his face.

"Are you American?" she asked him.

"I have a U.S. passport," he said flatly. "Although I have never lived in the United States for more than six months at a time. One might say I'm homeless."

Well you poor little thing, Chloe was tempted to say, but chose not to respond. He waited.

"You have a bubbly friend," he said. "Annie, is it? She told me you were depressed and I should come cheer you up."

Chloe wanted to slit both their throats.

"Would you like to dance?" He turned to her with his right hand out, palm up.

"No," she said. She looked at him and was dismayed to find he had a truly fine face. A delicate face with tiny cheekbones, straight nose and razor-thin mouth. His eyes were disturbingly sweet.

"But I'm sure I could get you another drink," he said. Was he reading her mind? She didn't like it. And the indifferent, slicing edge in his tone made her uncomfortable. It did not go with his face.

She held out her glass and told him what she was drinking. When he stepped off the balcony she watched his back. He was straight and stiff in the sports jacket. But then maybe it was the cut of the jacket.

In the room someone was shouting to turn up the stereo. A song had begun that sounded like a drummy space-age version of the theme from *Batman and Robin*.

A man started to shout in a low-pitched voice:

> "She came from Planet Claire
> I knew she came from there
> She drove a Plymouth Satellite
> Faster than the speed of light."

Now the dancers were hopping from foot to foot, trying to bring shoulder to opposite knee.

"Planet Claire has pink air," sang the man.

The fellow came back with Chloe's drink and a large straight vodka for himself. She could smell the vodka on his breath.

"This song," she gestured with her head. "It doesn't make any sense."

He shrugged. "It doesn't make any difference. Actually, I think that may be the point. In any case les Français adorent les B-52's." He pronounced it *Bee-Feeftee-Tooze*.

"I believe they're from Georgia," he said.

"Georgia!"

Annie came out to the balcony. She was wiping sweat from her hairline with a cocktail napkin.

"My dear!" Annie said. It was a habit. They called each other "my dear" or "my darling."

"You would not be*lieve!*" Annie was out of breath. "If I had known what they were wearing over here, I would have hit my grandmother's attic. She's not so old, my grandma. She's got her fifties getups stashed away up in the attic. *Mar*vellous things that would've fit in just right here." She tossed her head to the side. "Too late now."

The guy was looking at Annie strangely, frowning a bit, as though he'd just caught a whiff of an unfamiliar smell.

"Hey, old Surge!" Annie tapped his arm. "Well, have fun, children." She was off, leading her body away by the hips.

"Bubbly," he said. He could have been judging a somewhat cheap, but pardonable champagne.

"Surge?" Chloe said.

"Serge," he pronounced in French. Perfect, nonrolled "r" and long, sharp "e." "It's actually Sergei, in Serb."

"Se*r*gei," she rolled the "r," overdoing it. "Okay."

Serb, she was thinking. Serb. She'd forgotten but she'd remember. She was relaxing a bit, taking it in. The drink helped; her mood lightened. The tone of his voice wasn't so disturbing any more. Serb! Archduke Ferdinand, she thought, Sarajevo, 1914. And then Tito threw all the rich people out after World War II.

"So who do you know here?" Serge asked.

"Nobody. Annie met this guy in a bookstore. She meets people easily. She brought me along."

"That must be Luc," Serge said. "He meets people easily too."

"Yeah, Luc."

He slid his elbows closer to hers along the railing. "Believe me, I know how you feel. So displaced. I truly do."

"Except you speak French like you were born here," she said.

"It makes no difference," he said. Just the corners of his mouth were smiling. "It doesn't help at all."

"I lived here before," Chloe said, and wondered why she'd told him. She didn't like to tell people this. "Six years," she added, "but I was pretty young."

"Your father works for IBM," Serge said rather tauntingly. "Or for the government."

"No. One of his plays was being produced over here; they asked him to oversee the production. Then we stayed on a bit."

She was expecting the next question: Your father's a playwright? She'd say, My father's dead. He'd say, Oh, I'm sorry. It's okay, she'd say. Then he'd ask her the name of the play. And she would tell him the name of her father's most famous play, the one Dominique had starred in, which had been banned in France for years because of its touchy subject matter. Riva, the half-Jewish hustler told it like it was: not *every* Frenchman was a *Résistant*.

But Serge didn't ask about her father or the play. He asked her where she'd gone to school in Paris. École Active Bilingue, she told him. First through sixth grade.

"How funny," he said, "I went to Bilingue for a few years. But later. I was thrown out for insubordination."

Chloe suddenly remembered the headmistress and her long crimson nails. She had a big chest and short legs. Everyone was terrified of her. Did Serge remember her? Was she still there then?

"I remember her," Serge said. "Mme. de Saint-Simon." He made claws of his hands. "I remember the nails too."

Chloe smiled. They had something in common. She was wondering why she'd suddenly remembered the school so vividly. She'd packed all those memories away somewhere.

"Alors, on danse?" Serge said.

"Okay, let's dance."

Serge moved like the others except his feet glided along the floor as though he were on ice skates. Chloe felt like an anachronism. Back at school they were still imitating John Travolta in

Saturday Night Fever. She barely moved and watched Serge so she could practice at Dominique's, alone.

It got late, people began to leave. Chloe stood by the window and waited for Annie who was talking to Luc, the host. Serge had gone off a while ago and had not come back. Just as she was wondering if he'd left she saw him coming toward her with an overcoat slung over his arm. She was not drunk, she was tired and wanted to go to sleep. Gloom was setting in again and she did not know if she was pleased he was coming back. He had a fresh vodka in his hand.

"May I offer you a ride home?"

She wanted to ask Annie how long she was planning to stay.

"Hold on a second," she said, and walked toward Annie.

"Annie," she said, standing behind her friend and placing a hand on her shoulder. "He wants to give me a ride."

"Don't worry about me," Annie said, figuring Chloe had already made a decision, "I'll be fine."

"No, listen," Chloe stopped, feeling Serge approaching. He went around her and began talking fast in French to Luc.

"Mais oui, pas de problème," Luc said, holding out his arm as though he were quieting a discussion. "Annie peut rester ici ce soir." And then to Chloe, "Annie can stay 'ere. My sister room is free."

Chloe and Annie watched each other as Serge led Chloe to the door. "Call me in the morning," Annie called. "I'll be downstairs with the kids."

III

She wanted to put her Frye boots up on the dashboard, a habit she'd acquired riding shotgun in her own car. She restrained herself. Serge's car was a black Lancia with smoked windows and creamy leather seats.

It was not his car, actually, he'd told her. It was his brother's, who was out of town for a few weeks. Chloe didn't know much about cars, had never heard of Lancias, but it seemed like a nice car to her.

Serge drove fast and did not stop for red lights unless it was absolutely necessary: a cop or another car coming at them.

He drove down the Champs-Élysées and across Place de la Concorde where the streetlights were blazing.

"Many of my ancestors on my mother's side were decapitated right here on this Place," Serge said.

"You drive like a fucking Frenchman," Chloe said. She thought maybe she shouldn't swear so much in front of him but everything about his attitude made her want to swear. She thought her swearing was like his driving; it was a waste of energy and didn't prove a thing.

He asked her about her living situation. Chloe told him about Dominique Augier. Had he heard of her? He said, Vaguely. She's an actress. Pretty famous in Europe. She told Serge how Dominique had gotten her start in one of her father's plays.

"What do you have planned for today?" he asked.

Tomorrow? As far as Chloe was concerned, today lasted until the sun came up again, then that was tomorrow. The next sun, she imagined, wouldn't be coming up for at least another hour.

Tomorrow was Sunday. She had to read fifty pages of *Du Côté de Chez Swann* for Monday.

"I have to study," she said. She had already considered buying an English translation to read along with the original. Was that cheating? Serge wouldn't think so.

"You have to study!" He let out a screechy peal of laughter, made a full circle of Place de la Concorde, and headed back up the Champs-Élysées.

"We're going to the beach. I'm taking you to Normandie."

It seemed crazy but she didn't argue with him. She was afraid of going back to Dominique's so late and waking her up. Dominique was an insomniac, subject to fits of rage if the little sleep she did get was disturbed.

Chloe had been at Dominique's a week, had slept there only twice because it was easier to stay at Annie's if it got late. Annie's little maid's room was under the roof, six flights above the Americans' apartment. Most of the larger Parisian buildings had a top floor, which was accessible only from the service stairwell, where chic residents housed their servants. Sometimes the chic residents rented the rooms out at a cheap price to students or seniors who couldn't afford to live anywhere else. The rooms had a sink, never a shower or toilet. The toilet was down the hall, and the shower was wherever you could find one. But Annie's American family had installed a shower in her little room, which made life a good deal easier for Annie's friends on the Program who weren't so fortunate.

They were on the highway an hour before the sun blasted into the colorless sky. The highway was straight and flat for endless miles. They listened to Serge's brother's cassettes on the four-speaker stereo. A song caught Chloe's attention. It had a simple, catchy beat and a hypnotic tune that repeated itself like an echo. A soaring male voice began to sing of loneliness in such a clear and convincing way you couldn't help but believe he meant what he was saying.

He sang about being alone and lost on an island in the middle of a sea. A thought hit Chloe. She had thirty francs in her back pocket; just about enough to take a taxi home from the party. Her passport was at Dominique's, in her wallet, and she had no credit cards. She'd never owned any.

"I'll send an SOS to the world," sang the voice.

"I hope that someone gets my
Message in a bottle."

Chloe waited to panic. Panic never came. She felt light-headed, and needy, and physically not connected to Serge, the Lancia, the endless highway, the burning sunrise. The only thing that touched her was the song.

Two weeks ago she'd landed at Roissy-Charles de Gaulle. A week ago she'd moved in with Dominique. Yesterday she'd been somewhere, today somewhere else. Places to fill the hours in a day. It didn't make a damn bit of difference to her, really, where and how she spent her time because in her mind she couldn't shake the image of herself standing with Andy, on the other side of the customs gate at Kennedy airport. But from there, what? After the gate? Void.

Serge began to chat about this and that. Chloe pressed rewind on the tape player.

"The hostage crisis is causing trouble for the dollar abroad," he said. "Can you imagine, getting less than four francs to every dollar? It's a scandal. What a time you picked to come to France."

It occurred to her that she had not picked the time, it had picked her. She listened to the song.

"Woke up this morning
Can't believe what I saw
A hundred million bottles
Washed up on the shore."

Serge talked about his family. His mother lived in London and his father spent most of the time traveling on business. Serge hardly saw them but they sent him a compunction check every month, he said. Serge was studying at the American College in Paris, but that was just an excuse to stay in France. The only class he went to regularly was pottery. He liked to work with clay.

"How do you like our Lancia? Lancias are the poor man's Ferrari," he said.

"It's nice," she said vaguely. She said she liked this song very much. Serge told her it was by the Police. His brother was crazy about the Police but Serge didn't care for their style.

An hour later Serge pulled up in front of a cream-colored stucco house that had black wood beams crisscrossed between the windows on every floor. It was perched on a sandy bluff, thirty feet above the beach. The tide was out, and the ocean seemed a mile from the shoreline.

Chloe stepped out of the car and breathed the windy salty air. It reminded her of home. Serge picked a key from his silver key ring and unlocked the back door.

They were standing in a foyer among empty coatracks and umbrella stands. Three pairs of yellow plastic boots were lined up by size next to the door. It was cold in the house.

In the living room there was a long plush couch, a glass coffee table between the couch and the red brick fireplace, handcarved wooden cabinets along the walls, and a crystal chandelier hanging from the center of the ceiling. Serge went to the fireplace and ignited the twigs and bits of paper which had been carefully arranged beneath the larger logs. The dry wood crackled loudly. Serge opened one of the cabinets and brought forth two snifters and a frosted bottle of Cognac. Chloe sat on the couch, leaning toward the fire.

"Our groundskeeper watches over the house. He leaves everything prepared in case someone shows up," Serge said. He circled the room, touching the carvings in the wood cabinets, and stopped at a high bay window that looked onto the beach.

"No one comes here anymore," he said.

"It's a beautiful house," Chloe said. "It reminds me a little of where I live back in the States. We're near the beach."

"Where do you live, back in the States?" he asked.

"I go to college in Connecticut but my mother's house is in East Whitman, Long Island."

"Aha!" he said. "Quite the Place to Be in the summertime, isn't it?"

"I went to high school out there," Chloe said, sighing, because that was the line she got from every jerk in college who asked her

"That's ridiculous," she said. "I don't even know if I like you yet."

Serge said, "You don't have to fall in *love* with me. Don't you think we might get along? I'm lonely, truly I am. Why, any one of my model friends would jump at such an opportunity."

Out went the flicker. "I don't give a fuck about your models, you know. I don't give a fuck about your money either." Not completely true, Chloe, she thought.

He turned back toward the house. Chloe walked along the beach a while and then followed him. She saw no alternative.

He waited for her at the veranda steps. "No reason to get upset," he said. "My, you have pride, I'd say. I have no pride. Let's have a nice Cognac and talk about other things."

"Fuck you," she said mildly. She couldn't look him straight in the eyes. "You don't even know who I am."

"I don't care who you are. I like secrets," he said.

* * *

He lit the already prepared firewood in the master bedroom's fireplace, and pulled the curtains. Chloe kicked off her boots and slipped into the bed, over the sheets and blankets, under the quilt. The ocean sounds outside the window eased her mind.

Serge slid in beside her. She turned her back to him. He came toward her, pressed against her back. His hands went up under her sweater. He felt around her breasts and tried to roll her onto her back.

I don't want to sleep with you Serge, she wanted to say, and get it over with. But she was afraid he'd leave her there. She was already counting the days before her next period, trying to figure out if it was safe. He tugged at her zipper.

As she felt the tugging she decided: This is it. This is the very last time.

She had an overwhelming desire to sleep. Sleep and sleep. And then she said, "No." And pushed him away from her.

"What do you mean, no?"

She thought, Oh Christ, here it comes, the grueling three-hour fight; the bastard isn't going to let me sleep.

"You won't even suck my cock?" he said.

"I'm tired," she said. "I didn't ask you to bring me here and I don't want to fuck you. I'm just plain tired of fucking for the hell of it. It's just not worth it." And leave me here if you want to, she thought, I'll figure something out.

"You nasty little tease," Serge said mildly, as though it were so unimportant he was already thinking about something else. "Nasty little girl."

He rolled away from her and puffed up his pillow, getting ready for sleep.

IV

Serge insisted they have a late lunch in his favorite boardwalk restaurant, which stayed open out of season, and where his father kept a permanent charge account. They sat on the porch that was enclosed in thick glass and watched the wind sweep across the sand and the waves. While Serge ordered for both of them, Chloe stared out at the dark sky and water, ten shades of grey, and thought about Annie, who was in Paris preparing Sunday dinner for her three little charges.

Annie had been worried all day, and angry because she did not like to worry. She'd snapped at the children for no reason and now they were sitting at the kitchen table waiting for their hamburgers, afraid to talk and get yelled at. Poor little kids always getting the shit-end of their grown-ups' moods, thought Annie. For dessert she'd let them have the fudge brownies she'd been saving. Annie remembered her grandma yelling and then feeding her home-baked goodies. There was nothing like home-baked goodies to lighten a gloomy mood and wipe out grudges.

The children's mother, Kathy-Sue Smith, had noticed that something was bothering Annie and had asked her about it earlier in the day. Annie did not like to impose her feelings on anybody, but she also wondered if she had any right to be worried in the first place, and told Kathy-Sue about Chloe's ride home. Kathy-Sue said Annie might be overreacting, being that Paris was not home turf. Why didn't she call the woman Chloe was staying with? Annie shook her head, it was Sunday, and that was the whole point. Chloe would have called if she'd gotten home.

What Annie couldn't imagine was what Chloe could see in that fellow. Maybe Serge harbored a gentle, sensitive soul under all that pomp. Annie doubted it. He certainly lacked humor. But a psychopath? She didn't think he had it in him. If it came down to it, Annie was sure Chloe could break him in two.

Kathy-Sue floated into the kitchen in her silver and black evening dress. Her high heels clicked on the tile floor. She had white-blonde hair and round velvety eyes, a long thin body and a round head. She reminded Annie of a sunflower.

She swooped down on her children, kissing them on the forehead. The veils of the dress hung from her shoulders like delicate wings. Annie put the burgers on buns and brought the plates, all three at once, to the table. Kathy-Sue put a light hand on Annie's arm and whispered, "Charles has been on the phone for half an hour. Business. Can you imagine, on Sunday?"

Annie said nothing.

"I'm sure your friend is trying to call right now." Kathy-Sue lifted her three-year-old daughter and sat down with the child on her lap.

"Annie will brush your hair out tonight and she'll read you a story because Momma's going out. Won't that be nice, Sandra?"

"Uh-huh," Sandra said, about to cry. Kathy-Sue looked up at Annie, exposing a wide section of white below her pupils. Sandra didn't like it at all when her momma went out.

Kathy-Sue put the little girl back on the seat.

"Well, I guess I should get Charles off the phone. I'll be back in a second." She wiggled the tips of her fingers at all of them. Annie knew Kathy-Sue would only stick her head in on her way out the door because she could not bear the look of desolation that would appear on Sandra's face.

Once the Smiths had left, Annie tried to be cheerful and asked the children about school tomorrow. She barely listened to their answers. She was troubled by her own questions to herself. It was a bad habit, cross-examining her own answers:

—Annie, you're too self-involved. Why are you so upset?

—Because you're worried about Chloe, and angry because she hasn't called.

—No, Annie. You're angry at her because she takes chances and you don't. Take Luc, for example. He offers you his sister's room, mentions in passing that he'd love to have you sleep with him in his own room, and you say no to both and ask him to walk you to the subway as soon as it's light out.

—But you had your responsibility toward Kathy-Sue and the kids. Don't forget that. You're a responsible human being, Annie.

When the phone rang Annie jumped up and knocked over her chair. Sandra began to wail. Annie asked the elder boy to take Sandra on his lap. He did so grumbling. Chloe's voice crackled at the end of the line.

"Oh God, Annie, you wouldn't believe this, we're in Normandy!" Chloe said.

"Well, damn. My dear girl, sounds to me more like you flew back to the States."

Annie listened to a stream of curses involving a beach and a house and a restaurant.

"Just get him to bring you back," Annie said, trying to sound reprimanding, though at this point she was holding back a laugh.

Chloe yelled that the goddamned French phone system was trying to fuck her. She said she was in some restaurant's phone booth and Serge was paying for the call.

"Just make him drive you back right now," Annie said again. "And call me from Dominique's." The line went dead.

The brownie trick worked wonders. Annie watched the children's faces redden and there were squeals of anticipation. Then total silence as they concentrated on getting the right amount of vanilla ice cream with each bite of brownie. Annie knew she shouldn't but the temptation was too much. She had a little slice of brownie, and then another little slice.

Later, when they were all in bed, she curled up on the living-room couch and began *Du Côté de Chez Swann* for the third time that week. What an ordeal, that book. May as well be trying to read Mao in Chinese. At the Program the professor had said, "Don't worry about every sentence. Your aptitudes vary. Do what you can. We don't want you spending all your time with your noses in a book. You're in Paris to study a culture and a people."

Well Chloe was certainly doing that. It took guts. Or being nuts.

* * *

Chloe called at eleven-thirty to tell Annie that she was back at Dominique's. She whispered that she did not want to stay on the phone long. "I don't know if I like that guy or not. But Christ he has more money than the Catholic Church." She kissed the mouthpiece. "I'll see you tomorrow," she said.

Soon afterwards the Smiths came home. Annie climbed the six flights of back stairs to her room. She did not use the service elevator which was black and had grills like a cage. It groaned and jolted at every floor. The hall lights were on a timer and Annie was afraid of getting stuck between floors in the dark.

She unlocked the door of her room and switched on the light. From her window she could see the Eiffel Tower, which reminded her every morning that she indeed was in Paris, and made her happier than she'd ever been in her life.

Once her clothes were carefully folded on the shelf in the closet, she slipped on her long cotton nightie and brushed her teeth. Looking at herself in the mirror above the sink, she thought it was a pity that she did not have larger eyes and that her forehead wasn't broader. But she liked her curly hair and profile.

There was a gentle knock at the door. It had to be the Arab next door because the old lady across the hall would be asleep by now. Annie put on her robe.

The Algerian or Tunisian or whatever he was made her nervous. At the Program the girls were told to avoid Arabs at all costs. She didn't know what to do.

"Excuse me," a soft male voice said in French, "I heard you come in. This is your neighbor." He had a strange guttural accent. Annie opened the door and peeked around its edge.

"I am studying for the Law exams (les examins de Droit, he said) and have run out of coffee." He smiled shyly. "And therefore, I asked myself, maybe my neighbor can lend me a bit of coffee?"

Annie stepped away from the door and gestured for him to come in. She'd only passed him in the hall and now in the light, she saw he was quite young. Probably nineteen or twenty. His skin was dark and his eyes were small and slightly slanted. He had very sharp, high cheekbones and dark grey circles under his eyes.

He would not come in farther than three feet.

"I am so tired for I work at night as well; I am guardian of a factory." He seemed quite proud of this. When he spoke he made rapid, circular gestures with his arms.

Suddenly Annie felt sorry for him. He was like her, alone, a foreigner with no one to talk to in the middle of the night.

"Well, if you come in I'll make coffee for you here," she said. He shuffled his feet.

"I did not want to disturb you."

"Not at all," Annie said. She boiled water in her hot pot and poured herself a glass of wine. He sat in her one chair and looked about.

"What luckiness," he said, shaking his hand as though he'd burned it, "you have a shower." He used *vous*.

"Yes," Annie said. "If you're ever in a pinch, you're welcome to use it."

He blushed, then she blushed.

"I mean to say, when I'm not here," she said quickly, feeling she was making things worse.

"Would you like a glass of wine?" she asked him.

"I do not drink alcohol," he said, "but thank you." He touched his heart with his hand.

He sipped his coffee in silence, then looked up at Annie apologetically.

"My name is Azzedine. I am Tunisian."

"Moi, je m'appelle Annie. Je suis américaine." Elementary French 101, Annie thought, smiling.

"Ah," he said. "I had thought that you were American."

They talked for a half hour. He told her his friends called him Azzed, and she should do the same. He was in his second year of law school, which was different from America because here you went straight from secondary studies to your specialized field.

In other words, Annie figured, he was a sophomore in college.

Azzed told her his family was very proud of him. He wanted to pass the bar exam in France and then maybe go to the United States to study International Law.

"Because the image Tunisians have in France is very bad," he said, shaking his head. "We are a civilized people. It is they that make us uncivilized."

Annie thought he was being childishly idealistic but said nothing since he was in her room and who knew? Maybe he was violent. In any case he was proud. And good-looking.

He got up to leave. He handed her back the cup and said he would knock next time he made a cous-cous next door. He had very nice friends and she should meet them.

"Let me know ahead of time and I'll bring my friend who is very nice too," she said, thinking of Chloe. She wondered how Chloe felt about Arabs.

V

Chloe never looked through the mail bin which sat on the ledge outside the sliding window of the Program's main office. It embarrassed her to get so excited hoping someone would write and then being let down because no one did. She'd written four or five letters since she'd arrived, two to Andy, one to her brother, a couple to Falcon, but hadn't mailed any of them. So what did she expect?

But Monday before the Contemporary French Novel class, Annie came up behind her and poked her in the ribs. Chloe was looking out through the sliding doors at the garden in the center of the building. It was drizzling outside.

Annie handed Chloe a light business-size envelope. It was from Sacred Heart University. Andy had written out the Program's address in careful block letters below her capitalized name. It was so uncharacteristic of Andy to apply himself to anything. Chloe's eyes filled with tears.

She sat on crooked wooden stairs that led up to the classrooms and read the letter. It was written on notebook paper, the sheet had been ripped away from the binding and was missing its lower left corner. It had been folded many times, at different angles. Chloe imagined Andy had hid it in a pocket when his privacy had been interrupted by any one of his curious friends. Slipped in between the folded letter were two snapshots of Andy playing basketball.

Dear Chloe,

Hi. I'm sitting here in Jazz class and the only way I can keep
my eyes open is to think of you and write. This class is pitiful
and to make it worse Johnson is next to me snoring. So how are
things in France? I hope fine. I really miss you. Everything
here is fine except my car got robbed. They broke the windshield with a bat or something, smashed out my glove com-
partment and they also stole my father's $100 coat.

I got 2 B's, 2 C's and a D last semester. I didn't deserve the
D and I'll try to sweet-talk the old bitch into changing it.

At this point Andy must have stopped because the ink color
changed from blue to black and his writing began to climb up and
down the lines like musical notes.

After I dropped you at the airport I was in a total daze. I
couldn't stop thinking about you. Believe me Chloe I feel a lot
of things inside I don't show them and I'm not sure why. I feel
really weird inside when I think of you. I miss you so much. I
have three pictures of you now on the wall next to my bed.
Remember the ones I took outside during Christmas break?
Your the first thing I see every day but it's not as good as the
real thing. I try to think time will fly by but it seems like
you've been gone so long and it's been just over a week.

Excuse my writing, I'm writing on my kneecap. I'm at work
parking cars at the Milford HiAlai, I'm sitting freezing my ass
off in this booth waiting for these jerks to come get their cars
so I can go home. I drink pretty much before I come to work
because it's so fucking cold.

And back to blue:

I guess that's it for now. I'm not going to read this letter over
or I probably wouldn't send it. I'm on my way to class, believe
it or not. Just remember I love you.

                                                    Andy

P.S.—I got these pictures from an intersquad scrimmage and I
thought you might like them.

One of the pictures had captured Andy in a jump, his hands
above the rim of the basket, the ball already halfway through the

net. His feet were parallel to the court, at least three feet in the air.
The other picture was a full-face of Andy hunched over at the foul
line, about to make a shot. He was holding the ball level with his
waist, his eyes focused upward on the basket that must have been
right above the photographer's head. Andy seemed poised and yet
bewildered, his mouth was hanging open slightly and his eyes had
that fixed expression, concentrating maybe just a little too hard on
the basket in front of him. He had the same look on his face when
he made love.

Chloe wanted to write him back immediately. Write him a love
letter before the passion of the moment wore thin in the face of
her doubts. When she wrote to him she felt she was cheating him,
and ended up not mailing the letters. She wanted to be in love
with him, because she respected him and was grateful to him; she
did not want to lose him.

But there was so much she couldn't say to him, so much that was
just not worth trying to explain. Sometimes she tried to hint at the
fact that eventually they would go their own ways, but that they
would always remain close friends. She hoped desperately that
someday she would find somebody who would understand her and
whom she would understand without forcing it, without so many
words. And they wouldn't be carrying along all this baggage, this
mutual past that did nothing but bog Andy and her down.

The truth was, she would leave Andy for good in one second for
that Right Person. But she would not admit this to herself. Andy
fulfilled a selfish need for the moment: He was an anchor. And
though a ship's anchor can't prevent the ship from rocking and
tossing about in a storm, at least it keeps the ship from being
carried out to sea.

* * *

February 18, 1980

My Dear Andy,

I got your letter this morning, let me tell you it was the
nicest thing that's happened to me since I've been here. I had
a bad time adjusting at first, but things are getting better. I'm
living with a friend of my mother's now, she doesn't charge
me rent, which is great. Otherwise I don't know what I would
have done. The dollar is *very* low because the U.S. for once is

on the shit-end of the stick and they're letting us have it for all the times *they*'ve been on the shit-end of the stick.

People here care a lot about how they look and they're very polite. Americans always say the French are all drunks but it's not true. It seems to me (at least from the ones I've met) that they drink more for taste than to get drunk. Sometimes I want to get drunk and I feel weird about it. Like I'm an alcoholic or something. So I'm not drinking anything but wine anymore.

For a long time I couldn't stop thinking about being with you at the airport, wishing I still was there with a chance to change my mind. I guess I just can't quit in the middle of an idea.

The world looks different from over here. I never realized how one-sided our view is back at home. Do you know what I'm talking about?

I miss you, Andy. If you were here you'd just be you, the way you always are, and you'd never let them make you feel insecure.

I miss sleeping with you so much. I think something weird's happening to me (you'll be happy to hear), I don't feel like sleeping with anybody. I hope my sex drive comes back by the time I get home.

God summer is so far away. I want to come home already. Do you think next summer will be just like last summer? I hope nothing changes. Please write as often as you like, whenever you can. It makes me feel so good to hear from you.

                                        Love, Chloe

Andy read it through again. In the tiny booth he could see his breath when he exhaled. On the ledge in front of him were empty and half-empty cups and paper bags from all the fast-food joints in the area. He kicked them onto the floor and placed the soles of his boots there. He held the letter against his knee. Small comfort on a night like this. He took the half-pint of Jack Daniel's out of his jacket pocket and had himself a long swig that made his eyes sting. He wondered how he'd ever gotten himself into this thing with her. He wasn't sorry for it. She warmed him in a way almost as much as the Jack Daniel's did.

He read the letter through a third time, looking for meanings that weren't apparent to him the first two times. Chloe was good at that. He was constantly afraid she would hint at something he was supposed to understand but wouldn't. Not because he was stupid but because he didn't want to know. The letters blurred. He felt his eyes watering and wondered if it was the Jack Daniel's, the cold, or her causing it.

VI

"Well if you don't like him why did you make a date with him then?" Annie asked, glancing nervously over her shoulder at the double doors, the heavy portes cochères that were the entrance to the Program's outside hall.

"Well shit," Chloe said, "you have something better to do on a Friday night? You have to baby-sit your kiddies, you should talk."

She had agreed to meet Serge at the Program at four. It was now four-twenty and she could tell Annie wanted to leave. Chloe hoped Serge would not show up in the next ten minutes; she would leave with Annie, go back to the Smiths' apartment, and watch Annie watch the Smith kids.

All week Serge had been calling Chloe at Dominique's. He left embarrassing messages on Dominique's answering machine (*Chloé! You're breaking my heart. Naughty girl, why are you avoiding me?*) which infuriated Dominique; and called late at night, which really infuriated Dominique; and completely disregarded the rules Chloe had spent fifteen minutes explaining to him before she would give him Dominique's phone number.

"Leesten," Dominique finally said, "go out with the fucking ass'ole if for nothing else than just to get him to stop deranging ME!"

"Well at least maybe I'll get to eat well," Chloe said to Annie.

"Nobody needs to eat *that* well." Annie made a clucking sound by tightening her jaw muscles.

Chloe wondered why Serge was interested in her. Her first

suspicion, of course, was that he wanted to sleep with her. But they'd been through that once already, that morning at the beach. Sex didn't seem to matter to him. But maybe it wasn't the sex itself, but the conquest.

He tickled her vanity. She was suspicious and afraid of her vanity. It was a restless lunatic that had to be kept locked up, away from the world, like Mrs. Rochester, in the attic.

She thought Serge sensed she was a romantic. That she loved the idea of having her eyes opened to the glittering world of Paris at night.

"Let's see," Annie rubbed her chin. "From the Michelin Guide: We say have him take you to the Tour D'Argent. While you gourmandise over your three-star meal you can watch the bateaux mouches cruise down the Seine. Plus you get a view of your favorite cathedral, Notre-Dame."

They heard a screech of tires. They turned and saw the black Lancia jolt to a stop, raising dust in front of the doors. Of course the other students standing around saw too. Chloe ducked into the collar of her coat.

"You want a ride home?" Chloe said.

"Why not? No experience should be missed. Who knows? I may be telling my grandchildren about this."

Chloe walked out with her head down. She knocked on the smoked window. Serge lowered it without looking at her. The rock and roll from the four-speaker stereo blasted into the street and through the open doors into the quiet hall.

"You're making people look at us," Chloe said.

"Am I?" He still did not look at her.

"Can we please give Annie a ride home? She's been waiting with me for over a half hour."

"Where does Annie live?"

"In the sixteenth, off Victor Hugo." She put her hands on the window and leaned toward him.

"Wrong direction," he said, looking at her fingers on the glass. "We're going to the American College. It's Happy Hour over there and someone's waiting for me with hash."

"So she can come to the College. You can drop her after or she can take the Metro from there." Annie doesn't really go out much, it'll be nice for her, Chloe thought.

He finally looked at her with his fine blue eyes. The corners of his mouth were twitching into a small smile that could just as well have been a snarl. Chloe leaned toward the car waiting for him to say something.

"So where is Annie?" he said.

Serge found a parking spot half a block down the avenue from the College. As they approached Chloe had an anxiety attack that was not unpleasant and reminded her of the way she had felt before going on stage. In front of the College there were rows of motorcycles and motorscooters parked on the sidewalk. Small groups stood around admiring the bigger motorcycles and talking to their owners who protectively stood guard.

The outside hall was larger than the one at the Program. It was long and had a high arching ceiling, like a medieval banquet hall.

Diversity was Cromwell's slogan. The diversity of this group milling about the hall made Cromwell's slogan seem foolish and pretentious to Chloe as she looked around. She was reminded of the market scene in *Casablanca*.

There were preppie-types in sports jackets and tailored pants, the girls in pleated skirts and bright sweaters; hippie-types with holes in their sneakers and embroidered jeans and jackets; Fascist Youth–types in black leather and chains; chic-chic French-looking people in the height-of-fashion; and a fair number of well-dressed and not at all well-dressed Semitic men who had no female counterparts.

Serge led them to the bar in the back of the hall.

"You should be able to tell the Iranians from the Arabs," Serge said. "Just by their clothes. And you have to watch out for the Arabs. They're pigs. Drooling like dogs over Western girls whom in fact they despise and think are whores. The Arabs can be quite dangerous. You see, the Arabs pretend they're Iranians to impress you naive American girls. They'll latch on like monkeys and never leave you alone if you pay any attention to them at all.

"However," he went on as he paid for their first round at the bar, "the Iranians are basically harmless. They're the ex-Shah's people. They've been thrown out of Iran and have nowhere to go. In general I'd say they're very well off. One fellow gets driven to school in a Rolls. See the Iranians?" He pointed with his chin to a couple of the well-dressed, dark young men.

Chloe watched the young Iranians' haughty yet insecure demeanor, remembered the American hostages, and had the sensation she was witnessing a historical moment. Back in the States even the most politically aware did not understand or identify with the insecurity of smaller, less powerful countries. "As long as we're indomitable, we're right," was the way Chloe thought Americans felt. And there was a perfect example: *Americans,* as though the "North" part was strictly understood. Seeing the haughty, nervous Rich Iranians made her wonder if the revolutionaries hadn't had a very good reason to storm the U.S. Embassy. Which made her sad for her country, sad for the hostages, who had to suffer for her country's enormous, childish egotism.

"And that, over there, is probably an Algerian, or a Tunisian," Serge went on. "One can't tell them apart." He pointed a finger at a man older than the students who was leaning against the wall smoking. He wore a dirty green army jacket and had an unshaved face. His eyes were shifty and his posture hunched.

Chloe remembered being little on the Paris metro, looking up and seeing a dirty, scarred face smiling down at her. The scar ran from the man's left eye to below his right cheekbone. He was an Arab. He put his hand between her legs and squeezed. Chloe had peed in her pants.

She looked away from the man in the army jacket and paid attention to her drink. Serge went off to find his connection, and Annie and she stayed at the bar. Annie drank gin and tonics, which were cheap at the American College Happy Hour. Chloe stuck to beer.

After the third they ordered a fourth and went for a walk, taking their drinks. Chloe was surprised at Annie drinking so much, but said nothing as she was happy to have someone to drink with.

"I don't like him," Annie said. They were heading for the steps that led to the entrance to the school's main lobby.

"Where does *he* get off talking about Arabs that way, that preppie cretin. What does *he* know about Arabs? He probably doesn't even know how to put on his own underwear. I have a Tunisian living next door to me. I've gotten to know him pretty well over the past few weeks, and he's nothing like that. He's nothing like that at all!"

Chloe was about to tell Annie the story about the Arab in the subway, and tell her she was too naive and gullible and should be more careful who she made friends with when a girl sitting on the steps caught her attention. The girl had a charming, innocent face that looked like it had gone through a terrible time. She was crying.

"For three days the poor old lady just disappeared. Nobody called to tell me. Nothing!" She wiped her face and looked up at the tall fellow standing above her.

"Then this morning they turned off the electricity, the phone, the gas . . . Then like an hour ago the old lady's daughter comes by and tells me the old lady died of a stroke this morning. She was in the hospital for THREE FUCKING DAYS and nobody told me! I bet you anything that bitch daughter didn't even go see her. You know why? 'Cause she lives next door and she *never* comes by to see how the old lady's doing.

"So the daughter tells me like an hour ago that I have three days to move out. They're selling the apartment. Oh man."

She covered her face with her hands. Her long blonde hair slid off her shoulders. The tall fellow seemed at a loss. He stood over her, passing his black motorcycle helmet from one arm to the other.

"I'm sorry, Veritas," he said. He watched her sadly through thick, steel-rimmed glasses as her shoulders shook. "I'm sure the old lady didn't expect you to come see her. You were just her tenant."

The girl looked at him almost angrily. "How do you know?"

"I can help you look for a new place. We can drive around on my moto. That part won't be too bad. I wish I could put you up but I'm in rather a bad spot myself. The wife threw me out and I'm profiting from the good nature of my friend Cédric who has lent me his kitchen floor."

Chloe thought he had a child's face. He had sorrowful eyes behind the glasses, a big triangular nose that stuck out from his rain-straight hair. It fell from the top of his head, over the tops of his glasses and ears. She couldn't imagine him having a wife and

thought it must be an idiomatic expression he had simply trans-
lated from French. His English was laced with French idioms.

"And I'm basically broke," the girl said.

"And you're illegal, Veritas, no?" the fellow said. "Ee-*lee*-gal,"
he said.

"Yeah, yeah. I had a tourist visa."

Serge came out of the crowd and stopped in front of the girl.

"Well hello, Vero," he said. His tone was sweet in a condescending way. And flirting, Chloe thought. "You don't look happy,
Vero," he said.

Vero told him about the old lady and the apartment.

"Well that's too bad, Vero," he said in the same caressing, condescending way. "You want to come outside with us and smoke a
little hashish? Like we used to?"

Vero said, *Sure!* But what about Jeff, can he come?"

Chloe had fogotten about Annie, who'd been standing next to
her listening the whole time. She was staring at Serge with open
disgust.

"I don't smoke hashish," Jeff said. "But if you don't mind I'll
come along for the fresh air."

On the way out, Annie asked him, "Are you American? You must
be with a name like Jeff."

"I suppose," he said, walking sideways tripping over his legs like
a very young colt. "It's Geoffrey. But I don't really give a damn
what people call me."

Chloe was surprised that Annie did not leave them. She came
along even when Serge suggested they pile into the Lancia to
smoke, since it was safer to take a drive.

Chloe and Geoffrey were the last to get in; she offered him the
front seat but he declined.

Serge filled the little stone pipe and drove at the same time. He
unfolded the tin foil and pinched a piece of the dark green hash off
the chunk, stuffed and lit the pipe and passed it to Chloe. She
smoked, passed it back to Vero who cupped the bowl in her palm
and inhaled till she couldn't anymore.

Annie still had her gin and tonic. She held the cup high in one
hand and took the pipe with the other. "Pot makes me crazy," she
said to no one in particular.

"This isn't pot," Vero said, holding her breath still. "It's hash. You can't get good pot over here." She blew out without coughing. "I brought an ounce of beautiful sensamilla over with me from California. Right Serge? Tell me that stuff wasn't great. Lasted about four months. I was proud of myself."

"You brought it from California?" Chloe said, looking back at her. Chloe was taken by Vero's face, the sweet clearness of her grey eyes.

"Sure," Vero said, "in my crotch."

"Well I say!" Annie said, acting shocked. Chloe did not think Annie was really all that shocked, but felt she *should* be shocked and therefore expressed shock. It was ingrained in her personality, an automatic reaction.

Chloe thought, You're already thinking too much.

Annie passed the pipe to Geoffrey who held up his hand like a policeman.

"No thank you. THC makes me introspect to the point where I begin to doubt my own existence." He was laughing and his knees were digging into Chloe's back, through the seat.

The hash warmth was rising in circles around her, beginning in the center of her stomach. It surrounded her like a cloud. She watched Vero's face lighten. It became smoother, pinker, prettier. Poor people like us who need so much, she thought.

"Annie," she said, "is there any way at all you could put Vero up for a few days?"

Chloe didn't say more because Annie and she understood each other. It was as though Annie were putting up an old friend of Chloe's, on Chloe's recognizance, though they had both met Vero at the same time.

"I don't see why not," Annie smiled at Vero. Annie told her about the little maid's room in the sixteenth, about her obligation to the Smiths. "It's their place. I couldn't put you up for more than a few days. I'd feel I was taking advantage of them."

Vero began to cry again. "Oh," she sighed. "I wouldn't impose myself, I promise. I can't believe it. You guys don't even know me."

"I must say, what an American thing to do," Geoffrey said. He was quite pleased, Chloe could tell, that the burden was off his hands.

"Oh my God," Vero went on, "you don't know how much I

didn't want to go back there tonight. I know her energy is still there. Poor old lady, I bet I'd still hear her clunking down the hall."

The light was fading, cold and colorless. They had driven down the left bank, past the Eiffel Tower and the new developments of skyscrapers that demarcated the beginning of suburbia. The landscape was becoming desolate. Chloe felt Serge's presence beside her like a cold draft.

His face was pale and set, expressionless. In the back seat they were all feeling better for Vero; but what could this possibly mean to him, she wondered. He's probably thinking what fools we are. He had not said a word the whole time.

"How're you doing?" she asked him, touching his elbow.

"Why do you say that all the time? 'How're you doing?' It doesn't mean anything," he said.

In the back they were chatting away. Annie was telling them about the Program.

"Next week you must all come to Cédric's for dinner," Geoffrey said. "We're completely in the poorhouse, so we'll just make do. We'll eat fried potatoes like Russians during the war."

"Why, how charming!" Annie said, laughing.

It seemed to Chloe that they were talking awfully fast and she was thinking awfully slowly.

Night began to set in. The tenuous time between day and night had always been Chloe's weakest time. When she was sick, the fever went up; when she was sad, her blues turned black. Now suddenly she was miserable at the thought of spending the evening alone with Serge.

"I'm dropping you all at the College. Chloe and I have dinner reservations," he said, crossing the river at the next bridge and heading back down the right bank.

"Serge?" Annie leaned into the space between the front seats. "Why do you hate Arabs?"

"They're pigs. But I don't hate them because they don't interest me in the least."

"Well, they interest me and I'd like to know why it is that people don't give them a chance," Annie said.

"Annie has an Arab friend," Chloe said.

"He's not really a friend," Annie said.

"But you like him. You should be careful, Annie. Because they're horny bastards, let me tell you. When I was living here as a kid I got my ass grabbed in the metro and it scared me half to death. Can you imagine? I was only a tiny kid."

"You lived here before?" Geoffrey said from the back.

"Yes."

"But still," Annie said, "that was only one Arab."

"Good point," Geoffrey said. "But I've lived in Paris fifteen years and I can tell you from experience the North Africans' reputation didn't fall on them from the sky. You know they are terribly repressed. Socially and sexually. You should see how they treat their women. Most of them actually don't have women here; they leave them behind and come to France to find work. But there's no work. And Western women taunt them. They get furious when aroused."

"But still, I don't think it's fair to judge all Arabs because a few of them are bad," Annie said.

"You don't have to justify yourself," Chloe said. "If you like the guy, you like the guy. If he slits your throat while you're sleeping some night, you'll know better next time."

Chloe hadn't meant for that to come off the way it did. Annie sat back and sulked. Chloe apologized.

Geoffrey tried to lighten the air by talking about his studies in Physics at the *Faculté des Sciences.*

"I'm dyslexic in both English and French. They say it's a common trait in genii," he said.

"Your wife doesn't think you're a genius," Vero said without malice.

"And that's the sad truth," Geoffrey said. "When we get divorced—I presume that's what she wants, my lovely wife—her papa's a big lawyer. When we get divorced I'm going to apply to Massachusetts Institute of Technology, which is the best science academy in America, as far as I'm concerned. And one of you very nice American girls is going to have to aid me with my essay."

Chloe wanted him to talk about his wife. She was curious about his story. Curious and dreading what he would say, the way the proletariat was curious to watch the aristocrats be guillotined, thinking, "My God, how awful!" and, "But I'm glad it's not me. Because it *could* have been me."

VII

"Do you know Serge well?" Annie asked Vero. They were climbing the back stairs to Annie's room.

"Just to get stoned with," Vero said.

Well, that's a good thing, at least, Annie thought. At least she isn't a good friend of his. That simpleminded aristocrat. No wonder there are revolutions.

Annie thought of Chloe looking at her through the tinted car window as Serge drove off, making the tires screech. Chloe looked about as happy as the calf on the wagon bound for market.

Just as Serge's car disappeared down the avenue, Geoffrey came around the corner pushing a tall red motorcycle. He straddled it and rocked back and forth, pushing with the heels and then the toes of his boots. While he was rocking, he asked Annie about Chloe. Vero stood leaning on one leg with a limp hand on her hip, listening with a sorrowful look on her face.

"Are they going out together?" Geoffrey asked, nodding in the car's direction.

"No," Annie said. In the car Chloe had barely said five words. But Annie had noticed that every time Chloe turned and looked at the backseat, Geoffrey was watching her.

"You've known each other a long time, then?" he asked.

"Since freshman year. I guess that's a pretty long time," Annie said.

"She has wonderful strange eyes," Geoffrey said. "They're rather mysterious but without intending to be. Quite vulnerable, I

imagine. She has that look, you know, like she's gone through a bad
time."

And there you have it, thought Annie. Chloe attracting strange
people because she has strange eyes.

"She has," Annie said, thinking she'd said too much.

Geoffrey said, "Ah." He kicked the starter angrily, his whole
body jerking into the kick.

VVROOMMVRROOM.

"Your Program," he yelled, "is it the one on Rue Vavin? Because
I know there's another American program on Rue de Passy."

"It's the one on Rue Vavin," Annie said. She could see it already.
Geoffrey flying through the portes cochères on that red terror,
shaking up the Program walls.

"Ah," Geoffrey said, "I was serious about dinner at Cédric's.
He's very shy but he loves the company of women. He loves to
cook but he's not very good at it. I'll talk to him and tomorrow I'll
come by the Program and if I can't find you, I'll leave a message."

And Annie would bet her last red cent that he'd be there tomorrow, and that he'd find out when Chloe had class, and he'd patiently wait. He had that look in his eyes himself. The Lost Soul
Look. Chloe was a magnet for lost souls.

Annie left Vero upstairs and went down to talk to Kathy-Sue.
Annie could easily not tell her, but she felt she should. Kathy-Sue
trusted her and Annie wanted to be trustworthy.

Kathy-Sue not only said, "By all means," she said, "bring her
down to meet the children. The children love to be around young
people." Annie went back upstairs to get her.

They had a nice conversation with Kathy-Sue in the kitchen
while she fed the children. Kathy-Sue liked to cook for the children herself when she had time.

"Vero," Kathy-Sue pondered with a hand to her chin. "What an
interesting name."

"Not really," Vero said, laughing and at ease. "It's Veronica." She
said this as though it were a monstrous confession. "Back in grade
school they used to give me so much grief you know, because of
the Archie comics? Veronica was the spoiled-rotten one. The bad
girl. So I started writing Vero on stuff and pretty soon people

forgot. What a pain in the butt I had to live with before that, though."

Kathy-Sue nodded slowly. It was a good thing Kathy-Sue liked outspoken people, Annie thought.

"I didn't know that," Annie said, as though she should have.

Annie was in one of her violent baking moods. These moods came on as a reaction to frustration, because Annie was not good at expressing anger. Her conversation with Serge had left her feeling he'd led her down a dead-end street. It was like facing a brick wall, because—the worst part of it—he simply did not care. Not about Arabs, not about Annie, and certainly not about what she had to say.

Annie wanted to make hundreds of gooey chocolate chip cookies to give the kiddies and to take upstairs to Azzed.

Kathy-Sue and Charles were gone now and the kiddies were in the living room, lying on the rug in front of the TV. Annie remembered she had a guest and was displeased because having another person in the kitchen when one is baking is a terrible pain. The other person is either an expert cookie-maker and has the world's only worthwhile recipe, or s/he can't bake at all and stands over you and pours ingredients in when you're not looking, "to be helpful."

Annie heard Vero behind her and turned from the cabinets. Vero had found an apron and was washing the pots and pans Kathy-Sue had left in the sink. Annie said, "It *really* annoys me that one can't find chocolate chips in France. You know, Nestlé's?" She described the package by making a rectangle of her hands, thumbs extended.

"You can make do with a bar of dark chocolate," Vero said. "You have to crunch it up."

"It won't be the same," Annie said, already looking through the cabinets. She found a bar of dark chocolate and Vero crunched it up with a meat cleaver. Then Vero sat down at the round table and talked and talked while Annie made her cookies.

"They don't look like chocolate chips now, but once they melt, it's all the same, right?" Vero said.

Vero talked about her family. Her father was a professor of philosophy at the University of California at Santa Cruz.

"I'm a fac brat," Vero said. "My parents are real old." Annie wondered what Vero thought was old, thinking of her own grandma. She didn't interrupt.

"They were really pro-Vietnam. They were as unbending as Goddam oak trees on the subject. Then my big brother got killed over there and they went completely apeshit. They started dropping acid and dressing like hippies. Going on peace marches. Totally weird. I was a mistake I think. When all that happened they forgot about me. Now I'm eighteen and my father looks at me like I fell from the sky. He doesn't know what to do with me."

Vero talked about dropping acid. She told Annie she could tell just by looking at people whether they'd ever dropped acid or not.

"I can tell you haven't," she said, smiling in an elfish way.

Right you are there, Annie thought. All this while Annie baked and smiled to herself, thinking she was here in Paris, baking for an Arab while listening to a flowerchild talk about her acid experiences. Six months ago she wouldn't have believed it.

"Azzed studies law and has very little money," Annie told Vero. They were climbing the dark stairs again, this time Annie was holding a large plate that was covered in tinfoil.

She had disclosed information about Azzed little by little, tentatively. Annie was very talkative, but deep down, very secretive. So far she'd told Vero that he was Tunisian and that he lived next door. That sometimes late at night they had talks while he drank coffee and she drank wine to fall asleep.

"He doesn't drink," she said, "and I'm sure he's never had a chocolate chip cookie." Annie was very pleased with the way they had turned out. Even with fake chocolate chips.

"Does he get stoned?" Vero asked.

Annie turned and looked at Vero for a second. Vero's expression was complacent and void of malice. Annie was afraid of malice when it came to Azzed. Though there was nothing between them, Annie took personally everything bad she'd heard about Arabs in the past two weeks.

"I don't know," she said. "I would presume he gets high. Don't Muslims smoke hashish? Drinking is against the religion, isn't it? God, I don't know anything about it. I'm Catholic, what can I tell you? I never even met a Jew till I went to college."

"You're Catholic? So am I. Though I don't think I've been to church since my baptism."

When they got to the top floor Annie saw the yellow strip of light beneath Azzed's door. She noticed that she was not out of breath. She was getting used to climbing the stairs.

Breathily, Vero said, "See, I have some hash. I didn't bring it out in the car because fuck Serge anyway; you know what I mean? He's rich. But if your friend wants to get stoned, I'd be happy to get stoned again myself."

"Gee, what if he doesn't smoke? He'll think I'm a derelict."

"Oh, grow up," Vero said, pushing the air down with a flat hand.

Annie knocked on Azzed's door.

VIII

"Annie?" Azzed called out. "Entre. C'est ouvert!"

They went in, Annie in front with the plate, and then Vero. Annie's heart was beating a little fast. She could feel it in her temples.

"On a fait des biscuits américains ce soir. Ils s'appellent chocolate chips," Annie said.

"Chocolate sheep?" he said, looking up from a book. She handed him the plate. He was sitting on his mattress under the slanting roof with his legs crossed beneath him. There were books everywhere.

"Sit, sit," he said in French, gesticulating wildly with hands the color of ashes. He pushed the books out of the way, piling them. He had nothing in the room except for the mattress, the books, a night table, an electric stove, dishes and pans in the sink, and old orange crates where he kept his groceries.

"I am sorry but if I had known you were bringing a friend, I would have made an effort to clean up," he shrugged exaggeratedly. At first Annie had thought his gestures fake and ingratiating but now she knew it was just part of him, an Arab trait. Like the Italians talk with their hands.

He pinched his fingers together as though he were holding a very small object, and pressed them to his heart.

"I have nothing to give *you*," he said.

"Oh, but we don't want anything," Annie said quickly. "I was making cookies anyway and thought of you. This is my friend, Vero."

"Bonjour," he said, though it was the middle of the night.

Vero took a step back and leaning on that back leg, made a 180-degree circle with her arm.

"Hey," she said.

"Vero has lost her apartment and is staying with me a few days," Annie said.

"She is very fortunate." Azzed smiled at both of them. His smile made Annie nervous. His smiles always seemed full of hidden meanings. And he had bad teeth. It was a pity because otherwise, he was by far the best-looking fellow she had ever seen.

He was still holding the plate balanced on his knee. Awkwardly, it seemed, as though it were fragile.

"Don't you want to try one?" Annie said.

"It was too nice of you. You should not have troubled yourself. Je suis gêné."

He put the plate down and carefully pulled back the tinfoil.

"Ask him if he wants to get stoned," Vero said, poking Annie with her elbow. Vero sat down on the floor and crossed her legs.

Good Lord, how forward can one be? Annie asked him, "Vero has some hashish and would like to smoke with you if you smoke."

"Hashish? Of course," he said. Big smile.

"Well, in that case, I'm going to get my wine."

Annie came back with two glasses and a bottle that was half full.

The girls drank and Vero and Azzed smoked. His face relaxed, which softened his features. They laughed a good deal and ate all the cookies. Azzed ate slowly, stopping at times in midbite to concentrate on the taste. Annie was thrilled.

She watched Vero fill the pipe and light it. And fill it again. She talked her street French, dragging the vowels, saying whatever passed through her head. Annie watched and wondered what made some people so easy to be with and others so difficult. She herself was easy, she knew. But she was, underneath it all, uptight. She was always aware and thinking of social rules, even when she was breaking them. She felt a little funny around Vero, who was so happy and complacent in her world without rules. Annie found herself examining people like Vero, taking it in from the "outside."

(Annie did not see herself as an "in" person.) Annie felt safe being aware of The Rules, especially since she intended to break them once in a while, without getting caught.

Annie sat uncomfortably on the edge of the mattress next to Azzed. Often he turned his head and looked at her and his eyes made her heart beat in her temples again. His pupils were black but his irises were blacker. His eyes were saying, "I want to fuck you Annie," though he'd never remotely approached the subject. "I want to do dirty things to you. Roll you onto your stomach right here on this mattress and stick it in from behind."

Annie looked away.

"Ha, ha!" Vero kicked her feet up and let them drop. "A-zed. You got the *whole* alphabet in there!"

Not long after that Annie pulled Vero up and took her back next door. Annie folded a blanket on the floor and covered it with her down sleeping bag.

"You sleep on the bed," Annie said.

"No way! Not a chance, kiddo," Vero said, dropping onto the sleeping bag. She winked at Annie.

"Hey," she said, "he's real sweet."

Then they heard him call from his door. "Annie," he said in a clear loud whisper.

She went out into the dark hall.

She felt her way along the wall, the few feet between her door and his. She could see his silhouette and his hand holding his door cracked and the yellow strip of light, vertical now, splitting the blackness.

"Stay with me," he said.

Annie's automatic reaction, the first one before thought, was outrage. Then for about fifteen seconds she was so shaken up she couldn't speak.

"That way nobody will have to sleep on the floor." Slinkily he leaned toward her.

Annie, what are you THINKING ABOUT? her brain shouted.

He kissed her gaping mouth. His mouth was warm and very wet. He smelled like old books and dust and shaving soap. Then he breathed the sweet hash breath on her face. He kissed her again harder as though he were breathing her in. She locked her knees because they were shaking. He held the back of her neck, tilting her head back and then farther back, kissing her till she lost her sense of time and an hour or a second could have passed. She ran spread fingers through his very curly, very short hair, which she realized she had expected would be oily, but wasn't.

Then something clicked and she was afraid again. Because he was firm and dark and passionate.

She pulled away, pushing him back gently.

"Je ne peux pas," she said. "I can't."

He said nothing.

"Goodnight, Azzed," she whispered, thinking about his name.

"Bonsoir," he said. She thought she could feel him smiling in the darkness. The farther she backed away the more frightened she became. Because now he probably knew she would do it. He'd won. It was just a question of time.

Back in her room she lay in bed hearing him move about on the other side of the thin wall. Azzed.

She crossed her arms above her head under the pillow and stared at the blackness that was not as black as his eyes.

"Why didn't you stay with him?" Vero said from the floor.

"Because." Annie didn't know what to say to that. "Because I don't know him very well."

Now that she was back here at home and safe she felt self-righteous. What with Vero right here, next door. It just couldn't have worked.

"Well there you have one good way of getting to know him better," Vero said. Then she laughed quietly. "Don't KNOW him that well. She-it. I've slept with guys I never saw before or since. Sometimes it's just great that way. And then I guess sometimes it's not."

—Ah, Annie, what are you going to do, surrounded by these free spirits? her mind said.

—Free spirits, my ass. Get up and go back to him. This has nothing to do with them. Chicken chicken chicken.

She pictured him naked sliding into his bed. She wondered if his sheets were dirty. She slid her leg up without lifting it, noiselessly. She was wet. She wiped the wet with her flannel nightie.

"One person I'd really like to sleep with is Geoffrey," Vero said.

"I bet he'd be a great lay. You know why, because he's so sensitive. He won't fuck. He's all screwed up over his wife and kid."

"His kid?" Annie said, sitting up.

"Yeah, he has a kid. A tiny kid about two or so."

"Oh my God," Annie said.

IX

The first time in her life Chloe had truly worried about her appearance was at the party Annie had taken her to. This was the second time, and far worse. Sitting back in the plush velvety seat in the disco at Castel's, she looked down at her eternal jeans, sweater, Frye boots, and felt like a farmgirl gone barefoot to town for the yearly harvest feast; big-boned, red-faced, and vulgar.

They had had a lovely dinner in a small restaurant. They had talked to each other comfortably about nothing important. But now she sat next to Serge and he was not speaking to her. She watched the girls come and go. None of them sat at the table for more than a few minutes. None of them said a word to her. And she knew it wasn't because she threatened them. They all looked like Mata Hari, decked in silk and jewels, sparkling like Christmas trees.

When she tried to speak to the table of young men her comments went ignored. Serge's friends smoked and drank endless bottles of champagne and talked about money. Chloe listened in disbelief. This seemed the most perfect parody of snobbism she'd ever seen. And worse than that, she was feeling envious of the girls; their clothes, their names, their money. She had never felt envy before because she had never thought she lacked anything. And it made her miss her father terribly.

"I'm tired of spring skiing," one of Serge's friends said in French. "This spring I'm going to Greece." His voice displayed no enthusiasm at the prospect.

"What a fine idea," Serge said blandly.

It seemed they were all trying to outbore each other.

Chloe watched a girl sit down across from her and light a cigarette. She tilted her head way back and blew the smoke toward the
ceiling. Except for smoking she did not move at all. She was as
delicate and quiet as an orchid. Chloe got up.

"Give me the coat-check thing," she said to Serge, putting out
her hand. When she was embarrassed or forced to lie she had the
sensation of standing behind herself. As though there were two of
her, the one in front a puppet being manipulated by the one in
back. Right then she could feel the one in back forcing the one in
front to move her lips.

"Give me the coat-check thing."

Serge looked up, perplexed for a moment, as though he could
not remember who she was.

"Oh," he said, and got up.

He led the way up the stairs. She did not turn and say good-bye
or nice to have met you to his friends at the table. She could hear
them behind her talking as though nothing had happened, as
though she'd never been there.

Serge gave the coat-check girl the ticket and she handed him
Chloe's old linty pea coat. Chloe snatched it from the girl and
holding it to her hip, headed down the hallway to the door. Serge
followed her.

"Are you not feeling well?" he said.

"I'm feeling fine," she said. "I just think you're a bunch of assholes and I don't need this shit. It's bad for my head."

"We've known each other a very long time. Family connections.
It's hard for outsiders to break in."

"What the FUCK ever made you think I wanted to *break in?*"
She tried to be calm as she stared him down. Her eyes were
burning and she was afraid she would cry. At that moment she
would rather have jumped in front of a car than let him see her
cry.

"Let me take you home," he said mildly.

"No fucking way." She turned her back on him and pushed the
door. Good Goddamn thing you brought money this time, she told
herself. Good Goddamn thing you live in this neighborhood and

you know your way home. She wanted to walk. She felt she could walk a circle around Paris and then some.

She left him standing in the doorway. The woman-guard stared at her from behind her window. She walked out slamming the door.

She remembered that as a little kid she used to watch her parents get dressed up to go out dancing. They went to Castel's a good deal. They knew Monsieur Castel personally and were treated the way famous people are treated.

She had been sitting next to Serge when Jean Castel walked by their table. Serge pointed him out the same way he pointed out the sons and daughters of the Very Rich, leaning over and whispering in her ear. She had wanted to go up to Castel and say, "I am John Raymond's daughter, and my mother says hello." But she had been afraid. He may not remember them, she thought. He may think I'm catering to these assholes, trying to live up to their standards.

She walked down the street with her eyes to the cobblestones, swearing at herself for being a chickenshit. She felt estranged and conspicuous and avoided the eyes of the people she passed. She imagined her mother and father weaving their way down this narrow street, drunk, happy, in love. And she imagined the street two hundred years ago, the coaches, the hand-lit streetlights; other people drunk, happy, in love.

She wondered why some were born able to stand loneliness, and some just weren't. She could not remember a time when she had wanted to be alone.

When they had lived in Paris, her parents had been famous for their wonderful parties. During the parties Chloe could never sleep. She'd drag her blanket quietly past her nurse's room, up the short flight of stairs to the living room, and curl up inconspicuously on a corner of the couch and watch the grown-ups carouse. Sometimes they sent her back to bed, but usually they let her be. Because the music and the laughter put her quickly to sleep. Being at the party, she felt included in the fun.

She felt left out being back in Paris without her father. She felt entirely excluded from the life they'd had. She hated to admit that she'd hoped to gain some of it back through Serge. She refused to be his whore under any guise or principle. Fuck him, she thought.

Really. But then Serge appeared beside her, falling in pace, not out of breath, and wearing his coat.

"I didn't want you to leave like that," he said.

She was flattered he had come after her. She kept walking fast, staring straight ahead as if she knew exactly where she was going though she was not even looking at the streets.

"You don't know who I am," she said. "You have no right to treat me like that. Even if I'm *no* one."

"But you're *not* no one. You're strong and you're determined. You're interested in things. You care about the world."

"I don't give a shit about the world. I don't give a shit about anything except my father and his work."

Am I lying? she thought.

"But he's dead." She could never get used to those words. "Did you ever bother to ask me about him? No. You don't give a damn. But why should you? Let me just tell you something. He did more with his plays, bleeding for this fucking world than you or your Goddamn friends and me and anybody else will do in our whole lives."

And she started to cry. But now it was not out of humiliation, it was for her father and for the past. Which was always the best reason she could find to cry.

She kept walking fast, crying and talking about him. Then suddenly it stopped, as though a bucket of ice water had been thrown in her face. She realized she had no desire to tell Serge anything about herself. There was no point to it.

"I think it's wonderful that you can *feel* that way," he said softly. Then he started and she didn't know what to do. She could have walked away, she supposed. But she did not think it was right, and it seemed they were finally getting somewhere.

He told her that nothing interested him. That he was a complete failure. His parents were terrified that he was going to kill himself. He'd been hooked on heroin once already, and the temptation to go back to it was overwhelming at times.

He had tried going to college in the States (an expensive private college that Chloe knew had a reputation for accepting students on the basis of their bank accounts rather than their transcripts) but had quit in the middle of his first year because a townie who didn't like his face smashed his jaw in one of the local bars. Serge didn't remember why the guy did it, because he'd been drunk out of his mind.

He had never lived with his parents and he blamed his screwed-up head on them. He'd had a slew of nannies he couldn't remember, and one Baba who was the only person in the world he cared about. Baba was his maternal grandmother, a Serb princess who never learned to speak English but spoke French perfectly, and believed in the "old ways."

Baba was dead. He showed Chloe a picture of her he carried in his wallet.

"I'm sorry for you that she died," Chloe said.

They ended up in a dark bar somewhere in the Latin Quarter, drinking Cognacs that Serge paid for.

He stared at her solemnly from across the table. There was a candle between them that made him squint uncomfortably. He placed his palm over the glass and waited for it to burn out. He looked very sad and Chloe felt sorry for him, though she did not see why she should.

"You're interested in pottery, ceramics, aren't you? Why don't you start collecting? You could open a gallery."

He frowned at her.

* * *

They drank an enormous amount of Cognac. Before she knew it she was back at his studio on Avenue de Wagram, leaning over the balcony railing trying to focus on the Arc de Triomphe.

Serge was reciting poetry, sitting on the balcony with his head against the railing. The lines he was reciting made him cry and once in a while he blew his nose in a white handkerchief that had his initials on it.

He pulled out an old photo album and showed her pictures of Baba as a little girl on the country estate. Of Serge as a little boy with Baba in Rome. In St. Tropez. In Kitzbühel.

Chloe woke up fully dressed, feet hanging over the edge of the bed. She sat up and looked around at his apartment. It was severely furnished, with a long glass table and two heavy, hand-carved wooden chairs, the double bed, a couch, and a glass coffee table.

As soon as she moved Serge woke up. He barely spoke to her,

and she had the terrible morning-after-a-one-night-stand feeling, even though nothing had happened between them.

He walked about putting things away, getting ready to take a shower. She watched him from the bed. He's probably regretting last night, she thought.

"Are you regretting having been open with me last night?"

"Having been open with you?" he said, looking around for something. "It's much too early for me to be thinking yet, if you don't mind."

She sat silently while he stripped naked in front of the open closet and wrapped a towel that was hanging there around his waist as though she weren't there.

"I'm going to take a shower," he said. "Do you want to take a shower with me?"

She shook her head.

"If you wait," he said, "we'll go down to the café for breakfast."

"Fine," she said.

When he came back from his shower he stood by the bed wrapped in the towel, looking down at her and drying his hair with his hand. When he stopped ruffling his hair it stuck out around his head untame.

"Why are you so squeamish about sex?" he asked her, smiling.

"Squeamish!" That was the first time anyone had called *her* squeamish. She tried to remember if he'd made a pass at her, but after the scene on the balcony her mind was blank.

"I'm not squeamish at all," she shrugged. "I already told you, I'm sick up to here of casual sex." She touched her hand horizontally to her forehead. " 'The fucking you get isn't worth the fucking you get,' you know what I mean?"

He went back to the closet and searched through it; again as though she'd said nothing, weren't there.

He did not seem to care one way or the other so she did not elaborate. If she talked to him in a confiding tone she would certainly be leaving herself open to ridicule.

The truth was her period had stopped, and with it, her sex drive. Or maybe it was the other way around. She was eating more and gaining a little weight. Sometimes she was terrified by the thoughts she put in her own head: Maybe I'm pregnant! But that

would be impossible, unless it's tubal. Because she'd had her period once since she'd been in Paris. Maybe I have a tumor!

She thought of going to see the doctor her family had used when
they'd lived in Paris. He'd probably tell her the usual stuff, change
of climate, traveling, nerves all chase menstruation away. She was
afraid he'd try to send her to a shrink.

"I'd forgotten how puritan American girls are," Serge said from
the closet.

"I'm no sweet virgin, believe me," she said defensively. "I've
slept with more guys than you'd care to know about and there are
very few I'm sorry about." You're lying to him, she thought.

"Well well well," he said, and smiled.

If the disappearance of her sex drive had been limited to Serge,
she wouldn't have been too concerned. The problem was in general she could not think about sex anymore. She could not imagine
being touched by anyone. Not even Joe or Andy. The thought
exhausted her.

She watched Serge dress. He chose a starched white shirt and
grey tailored slacks, a red and blue tie and a tweed jacket. She got
up without bothering to inspect herself in his mirror. She felt like a
month-old Camembert, but at this point didn't care.

They went down to the café.

X

Chloe took her boots off outside the front door of Dominique's apartment. She had no watch but from the quiet in the streets she knew the children were still in Saturday morning classes, that it was before noon. Dominique stayed in bed until noon on weekends, reading and padding back and forth down the long hallway to the kitchen for coffee.

Chloe was exhausted and dizzy-drunk still and wanted to avoid having to explain to Dominique. She snuck into the living room which she had to cross to get to her bedroom, tiptoeing with her boots tucked under her arm, and was caught like a rabbit by Dominique's hard, cold pistol stare. Dominique was sitting on the couch with a drink set in front of her on the coffee table. Chloe stared at the drink which she presumed was scotch while Dominique stared at her unblinkingly, eyes ragged and bloodshot, mouth shut, face taut, as though if she relaxed, the whole thing would fall apart. For the first time since Chloe could remember, Dominique looked her age.

"Hi, Dom," Chloe said. She backed herself into the dining table.

"You know you are not a responsible guest. Toward me as your host you are not responsible." Dominique leaned forward and took a sip of the drink.

"The fucking *frigidair* is disgusting. You 'ave a milk in there already it must be a month old. And you leave the Roquefort and I don't know what other cheese in there that smell like dirty feet, you know, and they shouldn't be in the *frigidair* in the first place."

Chloe stood pinned against the table with nothing to say. Dominique was right.

"I'm sorry," she said lamely, the child's automatic response.

"You never bring anything 'ome. You don't *con*tribute. No flowers, no oranges to make fresh juice which I love. Maybe I shouldn't expect it of you but maybe you should realize that you are not at 'ome and should be more *con*siderate. It disappoints me terribly that you are so not *con*siderate of me."

Dominique closed her eyes and pressed her eyelids with the tips of her fingers. Chloe stared at her, feeling like a complete dope. Her excuse, as lame as it sounded, was that she had avoided Dominique and the apartment because she felt she was an imposition. She had tried to make herself as inobtrusive as possible.

"That boy who calls and leaves ridiculous messages on my answering machine, you are going out with him?"

"No," Chloe said. "When I don't come home it's because it's very late and I'm afraid of waking you up. Most of the time I stay with my friend from Cromwell, Annie."

"Ah, je m'en fous, tu sais," she threw up her hands. "It's not my business who you sleep with. I'm not your mother."

Chloe didn't like the way Dominique said "your mother." She couldn't pinpoint why, but it sounded like an insult. The comment didn't make sense in the first place because Dominique was very much aware that Chloe's mother had never made any noise about who Chloe slept with.

"That boy," Dominique said, nodding toward the front door, "on the machine he sounds like a pompous faggot."

Chloe laughed. "He's okay, I guess."

"You want a drink?" Dominique asked. Chloe shook her head. "I'm still drunk from last night. He took me to Castel's."

"To Castel's? What a shithole that place has become. I went a while ago for the first time in years; I think, even since your parents were here. Now it's an international jet-set crowd, mostly kids. Horrible." She shook the thought away and leaned back into the sofa with eyes closed.

"I don't know what 'appened to the old days," she said. "Paris used to be so much *fun*. There's no money around, I suppose. *Merde*. I feel so old today. I didn't go to sleep yet. I didn't even try to go to bed. Maybe that's why I feel so old, no?" she smiled wanly.

Chloe came forward and sat across from her on a low stool.

"What's wrong, Dom?" She was usually a decisive person. Dominique was one of the few who made her feel like she was walking in a labyrinth of mirrors. She had no idea if she was saying the right thing, if she was making the right move in the right direction.

"My father's in the hospital since yesterday morning. He had a *hémorragie* in the brain." Dom looked at her watch. "And I 'ave to go back there soon. I keep saying to myself if it was me dying in the 'ospital, he wouldn't come. Now I'm not sure anymore. Dying does strange things to people." She laughed bitterly at her joke.

"My father wants to die without guilt. So now he wants me to love him and make peace. He passes *me* the guilt. He doesn't think I 'ave enough with my *own?*"

"I never met your father," Chloe said, thinking this strange, since she'd known Dominique her whole life.

"You didn't miss anything," Dominique said.

"Maybe he won't die," Chloe said. She felt like crying all of a sudden. She was reminded of how the hopelessness of hoping was so much more heartbreaking in the end than the death itself.

"I suppose maybe you're right. But then he'll be like a cabbage with a brain. No. Better if he dies and leave us all alone."

They stared across the coffee table at each other.

"Tell me what you want me to get for the apartment and I'll do it today," Chloe said. "I apologize for being so rude. I was trying to stay out of your way."

Chloe saw Dominique's flowers in the vase on the coffee table. They were scrawny. They looked like Dominique, for show, always beautiful, but now under pressure, you could tell they'd seen better days. It made her heart ache.

"Oh shit, I don't care. You should be old enough by now to 'ave an idea," Dominique said impatiently. "Your mother didn't teach you anything, did she?"

Chloe couldn't decide whether she deserved this or not. But she didn't want to fight.

First she'd get flowers. Beautiful long-stemmed colorful fragrant flowers.

"During the Occupation," Dominique said, "at first they made us wear the yellow star. My father said, 'You 'ave to wear it,' and I pulled it off. He put it back, I pulled it off. Because at school the kids laughed and yelled terrible names. I had fights, you can't imagine the fights. I was horrified he made me wear it. I was horrified it was *his* fault I had to wear it in the first place. Both my parents spoke French with such a Yiddish accent I had to go to the store with the food stamps.

"When they started deportation my father wanted to escape from France. Can you imagine? He thought we'd be safer there. With his brother they flipped a coin because there were too many of us to all get out. The whole family on the brother's side went to the Spanish border. Everyone died in Auschwitz. It's not a new story. Every Jew I know in Europe lost somebody in the camps. My father thought Poles won't turn in Poles. French will turn in Polish Jews but not French Jews. It's a lie. Everybody turned everybody in. For gold coins. For bread. For favors. Life wasn't worth a good shit then.

"We were lucky. We went south, over the line. And then to Grenoble. After the War there's blood on everybody's hands. *Your* father got that right, about the Occupation. I never forget what a scandal his play was."

There were tears streaming down her face but her expression did not change; tired, wasted, not sad.

"I loved your father," she said. "He changed my life. You know, that character Riva that I played? That was me! He created her as though he had known me before he wrote the play. But it's impossible, isn't it?"

Outside the bells of Saint Sulpice Church were ringing. Then in the street the children came out of school, screaming and laughing, making the noise of a million bees.

They sat quiet for a moment. Dom wiped her face with the sleeve of her robe.

"You're still acting?" she asked.

"No. Not since he died."

"I saw you a few times, with him, out in Long Island. You're lazy, but you have a serious untrained talent. Like me when I was your age. Except you have natural beauty and I did not. You have to work at it. You know that? You want to act?"

Chloe had her excuse, which was her recurring nightmare. But Dom was not one to go for self-indulgent psychoanalysis. Chloe stared at her and tried to find something to say that would not make Dom laugh.

"I don't know," she said. Her heart began to pound at the thought of what she'd given up.

"When he died, everything seemed to stop. I'm too scared now."

"Before it was for games. Now without him it's different. They can hurt you. I know it's very hard. Even for me, it's hard." Dominique stood up and went toward the window, arching her back. "I have to go back to the fucking 'ospital."

She pressed her nose against the glass.

"Yes. I really loved your father," she said dreamily.

Chloe was overcome by a nauseous feeling, like seasickness. It came a split second before the thought that caused it: There had been something between them. All along. Could it be? There was no one she could ask. No one would tell her even if they knew. She felt the blood had drained from her completely.

After Dominique left she went out to the bank and cashed a hundred-dollar traveler's check. She spent over half of it on things for the apartment. Flowers, Chivas Regal, fresh oranges, fruit for the fruit bowl, coffee beans . . .

She still did not feel well when she got home. She arranged the flowers, threw out the old ones, and went to bed.

* * *

She woke up choking back a scream. She sat up in the almost dark room blinking and sweating, and tried to remember where she was. Behind her the curtains swished and flapped and the color that seeped in was between night and day and it could have been dusk or dawn. She tried to reconstruct the dream to prove it had been a dream and meant nothing. The feeling it had left behind would not go away.

In the dream she had been at a summer resort, sitting at a round stone table that had a closed parasol sticking in the hole at the center of it. The table was one of many on the veranda, but there were no other people. Tall white apartment buildings encircled the veranda, and a lawn sparkled emerald and sloped down to a smooth lake.

She was sipping a cold drink that was too sweet, waiting for Joe to come back from a basketball game. It seemed he'd been gone a long time and she was getting impatient. She did not feel like a whole person without him.

"Chloe," she heard a soft but gruff voice behind her. When she turned the sun stung her eyes. She put her hand up to her forehead but it did not help much.

It was her father.

"Chloe," he said. "Honey, there's somebody I'd like you to meet."

She wiped her burning eyes and squinting saw a young woman who couldn't have been more than three years older than she. The woman looked like Vero, though this did not occur to her at the time.

"This is Mara," her father said.

"We're on our honeymoon," Mara said, smiling.

Chloe tried to stand up to face them but could not get out of the chair. She spoke to her father, not to Mara.

"You could have picked another place to go," she said, trying not to sound angry because she did not want to hurt his feelings.

They sat down across the table.

"Yes," her father said, "we just got married a few days ago and I really wanted Mara to meet you." His voice was gentle, almost ingratiating which was not like him, as though what Chloe thought of all this really meant a lot to him. He and Mara were holding hands on the table. Chloe felt sick looking at their hands. She had lost him. But if only Mara would go away, she'd convince him, get him back.

"Daddy," she said, "Mom's here. Maybe you should go see her alone. You can't tell her about this, she'll die. You can just go see her alone and then leave."

"Why, honey?" he said evenly. "I'm a different person now. Being away so long has changed me. She'll understand that."

Chloe started to cry. "No she won't understand. She hasn't changed at all. She's still waiting for you. All she does is wait for you to come back."

"It was such a beautiful wedding," Mara said, still smiling.

"Daddy, please, you have to go away before she finds out!" Chloe was crying so hard she could barely talk. "She'll d-d-die, Daddy."

Then she was trying to get away from Joe. He was holding her by the arm and she was jerking trying to run toward the closest white building to stop her father and Mara from finding her mother. Her arm hurt.

"Cut it out!" Joe was shouting. "It's always best to get the truth out. Only the *truth* counts. And it's none of your business. There's no law says people have to love each other forever!"

She was still trying to jerk away, hearing him, when she saw her mother topple in slow motion from one of the highest windows. She fell in silence, bouncing like a black rag doll against the white wall.

*   *   *

"Saturday, March 1," she wrote. Dominique was not back from the hospital and there was not a human sound in the apartment. The curtains continued to swell and flap, the alarm clock ticked on, the radiator groaned once in a while. She felt removed from the world and afraid of what she was going to write. Her instinct was to call up and get ahold of anybody she could and go out, leave. She started to write, thinking of Edgar Allan Poe as beads of sweat formed at her hairline.

My Dearest Eric,

Today I came home to Dominique's and found her terribly upset. Her father is in the hospital and will probably die. You know how crazy she can be, and the whole thing has upset me pretty badly.

I took a nap after she left this afternoon and I had a nightmare that was so awful I can still feel it now. It was about Mom. It made me think about how fragile she is and how stupid I am. You're probably the strongest one of us all and I think we both need you very much. I think I have to write to Mom but I don't know how to start.

I wrote you a letter but didn't mail it, when I first got here. It was a weird letter and I know how you don't like to be reminded of bad things. But being here has made me think about you and Mom and how fucked up it is that none of us can talk to each other. I worry so much that something awful could happen to one of us, with me so far away, and that we'll never see each other again. There's so little time in life when you think about it. We've wasted so much time.

I don't have anybody but you and Mom. I'm proud to have you as my brother even though I've never told you this. We're old enough now to be friends. And right now I need you and miss you very much. I hope you'll write to me and tell me how you are, tell me what you're doing. Do you have a girlfriend up at school? Tell me what you're thinking about. What I'm thinking about right now is that we should stick together no matter what, because that's what Daddy would have wanted us to do.

Love,
Chloe

XI

In Linguistics and Poetry class, there were days when the old professor was so drunk he could barely stand up. When he could do nothing else he stood at the front of the class, tottering and holding on to a desk, and incanted verses from the great French poets of the late nineteenth and early twentieth centuries. His passion made the American students cringe with embarrassment.

One afternoon he got angry during one of his recitations when he heard giggles from the back of the class. Chloe's heart sank for him. She soon realized he was not the fool.

Arching his back slightly, he gazed down at his students and said, "It seems to me we are wasting each other's time. If you want to dissect, I suggest you study biology. This is not a biology lab. There's nothing to dissect here. We're here to *enjoy* and *feel* these poems." And with a burst of emotion, he began to recite: *"La musique souvent me prend comme une mer!"*

He pitched forward and righted himself with the help of the desk, keeping his thumb and index finger pressed there for support. Chloe watched his face while, like the most accomplished actor, it took on the moods of the verses he put forth to the class. When he finished the poem and caught his breath, his eyes were all fogged up. "You see, children, as Baudelaire that wonderful man tells us in this gem of a poem, music carries one off like the sea. The music of words—changeable and temperamental. We should all be small boats at the mercy of this temperamental sea!"

Chloe walked out of class with her head buzzing like a crowded beehive. Francis Morgan had been telling her to take a poetry class for years. She hated poetry classes because she was too intimidated by the professors and the poems to begin enjoying them. Francis told her she had an acute case of poetry anxiety. The old drunken professor was right. She was always dissecting, looking for those Hidden Meanings, instead of listening to the music of the words. This one class had validated an otherwise worthless scholastic semester. She was in a profoundly good mood.

Outside in the main hall she found Geoffrey leaning against the wall with one leg bent and a helmet balanced on that knee.

"Well hello hello," he said. "I was about to leave a note for you girls when I heard a class being let out and decided to wait and see if either of you were in it."

"Do you know that poem "La Musique" by Baudelaire?"

" 'La musique souvent me prend comme une mer'—that one?"

"Yes! That one," she laughed in surprise.

"There are many more of his that are better than that one," he said.

"Impossible."

"Truly. I'll lend you *Les Fleurs du mal.* You'll see."

"Do you have another helmet?"

"Why yes I do."

As they headed out the door he told her that Cédric would be delighted to have a dinner, but it would have to wait a week. This week he was completely swamped with exams. "Will you be bringing Serge?" Geoffrey asked tentatively.

"No," she said. "He feels uncomfortable around the people I feel the most comfortable with. It makes me uncomfortable."

Geoffrey nodded pensively.

At the tall and slender motorcycle he turned his backpack around so that it hung against his stomach.

"I'm on my way to Beaubourg to pick up my roller skates. I lost a wheel jumping a flight of steps in Montmartre last week. Boy, did I take a spill." He shook his hand vigorously with a limp wrist. "My friend Thierry owns a moto and bike shop near Beaubourg. You know the Centre Pompidou?"

"I haven't been there yet. They started building it after we left France."

"Fascinating place. Absolutely fascinating. It's so un-French. But then, it's *so* French. Parisians threw a shit fit when Eiffel began constructing his monstrosity. It's a tradition."

She stood by the motorcycle while he straddled it and kicked violently at the starter. She stuck her head in the helmet he'd handed her; the bike coughed and spat and then roared. He yelled over his shoulder for her to get on as he lowered the rear footpegs. She glanced back at the Program. Three classmates stood staring at the noisy bike. She was very embarrassed and also very pleased. She had always adored motorcycles.

"This is Lucy," Geoffrey yelled, leaning forward over the handlebars. "I've been putting her together for a long time. She keeps my mind off my other woman. Lucy's short for Lucifer. She's a Suzuki S.P. 370."

"I want to learn how to ride," Chloe yelled at his helmet.

"If you like, but not Lucy. We'll borrow a moto from Thierry. Lucy's a little large to start on." When he gunned the throttle Lucy reared like a wild horse.

"Top light," he yelled, standing and leaning forward like a jockey. "My girl has a big ass."

From the back of the motorcycle Paris seemed like a different city. They were one with it, with the dirt and fumes and cars. Inside a car you were shielded from all this, separate.

Geoffrey was a careful, respectful biker. She imagined that without a passenger he would be much more reckless. He judged his space between cars generously, because her knees stuck out several inches farther than his.

After skirting the Luxembourg Garden he flew down Boulevard Saint Michel, and traversed the Seine to the Right Bank through the center of the Ile de la Cité. As they idled at a red light, Chloe took a long look at the Palais de Justice. In school, when she was little, they told the children that's where they would be sent if they were bad. It seemed terribly solemn and serious behind its black and gold gates.

She yelled, "I used to skate a lot. I learned right over there," she pointed to the right. "On that bridge they built when they tore down the old footbridge the Nazis built. You know the one that's closed to traffic, between the two islands?"

"You don't say!"

"I used to be able to jump the first flight of steps at the Trocadéro. I was a real show-off. It impressed the tourists. Sometimes they took pictures."

"Imagine that. I was there too!"

Geoffrey parked Lucy on the sidewalk outside his friend's shop. There were tires and bicycles and chains and other motorcycle parts hanging in the window.

"Thierry builds custom-made skates. Not these disco contraptions you see around. Not made for parquet floors, if you know what I mean."

In the shop Geoffrey changed completely. He seemed in control, not at all shy or nervous. Thierry was short and dark and greasy-looking. He was wearing a black T-shirt with cutoff sleeves and black jeans that could have been painted on him. He and Geoffrey talked shop for a while in a rapid, slurry slang she was not used to and could barely understand. Thierry didn't acknowledge that she was there.

While they talked on in a most casual way, Thierry bent down behind his counter and came up with two pairs of skates that looked like mini racing cars. He placed them in front of Geoffrey who began to inspect the wheels on the larger pair.

"Try those on," Geoffrey said to her, sliding the other pair toward her down the counter.

"Geoffrey," she nudged him, "I can't skate in those!" The white boots looked like basketball sneakers, not like ice-skate boots. They were tall, made of soft leather, and had blue soles and a blue curving stripe up the sides. The wheels were also blue, and two inches wide. The sole plate, because of the complex shock system, was at least three inches off the ground.

"Sshh," Geoffrey said. "You're getting a fifty percent discount. These cost eight hundred francs new, and look, they've never been used. You're getting them for four hundred."

"Four hundred! You're crazy, that's over a hundred dollars."

"Ben alors, quoi? Elle les essaye ou pas?" Thierry said in his *voyou* French. Gripping the counter with one hand, she slid into them. The boots were tight but with skates that was a good thing. She thought of the hundred dollars she already knew she was going to spend though she could not afford to. After all, a hundred dollars was only a gram of cocaine, gone in a night. The skates slid off by themselves with her feet in them.

"Geoffrey, I haven't skated in years . . ." she rolled off toward a
row of tires.

"You can sell them tomorrow for six hundred francs to another
friend of mine," he said quickly, catching her arm and pulling her
back to the counter.

"I don't have any money with me."

While Geoffrey wrote out a check and discussed his bike with
Thierry, she practiced just rolling back and forth without holding
on. Geoffrey put her sneakers in his backpack with his own.

"Later on we'll stop by your place and you can pick up a traveler's check or whatever you have, and get cash somehow before
tomorrow because otherwise my check will bounce. I have another friend who'll buy the skates tomorrow for six hundred, I
guarantee. That's if you decide you don't want them."

They left Lucy in front of the shop. The street had recently been
repaved with large, flat slabs. It was closed to cars. She held on to
the hem of Geoffrey's army jacket and concentrated on not tripping over herself. Slowly she began to get the new sense of balance, pushing out tentatively with one foot, then the other. The
ground seemed very far away, and she felt old.

She could not skate at all on the cobblestones around the Centre
Pompidou. She felt like a cripple. In front of the Centre on the
open square there were mimes and jugglers and musicians and
beggars and four gorgeous women modeling fur coats. There were
so many people milling about it seemed like a Sunday, though it
was the middle of the week.

At first the Centre's gaudy colors were like a slap in the face.
Miami Beach pinks, reds, blues. Its entrails were hanging out,
visible to the public, wiring, piping, escalators, as though the work-
ers had gone on strike in the middle of the job.

"It's really horrible," she said. But she couldn't stop staring at it.
Surrounding the Centre the little somber Parisian buildings
cringed in horror.

"I love it it's so horrible," Geoffrey said. "I do love it."

"It doesn't fit in!" Chloe insisted.

"It fits in perfectly," he said.

Geoffrey wanted to give her a tour of the inside. She didn't want

to stop skating for fear she would never put the skates on again.
"We can come back another time," she said.

They skated down Boulevard de Sébastopol toward the Place du
Châtelet. On Sébastopol's wide sidewalk she could manage by
herself, though she almost ran into a blindman at one cross street.
Cross streets were the worst because of the cobblestones. She
could not watch the ground and watch where she was going at the
same time. If the light was red for pedestrians she resorted to
banging into whatever was stationary, parked cars, signposts, or
Geoffrey, because she couldn't yet manage the slide into a brake
stop.

They came to a No Parking signpost that had a heavy black
motorcycle chained to it. Geoffrey held the pole at arm's length
and leaning in, made slow, descending circles around the pole and
the bike.

"My wife lives here," he said. "This is my old home."

At Châtelet she panicked because there were so many cars.
Geoffrey had to hold her hand as they crossed at the red light.
They skated down the Rue de Rivoli, beneath the arcade where
shoppers stopped to stare at them. Anything out of the ordinary
made people stare. It reminded Chloe of being on stage. Geoffrey
skated better than any person she'd ever seen. He skated better
than he walked.

After Concorde they took hilly side streets that were not
crowded with pedestrians. They had reached the posh residential
quartiers. The whole while, until they reached the Trocadéro,
Geoffrey recited heartbreaking verses from *Les Fleurs du mal*. He
also recited a poem by Apollinaire from beginning to end. They
were all about loves lost and hope never to be found again.

> "Sous le pont Mirabeau coule la Seine
> Et nos amours
> Faut-il qu'il m'en souvienne
> La joie venait toujours après la peine"

In fifth grade Chloe had memorized "Le Pont Mirabeau" in her
French class. Now she could remember nothing of it but a childish
vision of two lovers standing facing each other on a lower quai,
watching the murky river flow beneath the low arches of a bridge.
It was a terrible shame, she realized now, that her brother and she

had tried to forget about France and everything they knew, just so they might fit in better with the kids in their public American high schools. Now they were forever separated from France. It was too late.

At the Trocadéro she leaned against the low wall at the end of the large open pavilion in the center of the Palais de Chaillot. The pavilion was like a balcony which faced the river, and the Eiffel Tower directly across. On each side of the low wall, steps led down to the sloping gardens and fountain. These were the steps she'd jumped as a child. Looking at them now, she was quite proud of herself. She did not remember being such a fearless little girl. But she recalled coming home with sprained ankles and wrists that her father would test with gentle movements, and wrap in Ace bandages once he was satisfied that nothing was broken. He liked playing medic, and she liked playing wounded soldier.

She watched the smaller kids skate and felt nostalgic for the days when the ground did not seem such a long way to fall. Old smells came back to her, the grime of old motor oil, tar mixed in with the dust that covered the streets and became ingrained in you when you became a moving vehicle yourself. They were pleasant, oddly familiar smells. Getting street dirty was great fun.

Geoffrey shot past like a cannonball and flew off the edge of the steps. She watched him hit the landing with one skate in the air, and speed around the corner without missing a beat.

Across the river people milled around under the four legs of the Eiffel Tower like ants beneath an elephant. Geoffrey climbed the steps on his toe stops and joined her at the wall.

"This used to be my favorite thing in the world," she said.

"It does give you a sense of freedom, however temporary."

She felt she'd known him a long, long time. Their conversation was pointed, lacking small talk. It made her feel naked. She thought it was dangerous for two people so inclined to go straight to the point to spend too much time together. Geoffrey was exposing himself to her from the inside out. Males were not like this; she felt very strange.

"For me," he said, "a good day is when I can cross a bridge without contemplating throwing myself in, skates and all." He laughed. "I practice on the steps."

"What do your parents think of her kicking you out?"

"Oh, my parents," he shrugged in that je m'en fous way. "They don't have time to worry about it."

He told her his mother was the dean of the American College, which was why he'd been there that Friday; and his father had been a very good brain surgeon in Detroit who'd just up and quit one day. Now he was a painter. "His vision is obscure," Geoffrey said. Without looking at her, nonchalantly, he asked her what she found in Serge. She became angry.

"You should be careful of him. Besides the fact that I'm furiously jealous and possessive of all my friends, I think he's dangerous because he's involved with serious drugs and it would be awful if you got yourself in trouble."

"He's through with the drugs. He already told me about it," she said shortly. Geoffrey didn't seem put off by her tone. Maybe he's used to being yelled at, she thought. She knew instinctively that his lack of reaction would only incite more anger on her part. It had been that way with her brother. There were some people who never outgrew the need to be reprimanded. She was thankful that Eric refused to take shit from her anymore.

Chloe said, "It's terrible to realize after such a long time that you've made a terrible mistake." She was thinking of Joe, and of Geoffrey and his wife.

"Ché is not a mistake," Geoffrey said.

"Ché!?"

"My son."

"Your son. You're nuts."

"Why?"

"You knocked her up and so you married her."

"No. We wanted to have a child."

"I don't believe you. God what a name."

"My father only listens to Country Western music. He has an album that has a song on it called 'A Boy Named Sue.' Maybe it will have that kind of effect on my son."

She rolled the skates back and forth into the wall.

Geoffrey was a barrel of incongruities. He had such grace and strength when he skated, but on his own feet he could barely walk without tripping over himself. He seemed so young but his eyes were so old and tired.

"Friday afternoon I have to pick up my son and take him to my mother's for the weekend. So Estelle can have a break. Will you come to Estelle's with me to pick him up?" He didn't look at her, he stared blindly at the river in the distance, below.

"Why?"

"Because I'm a weak shithead and I can't bear to face her alone."

"It's going to put me in the middle," Chloe said.

"It will put you in the middle only if you want it to."

"Why don't you take Vero?" she asked, thinking this was really a shitty tactical maneuver to find out more about his relationship with Vero. She didn't know why she was so fascinated by the whole thing.

"Because Vero's still very young and she's looking for a replacement daddy. I'm already a daddy and can't handle it, at that."

"I'm no fucking powerhouse," Chloe said. And then after thinking about it for a while, "It's going to put me in the middle if I go with you to your wife's."

"No it's not."

"Yes it is. She'll think I'm the new girlfriend and it'll make trouble for you."

"You remember that black moto that's parked outside her apartment?"

She remembered him skating circles around the bike and the pole.

"That's Franck's Honda. He's my best friend from the fac and from the lycée as well. I've known him since I've been in France. I know it's his moto because I helped him put it on the road. It was a pile of shit when he got it. See, I work in a garage putting together and feeding cars so I can have money to eat so I can have energy to study. It's ridiculous. Why don't I become a clochard and live with a bottle of wine under a bridge?

"And since she threw me out I see Franck's moto parked there every day, in front of my wife's apartment. And it's there at night, too. It's beginning to obsess me. I ask myself, what's going on up there? What does my son think his Tonton Franck is doing with his mommy?"

"If you ask me I'd say they're screwing."

Geoffrey's face turned to hers and froze there in shock.

"I have a bad time accepting that," he said quietly.

She winced at her cruelty. An image slashed through her mind: Joe in his room sitting at the feet of the girl who had the cornered-rat look in her eyes. Chloe wondered why it was that people refuse to accept what's most blatantly obvious. It seemed like a breach of humanity. Joe was not humane. Neither was Geoffrey's wife. How could people be so cruel?

"I'm sorry," she said. She felt like a monster.

"For what?"

"For saying that. Listen, I don't want to get involved in this. I came back here to get myself out of a seriously bad scene. A situation too much like yours to be funny. Except, you see, you had a baby and I had an abortion."

It was getting easier and easier to say. She no longer felt like an axe was about to fall on her head from the sky.

"Let's go," Geoffrey said, slinking away from the wall like a beaten dog.

They skated along the Left Bank quai.

"Will you come with me on Friday to pick up my son?"

She felt a terrible compassion for him. It made her angry. Because he'd been stupid enough to go ahead and do it. He'd believed in his dream. He loved his wife. And Chloe thanked everything and everyone in the world that when she'd walked in and found the girl lying on Joe's bed, her ties with him had stopped there. There was no child.

By the time they got back to Lucy the sky was pitch black and the lampadaires were glowing warm and yellow in the night.

XII

The black motorcycle was not parked in front of the building when they arrived to pick up the son. The apartment was on the sixth—the top floor. As they rode up in the antique elevator, Chloe noticed that Geoffrey was quivering. Her emotions were in a whirl. She pitied him and disliked him intensely for bringing her to witness this scene. She was also scared to death of his wife.

Geoffrey rang the bell and stepped back, tripping on the mat.

"Maybe I'll wait for you out here," Chloe whispered.

"No, no, no," he said.

It was too late to back out now anyway.

A woman around five-two, maybe a couple of inches shorter than Chloe, opened the door a foot and held it there. She said "Ah" as though she'd been waiting for hours, and opened it all the way. Chloe now saw that she was heavyset and blonde. She disappeared into the dark apartment and left them to come in on their own.

It was something between a penthouse and a garret, with large slanted windows giving a view of slate-grey rooftops and narrow side streets. The room was dark because the sky was overcast, and there were plants hanging over all the windows; very green, opulent plants. Beautiful plants made Chloe nervous because they suggested care, tidiness, organization.

"Ché, mon chéri! Viens voir, c'est ton papa qui est là!" Estelle called from down the hall in a high-pitched, enthusiastic voice. Chloe thought it was more for their benefit than for Ché's.

She scanned the room guiltily. There was a wooden staircase

that led up to a loft area. She presumed this was Estelle's bedroom, which had also been Geoffrey's, which Estelle was now sharing with Tonton Franck.

Estelle came down the narrow hall carrying a little blond child on her hip. She had large breasts. Ché looked like a perfect cross of the two of them. He had his mother's blunt features and Geoffrey's deep-set, fragile eyes. Estelle put him down like a parcel and approached Geoffrey. She kissed him formally on both cheeks and put her hand out to Chloe.

"Joff m'a tant parlé de vous," she said.

She used vous though she was only about a year older than Chloe. Estelle's expression was flat, clear, hard. She looked much older than her age. She looked angry.

Chloe wondered how Geoffrey could have told his wife so much about her when they'd only met a week ago.

"Franck will come fetch him on Sunday so you don't have to worry about that," she said in French to Geoffrey. On to the next subject, Chloe thought. Get it all over with. His wife was a good diplomat. She spoke a rapid French. Chloe wondered if this was meant to exclude her.

"You have the most beautiful plants I've ever seen," Chloe said, also in French.

"Thank you," Estelle said. "You know it's not difficult to take care of them when one's home all the time." Chloe found it difficult to smile at her.

"And it's a lovely apartment. You're very lucky."

"Thanks to my father," she said pointedly, looking at her husband.

"Yes. Estelle's papa bought it for us as a wedding gift," he said, not without humor. It did seem funny to Chloe that Estelle would expect Geoffrey, at seventeen, to support the three of them and be able to pay for such an apartment.

"Écoute, Joff. I want more time for myself. It's exhausting, you know. I want you to take him during the week."

"My dear, I have to work during the week."

"Well, take him to your mother's, then."

"My mother has to work during the week, too."

"Did you bring the shoes for him this time? You forgot again.

Ché's outgrowing his shoes so fast—I don't have time to do everything."

Geoffrey was looking out the window at the rooftops.

"Come here," he said in English. Chloe wondered if English was a safety switch for Geoffrey the way it was for her.

"See the light-blue building there? That's Ché's school. I used to take him every morning, on my way to the fac."

They were leaning toward each other, looking.

"It's a miracle you got him there at all," Estelle said behind them. Chloe thought, she understands English perfectly.

"Il a vraiment la tête d'un scientifique. Always the head in the clouds." Now she was smiling.

Estelle was the expert mother and the expert wife. There was nothing you could teach her on either of these topics. And it all seemed to drive her crazy. Maybe that's why he wanted me to come, Chloe thought. Estelle would think she knew everything about Geoffrey's relationship with Chloe, but she would be wrong. Because they never would be lovers. But maybe Geoffrey would tell his wife they were lovers to get her back for Uncle Franck.

Chloe had forgotten about the son. She looked down and around for him. She found him standing in a corner holding a knitted cap.

"Hello, Ché." She wriggled her fingers. He turned and faced the wall. She felt rejected.

"He's very shy with strangers," Estelle said. She went to him and scooped him brusquely into her arms.

"Pourquoi Ché veut pas dire bonjour, hein, mon grand?" she nuzzled him. Chloe took Estelle's high-pitched baby talk as a personal affront, as though Estelle knew her inside out: See, look how it would have been. The righteousness of motherhood, the clean, safe life. Chloe was envious in spite of herself.

"You're ready to go, Geoffrey?" she said. He was off floundering in his memories, overwhelmed. Her instinct was to fight over him, which was absurd. She wanted nothing to do with this. But Geoffrey needed someone to fight for him because he couldn't do it himself. Sometimes Chloe didn't like herself or her instincts at all.

"Bon. Euh . . . Alors, on y va," Geoffrey said.

"Ché, go get your coat," Estelle said. "You let him dress himself, oké? Tell your mother he can dress himself. Every time he comes back from her he's lazy. He's old enough to do it. Tell your mother

Franck will come fetch him on Sunday. And don't forget, no moto with Ché."

"Be serious, Estelle. You know I'd never take him on the moto."

"Where are you sleeping anyhow, these days?" she asked, looking at Chloe. Chloe wanted to shout, DON'T TELL HER, it's none of her Goddamn business!

"At Cédric's."

"Ah, still at Cédric's. Well. Thank your mother for me. Give maman a big bisou." Kiss kiss all over Ché's little white face. She passed him to Geoffrey. He was all bundled up in his coat and knitted cap.

On the crowded bus they were forced to stand. Chloe looked at the child's blank face which was even with hers as he sat on Geoffrey's arm. Geoffrey was staring out the window away from his son, as though he were trying to ignore the fact that the child was there at all.

"Do you like to stay at your grandmother's, Ché?" she asked. Geoffrey had not said a word to him. Chloe thought it was important to talk to small children so they would not feel left out. And children usually liked her because she talked to them seriously, as adults.

She gently touched Ché's knee. He hid his face in the folds of Geoffrey's jacket. Chloe took this as passive aggression against her.

"I think it's better if you don't talk to him," Geoffrey said. "He's very confused right now and I don't want him to get attached to other females."

Chloe felt insulted by the entire family.

Geoffrey's parents' apartment was a large loft with a high ceiling. There was a hallway that led to two bedrooms with bunk beds, but the living area was the loft space, which was also the master bedroom, and where his father painted. There was dust everywhere.

His father was a perfect caricature of the painter; dusty, paint-smeared frock, arched back (from looking up at canvases), eccentric goatee, and French beret. "Your mother went to the store," he said, and continued to dab at his palette and apply paint to a seven-foot canvas. There were seven- and eight-foot canvases stacked all along the wall. They seemed to depict aspects of the human anat-

omy, spines, kidneys, brains; all infested with amoebic creatures.
Chloe thought, he was surgeon too long.

She heard a key turn in the door. She looked at Geoffrey's
mother in complete surprise as she stood in front of her, loaded
down with grocery sacks. She was Mrs. Creeger, Chloe's sixth-
grade English teacher at École Active Bilingue. Mrs. Creeger had
been the one who'd explained "drink-drank-drunk" and "there-
they're-their" and "accept-except" to her. She was the best English teacher Chloe had ever had. Chloe had actually taken home
report cards that weren't marked C— or D for Conduct ("this
child is belligerent and noisy in class"). And Mrs. Creeger had
invited Chloe's father to come speak at the school. Her father had
been curious to meet this English teacher who'd tamed his wild
kid. He'd spoken to the assembled sixth-through-eighth-grade English students about playwrighting, from script to performance.
He'd even cried a bit, Chloe remembered. The ladies of the English department hovered around him like sea birds around a big
fish. They'd taken him to lunch at the cafeteria. He'd eaten the
salty food, though at that time, because of his failing heart, he was
already restricted to a salt-free diet. He knew how to be polite.
That day was one of Chloe's best memories of École Active Bilingue.

They stood six feet from each other, staring.

"Mrs. Creeger!"

"My, my," she said, shaking her head slowly with a gentle smile
parting her lips. She had a lovely delicate face with deep wrinkles
around her eyes and mouth, which gave the impression she
worked too hard, or spent too much time in the sun.

"My, you have grown up," she said.

Chloe was thankful that in the long conversation that followed,
Mrs. Creeger never mentioned her father.

Chloe was invited back for dinner "anytime." As Geoffrey and
she departed, leaving his son behind, she wondered what strange
turn of fate had brought her into Geoffrey's life.

XIII

Dominique's father died the following Monday. For two days she floated around the apartment on painkillers she'd stolen from the medicine drawer by his deathbed.

"This is a drug very much like Soma," she told Chloe. "It doesn't put you to sleep but you feel . . ." she made her arms into bird wings and flapped in slow motion around the living room. "In France they only give it to you if you're dying. What a waste. All my neurotic actress girlfriends are calling me every two minutes to get my pills. Because they're not stupid; they know me, I have no morals. My father doesn't need the pills anymore. But I'm not giving my pills to anyone. Here, I give one to you. If you tell your mother, she shoots me."

Chloe put the pill in her closet, on a shelf under sweaters.

Wednesday Dominique pulled herself together enough to call a travel agency. She'd decided overnight to take a vacation.

"I must get away from my surviving family. Now that he's dead, they're even more unbearable."

On Thursday morning she packed a suitcase, grabbed her fur-lined raincoat, and left for three weeks. New York, and then to the sun—wherever she could go for free, she told Chloe.

At the Program that afternoon, Chloe told Annie that Vero could come stay in the apartment for a while, since Dom was gone. "You must be getting pretty sick of sharing your little room," Chloe said.

It wasn't so. Vero had offered to move out several times, but

Annie had told her to stay as long as she wanted to. As long as Vero was there, Annie felt she had an excuse to refuse Azzed. Poor Azzed was becoming resigned to the fact that Annie was not going to sleep with him, and Annie was secretly resigning herself to the fact that she would. It was just a question of putting her resolve into action. With Vero moving out, the hour of reckoning would be at hand. Annie was scared to death.

Annie went home from the Program and baked a batch of brownies for Cédric's party. Vero was not there—she never was during the day. While Annie baked and thought, she drank several glasses of wine. By the time she left for Cédric's, she was feeling no pain.

She was the first to arrive. She sat in the kitchen-living room, which had nothing in it but appliances and a long wooden table, while Cédric chopped vegetables on a tiny cutting board next to the sink. He was a very tall person with long, large bones. His eyes were round and bulged from his face, and he never quite shut his mouth, which gave the impression he'd once, as a child, been stupefied by something which he'd never quite gotten over. Annie thought he looked hungry.

They spoke in French because Cédric did not speak English. She asked him about the French university system because she was considering returning to Paris for graduate school. On the floor by his long feet was a mattress with tangled sheets spread over it. Annie figured this was where Geoffrey slept.

Cédric told her the students were graded strictly on an exam basis. There were so many students (college was free) that it was the only way to do it. You didn't even have to go to class as long as you passed the exams. Cédric said Geoffrey was in the top fifth of his class. All the while Cédric chopped and threw vegetables into a large tin pot.

"I'm making ratatouille," he explained. "And rice. I'm a vegetarian."

Annie thought he looked anemic and should be eating red meat, but did not tell him so.

"Joff is bringing a salade and the other girls are bringing wine, I think. Tu sais, Joff has taugl.t me a few American words, but I think they're the kind you don't repeat in the presence of ladies. Yesterday he taught me shaddap you *matherfacker*. What does that mean, exactly?"

Vero and Chloe each brought two bottles of wine that were eagerly consumed with the ratatouille which was spicy and delicious, but not very filling. By the time they got to Annie's brownies, Cédric brought out an old beat-up guitar with a bandaged body and began strumming and singing in a soft deep voice. He sang children's rhymes, scatological verses French kids learn in elementary school and at summer camp. Geoffrey sang along, drumming his plate with his fork and spoon. Annie watched Chloe across the table. She was remembering bits and pieces of the songs and laughing with delight.

Someone upstairs began rapping on a heating pipe. The noise reverberated through the rugless two-room apartment. Geoffrey banged harder on his plate and on his glass, stamped his feet, the rest joining in till they couldn't hear Cédric or the guitar anymore.

"Ah NON, ça alors! Ça suffit!" Cédric brought his fist down on the table. With guitar in hand he went to the window, opened it, and leaned out to his waist, facing up.

"Alors, la mal-baisée d'en haut, t'as pas fini de faire chier le peuple?!" He shut the window with a bang. The clanging stopped. He returned to his place at the head of the table.

Cédric explained, "No, it's true, in the end. Once a year we make a little noise and she throws a fit. She doesn't want anyone to have a good time because, simply, her husband doesn't lay her. She takes it out on the rest of the population. She's the kind who turned in Jews, I swear."

Geoffrey went out for more wine.

"Did Annie tell you?" Chloe was saying to Vero, "the lady I live with went to the States for three weeks. If you want to give Annie a break, you're welcome to come stay with me for a while."

They were sitting next to each other, always following each other around with their eyes. Annie was interested because the situation was absurd. Geoffrey kept approaching Chloe like a puppy looking for affection, and Chloe kept backing away, hiding behind Vero and putting her in the middle. Yet Annie could tell that Chloe liked Geoffrey a good deal, but it seemed she was almost afraid of him. And Vero had confessed her unrequited love for Geoffrey to Annie numerous times. Vero was soft and glowing. She had a mother's arms. Geoffrey was by no means threatening. Annie couldn't figure it out.

Thinking about going back to her maid's room alone filled her with dread. And anticipation. She couldn't tell which emotion was stronger.

With the fifth and sixth bottles of wine the table grew rowdy. Geoffrey began talking politics.

"I am a man without a country," he said glumly. "I am not American, I'm not French. What am I? I'm nothing. I don't particularly care to be associated with the U.S., a nation, my dear friends, which was founded on the principles of genocide and slavery."

"GENOCIDE!" Annie cried. She was aghast. She'd never heard such a thing. Even in the radical circles at Cromwell she didn't think they spoke this way. Maybe they might for effect, but not seriously?

"Parfaitement!" Geoffrey said. "What do you call the American Indian, dogshit? May as well. And your blacks? May as well call them dogshit too."

"How can you *say* that?" Annie said. "*I* certainly don't feel that way." Need she tell the table that she had never met a Jew, let alone a black person, before she'd gone to Cromwell?

Geoffrey was on a rampage. He wasn't listening to her. Nobody ever listened to her.

"And now they have an actor running for President who can't even act! The Republicans say the Democrats are weak, BOMB those fucking Iranians. Who the FUCK do they think they're fucking with? they say. THIS IS THE USA! That's a great attitude for the future. We're going to get very far with an attitude like that."

"You can vote against the Republicans," Annie replied. "You can vote absentee instead of bitching and moaning and doing nothing."

"I refuse to vote just for the sake of voting AGAINST something. You only have two parties in the U.S. And they're exactly the same. You have no choice at all. If you had an Anarchist or Communist party, maybe I'd vote."

Oh my God, he's a Communist! Annie thought. "But we DO have a Communist party," she insisted.

"But it doesn't *mean* a shit in the toilet," Geoffrey said. He slid closer to Chloe on the bench and Chloe moved closer to Vero, trying to make a space between Geoffrey's arm and her own. Vero was watching Geoffrey intently.

"It's true that it doesn't mean anything," Chloe said.

"It doesn't matter," he said, shrugging the whole thing off. "Your CIA and their KGB are going to blow up the whole fucking world anyway."

Annie burst into tears. "It's not true!" she shook her head.

"The fuck it isn't!" Geoffrey insisted. "The U.S. wants to bring more bombs over here and plant them on European soil!"

"Why does Europe hate us suddenly?" Annie said. "We saved your goddarn asses during both World Wars. My grandfather and Chloe's father were in WW II, getting their rear ends shot off for Europe."

"The Russians 'saved' Europe too. It's all colonialist horseshit." In a softer tone, he added, "No disrespect to your families."

"Non mais, dites, ça va pas?" Cédric leaned forward. "La politique, on en a rien a foutre, Joff. Regarde, elle pleure." Cédric was seriously offended that a guest was crying in his house. He wrapped his long arms around Annie's shoulders and shook her.

Retreating, leaning back, Geoffrey said, "It's not your fault you're so misinformed."

Annie cried in her hands while Cédric bounced her from side to side in her seat. It was ridiculous but she could not stop herself. She couldn't remember the last time she'd cried.

"What's the matter with you?" It was Chloe leaning over her. "I don't know what's wrong with her," she told the rest of them. "She never cries."

"It's nothing," Annie said, looking up at a spot on the ceiling.

"I think the Iranians are giving us a good, long-deserved kick in the ass. The Shah was backed by the U.S. He was no prince charming, he was a fascist pig. It's a very sad time," Geoffrey said. "I'm very sorry to have upset you. I think you should read the French newspapers while you're here. Not just the *Herald Tribune*. See what the world thinks of the U.S. I'm telling you, it's a bad time."

"Bon alors, c'est fini? Drink," Cédric said, and poured.

In five minutes the whole thing was forgotten. Annie was in high spirits again, laughing at the jokes. In the back of her mind an ugly doubt was spreading. What if they *were* misinformed back home?

She wasn't saying Geoffrey was right; he was a radical lunatic. But on the French news the other night, she'd watched a clip on the Republican candidate Geoffrey had mentioned. She had thought it was a joke, an early April Fool. The French had treated it as a joke. They showed a clip from one of the man's old movies. He was talking to a chimpanzee that was sitting on his lap. The French reporter laughed and then turned dead serious as the screen flashed a still of the hostages with hands tied and hoods over their heads. "Can this new candidate remedy this situation? The Americans seem to hope so."

They were making fun of the U.S.! Annie was afraid. It was a strange and ugly time to be an American away from home.

Azzed was standing in his doorway, a dark shape in a rectangle of yellow light. What am I doing here, she asked herself. The rest of them had stayed on Cédric's floor. Azzed stepped into his room; she stumbled and her shoulder hit the doorframe.

"You're completely drunk," he said. It was a simple statement devoid of judgmental undertones. She was thankful for that.

"Completely," she said.

In the room she pushed his books off the bed and sat on the mattress under the slanting eave.

"Vero's gone, finally," she said.

"Yes?" he said, approaching.

She watched him, looking up and trying to focus because she did not want to miss a second of this.

"What do you think of the hostage thing in Iran?" she asked him. He stopped and looked over his shoulder.

"Me?"

She laughed. His reaction seemed funny.

"I haven't thought about it," he said. "I'm sorry for the hostages."

"That's good because so am I," she said, hoping that she would not start crying again.

He sat beside her, very close. She felt his warmth and it made her sweat under the arms. She didn't know what to do. She closed her eyes and the room spun slightly. His breath was on her neck, her face. She smelled his shaving soap and the dusty books, and leaned back forgetting there was no wall. She fell onto the mattress with her eyes still shut. She was afraid to look at him. It was a terrible thing to be so inexperienced.

XIV

March 30, 1980

My Dear Sister,

Are you going to stay in Europe and travel this summer or are you coming home? I hope you come home because I really miss you and so does Mom. She brags about how smart and perfect you are all the time. As soon as you're gone she forgets how much you two fight.

I'm disappointed in myself because I haven't worked as hard as I should at school. I've decided to major in political science because that's what I like the best. I'm doing well but I still have goofed off too much. It's hard to be good when you're living with a bunch of wild maniacs. I wrote you two other letters which I tore up because I didn't like them. I told myself I had to write to you at least once. I'm so bad at it.

I'm mad about a lot of things in this world. I can not believe what's going on in Iran. The world is shitting on America and I don't like it. I just can't understand the attitude of the majority of students here. I've been talking to a lot of people about the draft. They all say that if the draft is put into action they will leave for Canada. Not very patriotic. What happens if half our generation leaves for Canada? What will the world think then? I'm against a peacetime draft but if there is one I'll go. I think I sound like a conservative shit. I'm not. It's just that everybody wants freedom around here, but they're spoiled, now they want it for free. What do they think over there?

I believe we are witnessing the decline of America. I bet you're asking yourself why I'm saying all this. I don't know myself. This is a strange letter but I decided to write you no matter what I wrote. I've just been thinking about this too much I guess.

I think Mom loves you very much. You should try to be nicer to her. When she bugs you just pretend you're listening and don't talk back. I don't know why it's so hard for you guys to get along. You're too much alike, that's what I think.

This is something I don't like to talk about, but Dad told me never to let her give up the house. He said the house is the most important thing. I didn't understand what he meant by that but now I think I do. We have enough to worry about without fighting between ourselves too. We have to stay a family and the house is what keeps it together. That's why I work my ass off in the garden every summer. Now we have the nicest garden in the whole neighborhood, Goddamnit! And that makes me feel good.

I think you should write to her and tell her about Paris and how you're doing. She was so happy when I told her you wrote to me. It was funny, she told Dominique if she wasn't nice to you, she would never talk to her again. I miss you a lot too and can't wait till you come home.

Love,
Eric

P.S. I'm being chased by three good-looking mamas and I love it!

His handwriting astounded her. For years Eric's hand had been fragile and shaky, due to his insecurity discerning French from English spelling. He had refused to speak French for several years, when they'd first moved to Paris, and once he'd started to speak, he refused to write or read in either language.

In the letter his script sailed confidently across the page, slanting to the right in swift angles and curves. He'd grown up. She hadn't seen it before.

She felt a terrible loss, as though she'd let something crucial pass her by. She had not pushed him to open up to her. Maybe she *was* too much like her mother, solipsistic in her grief. It was a load she could barely carry herself. She believed with staunch self-righteousness that their mother should have been available to both of them, regardless. Eric was the strongest of them. She could see him thinking, *I will keep this house together no matter what,* out in the garden with the clippers and Locke lawnmower, making endless circles of the house. He was a stubborn, heroic fool. They did have the nicest garden in the whole neighborhood. She could hear her father joking harshly a long time ago, as he hammered away at some unhinged shutter, or as he sealed off the grackles' nest under the roof so the babies would starve. Eric stood below him, sheepishly suggesting alternatives while Chloe cried.

"You dumbhead. What a city kid you are. What're you ever going to do if I'm not around to take care of this place?"

Their father did not like these jobs himself, she knew. She could tell by the way he lumbered over them, the set expression on his face, jaw forward as though to receive a punch.

Eric had taken over the garden to prove to him he could.

Once back in the States, the kids in school called Eric the Frog. He wanted to play football, and had just about figured out the rules when they introduced plays. He settled for running track instead. And that became his passion; he ran and ran with the same devotion and concentration he later gave the garden.

And Geoffrey, by trying to assimilate himself into French society and rejecting the States, had done the exact same thing. But once you were borderline something, anything, Chloe thought, you remained borderline all your life. Geoffrey wasn't completely French by any means, and Eric and she were not completely American.

Chloe wanted to be home. Eric was asking her for her opinion. She didn't know what to tell him about the "mood" in France. She hated politics and politicians, and both had never seemed a subjective matter to her before. Politically, she had always thought of herself as a mass of seaweed floating in the sea. Whatever she thought would never make a difference anyway, so why bother?

But now, it suddenly seemed terribly important. She was, after all, a type of ambassador.

She wrote Eric that she thought it was time to change things. At home, people only saw one side of the world, the U.S. side. "It's different over here. People are sick of getting pushed around by us. It isn't like it used to be after WW II. I think the French are still mad at us for saving their chickenshit asses." (She added the last sentence because of their father.)

She wrote that she didn't think what the Iranians did was right. But maybe we should look at *why* they did it. And to add to the confusion of this whole mess, she wrote that she loved him, and everyone like him, for believing that no matter what, you had to protect and stick up for your home and your land.

She did not know what to do about her mother. She tried to write but the words came out angry and stilted.

She did not want to be angry. She desperately wanted to patch things up. The wounds were messy and deep.

She looked at it like this; if you want something because it's pretty, like a flame, you reach out for it and touch it. You get burned. After a couple of times, you stop reaching for it. That was her mother.

"Mama, come put me to bed!" On Sunday nights when the nurse had off, Chloe couldn't sleep.

"Go put yourself to bed!"

Her mother was too honest, she held nothing back, regardless of the damage.

"Kids bore me to death. I hope you get more interesting as you get older."

It was not like this all the time, obviously. But Chloe's memory was like a child's playbox filled to the top with pieces of various jigsaw puzzles. Who even knew if any number of the pieces put together would ever make a complete picture. It wasn't worth sorting through the box.

Once, when Chloe was already much older, her mother had said, "You don't mean shit to me. Given the choice I would have taken your father. Anytime. He came first, first, and first. If I'd stayed home with you kids when he wanted to go out, he would have left me for someone else. I had to be with him because he wanted me to be with him."

Chloe's mind flashed onto Dominique and her guts froze. Couldn't her mother have managed to do both?

"Your mother loves you kids more than anything in the world." This was her father. *"She loves you like a mother lion loves her babies. It's so instinctual she doesn't even realize it herself."*

"Well what about you, Daddy?"

"I think about how much I love you all the time. It's much more mental. I overintellectualize it."

Chloe didn't believe him.

The day he died she had stood three feet from her mother who was lying on the couch. Chloe felt immovable and cold as a donjon tower. "You have no right to behave this way," she told her. "Eric needs you. Especially now." She would not admit that she needed her herself.

Her mother stared at her with utter hatred. "Eric is a complete introverted fuck-up because of you. You've been pushing him around all his life. Now you run around fucking everybody and carrying on, bringing maniacs into this house and you dare talk to ME about caring?"

Everything she said was true. There were people sitting around her, watching this scene. Relatives, friends, even Jack was there. They told Chloe not to listen, it was the shock speaking. Chloe knew it was not the shock. She'd gotten burned for good.

She sat with the sheet of paper in front of her on the table. "Dear Mom," she had written for the third time. By now it was useless. She felt Vero approaching behind her, then Vero's hand pressing lightly on her shoulder.

"Is something wrong?" she asked. Chloe handed Eric's letter to her. They'd been sharing everything for a week, now. It was like being little again, and having a girlfriend come to spend the weekend. That was when sharing became fun, the way it was not with a sibling.

They traded clothes, and shopped in flea markets and open food markets, invented elaborate meals which they prepared for guests, Geoffrey, Annie, or sometimes just for themselves. Having Vero at Dominique's made every day, even when Chloe had to go to school, seem like a vacation.

They both cried a good deal. Chloe, when she was drunk and reminiscing, cried in outrage in a gut-wrenching way. Vero, when she saw a lonely dog chained to a parking meter, and at the Homage to Monet exhibit, where they'd spent a full afternoon and had gone back the next day. Vero cried lightheartedly, making fun of herself for being sentimental. You couldn't cry like this with boys. Chloe couldn't remember the last time she'd had a sleep-over girlfriend like Vero.

Vero finished reading Eric's letter and looked up with cloudy eyes. Wiping them quickly, she'd said, "You're so lucky. You've got forever to work things out with him. My brother was eleven years older than me. I hardly remember a thing but I wish so much that I had known him better. I was so little, what could I have talked to him about? Sometimes I dream about Ted and we have long talks about my folks. He tells me what I should be doing with my life. Like going to college. What the fuck. Maybe next year." She smiled in her self-effacing, melancholy way. Chloe felt selfish and spoiled for having Eric, and suddenly possessive of him; as though she'd found a treasure that was not hers to keep. She didn't deserve him.

Taking the letter from Vero's hands, she went to her closet and put the letter in with her passport and traveler's checks. Under the sweaters at the back of the shelf she found the pill Dom had given her. She held it in her fist and took it out to Vero to see if she wanted it.

They decided to each take half. On the thin formica counter in the kitchen they split the pill with a butcher knife. On Dom's old scratchy stereo Vero played one of the albums she'd brought with her, and gave Chloe a lesson on New Wave dancing. I'll show that Serge, Chloe thought. And what a scream it will be to dance like this at the disco parties back at Cromwell!

"It's just like the twist," Vero explained, "just crazy. See?" She went limp at the hips and knees. "Pretend you're a noodle."

They wandered aimlessly through the Latin Quarter and ended up on the lower quai beneath Notre-Dame. The sun was out and there were people sitting with their coats off, backs against the rampart. Treading heavily over the uneven cobblestones, they found a spot in the sun on the wide ridge just above the river. The trees on the upper quai were beginning to sprout round green buds. The sun rays reflected off the ripples in the water like sparks from a yellow fire. Chloe felt very small from Dom's pill. Relaxed, with a heightened sense of sound. She could hear the spring getting ready to burst through the weakening cold. People behind them were talking comfortably. She lay on her stomach on the wide ridge with her head on Vero's lap, face turned to the water. Vero's boot heels bounced back and forth against the embankment.

Vero began to sing in a delicate, high voice. She was not singing loudly but the echo carried over the stones and bounded back at them from the other side of the river, and from the arches beneath the bridge.

> "Sitting in a park in Paris, France
> Reading the news and it sure looks bad
> They won't give peace a chance
> That was just a dream some of us had
> Still a lot of lands to see
> But I wouldn't want to stay here
> It's too old and cold and settled in its ways here
> 　　Oh, but California
> California I'm coming home . . ."

When Vero finished Chloe waited in stunned silence while the last echoes of the song came back to them from across the river. Behind them someone clapped.

Vero took an apple out of the pocket of her jacket and bit into it with a loud crunch. It was a bright green, shiny apple. When she finished, instead of throwing the core into the river she put it back in her pocket. Behind them a man said in French, "You see, I told you they were American. Only Americans do things like that. We throw everything right in the Seine—hop!"

"Eh, chante nous-en une autre," the same voice said. Chloe, propped on her elbows now, watched Vero smile and glow with her little success.

She sang "Bridge Over Troubled Waters." Better, Chloe thought, than she'd ever heard it sung in her life.

XV

Vero went to Neuilly for the weekend, to house-sit for an American couple she knew. Chloe said she'd come house-sit with her Saturday night. Friday she agreed to meet Serge at his apartment, after school.

She liked meeting him at his apartment, because it was easier to leave if she felt uncomfortable. If he took her off somewhere, to some quartier she did not know, it was much harder for her to get away from him. With Serge you never knew what kind of mood he was going to lay on you.

She had her books with her in a red canvas bag. Around Serge, her books made her feel secure; the way money made him feel secure. He stood by the table and poured a ruby wine into two round crystal glasses. He handed her one, and she set her book bag down on the closest of the imposing chairs.

"I have a friend who's gotten ahold of some genuine Colombian weed. A rarity in France. Are you in the mood for a good party?"

She was greedy about having a good time. Good food, good wine, good pot.

"Sure," she said. After all, it was Friday night.

"There's one problem. I was unable to get cash today. My check will clear by tomorrow morning. Could you advance me some cash?"

"How much do you need?" She worried that she would not have enough on her. Who knew how much the French would charge for Colombian? She didn't want him to think she had *no* money.

"A hundred and fifty francs for the pot," he said. "We're splitting it three ways. That would be for our share. Of course, I'll reimburse you in the morning."

She had a hundred and sixty on her. She'd just cashed a traveler's check that morning. She told him that if she lent him the money, she wouldn't have enough to get home tonight.

"You can spend the night here," he said. "It's not like you haven't done that before. If it's early, you can take the subway, if it's not, stay here, and I'll get you the cash first thing in the morning."

She was not thrilled at the prospect of spending the night with him, or at having only ten francs mad money on her. But she was in France, after all. She had to be adventurous if she wanted to observe and enjoy new things.

A friend of Serge's called Marc de Something came to pick them up. He brought a bottle of Cognac with him that was labeled by hand. Marc had black curly hair and puffy cheeks. He was well mannered and didn't intrigue or repel Chloe; he was innocuous. She was disappointed.

Marc mentioned that he'd taken the bottle from his father's cellars. They drank from crystal snifters. The Cognac was golden brown and smooth as honey. It warmed from bottom to top. Soon they wanted to leave. Chloe wanted to bring the bottle. In the elevator she drank right from the neck of it which was a serious breach in etiquette. She was sick of their etiquette and didn't give a damn.

Marc had a black Golf, the better German version of the VW Rabbit. She found out it was the better car when she mentioned that she had a Rabbit as well and Marc snickered.

"Mais c'est pas du *tout* la même chose," he said.

"Oh," she said. They'd put her in the backseat. She did not pay attention to where they were going. She took sips from the bottle and relaxed, sitting with her back to the window and her legs stretched out on the seat.

They took her to an art-deco apartment. There was glass everywhere. Glass doors downstairs in the lobby and glass railings along the wide chrome stairs. She did not remember how many flights they'd climbed; they were standing in front of a white door and Serge was ringing the bell.

This new friend had an imposing round glass table directly across the room from a plush beige living-room set. The coffee table was glass as well. There was a Chinese or Japanese screen of dark wood separating the sleeping from the living area. The apartment seemed much bigger than it was. The new friend Gilles seemed all right to her if a bit faggy. The three of them sported an attitude of complete boredom, as though they had found nothing worth wasting emotion on.

They ignored her, but she didn't take it personally because they were like that with all females. She sat at the round glass table with Serge to her left and Marc to her right. The three de Somethings were drinking something else now, out of tall crystal glasses. She was still sipping at the bottle of Cognac. Gilles asked her if she wanted a glass. Serge said, "She doesn't need one, she likes the bottle." His tone was oddly crisp, she thought.

Marc was rolling measly joints from the envelope of Colombian that was filled with seeds and stems. She told them they'd gotten a bum deal.

"That's not worth a hundred and fifty francs each!" she said.

"But what do you want?" Marc said. "One is not in the United States."

These two didn't speak a word of English. Or at least they insisted they didn't. Most French people told you they didn't even if they spoke rather well.

The pot made the room spin but by then it was too late to go back on what she'd already consumed. The pot was harsh and smelled lousy. This probably had something to do with why the room was spinning. She had to refuse the next joint as they passed it around. She was feeling very unsafe suddenly. Very out of control.

"Si tu viens à cette soirée," Marc said to Serge, "tu comprends, il faudra que tu portes ta bague."

"What's he talking about? What ring?" she asked Serge. Her voice sounded very loud, though maybe it wasn't really.

"It's a ball given in honor of the young nobility. One has to present oneself at the door with one's crest ring."

"Crest ring? You have a crest ring?"

"No I don't. But they do." He said to them in French, "I think I can find my papers, would that be all right?"

"Probablement," Gilles said, shrugging.

"God, you snobs," she said, laughing, and then in French, "How do you people prove you're the real thing and that your families didn't buy their titles from Napoleon? Didn't he sell titles to anyone who was willing to pay for them?"

They were silently furious for a moment. The room kept spinning.

"You're such a snob, Serge," she said. "You're as American as I am. Yugoslavia's better off without you, anyway."

Suddenly she remembered her book bag was in his apartment. He owed her a hundred and fifty francs and she was broke and maybe this was the wrong time and place to be laughing at him. But she couldn't help herself.

"Look at you three, the Flatulent Dukes!"

Serge's eyes froze on her.

"You're a peasant," he said. With a flat hand he tapped her cheek sharply three times. If she'd been sober, she would have been furious and would probably have slapped him back.

"Tu vois," Gilles said from across the table, leaning forward nonchalantly and placing his long fingers on the glass, "Marc et moi, on est pédé."

"What?" she said. He'd said, "You see, Marc and I are fags," completely without humor, as though he were explaining. The barrage that followed seemed right out of Ionesco. Gilles repeated, "Marc et moi, on est pédé," in an even, everyday tone, and then went on. "But we don't like to make love together unless there's a girl between us. You see, it gets boring otherwise."

"Comment?" she started laughing again, and looked at Serge. He was leaning back in his chair, tapping away at the table with his white fingernails.

"Yes," Marc joined in. "Won't it be fun? We'll have fun. You'll come sleep with us in that big bed." He nodded toward the screen. "And Serge will come too. N'est-ce pas?" He looked longly at Serge.

All this was in French and she was not sure she was grasping the humor. Marc grabbed her by the chin and turned her face toward him.

"Come now (allons donc), you're not going to tell me you've never done it before. Une partouze, c'est amusant!" Coaxingly,

"You don't *look* or act the squeamish type. Serge says you talk a big game."

She jerked her face away and stared at Serge. She laughed, but nervously now. "Serge," she said, "he thinks he's being really funny, or what?"

"Absolutely not." He could have been sitting at an executive conference, closing off a big deal. "He's dead serious."

"Then tell him to go fuck himself," she said.

Serge's mouth twisted into that weird, disturbing smile.

"We're going to do it," he said.

"The hell we are," Chloe said. She swung her arm around the table at the three of them. "You three can go in there and do what you want. I'll wait for you right here."

"Oh come on," Serge said. "You don't want to pay for all the goodies we give you?"

"But you're my friend," she said lamely. She suddenly felt sick all over. It flashed on and off in her head like a red light, He thinks I'm a whore!

"You're just a fucking peasant," Serge said. "Just a cute, fucking American peasant." He got up, went to the living room area, and began to unbutton his shirt. The other two followed him. All three slipped out of their clean cotton shirts. Their arms were skinny, torsos pale and muscularly undefined. They went on talking between themselves as though she weren't there.

If there were two of them, she could probably fight. If they were joking, they'd gone too far. If they were serious, she was in terrible trouble. She didn't know what to do. She was so dizzy she could not have found the door, or the phone fast enough to get away from them. She was paralyzed. What would she tell the cops when they arrived? She was drunk. But it was all a joke! the dukes would say.

Leaning heavily against the edge of the table she made her way around it, tripping in the thick carpet, to the tiny frame of the kitchen door. They didn't even look at her. She dropped onto the kitchen floor, crossed her legs and put her head between her arms. She tried to think while tears poured like acid from her eyes.

This is going to be rape, she thought. If they touch me this is rape. Where's Eric, if Eric were here they wouldn't do this. Where is everybody?

She felt a hand on her neck. First it was light then it began to tug at the collar of her shirt that was hanging loosely on her shoulder. Her reaction was to pull the collar back to cover her neck. She looked up and saw Serge standing in his boxer shorts, smiling that crazy sneer. She was trying to think of who to call afterwards. Who did you call after you were raped in France? She imagined Eric beating the bloody shit out of the three of them. He would, she knew it. Eric gave her strength. Oh God, Eric, if you could only see this, she thought.

Serge ran his hand up her shoulder to her neck.

"Don't touch me you motherfucker. If you touch me I'm going to have you thrown in jail." She said this slowly, with more conviction than she'd ever said anything.

Serge snickered loudly. "You don't think I can get myself *out* of jail just as fast as you can have me thrown *in?* I know more people than you do."

"That may be but I'm going to make so much fucking noise about this you're never going to forget it. Call me on it. Your father is going to love this one, Serge."

They stared at each other. As an afterthought, without malice, she added, "You're a faggot."

That was the part that got to him. He looked shocked. "I'm not a faggot," he said defensively. And just as she thought he was going to hit her he turned away.

"Elle ne veut pas," she heard him say.

"Vraiment pas?" one of the others said with disappointment.

"Vraiment pas."

Marc drove them back to Serge's apartment. She sat in the front this time. Marc kept touching her leg. He asked her quite nicely if she'd go home with him, without the others. She told him to go fuck himself.

"You shouldn't upset yourself so," he said.

"Go fuck yourself," she said. She pressed her whole body into the door, trying to block everything out. She felt so low and small the kindness in Marc's voice seemed like an enormous compliment. It was hard for her not to be thankful to him.

Serge unlocked the door and stepped aside to let her in. Never forget etiquette, she thought.

"Go ahead," she told him.

He went into the kitchen and poured himself something to drink. She was completely sober now and her mouth was parched. She looked at her bag on the chair and for a moment considered the one hundred and fifty francs. Serge came out of the kitchen with two golden glasses of champagne. She took the glass he handed her and drank it down. She went to the kitchen, found the bottle in the fridge, and poured herself another.

She heard him undressing by the closet.

"Come to bed now," he called to her.

"You go to bed," she said.

He went to bed. She heard him rustling around in the sheets.

"I won't let you stay here tonight unless you fuck me," he said.

She pressed her forehead into the refrigerator door.

"Don't be an asshole, Serge," she yelled to him. "Go to sleep and leave me alone."

She sat at the table, in one of the two large, imposing chairs, and drank the rest of the bottle. She fell asleep with her head between her crossed arms.

In the morning she woke him up and made him take her to his bank, no shower, no breakfast, no nothing. She was amazed that with a little determination and authority in her voice, he did what she wanted him to do.

She waited while he withdrew his cash. On the way out the door he handed her the one hundred and fifty francs.

"Would you like to have breakfast?" he asked her as though nothing had happened. She was completely drained of strength.

"Listen, Serge. Do us both a favor, don't call me anymore. Okay? And if I were you, I'd stay away from my neighborhood on Long Island."

He looked at her questioningly. This was making no sense at all to him.

"My brother will do more than break your fucking jaw," she said. She walked out into the street, without looking back, and hailed a taxi.

XVI

Three days before Dominique came back, Vero found a place to live in the Ninth Arrondissement on Rue de Clichy. The apartment was the ultimate in bourgeois chic. At the center of the building was a large courtyard with trees planted at each corner, and a fountain in the center. The family owned the ground and second floors of the far section of the building. The large bay windows of the ground floor looked out on a quaint garden with graveled walks and flowerbeds, and a round picnic table with a parasol for sunny days.

Vero's job, in return for room and board, was to wake the twenty-year-old son up every weekday morning at 7:30 to prevent him from sleeping through his musicology classes at the Sorbonne. Vero was to bring him his coffee and croissants on a breakfast tray, and try to talk him out of going back to sleep. According to his mother, he was quite a partier and not terribly interested in school.

This left Vero the rest of the twenty-four hours in every day to goof off with Chloe and Geoffrey. The day before Dominique returned, Chloe and Vero scrubbed and mopped and swept the entire apartment; they even Ajaxed the walls above the radiators, which hadn't been touched since the previous paint job. Chloe bought Chivas and fresh oranges and cream for coffee, and two hundred francs' worth of long-stemmed exotic flowers to fill the vase that had stood empty since Dominique's departure. The apartment looked like a new place.

Chloe did not want to drop a single crumb on the floor. She left the apartment sparkling like a picture from *Good Housekeeping*, and stayed with Vero the night before Dom was to return.

Since her catastrophic night with Serge she couldn't bear to be alone. The sickly, angry feeling stayed with her all the time. It sharpened into focus at night when she had nothing else to think about. In the day she kept busy with her friends and even talked about that night to try to give it distance. Geoffrey wanted to find the Lancia and piss in its gas tank. Chloe argued, though the thought made her laugh, that it wouldn't matter a damn to Serge since it wasn't even his car. And his brother and he could afford to dump it and buy another for all it meant to people like them.

That was what hurt the most. Nothing meant a damn to people like Serge. Today he probably couldn't remember that night at all. He'd called twice since, and left banal messages on Dom's answering machine. He gave up after that. But Chloe was sick from fury. She had the bizarre urge to speak to Serge, to try to wound him in some deep way. Make a lasting statement that would ease her conscience and leave her feeling victorious. She felt dirtied. Filthy. He'd thrown shit in her face. But Vero, who tended to be less outraged by fate, told her Serge was not worth wasting an ounce of energy over. "Chuck him," she said. "He's garbage." This helped a little bit. Chloe needed to be reassured constantly.

When she walked into the apartment the next morning she found Dom standing in the center of the living room.

"Really, I must say," she looked about, "this apartment is of a non-Dominiquian cleanliness."

Her vacation had done her wonders. She was tanned a rich dark bronze, her eyes were clear and calm. She had shed ten years the way some people shed ten pounds.

They had a cup of fresh coffee spiked with Chivas, and Dom told Chloe about the States. She had spent a weekend in East Whitman and had slept in Chloe's very room.

"Your mother she said to me, 'Dom, if you are not good to my little baby I never speak to you again.' What's the matter with her? She never used to have such concern for her little babies. Maybe she's senile already?"

Chloe laughed halfheartedly. Dominique looked her over care-

fully. When Dom was being funny, people usually laughed and
laughed to split their sides. If they didn't laugh immediately, there
was something wrong. She'd keep going till the wrong was reme-
died.

"It looks like to me you need a vacation. Shall I tell you how I got
my free Bahamas trip? I met a doctor from Queens on the aero-
plane. 'Queens,' I say to him, 'what's that?' He thought I was an
innocent French lady coming to New York for the first time. It's
okay with me if he wants to think that. He asks me for a date in
Queens to meet his mama. I say oké for the date, but not to meet
his mama. You ever went to Queens?"

"Driving through on the expressway."

"Very interesting place. I say I am going to the sun because New
York is too cold in wintertime. He says his vacation time is soon,
why don't we go together? I say why not? I hate the Bahamas but
it's better than Miami Beach. He is about thirty-two, I'd say. I told
him I'm thirty-five. Maybe he believes me, maybe not. For me, it's
oké if they're young, because the older they get the less they want
to fuck. True or not?"

Chloe didn't know what to say to this. She nodded with a stupid
smile.

"He was called Antonio Cappello. He's a nice Italian Catholic
boy with a severe mother complex. He's still living with her. He
wanted to be a priest to please his mama but then he thought he
could touch more people being a doctor. For DAYS he won't fuck
at all. I become worried maybe he's some kind of faggot. Then one
night in the Bahamas he drags me to the beach in a mad passion;
he takes me from the front, he takes from the back. 'Cappello,' I
say to him, 'you cannot find God through me.' Did you ever notice
how Catholic boys once they get going are unstoppable in bed?"

Chloe had tears streaming from her eyes at this point; in her
mind she saw Joe Gillan's parents sitting at this table being victim-
ized by Dominique's humor. Her stomach ached from laughing.

"No, but seriously, you are looking to me very *un*happy. In my
opinion you need a man. What happened to the rich little
shithead?" she asked. Chloe wavered for a second between telling
Dom and keeping the nightmare to herself.

"He's *really* an asshole," she said, and left it at that.

"I could have told you that a long time ago. Listen, oké? I have a dinner. I invite someone young and good for you. A Russian. How about it? He just ran away from the Sovietic Union. You like the Russian literature, maybe it will work, no?"

Chloe became exhausted at the thought of meeting anyone new. But she was touched by Dominique's offer and could see no way to refuse.

The night of the dinner Chloe had the flu. Dom fixed her a grog with a double dose of scotch. By the time the guests arrived Chloe felt much better, though her ears, sinuses, throat, eyes were besieged by fluids so that she had the impression she was gazing at the scene from the bottom of a pool.

Vladimir arrived with a rose for the hostess. He was a pale, slight fellow with delicate bone structure and deep black eyes. He seemed ailing. Chloe had never met a real Soviet Russian before and was quite fascinated, even if he was only an *ex*-Soviet Russian. When Dominique introduced them he bowed and kissed Chloe's hand. She was suddenly reminded of Serge and in a flash became so dizzy she was obliged to sit down.

The dinner guests consisted of Chloe's father's French publisher and his young man friend; an old boyfriend of Dominique's who was a professor of psychology at the Sorbonne who came with his new girlfriend, one of his admiring students; and Vladimir. They sat down to a beef stew with vegetables in a light tomato and wine sauce, which was a specialty of Dominique's. Dom hated garlic. "You fucking Americans put garlic in EVERYthing and then you call it French. Can you imagine? Your mother takes me to that stupid restaurant and they put garlic on the fucking lobster!"

Vladimir sat beside Chloe and talked quietly to her in his throaty French, rolling R's and swallowing vowels as though he were lifting an impossible weight while he spoke.

"I read *The Sound and the Fury* in four colors!" He proudly held up four fingers and leaned closer to her. "In Russian. I hear that in the United States the publishers would not print it in four colors because it was too expensive, and he was not very popular. Is this true?"

"I heard something like that, but I don't know much about it." She wasn't sure whether he wanted to ask or argue, and feeling weak, decided to feign complete ignorance. It was always safer with strangers. Especially foreign ones.

"Fukner is the most popular of all your writers in Russia."

"He definitely has the Russian temperament, it seems to me."

"Yes!" he clapped his hands. *"Heavy.* Full of the dark side of the soul. Always introspecting like that. Yes?" He explained "heavy" by holding his arms at his chest and pantomiming a large, weighty package. He lifted an index finger to her nose. "You are intelligent." He turned his back to her momentarily. "Dom," he called down the table, "you brought me an intelligent one."

"She's not intelligent at all. She's dumb as a broomstick. That's why she'll make a good actress."

"You're an actress!" This seemed to excite him terribly. "Dushetchka moya!" he patted her cheek.

"No I'm not."

The wine kept flowing. Chloe could not drink at all, it made her too dizzy, so she watched Vladimir get maudlin drunk. He began to describe the horrors of his life in the Soviet Union. But then he shed tears remembering the loved ones he'd left behind. He'd driven his Lada west from Moscow on a two-week visa and had never returned.

"You can't imagine what I had to do to get the two-week visa," he told her as though this were in the greatest confidence. In her weakened state she didn't think she could handle whatever it was he'd done to get out. She envisioned all sorts of gruesome sexual acts. There was something not quite right about Vladimir, though she could not tell what. He was certainly not dishonest.

"Come," he tugged at her sleeve, "you want to see my Lada? It's parked downstairs. I bet you have never seen a Soviet-made car."

She shook her head. "I have the flu. I'm very sick."

Feeling the need to breathe, she gathered the plates and brought them into the kitchen.

Dom was having a fight with her Moulinex coffee grinder, slapping its plastic head because it refused to grind.

"I want to tell you something," Dom said.

Chloe's stomach iced over. She felt hot and cold and terribly weak in the knees. The flu gave her a hallucinatory perspective on the most banal things.

"Of the whole gang that used to hang around your father, the

actors, the playwrights, everybody, I slept with every single one."
She stopped, slapped the Moulinex which began to whine, and
raised a finger at Chloe's face. "Except him."

Chloe leaned into the counter with the side of her head against
the cabinets.

"Everybody's so damn promiscuous in the business," she went
on. "They're always preaching monogamy and family. But there
was not one that I didn't sleep with. Except him. And don't think I
didn't try. Even though I love your mother. That 'as nothing to do
with it. I love the wives of all of them that I slept with. They were
all terrible 'ypocrites. Terrible. Your father was not. If he would
have fucked around with anybody, it would 'ave been me. So
believe me when I tell you he never did with anyone."

She dumped the powdered beans into the espresso pot and filled
it with water.

"There were always people around him. The actors who wanted
to work with him. He got all his ideas from people, always people.
But for him, there was *only* your mother. When he got *really* sick
—you probably don't know how frightened he was—he decided
right away to go 'ome to the States and live quiet somewhere not
too far from New York. He never trusted the fucking French
doctors and I don't blame him." She waved her hand, dismissing
all of it.

"What I am talking about? Shit. Just remember what I told you."

Chloe was afraid there was a shortwave radio inside Dom's head
that transmitted all Chloe's thoughts to her. She didn't know how
to protect herself against it. Dom had the strength to frighten her
into being a small child again. She had the same nightmarish vision
of herself hanging on to her mother's skirt, begging for love and
understanding and being tossed aside. But Dom was not her
mother. She only had one mother.

"I've always known that," she said in an even, unmoved tone.
She didn't sound like herself. Dom turned from concentrating on
the espresso pot and concentrated on Chloe's face, maybe to see if
she was lying. Chloe felt Dom's eyes staring at the wall behind her
head.

If she had slept with him she was doing a damn good job of
covering it up, Chloe thought. Chloe had been lied to before. In
these situations you never find out. Better to believe what you

want to believe than worry about it forever. She suddenly felt very close to her mother.

"My mother would not have liked you if she had had the slightest doubt about him. She never trusted you. But she trusted him."

"That's true," Dom nodded slowly. "Good point."

They left the kitchen and went back to the party. The professor of psychology was explaining in a loud voice how Sartre who'd just died recently had never gotten over his vagina dentita complex. Vladimir didn't seem the slightest bit interested. He seemed impatient to have Chloe back.

The talking buzzed in her ears and she'd reached that delirious state where being sick becomes almost pleasant. She wanted desperately to go to bed, but didn't want to insult Vladimir's susceptible Russian pride.

"Vladimir, listen, I must go to bed. I have a fever and am really not well."

He placed his cold delicate hand on her forehead.

"Pretty, intelligent girl," he said affectionately. Her forehead felt on fire beneath his touch. "I call you soon and we go to a café and discuss Tolstoy, yes?"

"Sure," she said. "I'm very sorry to be sick."

The next morning she was sipping tea with lemon at the dining-room table when Vladimir appeared in the doorway to the hall. He looked dazed and frazzled and his shirttails were hanging out of his pants which he hadn't bothered to zip.

"Good morning!" he said. "I think I drank too much." His black growth of beard cast a dark shadow over his sallow cheeks, which gave him an emaciated look.

"You want some Alka-Seltzer?"

"What is it, please?"

"For hangovers," she said. In French, "gueule de bois."

"Ah, what an American thing. It would go far in the Soviet Union."

A few moments later Dom came padding down the hall in one of her seductive negligees. She looked as dazed as Vladimir.

"I think we drank too much," Dom said.

The three behaved as though it were the most normal thing in the world for him to have spent the night with Dom.

"How is your flu?" he asked.

"Much better, thank you."

Dom and he started partying again. Vladimir had some black Lebanese hash which they smoked out of a pretty green stone pipe. Chloe couldn't take it and went back to bed. She closed her door tightly to catch as little as possible of their conversation. Dom began playing Billie Holiday records and Chloe heard them laughing hysterically about God knew what.

At nightfall Chloe got dressed, wearing a turtleneck beneath a sweatshirt, and prepared to leave for Vero's place. Vladimir was still there, sitting with Dom in the living room. He offered to drive her to Vero's.

On the way down in the elevator he told her that ever since he'd laid eyes on her, he was convinced that they would have a wonderful love affair.

"If you thought we were going to have a wonderful affair, you shouldn't have spent the night with Dominique."

He threw his arms up. "But it means nothing! Not to either of us!"

"But it means something to me. Anyway, you don't know her as well as I do. I don't want any bullshit in this department, even if it's prearranged and set up by her." Then she laughed wholeheartedly. "You're crazy! Both of you."

"Will you go out with me?"

"Absolutely not."

This did not discourage Vladimir from calling and leaving extensive wooing messages for her on Dom's machine.

XVII

It was the last day of classes before spring break. The afternoon was warm and sunny. Annie sat on the terrace of her after-class café, facing the Luxembourg, and once again contemplated her moral dilemma. She still had about ten minutes to change her mind, at which time Chloe would appear through the Luxembourg gates and join her on the terrace to discuss last-minute preparations for their spring-break trip. Tomorrow would begin their tour of France, organized by Geoffrey.

Annie was not going, but no one knew that yet. Azzed's spring vacation had turned out to be at the same time as hers.

But Geoffrey had been planning the trip for weeks. He spent long hours at Cédric's kitchen table, smoking non-filter Gauloises one after the other, burning candles for light while Chloe, Vero, and Annie listened. He described their itinerary with the clear-headed excitement of a leader planning a commando raid.

He had put together a car by taking the engine of a Deux-Chevaux and fitting it into the carcass of a Renault 6. The rest of the parts had come ad hoc from different discarded automobiles. He explained to them that Harry (the car) could only go 60 kilometers per hour, tops, but would make it to Nice and back, no problem. Geoffrey was bringing along his tools in case Harry broke down. There was nothing about Harry Geoffrey didn't know.

As they sat listening to him, Annie watched Vero's crush turn to admiration and awe. Chloe, on the other hand, was not so thrilled by the whole plan. She did not like camping, hated to depend on the weather, and did not believe for a second that Geoffrey's automobile-contraption would endure the trip. Annie had agreed to go along for moral support. She was rugged enough. And after all, she did want to see the countryside.

But all this had happened before her thing with Azzed became serious. She had avoided admitting this to herself for too long. Now Azzed was talking about the wonderful quiet hours they would be spending together once his exams were over. How there weren't enough hours in the day for him to think about her.

When she told Azzed about Geoffrey's trip he almost cried. At first she had thought he was jealous of Geoffrey, but then realized he was jealous of everybody who touched her life. Late at night when they would finally be alone together, they would lie in his bed and he'd run his fingers over her body, and beg her not to go with them. His hands in the dim light looked grey and sometimes even black against her white skin. Annie had dry skin and his was smooth and soft as waxed wood. She never had imagined that a man's touch could be so tender. Because he felt so good she capitulated.

It was difficult for her to capitulate to anyone. That was her nature.

She had bought herself a Eurail pass and in July she was getting on a train headed for a random European country. She had planned to do this from the very beginning. Before Azzed, before Geoffrey's spring trip.

She had to give up the spring trip and stay in Paris with Azzed to clear the way and give herself leverage for the fight they would have over the later, more important trip.

As of yet, Annie hadn't told a soul about the nature of her relationship with Azzed. It was so illicit and personal she could not bring herself to admit it even to Chloe, who was by far, when it came to sexual talk, the most relaxed person she knew.

She had put it off and put it off, hoping that a deus ex machina would fix things before it came time for the spring trip. Now the spring trip was imminent, and fate had not come to the rescue.

Annie watched the Luxembourg across the street. Chloe would appear through the gates at any moment. The thought of explaining herself sent Annie into a cold sweat. Chloe would be angry and hurt about Annie backing out of the trip at the last minute. But she would be FURIOUS that she had not been previously informed about Azzed.

From the terrace Annie watched mothers with prams and small children coming and going from the park. Several loitering Arabs stood around checking the ladies out. Suddenly there was Chloe with her red book bag, marching toward the pedestrian crossing. One of the Arabs said something to her and she turned around and yelled something back. He laughed sheepishly. She crossed the street and approached the café.

"Fucking assholes." She sat down.

Annie listened patiently while Chloe went on and on for at least fifteen minutes about her great news. Vero's French family had given her the key to their villa outside Saint-Tropez. Which meant NO CAMPING! Chloe was ecstatic. There were two bedrooms, so now they'd have to figure out who was going to sleep with whom. Annie sighed, preparing herself.

"Chloe, my dear," she said evenly, "I've decided that I can't go with you." She was thankful that there were other occupied tables on the terrace. Chloe wouldn't holler or stomp out with other people around. Probably. Chloe listened, placed her mug on its round coaster, concentrated on centering it, then looked up at Annie as though she'd just been slapped.

"WHY?"

Annie watched her face change from shock to hurt to anger in a matter of seconds.

"I wish you could have said something sooner, Goddamnit. We're leaving tomorrow morning already. It's going to be weird with just Vero and Geoffrey. Shit."

Annie put her hand over Chloe's. Chloe pulled back.

"Don't think this is easy. It's taken me weeks to figure this out. Please, listen. I can't leave Azzed right now. I'm going to Eurail it this summer and—"

"What?" A spark of interest glinted in Chloe's gloomy face.

"I don't want to leave Azzed here alone during his spring break." Annie's tactic, out of embarrassment or lack of experience in discussing such matters, was to play it as though her affair with Azzed were a given fact that Chloe should have taken for granted long ago.

"You're doing it with Azzed?" All at once the lights went on in her head, warming her eyes. "You're kidding!"

"I might have put it differently," Annie said, proper lady that she was. "But yes. Why would I be kidding?" She feigned impatience, as though all this were trivial stuff. She hoped it would camouflage her discomfort.

"Oh you little liar!" Chloe was smiling like an imp. "And I'm supposed to be your best friend. All this time you're telling me he's such a gentleman, you're *such* good friends, there's nothing sexual about it. You've been doing it all along and playing little miss innocent. Wait till I write your grandma and tell her you're doing the dirty deed—with a Muslim, no less. Oh boy!"

"I already wrote to her and told her about him. But no sex, please! Grandma would have an embolism on the spot."

"Jesus, Annie!" Her eyes went wide with a new thought. "What about birth control?"

Annie looked around at the other tables to see if anyone was listening, although they were speaking English.

"Does he make you squat in the corner and twirl your finger around in there?" Chloe threw her head back and roared at her joke. On the terrace several faces turned toward their table.

This was going too far. Annie slapped her hand.

"Stop it!" She felt her face turn purple. Trying to seem disappointed, she said, "Of all the people from Cromwell I know, of *everyone,* you're the one I thought I could talk to about this." It wasn't working very well because she couldn't stop giggling.

"I bet he has two wives back in Algeria."

"Tunisia."

"Tunisia. What the fuck's the difference. I bet he'll try to take you back there and sell you into white slavery." She reached across the table and plucked at one of Annie's front curls. "With this hair he could sell you for, let's see, a thousand dollars in gold and two camels, maybe."

Annie turned to shoo her hand away but Chloe kept plucking. *"Please come with me to Tunisia and meet my family,"* he'd told her. *"We're important people in my village. My father owns a taxi."*

—ANNIE! she shouted inside her head. KIDNAP YOU! DON'T BE AN ASS!

"You jerk," she said to Chloe. "And you're supposed to be so open-minded." The worst was over, at least. Annie tried to relax. She was beginning to enjoy holding center stage.

Chloe stopped laughing. "No, really," she said, "you'll get pregnant. Imagine that! Annie comes home to grandma with a café au lait baby."

"Hopefully not," Annie said primly. "Before we left Cromwell I got fitted for a diaphragm. Just in case."

Happy surprise flitted across Chloe's face. "You big hypocrite!" she shook a finger at her. "What's the world coming to. Planning ahead and everything."

"Do you remember, a long time ago you told me that I didn't know what I was missing? Do you remember?"

"I said that?" Her eyes went blank while she searched back in her head.

"Now I keep wondering how I could have lived without it for so long." God forgive me, Annie thought. She'd have to make up for all the times she'd missed and go to mass at Notre-Dame on Sunday.

"So the Arab's good in bed." Chloe leaned forward. "Tell me, does he try to penetrate your nether passage? I hear they prefer little boys."

Annie slapped her palm down on the table. The mugs and ashtray jiggled furiously.

"Stop it! Anyway, that's the Greeks."

Across the street in front of the Luxembourg the same dark-skinned character who had accosted Chloe was following a woman pushing a baby carriage. He was whispering things into her ear. Her face was flushed crimson and she kept trying to move to the side, away from him. But she couldn't abandon the carriage.

Patiently Annie looked from this scene to Chloe, who was shaking her head. Annie could see why Chloe felt the way she did about Arabs. It had been programmed into her head, as it was programmed into French mentality. Engrained, just as back home people were wary of blacks. Chloe was not wary of blacks because no one had taught her to be.

"Look at that fucking pig. They're like dogs in heat," Chloe said. "No wonder you're having a good time."

Prejudice, Annie thought, was not a cut-and-dried thing. Most

North Africans *were* sex-crazed lunatics when let loose in this fast-moving city. But *not* Azzed. Well maybe a little.

Annie sat thinking about the one question she had wanted to ask someone for weeks. Here was the perfect experienced person. Who else was she going to ask?

Speaking softly she said, "Presuming one sleeps with a man," she took a sip of her panachée, "who is, how can I say this? Well endowed, I guess I should say. Do you know what I mean?"

Loudly Chloe said, "No, what do you mean well endowed, what does that mean?"

Annie threw her her best Nun's Look: full of self-righteousness, backed by God himself. Chloe quieted down. This was serious and Annie wanted calm and no jokes.

"Well en-dow-ed," she said between her teeth. "Very big. Would that affect later relationships with men who might not be so big?"

"How big *is* he?" Chloe was completely captivated.

"Well," Annie took her time. "Very big." She certainly was not going to make a measured estimate with her hands, right here on the terrace in front of all these people. "But that's not the point," she said impatiently. "Will I be stretched out forever?"

"What," Chloe asked, "a kielbasa? A squash? What?"

Annie said nothing and shrugged. Chloe seemed flustered.

"Well. We're flexible, aren't we? I mean, no really. Babies come out of there. It goes back to normal. Right? I think."

"I hope so," Annie said. Then she laughed primly.

For posterity's sake, maybe one night she'd whip out a tape measure. Then she'd have figures to resort to. It would lend a sense of reality to the experience, a thing she was still having trouble believing herself.

"Well fuckin-A!" Chloe said. " 'Good-bye and good luck to you on your journey downward,' as my father used to say when he'd throw us into bed."

Annie was proud of herself.

"Let's take another glass," Chloe said. They had invented a series of direct translations, "take a glass" being the newest, for "prendre un verre."

Chloe went into a big-sister number. "My dear, if anything goes wrong, hear me? Anything. Like if he wants to come back to the States in your suitcase or something. You better let me know. Next time if you wait this long to tell me anything I'm going to be really pissed off. I don't know about this trip, man. Geoffrey's tin can on wheels isn't going to get us there and back. Well. Whenever I get bored or depressed I'll think of you and your kielbasa and lift my spirits."

"Yes. Slap me a string as soon as you get back."

That was another one: Translation of "Donne-moi un coup de fil." More simply, "Call me up."

XVIII

They left Cédric's apartment before dawn. Harry broke down at the Porte d'Orléans. They putted through the somber streets to Geoffrey's garage, which fortunately was in the same neighborhood.

Chloe and Vero sat in the car and tried to sleep while Geoffrey and his boss argued over, and fussed and fiddled with, Harry's transmission. Geoffrey arranged a "temporary repair," as he termed it, and by nine A.M. they were off for their second try. Geoffrey had lost some of his confidence and zeal, and decided not to brave the Autoroute du Soleil (out-of-season the fastest way to Marseille) but to head for Orléans and follow the Loire's banks southeast toward its source. Near Lyon they would pick up the Rhône and follow it due south to Avignon. Very scenic, Geoffrey said. And from Avignon, it was just a question of 100 kilometers or so to Marseille.

Along the Loire's less popular southerly stretches, the countryside was flat and quite green. The road was often lined with poplars for kilometers on end, which made it seem like a long, straight, green alleyway. For long stretches they would not pass a car or farm, and it felt to Chloe like they'd reached the end of the civilized world. She fretted that Harry would cough his last breath at any second.

Chloe tried not to think about Harry. She sat with her legs stretched out across the backseat, listening to Geoffrey telling jokes and Vero laughing, and watched the endless procession of vineyards and trees slowly approach as on a conveyor belt, pass the car in a flash, and slowly recede.

She was reminded of the trip to Florida she'd undertaken the spring of her freshman year. She'd gone off in a car with a girl from North Carolina, older and more responsible. On the road she'd been able to dissociate herself from her troubles. She was running from two disastrous affairs—one-night stands that had turned sour on her because the fellows had taken her needy, desperate talk seriously. They had wanted *a relationship,* commitments; she panicked and fled. Up until then she had managed to keep her drunken rampages from infringing on her daytime life. And at home, she'd had her mother who frightened and appalled her. How could one person represent your good conscience and your bad conscience at the same time? The road had forced her to stop momentarily, and think.

The road was doing it again. Sitting in Geoffrey's car she was assailed by the crushing feeling that she had not progressed an inch since then. She had made one big blundering circle of it. So what was all that pain worth? What did it mean? In Paris there was Serge who had treated her like the selfish opportunist she thought she was. There was Dom trying to press her crazy Vladimir on her. He'd taken to visiting Dom at night, then leaving at a certain hour and waiting for Chloe on the street, pacing back and forth, till she came home. And there was still her mother, to whom she still could not write.

The pleasant thing about the road was the temporary relief it brought. The time to breathe and think. When she'd returned to Cromwell after her Florida trip, she'd faced the two fellows and admitted her tendency to rush into things without considering the consequences. She could not love either of them; they didn't have the strength to support her. A month later, she'd met Joe Gillan, who'd come out of nowhere to be her knight and protector.

She realized now with nauseating accuracy that she wanted a new Joe Gillan, and would probably for the rest of her life.

Stupid and happy or intelligent and miserable? Stupid and happy, she decided. It was already, unfortunately, too late.

" 'Herr Bigsby ze great British RAF pilot is here today to tell us about ze var,' the German radio announcer says. 'Herr Bigsby, tell us about ze var, please.' "

She watched the back of Geoffrey's head, his straight, thick hair piled like a haystack. He did Bigsby with a cockney accent.

" 'Well, these fuckers were comin' at us, see—'

'Excuse me, sir, Fokkers. I sink you mean Fokkers, yes?'

'No, no, no. These fuckers were Messerschmitts.' "

Vero threw her head back and laughed and laughed. Her long blonde braid snaked over the back of the front seat. Chloe saw the flush in Vero's cheek. She was happy as could be when Geoffrey paid attention to her.

Geoffrey said, "All my jokes come from my brother-in-law. He's Irish."

They reached Marseille at midnight. Geoffrey had friends from the lycée living there, whom he'd contacted before the trip. They were a young couple, polite and hospitable, and cold. Was it Chloe's imagination? They were probably childhood friends of Estelle's, and here was Geoffrey with two new girls already.

Their apartment was on the outskirts of Marseille, in a modern ten-story building that resembled an American housing project. From their eighth-floor window you could see the twinkling white lights of the harbor. Geoffrey slept between the girls on the shag rug in the living room.

They left Marseille in the early morning and drove through winding, elevated roads toward the port of Cassis. The terrain was rocky and dry and smelled of spices and pine.

In Cassis they toured the old port. There were fishermen tending their nets on the quais who did not look up from their business as the strangers peered down at them. The clear air carried the smell of fish and seaweed. On a diagonal rock at the edge of the port the three sat down to a breakfast of fresh bread, saucisson, Camembert, and Côtes du Rhône wine picked up along the road. Geoffrey took out a Nikon camera and began clicking pictures of the girls sunning on the rock. "You look like lazy seals," he told them. He explained that recently he'd become so involved in photography he'd built himself a darkroom in his mother's apartment.

"You know, ladies, the most interesting thing down here on the coast is not the coast at all but the ancient villages *behind* the coast, in the mountains. We can base ourselves in the villa in Saint-

Tropez, and make our excursions from there. I personally don't find the tourist towns terribly exciting."

"Neither do I," Vero added quickly. She was so ready to agree with Geoffrey on all issues it was beginning to make Chloe feel like the fifth wheel, the party-pooper, the pain in the ass.

"But still I'd like to see the port of Saint-Tropez, since we're here. And Cannes too. I want to go to the beach."

"Sure, we'll do all that," Geoffrey said. He took a bite of cheese and a swig of wine. "You know, around here we can buy wine by the litre and keep it in the plastic vat you might have noticed in the back of the car, which I brought along expressly for that purpose. We can get the best local wine around for four francs or so a litre, and drink like kings for a pittance. Nothing like getting schlocked cheaply."

Vero's lovely bourgeois family's villa was not in Saint-Tropez proper, but a little farther down the coast in a compound of summer villas built on a hill overlooking the sea. It was one of twenty identical one-story brick houses with a grass deck in front and driveway in back.

All the rooms had tile floors. The main room had a fireplace, and iron furniture with plastic cushions. There were two bedrooms, one with a double bed, one with a single. The grass deck overlooked the private beach and jetty, which you could see from the dining table through the sliding glass doors.

They had filled the vat at a local winery and shopped for food in the open market of a tiny village they had passed through. In the early evening Vero and Chloe cooked, making do in the sparse kitchen, while Geoffrey sat at the dining table pondering over his maps.

The villa was cold and Geoffrey built a fire. A red glow illuminated the room. According to Chloe this was very near camping. They could have been in a brick cave whose mouth overlooked the sparkling aquamarine sea.

They drank a good deal of wine with dinner. Their drinking didn't put a dent in the ten-litre vat. Geoffrey kept adding logs to the fire. Vero sat across the table from Chloe, facing the fireplace. She was cutting dainty patterns out of notebook paper she'd found in a kitchen drawer.

With the heat at her back and her head filled with wine, Chloe felt something beginning to break apart and give way in her chest. Something resembling a terrible congestion. She did not understand it, but feared she would break down and weep, and in the rush of it, would completely lose control. Keeping control had been so terribly important till now. She looked at Geoffrey who was smoking a Gauloise, taking deep drags and exhaling slowly so that in the glow he seemed on fire inside. She was thinking about Estelle, certain all at once that he'd married her to fill some bottomless pit in his life. He and Chloe were dangerously similar. But all this was silly philosophizing because the bottom line was he *did* love Estelle. Whatever the reason. She wondered if philosophy kept people sane, or if it ended up making them crazy.

"My mother says people are never *really* crazy until they permit themselves to be. They give up, and let go." She said this as though it were profoundly related to what they had been talking about. She could not remember what that was.

Vero looked up from her cutting. The yellow flames flickered in her eyes. "It's *easy* to become crazy. Have you ever listened to real crazies? They're so convincing. I guess if they can make you believe them, that makes you crazy too. Or it makes *them* sane." She shrugged, went back to her cutting. She had a child's package of felt coloring pens on the table, which she'd also found in her rummaging. She began to color her dainty patterns.

"What do you mean?" Chloe pursued.

"I have a crazy cousin," Vero sighed like an old grandmother about to embark on a long tale. This was a real campfire night.

"He was in the booby hatch in England for a few years, that's where my aunt and uncle live. He's a couple of years older than me. My parents told me before I left the States, Watchit, because Al's out now, and if he finds out you're in Paris, he'll try to track you down. They don't want me hanging with him at all, see. He used to do all sorts of drugs. He was a good musician. Real good, lots of potential. He totally fucked himself up.

"So he tracks me down. He calls up my parents' friends in Boulogne, tells them he's a friend of Vero's from Santa Cruz, they give him the old lady's address. This was way before she died. So he shows up at the old lady's, gives me this honest-to-God-I-swear-this-is-true story. Al has these huge blue eyes . . ." Vero opened her eyes wide. "Full of life or energy or something. He tells me he's in Paris to meet Mick Jagger. Mick's giving him a contract on the Rolling Stones label, for some songs Al's written with his band. Mick's got to meet him in Paris for the final deal because in London he's got tax problems. They're meeting at the Ritz. Mick's going to show up either tonight or tomorrow morning. Al doesn't want to look cheap in front of Mick. Right now Al's got no cash or cards, so would I go with him and book him a room, wait with him till Mick shows up and pays him. Al's going to pay me right back for the room and everything. AND, I get to meet Mick Jagger. I say to myself, this does *not* sound too cool; but what the fuck? One day at the Ritz. And maybe it's true? I put it on my dad's Visa card that he gave me for total emergencies. We stayed there for three days. We never left the room."

Vero stopped, looked from Geoffrey to Chloe. They waited for her to go on.

"Al ordered up champagne and caviar and foie gras and Lord, I don't know what-all. Real straight he says to me, over and over, Mick's been delayed. He keeps calling this number, talks to Mick's agent. Three days pass and he keeps it up. I really believed him by then. Then on the third day the cops come up and drag Al away. He'd really been calling someone at Rolling Stones records, who finally called the police. And the Ritz called my dad.

"I went back to the old lady's like nothing had happened. I get a letter from my folks telling me maybe I should come home. Maybe the country's getting to me or something. See, I always liked Al. Always had a wicked crush on him. He's so cute, man. With those eyes, I swear. I went nuts. I really did." She seemed frightened.

Geoffrey exhaled a long vertical stream of smoke. "You were in Paris alone for the first time. In that awful old apartment with that crippled old lady. You were off your ground. It makes sense." He shrugged.

Chloe thought this was much too weird, even for her. Weirder than Serge or Dominique.

"That's like my best friend Franck and me," Geoffrey said in a conversational way. "He's very convincing when he pats me on the shoulders and says it's his sworn duty as godfather to my son, and my best friend, to watch over my wife. And like a complete asshole I believe him. Oh but Franck's not crazy at all. I'm crazy."

Chloe said, "I have fantasies that I'm back at Cromwell in one of those nice two-story New England, off-campus houses, raising a kid, happily married. It would be so nice. Joe's friends would respect me. I'd have enough money. You know sometimes I'm absolutely sure I've made a terrible terrible mistake." She felt her countenance crumbling.

Geoffrey was staring at her. "Either way," he said somberly, "some people spend their lives trying to self-annihilate." Then he laughed gleefully. "We're all batshit!"

"I'm going to get over it," Chloe said. Thinking, in the long run, that Geoffrey and she could only be detrimental to each other.

The three were laughing. Vero said in her sweet, self-effacing way, "We're the blind leading the blind. What a riot."

She had finished her coloring and handed each of them a crown. Each had its own delicate, intricate curving points and colors. Geoffrey's was yellow and red, Chloe's blue and green, Vero's brown and orange.

"For the king, the queen, and the *valet,*" she said.

"Who's the *valet?*" Chloe asked, sorry as soon as she'd said it.

"Me." Vero got up from the table and sauntered off with her sleeping bag under her arm. Geoffrey had placed his crown on top of his head. He poured more wine into two glasses. The wine in the vat looked thick and black as blood. In the glasses it had the shimmer of rubies.

"It's because of fucking Estelle that I'm having these Goddamn fantasies," Chloe said. "Ever since you took me to her apartment. How cozy her life is. You're the one who got fucked, my man." She hated the nasty twist in her tone.

"I got fucked," he agreed. And she didn't like the way he always agreed with her. She wished he'd fight back. He stared at the dying fire. There was a red square on each of his lenses.

She was getting rip-roaring drunk. She kept thinking, maybe I'll pass out before I explode. The more she drank, the more she felt like a dam with a large crack in its wall, spreading, the concrete giving way.

"We could help each other," Geoffrey said.

"The hell we could." She got up, tottering, and went off to find her bed. Sleep it off, block it out. The cold of the rest of the house was a slap in the face. Vero was not in the double bed. Chloe pushed at the door to the single room. It was locked. Fuck you, she thought, and kicked it. Back in the room with the double bed, she fumbled with her sleeping bag, laid it out, and crawled in fully dressed. She pulled its rim tight around her head. Let the fucker try to get in here.

She could not get herself to ask him to sleep on the bare floor. Like a specter he approached, making no sound. He lay down beside her. Later on, in his sleep, he placed a light arm over her middle. He pressed into her during the night. She woke up in the fetal position with the weight of him against her back.

*　*　*

The next day Vero acted like a martyr. Chloe found the first possible occasion to inform her that she and Geoffrey had not had sex. Vero seemed disappointed.

They spent the day touring ancient villages set high up on top of rocky mountains. There were castle ruins and defunct wineries, all covered with weeds and vines. Often, walking slowly through a silent village, Chloe felt a desire to cry. It was the quiet beauty of the village square with its center well, and solemn church. The villagers paid no attention to them, the tourists. Everything went on in its undisturbed way, as it had for centuries.

In Ramatuelle, at the edge of a cliff Geoffrey and Chloe stood looking down into the dry valley. He said, "I've always found such spiritual uplifting from being on the road. This time it's even better because you're here. I feel my spirit returning. I'm an incurable romantic." Looking out, he added as an afterthought, without malice, "I wish Vero weren't with us."

Chloe suddenly thought that he might think she would not sleep with him because of Vero being there. In a flash of nausea quite like seasickness she saw that this threesome was quite unsound. It passed.

"I won't sleep with you, Geoffrey," she said evenly. "It has nothing to do with her."

"But can we share a bed?"

"That's up to Vero." Chloe would much rather, she realized, sleep with her. But Chloe was angry at Vero because of last night.

Vero had gone ahead into the village, singing softly to herself. She was removing herself, to give her imaginary lovers space.

Chloe spent the rest of the day trying to convince her that she had the situation completely wrong.

Vero refused to relinquish her position in the single room. For three days they toured the countryside, returning at night with food to the cold house. Bedtime was an uncomfortable moment. But Vero always retired first, to the single bed. Chloe thought that Vero had stubbornly decided, since she wanted Geoffrey and could not have him, that Chloe should have him completely. The more she thought about this the angrier she became. By the time they got to Saint-Tropez on their last day, Chloe and Vero were barely speaking to each other. Saint-Tropez was a letdown. The quais of the harbor were crowded with Beautiful People out walking their adorable children and dogs. The port was crammed full of glorious yachts that made you feel unworthy.

There were sidewalk painters and jewelry vendors just like in Paris. None of the art was any good. Chloe was again reminded of Serge. She wanted to escape quickly, and return to the solitude of the villa, and the ancient unspoiled villages.

Geoffrey's mother owned a thirteenth-century farmhouse near Brive, on the border of the Périgord and Auvergne regions. The family was renovating the farmhouse stone by stone, and Geoffrey had told his mother he and his friends would be coming by to help out shortly before Easter.

To get to Brive, Geoffrey drove through the Massif Central.

The road wound and curved along the mountain's edge. Below the car, beyond the white posts that demarcated the edge of the road the valley dropped into a void. The car could manage 20 kilometers per hour on the uphill slants. Chloe sank below the window in the backseat. Vero, in front with Geoffrey, sang courageously in her pretty voice. Vertigo, along with agoraphobia, was one of Chloe's recent afflictions.

They drove through Roquefort cheese country, where sheep grazed on the rocky, undulating land, and then down into the gorges of the Tarn River. Down a forty-five degree incline that could not fit more than a single car going in either direction. Chloe had visions of the brakes giving out, of her life ending at the bottom of the dark blue river. Her mother would never know. Her mother would think she had run away forever, and die in guilt and misery. Chloe decided that if they lived through this expedition, she would find the first opportunity to call her mother and at least explain . . .

It was almost Easter. The lilacs would be budding at home.

They drove along the river, with a straight rock wall to their right. Chloe asked Geoffrey to slow down. You could not see around the bends and the road was too thin. Geoffrey laughed and Vero laughed. From the back window Chloe watched the dark foaming river below her. It made a sound like a waterfall.

Across the river the grey rock rose to unimaginable heights. At times a patch of green, an angled cluster of grapevines appeared. And then like a mirage there was a village at the river's edge, emerging out from the rock like Michelangelo's *Slaves;* somber, subdued, and eternal. In the car no one had spoken.

"My God, what do they eat? What do they live on?" Chloe whispered.

"Fishing, agriculture, I suppose," Geoffrey said.

"Agriculture! It's all rock. There's nothing."

Vero turned to her. "Up top," she pointed, as though she were reminding Chloe and her question had been ridiculous. It pinched her heart.

* * *

It was pitch black outside by the time they reached the farm. The air was damp and quite a bit cooler there than it had been on the coast. The golden light coming through the small windows of the farmhouse reminded Chloe of childhood fairytales of lost children finding shelter with good peasants. Inside the house a fire was going, and over the logs in the fireplace Mrs. Creeger was stirring lentil stew in a cast-iron pot.

The walls of the old farm were made of stone slabs, the roof was thatched, held up by diagonal beams. Mrs. Creeger looking up from her stew, explained that the work on the place had not come along as fast as she'd hoped. The renovations were being done by the family only, and it was so hard to coordinate vacations. Chloe gazed about the room in her near-catatonic state. They had traveled all day through that hazardous terrain, and her thoughts more than once had turned to her mother, who in an emergency would not be able to find her. Chloe had left Paris like a gypsy, with a romantic and childish desire to prove she could get along perfectly well on her own.

As she looked about the room all her hopes of finding a phone were destroyed. There was a metal sink against the far wall, and wood shelving beside the sink. A butcher-block partition split the room, and between it and the fireplace was a large oval table that could seat ten. A fine coat of plaster dust covered everything. There was no stove or refrigerator, and certainly no phone. Chloe felt like a dumb tourist American. She would not mention the phone until she had a better idea of the situation. She could not bear the thought of sounding like an ingrate to Mrs. Creeger, whom she held in awe. This was left over from Chloe's time in school, when Mrs. Creeger had permitted the student's imaginations to run wild in an attempt to tap that energy and turn it to good use. This method of teaching had worked particularly well with Chloe, who held, from her father, an aversion to restraint.

Just before they sat down to dinner a young man with a mass of black hair and glasses came through the door. He looked about at the new guests, nodded, and sat down at the table without saying a word. "Hello, Luke," Geoffrey said. Luke nodded again. "These are my friends," Geoffrey went on. No response. To the girls, "This is my brother Luke."

After dinner Luke took the plates to the sink. Chloe tried to intervene but he shook his head. Until they crossed the yard to the barn to sleep, Luke went about his business and paid no attention to anyone, including his mother.

He did not say hello when they arrived, and did not say good-bye when they left a week later. After a day Chloe asked Geoffrey if his brother was mute. Geoffrey said no, Luke was just shy.

In the barn there were three beds, one of them Luke's. Vero appropriated a double bed and got into her sleeping bag without a further word. Chloe slipped in beside her and called goodnight to Geoffrey in the dark.

The girls were given odd jobs around the farm. The first morning they raked and then broke up old dried branches for firewood. While Chloe stood raking the area by the barn, Vero approached her from behind. A little way up the hill Geoffrey and Luke and their mother were plowing a small field.

"I can't understand the way you treat him," Vero started in a low voice. "He loves you so much, you *act* like you love him, and then you lead him on."

Chloe stopped raking and turned to her. She was so taken aback she did not know how to respond.

"You don't understand, Vero," she said. It seemed such an ironic shame that this ridiculous romantic notion of Vero's should ruin their friendship, which Chloe had deemed far more important.

"We are not interested in each other in a sexual way. Can't you see that he's all scarred up? I am too."

"I don't get you," Vero shook her head solemnly. "If *you* can't see that he's in love with you, you're blind. You know, you're the only person I know that has everything. EVERYthing in the world. And you're still not happy."

Chloe thought she might hit her. She was squeezing the rake in her blistered hands. When that desire passed, she wanted to shake Vero and hug her and plead with her to understand. Jealousy was not by instinct part of Chloe's nature. She couldn't imagine how she might have caused it in this person she thought she knew and trusted so well. She did not think Geoffrey, or anybody else for that matter, was worth their friendship. But it seemed Vero had already decided otherwise.

"Oh Vero, how can you say that?" Chloe said. She felt betrayed, her hurt turning to anger. "I thought our friendship was clean of this kind of shit."

"But I'm in love with him," Vero started to cry.

"Vero he's still in love with his wife."

"I would try to get him over it if he wanted me," she said in her childish voice, full of hurt.

"People always seem to want what they can't have," Chloe said, "like babies. We're a bunch of babies."

She felt a dead weight in the pit of her stomach. Everything crumbled to that spot. She did not even want to cry over it, and turned her back on Vero and went to rake the far end of the rickety yard.

In the afternoon she climbed the hill to where Mrs. Creeger was planting potatoes. Chloe felt uneasy because she was getting tired of the manual work, and Mrs. Creeger never seemed to tire. She seemed to thrive on hard work. It was not a big field and its soil was

rutty and dry. Mrs. Creeger was wearing a large straw hat and her
sleeves were rolled up past the elbows. Under the hat Chloe could
only see the tip of her largish nose, which was Geoffrey's nose
exactly. Mrs. Creeger was taking her time, moving with difficulty
on her hands and knees, stuffing the potato halves in the soil with
her dry brown hands.

"It's late to be planting potatoes," she said, musing aloud. Her
voice was gentle and frail. "Usually I come down around Saint
Patty's Day. But this year I simply did not have time."

Chloe crouched, and Mrs. Creeger handed her a fistful of potato
halves from the burlap sack. Chloe had an aunt back in Pennsylva-
nia. This aunt on her mother's side was like Mrs. Creeger, always
fixing, cleaning, painting, building, making butter, milking cows,
all for amusement. One summer Chloe's mother used to watch for
the aunt from the window of their rented house. When she saw
Aunt Ellie's car approaching, she'd shout, "Everybody run, here
comes your aunt with something new to do!" And they'd hide and
giggle and wait till she left.

Being productive was a wonderful quality that tended to make
Chloe feel like a guilty bum.

"Mrs. Creeger, I want to call my mother."

Mrs. Creeger looked up from under the rim of her hat. She
handed Chloe another bunch of potatoes.

"I hope nothing is wrong," she said evenly.

Chloe wondered how much she knew about her relationship
with Geoffrey, if she knew Vero was in love with him. Maybe she
knew nothing at all and didn't care. Or maybe it was all plain as
day to everyone but Chloe.

"Nothing's wrong at all. You see, I thought it would be good to go
off from Paris without letting anyone know where I was going to
be. Now I regret it. I think it's the first time in my life my mother
doesn't know where I am."

This seemed to surprise Mrs. Creeger. "How *is* your mother?"
she asked.

"I suppose she's fine. I hope she's fine." Chloe was embarrassed.
"We've been having a bad time of it. Since my dad died." Chloe
flushed. Some people reacted badly to that word. But she knew no
other way to put it.

Mrs. Creeger nodded slowly, looking straight at Chloe with her pale blue eyes. "I know mothers grow to regret many things too," she said. She'd say no more. They went on planting. A while later she said, "I'll drive you into Brive this afternoon. We have a post office in town here, just a few kilometers away, but I'm afraid the lines are continually down. It's even difficult to call Paris."

Chloe thought it would be better not to think about what she would say to her mother. As before a performance she'd had to stop herself from thinking about it, or she would get stage fright.

The old lady behind the counter wrote down the number. Chloe, standing on her toes and gripping the counter top could barely see the top of the woman's grey head. She sat and waited to be paged to one of the booths. Her mind drifted off to Mrs. Creeger and their silent drive into town. Chloe wondered what Mrs. Creeger thought of her son being married, of the grandson who'd been forced upon her weekends. These were not things they could talk about. Chloe thought Mrs. Creeger was saintly. She imagined that most normal people, like herself, could not feel totally at ease around saints.

The woman called out Raymond from behind her counter. Chloe was directed to enter booth number 5. She pulled the door shut and said "Hello?" in a bewildered way.

"Hello?" her mother said.

"It's me, Mama! You wouldn't believe where I am!" She tried to explain but suddenly it seemed irrelevant.

"When are you coming home?"

"Mama, is everything all right?" she yelled. Her mother sounded like a voice on a car radio with bad reception.

"Will you come home soon?"

"School's not out yet." Her mother never seemed to know what month it was, when her children's exams were; all the things crucial in their lives seemed arbitrary to her.

"Darling, listen. Eric told me you wrote him two lovely letters. I'm sorry about the way I handed you that check. I didn't mean what I said about you being on your own. This is *your* house as much as it's mine."

Chloe laughed nervously. "I know, Mama."

"Darling, I promise if you come home I'll spoil you rotten for the rest of my life. OKAY?"

"Mom, I'll come home as soon as school's out. We haven't even had our exams yet! Can you hear me? I'll come home SOON."

"Yes, darling," her mother said. "Where are you?"

Chloe tried again. "This place is unbelievable, it's like the beginning of the world it's so old!"

"I saw Andy in the street. He asked if I knew when you were coming back. I felt like an idiot. He probably knows more about what you do than I."

Chloe's heart beat faster. She wanted to be there with all of them, she wanted to see Andy and her brother out drinking together.

"I miss you, Mama!" she said.

"I thought I was going to die without you," her mother said. The line began to crackle. They yelled at each other. When Chloe hung up her blood was pulsating. She sat down in the booth. It was too hot. She went out into the blinding sun and sat on the post office steps. She waited for Mrs. Creeger to come back from her shopping. Across the square there was a wedding procession entering the church. She blinked the tears out of her eyes. She felt as she had when she'd realized she was in love with Joe. That they were not nearly out of the woods. A whole long slew of mutual compromises would have to follow. She was exhausted.

They did a good deal of exploring in the next few days. There were caves to see, and fortress towns built in the twelfth and thirteenth centuries. The tension between Vero and Chloe did not ease. Chloe had gone back to sharing a bed with Geoffrey, who did not attempt to make love to her. She was grateful to him for that and many other things.

On their last evening, after a long dinner and much wine, Chloe decided to go for a walk up the bumpy dirt road. She felt the congestion giving way again, slipping out of her control. Outside the air was crisp and the stars shone coldly in the sky. She wondered what stars her mother would be seeing from the garden, and if the trees would be green yet. She wanted to make it home in time to see the lilacs.

She found a large rock to sit on. There was nothing for miles but the rolling land and the deep sky. She felt small, and nostalgic for all the things she had lost, the things she'd never had, and would probably never find.

She heard footsteps coming up the road. Vero appeared out of the night and sat beside her on the rock.

After a long silence Vero said, "I've decided not to go with you up to Brittany."

"What?"

"It's better."

"Well what are you going to do?"

"I have an old boyfriend in Lyon; I'm going to hitch up there tomorrow morning."

"But you can't hitch alone!" Chloe said in dismay. All at once she exploded from within, and large uncontrollable sobs rose out of her chest. She wept like a mad person with her face in Vero's lap. Not another word was said.

In bed that night, calmed and sleepy, she felt Geoffrey suddenly very close. As his mouth approached her face, she became frightened.

He whispered in her ear, "It's such a pity that we could not love each other together."

Chloe whispered back, "But we *do* love each other. You have no idea, Geoffrey, you've helped me more than you could ever know . . ."

* * *

The next morning they drove Vero to Tulle. Geoffrey asked her over and over if she were certain this was what she wanted to do, mentioning how dangerous it was for a girl to hitchhike alone. Vero wasn't listening. Chloe watched her slip on her backpack with the sleeping bag attached to the bottom of it, the movement causing her braid to slide and fall from her shoulder. In her jeans and hiking shoes she looked like a hippie. They had had one shower in ten days, at the municipal baths in Brive. Chloe didn't feel dirty at all.

Geoffrey made a U-turn. Chloe watched Vero through the back window, walking slowly toward the highway with her head down. She stopped and turned once, but did not wave. Chloe held up her hand, then dropped it. She was certain she would never see Vero again.

They passed a gourmet store with a red awning that displayed regional specialties in the window. Chloe asked Geoffrey to stop. She bought Dominique a large mason jar of round green prunes preserved in eau-de-vie. There was a big red bow tied around the top of the jar which she thought was very pretty. Vero would have approved.

They drove northwest for several hours, in complete silence. In Cognac, she asked him to stop once again, this time in front of a liquor store. She bought Dominique a bottle of Cognac.

"Thanks," she said. And they were silent again.

She wondered how difficult it would be to find her old Spanish nanny in Paris. She would go to the last address she had for Candida, and ask from there. It was time. And in the phone book she might look up the names of her old schoolmates, the few who may not have moved away. There were so many things she had to do. She was tired of feeling as though she were running late to catch a train. She thought she could forever be running late, and the train would always be about to leave, but never gone. And that was the nice thing about living. You could fix what you'd messed up. Unless you killed somebody.

"So tell me," she said, trying to sound lighthearted, "what exactly do you study at the fac? What's Physics?"

"The study of atoms, basically. You're a poet by nature. For example, you say, "the grass is green like an emerald sea." You try to describe it. I study *why* the grass is green. It's not really green at all. Its molecular structure makes it seem green to us."

"What?"

"If you think of it this way, nothing is real."

"Oh fuck you."

"Didn't you study the atom in high school?"

"Sure. But I failed the class."

"Would you like me to explain?"

"How long will it take?"

"Depends on how smart you are."

"Go ahead. Before you start, let me just warn you that I still don't know my multiplication tables past the twos."

For the next eight hours, while Chloe began to feel the old pinch and pull in her lower stomach which she'd by then stopped hoping for, Geoffrey explained the atom.

Andy

Summer and Christmas Vacations, 1980

Andy opened the fridge and leaned in, reaching for his orange juice as the phone on the counter decided to ring. The jolt made him drop the carton but he caught it before it spilled out on the floor.

"Yo, Ben!" he yelled angrily, "come get the phone!"

Ben came grumbling from the bathroom, half undressed. He was still in his sweatpants and had a towel hanging like a scarf around his neck.

"What the fuck, you the king now or what?" He slid the towel from his shoulders and snapped Andy in the ass with it. Grabbing the phone first by its cord, he picked up the receiver and said, "YEAH?"

Andy stood by drinking his OJ from the carton, waiting to find out who it was. He had been avoiding the phone and the local hangouts for a week, until last night when his idiot brother and basketball buddies had convinced him to hit the bars. Today was Chloe's due-date back, and Andy did not intend (especially after last night), even in his zeal, to blow it now by running to the phone every time it rang. Because it could easily be the other one, the one he had been hiding from, calling to apologize for punching him in the face; or calling to demand further explanation, which Andy knew she deserved. He was a basic shit. You're a shit, he told himself.

Ben covered the receiver and passed it to Andy at once: "It's

Clo." He shook his head disapprovingly, great authority that he was. Andy grabbed the phone from him.

"Hi," he said, trying to sound nonchalant and failing miserably. His throat was parched and his tongue felt like sandpaper. He coughed silently.

"Andy!" she said happily. He had never imagined that hearing her voice would make his heart beat so.

"It's so good to finally talk to you!" she said. He was suddenly so pleased he wanted to laugh aloud, but Ben's shadow just a foot behind him put a nasty twist on the feeling.

"Andy, I'm back!" she said.

"I'm psyched," he said. He thought he sounded like a mortician. But she was never put off by his inability to express himself. He felt desire rising in him like two small hands, one tickling his balls while the other gripped furiously at his throat.

"Listen, my mom did a number on me; she's having a dinner party tonight. To celebrate me being back. Will you come?" She waited.

Andy envisioned the dinner party at the long kitchen table, red candles burning at each end, glowing guests who spoke a different American than he understood. He would have to sit there, next to her probably, and wait his turn which would come afterwards, when they went out. First he'd have to listen to Chloe answer questions about life in Paris, and he'd be thinking grimly and weakly about his own radical infidelity, that little girl saying *I LOVE you, Andy,* tasting the words for the first time—and Chloe, lying in ecstasy under some suave and graceful Frenchman.

"No," he answered flatly. "Ben and I got a game down at the high school. We'll be done around ten."

He glanced over his shoulder at Ben who was, again, shaking his head. Andy shot him the finger. They had just come back from their game and Andy's sweats had turned cold and clammy.

"Well that's a fucking good start," Ben mumbled.

"What was that?" Chloe said.

"Nothing, Ben's talking about the game."

"Tell him hi and give him a kiss," she said.

"Fuck the kiss," Andy said, feeling better that she was not angry with him.

"Listen," he said, "okay if I come by at ten?"

He got potted on beer with Ben in front of the TV, waiting for ten o'clock.

"What're you gonna do if she wants to go down to the Beechouse?" Ben said.

"Take her, I guess."

"You know, Bro, there's better ways than this of dealing with this kind of situation."

"Yeah, you're such a fucking expert."

"Yeah, you fucking asshole, you don't call the chick for a week, and then you wonder why she punches you in the face in the middle of the bar in front of everybody."

Yeah, but—Andy was thinking of what to say. Yeah, but—oh fuck. So what? He kept trying to tell himself that; so what? In the old days it wouldn't have meant a shit to him. But that little fragile girl, her skin had the consistency of a just slightly unripe peach.

Yeah, but, for months, MONTHS he's been telling her that the way he felt about Chloe would never, could never change. The girl was too young to understand.

He remembered her as a tiny blonde child with bony legs who used to stand at the corner in front of her house with a red lunchbox dangling from her hand, waiting in the freezing cold for the schoolbus because her brother Lewis, Andy's buddy, wouldn't give her a ride.

"Listen, Linda, I really like you a lot. A whole lot. But you see, I have to wait for Chloe to get back. If she hadn't left, we'd still be together, see." This is what he'd told her. But was it true? He doubted it. He could envision another bleak semester at Sacred Heart, waiting every fucking weekend for Chloe to show up, and she never would . . .

"If she loves you so much and you love her, then why did she go away?" Linda would ask.

"Because things were fucked up for her at school, and it was even worse at home."

No, simply, the kid was just too young. He should never have broken his big-brother vow, and that was a fact.

It had to be every guy his age's dream. She had changed almost overnight from a bony little kid to a slim, long-legged beauty with an almost loping gait, as though she didn't know what to do with her new body; and she had eyes that were almost yellow; they changed shades with the weather, sad eyes that drooped slightly at the corners. She was a walking angel. How could his ego not succumb?

As soon as Andy came through the door, Chloe jumped up from the table and came toward him. He vaguely saw the reddish glow of candles and bright, intent faces turning toward him. He and she were the only ones standing. She brought him toward her mother, who was presiding at the head of the table.

"Hello, Andy," Mrs. Raymond said.

"Hello, Mrs. Raymond."

She said loudly to the whole table—there must have been ten people there—"THIS IS ANDY FLETCHER."

"Here, sit down for a second," Chloe said, squeezing his arm. "I'll get my sweater and we'll go out."

"Darling, are you sure you should go out? You must be exhausted," her mother said. Andy thought, well, that's a first.

"Oh Mom, come on." Chloe flew off and left him stranded; all eyes were upon him, the only one standing.

"Here, sit down for a minute," Mrs. Raymond said. She poured for him, into Chloe's glass, a large amount of rich red wine.

Next to him, on the other side, a greying woman with three pearl necklaces said, "Are you from around here?"

"Yes," he said. *Me and Chloe—Chloe and I?* A running joke through all their letters back and forth. "Chloe and I went to high school together," he said. He could never get it straight, but whatever sounded wrong was right.

Chloe rushed in holding her sweater, a new one he'd never seen. It was white with sequins sewn into a pattern of flowers on the back and sleeves.

"Ready?" she said nervously. He got a good look at her now, since she was the one standing and he was safely in her seat. Her beauty had become healthy. She glowed. The look was so different from Linda's, or anyone else's he knew. It was so powerful he imagined that some men would not feel safe around this kind of beauty. It could shrivel certain cocks he knew of.

And there was something else radically different. But what? He had never been good at details. It was her hair.

Once they were even more safely away from the house and in his car, he said, "Why did you cut your hair?"

Her hand automatically went up to it.

"You don't like it?" she said quickly. "My friend Annie found out that l'Oréal gives free haircuts to volunteers so their beauticians can practice, you know." She laughed in her old, nervous, silly way. He thought of the first time they'd had a date, when they'd driven out to Montauk in the middle of the day.

"Remember the time we went out to Montauk?" she said.

He thought, it is absolutely necessary that I tell her about Linda right now, before she guesses it. She had an uncanny ability to read through him like nobody else could.

"Andy, I missed you so much. You can't believe how strange it is to be in a strange place where habits are different. You wouldn't beLIEVE what happened to me. I'll tell you something, when Eric comes home from school he's going to hear about it, and some serious ass is going to be kicked . . ."

He was only half listening as she told him about a night she'd been attacked by three very rich boys.

"One of them hangs out here during the summer sometimes. I swear, Andy, I almost got raped."

He heard rape and was suddenly overwhelmed by a violent nausea: How could she let herself be so far away from him that she'd be subjected to such traumas? Why couldn't he BE there to prevent these things?

"Jesus CHRIST," he said.

He wanted to tell her everything about Linda to fill the gap time had made. But what if it enlarged the gap? He was ridden with anxiety and kept his mouth shut.

"Where do you want to go?" he asked her.

He hoped she would say *anywhere,* and then he could decide anywhere but the Beechouse bar, which was where Linda had punched him in the face the night before.

"Let's go to the Beechouse. Maybe Liz'll be out, and your brother. Let's go there."

Her enthusiasm crippled him.

It's your last night as a free man, Ben had said. *Come on out with the guys.* Had Andy gone to reconnoiter for tonight? He supposed in a way he had. A week earlier he'd received Chloe's last letter: *I know lots of things have happened to us both since I left, but maybe if we try a little we'll be able to work things out. I've missed you terribly.*

At the Beechouse he had gotten nice and drunk, leaning up against the small slit of wall between the ladies' and men's rooms, thinking how everything was going to be just fine as soon as Chloe came back. A dark shadow in the back of his mind kept reminding him that he had not dealt with the situation in a clean way: One two three. He should have said, Chloe's coming back in a week, we had a good time, Linda, but now it's over. OVER. Instead of avoiding her the way he had.

Then he saw Linda split from the crowd at the end of the bar and approach him. *She should not be in here!* he thought in outrage, *she's only seventeen!* He felt as though someone had poured a bucket of ice water over his head. He wanted to run but could not move, and looked around desperately for Ben. Nowhere in sight.

She stood in front of him, smiling in that sad, droopy-eyed way. "Where have you been?" she said sweetly. This wiped him out.

"Linda, Chloe's coming home tomorrow."

"What are you going to do about it?" Linda asked. She seemed panicked now and he felt absolutely sick.

"Chloe and me are going to try to work things out," he said flatly. He had not meant to sound so flat.

He couldn't believe he hadn't seen it coming, her little white fist shooting toward his cheek. It stung badly. He rubbed the spot as they stood staring at each other. Then she turned and disappeared in the crowd. He could not move from the wall, could look no one in the eyes.

"Oh, Andy!" Chloe leaned over the shift and kissed him wetly on the neck. "I'm so happy to be with you."

They had not sworn fidelity. Clearly she would not be angry at him for that. But she probably would shoot him for the way he'd dealt with it.

"Did you fuck a lot of girls while I was gone?"

"A few," he said evenly.

"Andy, I was very nuts for a while. I stopped getting my period completely. I wrote you that, didn't I?"

"Yes."

"Do you think we could pretend I never went away?"

"Yeah, just don't tell me about the guys you screwed over there."

She laughed heartily. "I didn't screw anybody!"

He did not believe her.

The Beechouse was not crowded yet though this did not seem to help the smoke much. The place could have been on fire.

They took a table not too near the dance floor and ordered drinks from a waitress who didn't look over sixteen. Andy looked around nervously, trying to keep low while Chloe talked.

"I was a stranger over there. It was weird at first because I didn't used to be a stranger there before."

The Beechouse suddenly seemed sad to him. The two of them were out of place now. This year the crowd seemed younger to him than it had the year before. The girls especially. He wondered who let them in. He felt his own age, too. The basketball games tolled heavily on his lower vertebrae, and on his legs, which never used to hurt him. He knew no one in the bar, though he sometimes saw a young face go by that suddenly seemed familiar; a younger brother or sister of someone he'd gone to school with, a basic clone of the older one. They were frightening. Chloe's mood lulled. She asked him if he knew where to get some coke. She had money left and wanted to blow it all in one shot. He found it depressing that she'd thought of coke, because maybe she was bored with him.

A while later, after they'd bought the coke, he brightened up quite a lot. They were toasting to shots, interlocking arms, and everything was all right when he spotted Linda leaning against his slit of wall between the bathrooms.

Chloe watched him watch Linda. Linda seemed sick she was so pale. Chloe looked over her right shoulder.

"Who's that?" she asked, looking back at him intently.

"Linda Abrams," he said, his voice steady. He would let it play itself out because his will was resigned to not fight Chloe's tonight.

"Lewis's little sister? My God, she's absolutely beautiful! I feel so old."

"That's what I said too," he said morosely.

This clicked something off in her, and leaning toward him, she opened her mouth as if to speak, but didn't. They sat in silence a few moments, and then she looked over her shoulder at Linda again.

"Andy?" she said lightly. "What's going on? Why is she staring at me like that, like she hates me?" He knew it was a terrible thing for her, to feel hated by people she didn't even know. It made her feel bad, that she was a bad person. But Chloe was thinking more particularly of Vero, because Linda reminded her of Vero. She had those same sad eyes that said, Why are you doing this to me?

"Does she do coke?" Chloe said.

"Yes."

"Give me the coke, then," she said. Coke was a perfect prideful way to approach somebody. It was no skin off your ass if you got rejected. Andy handed her the packet under the table.

"Be right back," she said.

He watched her go toward the bathrooms. He wanted to call her back and explain everything himself. Wasn't it a complete joke on him, he thought angrily, that what he loved the most about Chloe was what kept fucking him up? She always had the balls to face people head-on, the way he didn't. Chloe said something to Linda, Linda nodded, and the two of them went into the ladies' room.

Andy sat at the table and waited, considering the possibilities. He should escape right now. What could they be doing in there? They could be having a scratching fight.

He went to the bar and hid among the people. Ben, as usual, was never around when he was needed. Andy didn't know how long he stood there, how many people he talked to, or how many whiskeys he drank.

Later he felt a hand on his waist. It was Chloe back from the bathroom. She was not disheveled and there was no blood. Relief.

"That little girl is wrecked, Andy. I told her this didn't sound like you at all. Listen, if you've been seeing her just because you were lonely or something, she deserves an explanation, I—"

"Let's go outside."

They went out to the veranda and sat at a round table under a tree. The night was damp and chilly, but above the branches was a completely clear, brilliant sky.

"What'd she tell you?" He was furious and defensive now. It had taken the time to get to the table from the bar for him to decide that he'd just about had enough of all of it.

"She told me she loves you terribly, but you love me and I love you so there's no problem. That you spent lots of time together while I was away, in New York mostly, at Lewis's. She said you talked about me all the time."

"And what else?"

Chloe watched him. "That you didn't sleep together. Did you sleep together?"

He wondered if Linda had told her but Chloe wanted to hear it from him, or if Linda had more class than that and hadn't told her a thing. He gambled.

"No."

"Do you love her?"

"Not like that."

"But you might if I didn't exist. No wonder she wants me dead."

"Listen," he said. He took her hand and held it on the tabletop. "I laid a few girls up at school while you were gone. It didn't mean a shit to me. I've been waiting for you till I'm sick in the guts. Do you understand? Linda's a nice girl. I like her a lot. Please, please forget about it. You're back and that's all that matters to me."

"I think you fucked her. Because if you didn't, why would she be so wiped out? I think you fucked her and then didn't know how to get out of it when you found out I was coming back."

He tried to stare her down. They both looked away at the same time.

"Now *why* couldn't I be wrong for once in my life?" she said. Andy had to laugh.

It was so nice to be back in her soft white bed, with the curtains flapping above them and the pine tree swaying just the slightest bit, right outside. It was as though they were making love for the first time, shyly, even, and Andy made her turn out the light.

Afterwards he lay with his arms crossed above his head, and she placed her chin in the hairs on his chest. He could tell she was looking at him through the darkness.

"You know what I think? I think you do love her and don't even know it. If you'd told me right off, I wouldn't have thought it meant anything to you. But obviously it means a lot to you. I know you, Andy. God, I'm so jealous."

"I was scared," he said. A tear that he had not been expecting slipped out of his eye.

"See, what's wrong is that I come back tonight and already you're lying to me. We're covering things up so we can pretend it's still the same."

A second tear came and he did not try to stop it.

"You drive me out of my fucking mind," he said.

"You don't love me anymore."

He could have said yes, he could have said no. Either one would have worked, settled things. All she needed was an answer.

He said, "I don't know."

He knew perfectly well that he loved her and for the first time he understood what she'd gone through last summer, with Joe and himself. He would love her forever and he'd told her so before.

"You're a hero to me," she said quietly. "I think you're the most solid friend I've ever had."

"Oh Goddamnit, Clo, can't you see I'm just so tired of playing second string for you?"

She was immobile, with her head so light on his chest. He breathed and pulled her tightly to him.

"I knew you'd get me back someday," she said. He could barely hear her.

* * *

They moved apart, but without catastrophe. Their sadness was melancholy rather than violent. Once they had agreed to be free of each other, they were able, with a certain amount of discretion, to keep the relationship alive. Andy always felt sad after spending the night with her, but at the same time, as he drove away from her, he felt a great weight being lifted from him. They sometimes talked of getting back together, but both were frightened of committing themselves to promises they might not be able to keep.

For Andy that summer turned into a haze of booze and smoke and nameless girls.

Chloe had taken up roller skating. On Sunday and Wednesday nights you could always find her at the new disco skating rink, gliding around and around on the lacquered floor. Andy did not like to skate much, and spent most of his time watching. It amazed him that she was so good (he'd never thought of her as athletic), but what really killed him was that she skated like a street kid, not like a disco dolly. She'd made friends with a sixteen-year-old boy Andy had watched grow up. The boy was a skateboard champion. She and this kid Buddy skated like roller-derby maniacs, ducking, zigzagging between the people who were trying to learn to dance. Andy had heard that Buddy was teaching her to skateboard in empty pools, and to body surf on blue flag days. People said they were sleeping together. Andy would not put something like that past her, but never asked because he did not want to know.

They wrote back and forth from school. He found it much easier to be romantic by mail. Several times Chloe talked about coming down to see a game, but somehow never got around to it. She was writing a creative thesis which was taking up every minute of her spare time. They saw each other during vacations—on that neutral ground which belonged safely to both of them.

And then, second semester, Andy fell for an olive-skinned Italian gymnast called Maria. The only problem with the relationship was that her parents wanted her to marry a lawyer. Just before Christmas Maria found out she was pregnant. Andy staunchly refused to marry her, and all at once everyone turned against him. Their friends at school, and especially her parents, treated him as though he'd robbed a bank. He tried to persuade her to have an abortion, and she went weeping home to her parents. He drove back to East Whitman alone for Christmas break.

Four days after Christmas he ran into Chloe at the Beechouse Bar. She came in with her brother and another very pretty girl. Once they were settled at a table and the girl and her brother were comfortably engaged in conversation, Chloe left them and walked up to Andy, slowly looking about for enemies as was their custom. She smiled at him as though she'd seen him yesterday and the day before.

"Are you alone?" she asked. They always asked because neither wanted to cause the other trouble.

"I'm with Ben."

They sat together at the bar, talking in monotones. The room seemed empty with twenty people in it. The bartender gave them a free round for good luck.

"So how's your writing going?" Andy asked.

"Okay, I guess. It's a hell of a lot of work, writing a play. How's Maria?"

"She's home with her folks," he said uncomfortably.

Chloe looked at him without blinking. "Is something wrong?"

"She's pregnant."

She took a long sip of her beer.

They did not talk about it anymore. As usual, she knew instinctively what to push and what not to push, and left it up to him to bring it up again.

They talked quietly about easy things; Ben had transferred schools again. Andy's mother had four new dogs. The East Whitman b-ball team had a new star, a six-foot-seven black kid who most certainly would go pro.

Eric came to the bar to tell Chloe he wanted to leave. Andy offered to drive her home. Eric frowned at Chloe for a moment and then shrugged. Andy thought, He should be used to it by now. But brothers are brothers. Chloe kissed Eric on the cheek, Eric blushed. Once he was gone, she squeezed Andy's forearm on the bartop with her left hand.

"Look what Eric gave me for Christmas." On her wedding finger was a deep blue oval sapphire with a diamond on either side.

"Shit, you think you could show that to Ben? I'll take the money, thank you, instead of the ring," Andy said.

Later on they drove down a sandy side road to the beach. The icy wind howled and sent the sand scratching against the window panes. Andy held her hand in his lap. They were silent now and the lonely wind made his bones feel old.

"Clo, I'm freaked out. I can't believe this happened."

"What are you going to do?"

He sighed. "I want her to have an abortion. Her fucking parents hate me. See, I just can't handle getting married right now. Shit, I'm not even out of school." He wondered where he'd be two years from now; six months out of school with a toilet-paper degree in Phys Ed.

"She's acting all kinds of crazy," he said. "One second she wants to get married and the next she's crying and trying to beat me up."

"That's normal," Chloe said. "It's got something to do with her hormones changing. It's got nothing to do with you. People get pregnant, Andy. It's not your fault."

"It *is* my fault." It seemed paradoxical to him that aside from
Ben, Chloe was the only one on his side. They parked at the beach
and watched the waves topple over each other and crash into
foam on the sand. Chloe told him everything she knew about
pregnancy, about the different kinds of abortions and how much
they cost. She did not once throw him a slanty look.

"I feel sick," he said. It was the violence involved, and the guilt
he felt over having been its cause.

He turned the car around and headed back toward the highway.

"You want to stay over tonight? We don't have to sleep together," she said.

He wondered how old they would be before they would have to
stop this. One day she would get married. And probably so would
he. They were friends, but they were also often lovers, and it
seemed a terrible pity to him that they would not be able to invite
each other to their weddings.

Annie

Spring Semester, 1981

"What do you hope to achieve by joining the Peace Corps?" the grey-haired lady asked Annie.

Annie, who'd walked into her interview without the first clue as to what she would say, embarked on a speech that got her so heated up she walked out sweating.

"I spent seven months in Europe last year, you see. One thing that *really* got me was their attitude toward Americans. They think we're imperialistic, selfish, blind—all these things. Well, obviously Americans need desperately to widen their worldview—but the world needs to learn to give us a chance to grow up! I'd like *personally* to help improve our image. I think when students go abroad they're ambassadors, in a way—and just our group, in Paris, well I think we helped improve our image. Honestly, that trip was the *best* learning experience I've ever had (twinge of guilt)." Azzed, she thought, if you could hear me now.

Two weeks earlier she had spotted a green fluorescent poster on the library door: *Sign up for your Peace Corps Interview Now.* Well, why not? She'd gone up to Career Development and signed her name on a sheet, below one Abigail Goldfinch, whom she liked immediately though she had never seen her before.

Annie's interviewer seemed old to be a Peace Corps representative, but Annie liked this. It meant diversity.

"I think one of my major worries would be to learn not to inflict my values on a person from an entirely different culture. But really, what I would like so much is to convince one person—just one would be enough—that Americans *are* concerned, and want to help. Without attempting to colonialize, remold in *our* image, if you know what I mean."

Annie wondered if this old woman thought she was trying to pull her leg. Boy, it really might sound like a crock but she meant every word of it. The interview lasted an hour and a half because the person who'd signed up after Annie did not show up. Annie took this as a sign from above.

She walked around in a fog for three days, wondering why she'd done this, but finally she convinced herself that if, by chance, they accepted her, she would go.

"YOU ARE OUT OF YOUR FUCKING MIND!" Chloe said when she first found out about it. "They're going to send you into the heart of the jungle! HEART OF DARKNESS! DO YOU KNOW WHAT I'M TALKING ABOUT?"

"Well, that's not certain," Annie said primly, sipping at her tea. They were in the kitchen of their little house. "There's the Ivory Coast—wouldn't *that* be nice?"

"What do you think you are, a missionary? They don't need your Christian crap over there."

Annie wondered if living with Chloe had been such a good idea. It was now only February, and they had till June to go.

"Well yes, why not, a missionary! What's wrong with missionaries?" She could definitely see herself as the good Christian that she was, ministering to the poor and sick of the third world.

"Ah, shit. Goody two-shoes at it again," Chloe said, waving Annie off and heading back to her room to work on the twenty-ninth revision of her play.

Annie read *A Bend in the River,* and nasty thoughts kept sneaking up on her. They came in her dreams, or whenever she baked cakes with raisins in them. BUGS! YOU'RE GOING TO BE LIVING WITH THE SPIDERS AND SNAKES AND YOU'LL BE FORCED TO EAT GRUBS AND COCOA-COVERED ANTS!

But then, on the other hand, there was the Ivory Coast, the white sandy beaches and kind smiling natives. And there were the Arab countries, she might end up in Tunisia (Yeah, right, Chloe said, you can set up hut with Azzed). But the fact was they did not usually send white women to Arab countries.

With her luck she would end up in the jungle, surrounded by the only thing she feared in life: BUGS. Well, nobody could ever say she hadn't paid for her good times.

* * *

Le 25 janvier 1981 (Merry New Years, my Love!)

My Love, Annie,

I am so please to tell you I have learned much English. I have passed successfull all my examins. I wish to take all the money I am saving on a visit to your land.

If such a thing is possible, please write me soon. If no I take two weeks in Tunisia with my family.

You are coming back to Paris when you finish university yes?

My heart and dreams are on you always.

Je t'aime toujours,
Azzed.

"My dear girl, he's going to ask you to marry him so that he can become an American citizen." Chloe again. The prospect of having Azzed as a housemate for a month did not thrill her in the least. "I guess from now on we're going to have to wear clothes around here," she grumbled.

She nevertheless lent Annie her car to pick Azzed up at Kennedy airport. Annie got severely lost in the maze of parking lots and arrived a half hour late at the Air France terminal. She found Azzed sitting by a window, hunched over his smallish suitcase and Air France carryon bag. He did not appear nervous or worried at all; in fact he seemed to be having quite a time watching the lady-travelers' legs. When he spotted Annie hurrying toward him, he jumped up and hurdled over his bags, picked her right up off the ground, and swung her about until she had to beg him to stop. She was not one for public displays.

On the way back to Cromwell they almost had an accident on I-95 because he could not keep his hands to himself. She asked him to tell her in English what his plans were, hoping this would keep him occupied for a while. Whenever they passed beneath a road light, she gazed at him to make certain he was truly there. His face had aged slightly and he was even more handsome than before.

The wily look which had terrified her so in Paris now made her laugh. It was so much a part of his charm. He explained his trip to her in his guttural accent:

"I purchased a ticket both ways, good for one year. Ha ha!" He punched her in the arm, she swerved into the left lane. Behind them an angry Porsche blasted its horn. Annie was sweating.

"But you no worry, I must to go back to Paris in June, so that I can preparate myself for the examins. I'm much missing now, but no matter, for you, EVERYTHING. It is a wonderous system in France University, yes? You no go to class, you pass examins, you oké."

Thinking about how Chloe was going to react to this, Annie decided (as Grandma would put it) to cross that bridge when they came to it. This day was March 20, and spring vacation began the next morning. Chloe would be gone for two weeks; Azzed and Annie would have the little house, and the entire campus, for that matter, to themselves.

What timing, Annie thought. She felt the pull of her double life so drastically for a moment she suddenly wished he had not come. No one but Chloe knew about Azzed. What was she going to *do* with him when it came time to study? When it came time for the senior parties? What were people going to think? The important thing, first off, was to figure out how she felt about him now, after all this time. Already she could feel the urge which had remained dormant for so long. She wanted him. But the Love he talked about so freely in his letters, that romantic word, she did not believe it really existed. Affection, compassion, understanding, (lust,) yes. But Love?

As they drove up the little hill of a driveway in front of the house, Annie imagined she was seeing it through his eyes, for the first time, and was struck by how pretty and quaint it looked. Her plants were hanging in the lighted windows of the ground floor, and the porch seemed so clean and white in the moonlight. The house stood five minutes from the main campus, and a hundred years away from dorm life.

"C'est ta maison?" he said, completely impressed.

"Yes. We were lucky to get it." It was Annie's pull in the Housing Office, in fact, that had gotten them the ground-floor lease.

Annie opened the front door and found to her dismay—something new and different—Falcon spreading generous lines on her glass coffee table, and Chloe practicing her disjointed twist in front of the stereo speakers. Azzed followed Annie in. Azzed placed cocaine up there with heroin, junkie stuff. She was worried Falcon would make a bad impression. But her friends redeemed themselves: The stereo was turned down to a hum and the lines disappeared in a flash up Falcon's nose.

"Wow, we thought it would take you hours to get back," Chloe said. She came forward and put out her hand, keeping a distance. "How are you?"

"Very well, and you?" Azzed said, looking at her flushed face and then furtively glancing at her big titties. Chloe backed away, into the couch, and sat.

Falcon must have been informed, Annie thought. Good thing that he's so open-minded for a Kappa Phi—not the type to pass judgment or to be easily fazed.

The way Azzed was looking at Chloe made Annie a bit tense. There was lechery, definitely, in his eye. But then that was usually the case when Annie introduced her male friends to Chloe. The thing that made it all okay was that Chloe violently rejected looks and passes from Annie's friends. She resorted to her distant, frosty number. Annie had to admit that her looks were not her fault. Chloe's hips were made to hold and comfort and her breasts were made to feed babies.

"Okay, we're out of here," Chloe said. "It's nice to see you again," she said to Azzed. In Paris they had only met twice, in passing. Annie thought, It will be fine if they give each other a chance.

Falcon shook hands with him and they left. Off to a party. Annie felt a moment of stark depression. Azzed was invading her life and now she was left alone to entertain him. Should she make dinner? Should she take him out?

He said pensively in French, "Chloe is even prettier than before."

"Yes," Annie said.

"And you, you are even more beautiful than in my most fantastic dreams."

With that he knocked her down onto the rug, catching her

before she hit, in a graceful dip. Holding her by the shoulders, he bit lightly into her neck. She felt like Little Red Riding Hood.

Chloe did not come back that night, which was a good thing, and Annie mentally thanked her for it. All night long Annie's head kept bumping the wall where Chloe's head would have been on the other side. And her rear end kept bouncing on her squeaky bedsprings. And then it was his rear end and her feet smacking against the wood floor. There was the sucking sound of their wet bodies engaging and disengaging, of his mouth against the secret hidden parts of her, then came his crazy wolfish howls and her more subdued, choking wails. It was basically bad enough to be the soundtrack of a very dirty porno flick.

And it went on for two weeks. Annie was supposed to be at work at the Housing Office by four every day, and every day she showed up late. The old ladies tittered, but Annie simply could not get out of bed. She felt insane. This behavior was abnormal, it wasn't *done!* She had no self-control. In the afternoon, when she finally had to get angry and yell that she was going to lose her job, he let her go. And it took every ounce of strength she had left to find her clothes and put them on. Once outside in the fresh air, she felt certain that people were looking at her. They knew where she'd been! Her face felt mushy from too much time spent in bed, her eyes weak from the darkness of her room (she was one for shutting and locking everything before the act), and like a mole she wanted to return to that private, enclosed space.

In the privacy of her room he talked about the life they would share in Paris. They would find a nice garret in the Latin Quarter, work like slaves, and fuck like animals. And during vacation they would go to Tunisia and stay with his sister who'd just gotten married.

"You'll see she's very beautiful and very intelligent. Everyone in my family speaks French. And then by the end of next year I will have my degree. I will be a lawyer and after that we'll be rich."

Annie smiled at all this, listening contentedly while he massaged her back, legs, arms. She felt honored beyond her wildest dreams that he wanted to share all this with her. In the spirit of the moment she could not bring herself to shatter his hopes. At times she pointed out that he was being overly romantic, that it was not certain that she would go back. But she never mentioned her Peace Corps interview, because she did not know the outcome of it, and there was no reason to crush Azzed prematurely.

When classes began again, Annie had to put her foot down. "NO fooling around when Chloe's in her room. NO staying up all night because exams are coming up." She got Azzed a job at the Housing Office, sorting future freshman housing questionnaires. The money was miserable, but it was better than having him mope around the house all day. Chloe adapted quite well to having him around, though she began to wear her sweat clothes to and from her shower.

And then one morning she came into their bedroom in her nightgown and sat at the foot of the bed. Azzed was sitting up, naked to the waist with a sheet covering the rest, while Annie was running around in her birthday suit searching for the underwear he'd taken from her and thrown from the bed the night before.

"So tell me," Chloe said in French, "do your mother and sisters wear veils? If Annie marries you and you move back to Tunisia, will she have to wear a veil too?"

Azzed laughed and laughed until he almost fell off the bed.

"Really, Chloé," he finally said, "you think we're still like in *Ali Baba and the Forty Thieves!*"

"Definitely! I heard that if a woman gets raped, the guy who rapes her gets to keep her. I think they should do like when a robber gets caught. They cut off his hand, right? Well, the rapist should have his thing cut off."

"That's a good idea," he said. And then they laughed together while Annie slapped at them with her located bra.

"No, I guess we don't know anything about you guys," Chloe said. After that it got much better between them.

Azzed had been there almost four weeks when Annie developed a low-grade fever and a constant pain in her lower back. She had the most terrible time trying to pee. She felt she had to go all the time, but once she tried the pain was so bad it brought tears to her eyes. After several days of this she confided in Chloe, who rushed her in a fury to the Cromwell clinic.

Doctor Daniels, who was definitely a dyke, told Annie that she'd developed a kidney infection. "A good thing you came in when you did," Doctor Daniels pointed out. She told Annie that these infections were common enough in young ladies, not too serious if caught in time, and definitely worsened by frequent sexual activity. Annie blushed crimson.

Doctor Daniels prescribed antibiotics and abstinence. Annie took the antibiotics but could not abstain, as Azzed would hear nothing of it, and her desire was not slaked by the infection. On her painful walks to class she had to wonder at herself. More than five minutes on her feet and her lower back felt transpierced by butcher knives. Yet in the horizontal position with Azzed by her side, the pain dispersed. Every time she walked to class she kicked herself for ignoring Doctor's orders, and every morning, afternoon, and evening, she ignored Doctor's orders again.

She went back to Daniels. Daniels changed the antibiotics, but the infection remained.

"You're passing it back and forth to each other," Daniels said, employing a judgmental tone.

"But then why doesn't he get it?" Annie asked, blushing.

"That's quite often the case."

Annie decided to send Azzed off to her grandparents. It was the week before finals, and she needed all her faculties. He was affecting her studies as well as her kidneys.

She called her grandma and explained that Azzed was bored.

"Hmmm. Does he go to church?" grandma asked.

"No, Grandma. He's Muslim."

"Well, they have their own kind of church, don't they?" she said impatiently. She became offended easily now that she felt Annie was more educated than she.

"I guess so," Annie said. "What are you getting at?"

"Well, it's because of Grampa, see. He doesn't like to go by himself, and me with my arthritis, I just can't go every Sunday anymore."

"You can certainly ask him," Annie proposed.

She packed Azzed up and sent him off by train the next morning. It was only a question of three weeks until graduation. She begged him to understand. Anything to make her happy, he said.

Grandma called Annie three times a week to let her know how wonderful this Az was.

"He's been fixing the fence out back, and yesterday he raked the whole yard. And listen to this, he took Grampa to church last Sunday and sat through the whole mass. Grampa's letting him trim the rose bushes, and you know how Grampa is about his roses. I'm telling you, you're lucky to have a boy like that."

On May 15 Annie received her Peace Corps Packet:

CONGRATULATIONS! We are pleased to inform you that your application has been accepted. You have been assigned to a post in Zaire.

ZAIRE! She'd be sleeping with the giant frogs and boas. Worse than that, Chloe brought a friend of hers over who had been raised in Cameroun. He told Annie his marching ants story. From a distance they look like a tarred road. According to this friend, the ants pick up and rampage through native villages, and everyone is forced to evacuate. One time they forgot a prisoner in the village jail, and when they came back the next day, only his bones were left.

Annie wept. They comforted her by saying Cameroun was maybe different than Zaire. "I'm going anyway," she sighed courageously. "I feel I just have to go."

"To pay for your sins I presume," Chloe said disgustedly.

"No, to put it on my resume, asshole. Listen, if I hadn't been sleeping with Azzed, I never would have gotten this infection. God's punishing me."

"Everybody gets infections."

"But *I'm* not going to get sexually transmitted infections in Zaire."

"You'll just get amoebic dysentery instead."

Annie called the Peace Corps Office in Washington, D.C., and accepted the post. She and Chloe got drunk every night for an entire week before graduation, and by the end of that time Chloe admitted she was genuinely impressed.

"My friend the saint," she'd say. "If I ever have kids and I die, will you raise them?"

"I most certainly will. But don't talk like that."

Annie thought of Azzed constantly. On the phone she told him it would be best if they waited till after graduation to be together.

After that she would be entirely his. She knew it would be better that way. There were too many people to see, too many good-byes.

At one Senior Week champagne party, Joe Gillan cornered her and said in a condescending tone, "You've changed, Annie." As though it were a great loss and disappointment to everyone.

"I guess I've changed. I don't care what you people think anymore," she replied.

She mourned momentarily for her old self. Whatever sins she might have committed in the eyes of God, she would make up for in Zaire.

She decided that she would spend two weeks with Azzed, and tell him at the end of that time that he had to go back to Paris alone. She would explain about Love, and her need to keep searching. Our roads must split here, she'd say. I have a mission—maybe in her pain and discomfort she'd quote—*To explore strange new worlds, to boldly go where no man . . . .*

Falcon

Spring Semester, 1981

At the Phi Beta Kappa initiation luncheon, Falcon sat next to his father. His family had invaded a table in a far corner of the posh Honors College reception hall. Falcon peeked around his mother and maternal grandmother, who were directly across from him, and was relieved to find that in his immediate vicinity, he recognized no one. He was surrounded by pale and wizened students who could have passed as their own grandparents; they were not the sort Falcon associated with, not the kind who spent school nights down at Vito's bar. However, the room was enormous, and the chances were he knew more people than just Chloe in here. He felt immeasurably guilty. Falcon, you are the quintessential hypocrite, he said to himself. His father slapped him on the back.

"What a day, what a day," he said. His father was wearing his best pale grey suit, the one he wore to all family weddings. Clearly, the relatives were having a blast at the expense of Falcon's big success.

The day the "congratulations" notes had been mailed out, it so happened, Falcon hadn't gone to his mailbox. Chloe came running over to the Drug House, where Falcon had been living since the fall, crying and laughing and ready to go on a three-day binge because she'd made it—she'd gotten Phi Bete. Falcon (absolutely *certain* as he was that he could NEVER be Phi Bete) pooh-poohed her, beginning with a tirade on professorial hypocrisy. "All you have to do is lick a little ass around here and they give you an A for effort." Falcon's study habits were of the closet variety; they did not comply with Honor Society ethics. "Don't you know that Phi Bete doesn't *mean* anything anymore?" he'd told Chloe. She'd stared at him in outrage, mouth agape.

Well, obviously it couldn't mean too much if they've voted *me* in, he now thought.

"Sit up straight, Johnny," his grandmother said. Falcon looked up, startled. His grandmother's pink hat had two plastic cherries dangling from the front of it, over her forehead.

"Ah, come on, Nanny," his father said complacently. "We're celebrating here."

Falcon seriously asked himself HOW in the world might he ever be able to move back home with them. He'd spent too many vacations moping through end-of-school depressions which hit him like flu, watching TV in their dark, paneled TV room. The hum of the air-conditioning *and* the TV had never been able to camouflage the worried whisperings of his mother and grand-mother, who flitted by like shadows just out of sight.

He had a month left until graduation, four weeks to decide what to do with the rest of his life.

He looked down the table at his grandfather, who had become completely deaf in the last year. Why in the world had they brought him along? And who had dressed the poor guy? A gold-striped *Saturday Night Fever* shirt with a wide collar and puffy sleeves hung from his shoulders, and he was being strangled by a yellow tie the width and length of a broken dividing line.

Dad was sitting back, exploring. The look on his face told you that his son Johnny was by far the best kid in the bunch. My my, he was showing his Italian pride today. He had not touched his lunch of spinach quiche and green beans, but the grandparents were devouring everything in sight. Lunch was on the Honors College.

Falcon's father had stopped talking to him the day Falcon had called to say he'd quit hockey. Dad, the great Providence College hockey champ (All-American) lost his favorite topic of conversa-tion. He could no longer patronize his son. Three years down the road, Falcon was now thinking, Dad turns complacent because I made Phi Bete. Falcon had called home about that as well. "Dad," he'd said, "I'm withdrawing myself from the initiation lunch." It was just too hypocritical. What would he tell Chloe? His father dropped the phone and Falcon heard it bounce on the kitchen floor. "LUCILLE!" his father bellowed. Falcon heard his mother's little feet running toward the receiver. A long, terrible argument followed in which his mother pointed out that he was the first Falcone to ever get such an award. He finally yielded and agreed to present himself and be a part of the great honor which had been bestowed upon him.

It occurred to him suddenly that the speaker who was now tapping at his microphone would make them all stand up and say a pledge or some damn thing.

And what a joke! The speaker was one of Falcon's megaphone victims. He stalked them carefully from the roof of the Drug House across the street. When he spotted a good one shuffling down the street, he'd begin. "DIVEST NOW!" After a year of oppression wouldn't it be a shock to them to learn that they'd voted this troublemaker into their honorable institution?

"WILL THE INITIATES PLEASE COME FORWARD," said the man. Falcon's father nudged and prodded him until he stood. Ducking low into his sports jacket, he walked to the very front of the room, and found himself standing in a line of students on a little stage. He felt ridiculous. When he stopped being so uncomfortable, he noticed that *all* the initiates were embarrassed, and most of them were snickering loudly at the speech the man was making. It annoyed him profoundly that he was not the only one who did not take this seriously.

He felt a poke in his ribs. Turning just slightly, he saw Chloe, red with fury, standing behind him.

"You rotten fink! What are you doing here?"

He shrugged. "They made a mistake."

They listened in silence to the speech which was about the work ethic, striving toward goals, brotherhood; it was nothing he hadn't heard a million times before. But next to him Chloe was glassy-eyed, listening intently as though she wanted to remember the moment exactly. The snickers suddenly seemed peevish and disrespectful. It was *nice* that Phi Bete still meant something to somebody. He craned his neck and searched the back of the room for his father. His father stood almost a foot taller than the others, and Falcon found him immediately. Their eyes met, his father nodded, blinking slowly. Falcon smiled. They had not allowed such communication in years.

* * *

For the next few weeks, while his classmates ran around being ridiculously serious in their three-piece suits, interviewing for every imaginable Career Development suggestion, Falcon caught a tan on Drug Beach, the Drug House roof, and laughed at them derisively. His philosophy: You're a senior once in your life. No point licking ass until it's absolutely necessary. It was the old story of the grasshopper and the ant.

However, his coke stash began to run low just around the end of exam week. With ten days left before graduation, Falcon was moved to make a trip to Hartford to visit his connection.

With this fresh supply came a surge of energy. He took the train to New York City, and arrived at his cousin Alfy's apartment with half an ounce and a three-piece suit. Alfy was barely one year out of UVa., living in Queens with three other ex-football players. They all hated Manhattan. The apartment served as a flophouse to half a dozen UVa. graduates and future graduates looking for work in the Big City. Falcon's coke sold like popcorn at the movies. He maintained his basic high while he drank himself into a state of shock trying to figure out which "field" would best suit him. First off, he would have loans to pay back, but he intended to maintain his life-style.

It didn't take long for Alfy's place to sadden him. These tough-ass athletes were no different; they were experiencing post-par-tum as well. Nobody wanted to face a nine-to-fiver, starting at the bottom of the shit-heap all over again. Alfy's place was their fraternity away from home. Sticking together made it easier to pretend the four-year college stint was not up.

Alfy worked for Citibank. He put in a good word at the bank, and Falcon lined up an interview. Banking did not seem a bad choice for the time being. Later on he might apply to business school, or to law school, or to the CIA—who knew? But he needed money, and becoming a banker would not be difficult for him, even if it did not comply entirely with his ethics.

The Citibank AVP who interviewed him was a hockey buff. Banking was hardly discussed, but Falcon was called back immediately for a second round of interviews with the Higher-Ups. He snowed them (it must have been his vitality); it was just like college. He was offered a position in the fall training program.

That night, relieved but not quite happy with himself, he indulged beyond his regular limit. He watched from a broken, bleached director's chair while the scene at Alfy's went from bad to worse. Falcon was King of the Coke and the others treated him with deference. Most people, he mused, were awfully respectful if there was the slightest chance you might give them a free toot.

The place was upside down. Bare mattresses were spread all over the living room, there were people doing the worm to the theme from *Animal House*. Everywhere he looked there was a can of beer, empty, spilling, full. The sweet rancid smell covered everything.

What am I doing here? he thought. These people are stupid. This way of living is stupid. He clumsily made his way to one of the bedrooms and lay down in the dark on a strange bed.

There was no fucking way on earth he was going to be able to maintain a job, the way he partied! These people here had no clue. He felt around for a phone and found one on the bedside table. Lucky. As usual. He dialed Chloe's Cromwell number.

"I just wanted to tell you that life HAS TO GO ON after we get kicked off Fantasy Island."

"No shit, Falcon. Where are you? We're graduating tomorrow, do you realize that?"

He hadn't realized. But what the hell. "The days have been flying by my friend. I got a job at a bank; I haven't been *just* getting fucked up." He thought, it's just a question of this one last gram. He needed conviction, and that's why he'd called her.

"I got one more gram and then I'm quitting," he heard himself say. The quitting part did not frighten him as much as the thought of running out, being entirely with*out* his fine white witch for the first time in years.

"What?" Chloe yelled into his ear.

"I'm serious. I have to quit. I wanna grow up."

"Listen, Falcon, you can drive back to Long Island with me and stay for a while. As long as you want to."

She was always offering. Maybe that's why he'd called her.

"Yes. That's good. Tomorrow, right? After graduation. I'm going to catch the train later on. I'll be there. Aloha."

"I'm glad you're thinking seriously about it. I'm proud of you."

"Yes." He hung up. Thank Jesus it's not an opiate, he thought. Heroin-type withdrawals I can't deal with. Beach. Sun. Jack Daniel's. Everything will be all right. It was just a question of reorganizing one's perspective.

With that decided, he went back to the living room and spread half of his last gram out on a mirror that advertised some kind of Canadian beer. It was a trophy one of them had won in a Fort Lauderdale drinking contest. "Help yourselves," he said.

Someone suggested they head into Manhattan. Falcon thought it would be nice to get away from the apartment. Later on they could drop him at Penn Station and he'd be on his way. He ended up in the passenger seat of a two-door BMW with four other guys he hardly knew.

They were looking for Saint Mark's Bar & Grill. They knew Saint Mark's Place was either Eighth or Sixth Street. In the back of the car the three were yelling, the noise carried onto the street; girls were tooted, cabs cursed. The avenue seemed deserted, but in dark entryways and at street corners shadows moved. They saw some fearless types prancing about in black leather draped with chains. Junkies scoring here and there. The Puerto Ricans seemed very much at home chatting out in front of their bodegas. The scene made Falcon's backbone itch. "HEY, MAMA!" one of the guys behind him yelled out the window. A Puerto Rican girl in high heels and painted-on jeans was crossing the street. Circling for a parking space, they ended up on Avenue A. Falcon said, "Let's bag this scene and head uptown."

"Ah, you fucking pussy."

"Okay then, you guys have to cool out," he said over his shoulder, soggy-mouthed. "This isn't UVa."

At Sixth and A they were forced to stop for a red light. A beat-up old Ford pulled alongside them and all Falcon saw was eyes and teeth.

The driver of the Ford leaned out. "Hey, mang!" He banged on his door as he called to them. "Get out your car, mang! I want your car! Give me your car!"

"Yeah FUCK YOU!" The guy directly behind Falcon stuck his hand out Falcon's window and shot the guy the finger. Falcon rolled the window up.

"You're fucking nuts!" he yelled above the racket.

As the light turned green the BMW screeched and lurched past the Ford. They were forced to stop for the red at the next intersection. The Ford came up and gave the back end of the BMW a good whack.

After that the scene went into slow motion. Falcon had the feeling he did not exist. The three guys in the backseat somehow pushed him forward and clambered out. The driver, too, had gotten out. Falcon saw the Ford vomiting Puerto Ricans. It seemed like a hundred of them were coming forward toward the UVa. football players like a pack of grey, starving wolves. It was suddenly terribly hot inside the car. Falcon, for some reason, got out. Make peace, he thought. It was insane.

They started coming at them from all directions. From the dark doorways and street corners, they came toward the BMW which stood parked at a green light in the middle of the avenue. The UVa. guys sprinted back to the car. Falcon turned back and made it to the passenger door just as the grey shadows hungrily surrounded him. One of the three from the backseat, Bob, Dick, John, he couldn't remember, had taken the front and was trying to slam the door.

"What the fuck . . . ?"

The guys in the car stared at him with blank terror. He could not help but turn to face whatever it would be. Los lobos were closing in. What a dumb fucking idea to go out drinking with a bunch of bozos. One two three punches in the ribs and he went down. The strangest thing was that the Puerto Ricans made no noise. Not a sound. Then they were gone. The Ford was gone, the street was empty again. His hands squeezed his guts where they hurt. It seemed utterly incongruous to him that his shirt was soaking wet. He thought, oh fuck, it's blood. I'm dead.

* * *

He saw his feet way down at the end of his body, covered by a white sheet. They looked like two pointed breasts. The silence remained complete. He seemed to be pinned down, though he could not see how. His vision was limited to those two, distant white feet.

They opened the door and came silently into the room. They

made a semi-circle around the bed. To his right was Joey d'Orta, who'd run out into the street after his dog and got mowed down by a green garbage truck. Falcon had watched from his bicycle, a little boy paralyzed by fear or maybe curiosity. To his left was his buddy and Kappa Phi brother Larry Dowd, who'd hanged himself sophomore year from a beam in the attic of an off-campus house. In front of him stood his Falcone grandparents, who had died one year apart.

They all looked healthier than he had ever remembered them. Joey d'Orta was still wearing his blue baseball cap, the one he always wore and had been wearing that day. And Larry Dowd, who'd shocked the entire fraternity, did not look manic at all.

"How you doing, Falcon?" Dowd said. None of them would come closer than two feet.

"What're you all doing here?" he mumbled. Or he thought he mumbled because he wasn't sure he was actually making sounds.

"We came to get you," his grandmother said.

"Come give me a kiss, Granny."

She beckoned him with both arms, as though to take him against her plump chest. "Come, Johnny!" she said.

He felt himself going toward her. Not his body so much, but a part of him that was light as a feather, and completely without pain. A dim thought whispered to him in passing that if he left with them, he'd not be coming back. He forced himself back down into the pain.

"No!" he said, and opened his eyes. His mother swam in and out of focus as she sat there where Joey d'Orta had been. She crossed herself as he opened his eyes, and wept.

Behind her a male voice said, "Please don't tire him, he has to sleep."

"No," Falcon tried to sit up. "Talk to me, Mama."

His mother talked to him in her quiet voice. He felt sleep returning, and saw Dowd leaning toward him on the other side of the bed.

"You used to have this morbid fascination about what it would be like, remember?" Dowd said. "You're not afraid, are you?"

"No."

He wished he had the strength to explain to Dowd that it was quite the contrary. It would be so easy to just up and leave with him. Leave the pain behind.

"Things. Are okay. I'm going to quit." He was too tired. "Go away, Dowd. Don't bother me now."

He forced himself awake. His mother was still there, watching him. He did not want her to hear these things.

He wondered if he'd convinced Dowd and the others to go away or if they would be back. He would not, he decided, let them take him away without putting up a fight.

Chloe

Fall Semester, 1980—Commencement, Spring, 1981

Things had not changed in Francis Morgan's office. His stacks of books and papers and letters still looked too tall and dangerously crooked. A stamp of the foot or a loud sneeze could easily have sent everything flying.

Francis took his phone off the hook and sat back comfortably in his swivel chair. He said, "I want you to turn that father/daughter scene into a one-act play."

Chloe stared on impassively, as though he might be talking to someone else in the room because he most certainly could not be talking to her. He didn't give her time to let the words sink in.

"Problem is," he went on, "which department do we submit it to, as a thesis? Because obviously we have to get credit for it." He tapped the clean, unused eraser end of a pencil against the top of his glasses.

"Not Theater, that's for sure. First off, you don't have the Theater credits. And secondly, my colleagues over there are not particularly fond of you."

"Are not fond of me!"

"That's what I said. Imagine I'm Cromwell's football coach, or basketball coach—whatever. And I ask you, a big jock star, to come play for my college. You say, 'Sure!' But then you decide in the middle of your freshman year that you don't feel like playing anymore. I put my butt on the line to get you in . . . I think I might not like you very much."

He sighed, stretched, crossed his arms above his head. "They had big hopes for you over in the Theater department."

Chloe opened her mouth to yell out a protest, but Francis chuckled and went on speaking in his even tone.

"Problem is, we have a play. English department will pass it off to Theater, French department won't want anything to do with a one-act play in English. So what I suggest is you switch to a University Major. They permit up to ten a year. You create your own academic program, *and* your own thesis. So here's my idea: Your major would be English, French, and Russian Language and Literature, with an emphasis on the Spoken Word. Your play, 'a culmination of years of study in the field.' "

"What the *hell* are you talking about, Francis? You think I have time right now to go write some fucking proposal for some fuck—"

"Gee, you girls do swear. It's taken me years and years to get used to this co-ed living, sex before marriage, cohabitation; okay, so I'm old-fashioned. But the way you girls have learned to talk makes the hairs on the back of my neck stand on end."

"What it comes down to is you got so excited about learning you spread yourself too thin. A little French here, a little Russian there, a little . . ."

"I guess we're supposed to decide freshman year what we want to be when we grow up," she said morosely.

"According to your application essay, you already knew; you wanted to become a Great Actor."

She got up to leave. "Why do you keep having to remind me of this shit, Francis?"

"I'm sorry," Francis said, putting out his arm to sit her down again. "I'm sorry. I didn't mean that."

He softened his tone. "You can stick with English if you want to. You can make up the requirements this year, no problem. But then you can forget about writing the play. Do you want to write the play or not?"

"Francis, I can't write a fucking play. Be serious, I don't have the first *clue* how to write a play."

"Well obviously you're not going to launch yourself off into this unsupervised. I graciously accept the job of mentor and thesis adviser *if* you accept (graciously) the job of writing the play. See, I know you can. You write like hell but your ideas are very good, and your heart's in it. What do you say? We can really pull a number on our friends in the Theater department."

He sat back in his squeaky chair and waited patiently.

She didn't know what to say. She wanted to tell him to go to hell and march out of his office, but then she also wanted to jump up and kiss him for having this kind of confidence (though she didn't deserve it) in her. She did not like to turn down challenges. But on the other hand this was no time to be heroic.

"Yes or no?" he finally said.

She said nothing.

"Okay, so . . ." He took a blank sheet of typing paper and rolled it into his IBM. He began to type, dictating to himself.

"Dear Dean Harriman:

This is my application for consideration as a University Major. As I believe Mr. Morgan told you when he discussed my situation with you last spring when I was in Paris . . ."

"You bastard!" she yelled, "you already talked to the Dean!"

"Shut up. I'm thinking here.

"I have come to feel it essential that I design my own major. My interest in languages and literature finds its focus in my own playwriting . . .

"You're planning to study Russian this year, right? Perfect. We'll throw a little Dostoevsky and Tolstoy in the original in here . . ." He typed on furiously.

"You're going to have to defend this orally in front of the board, you realize?" he said over his shoulder.

She barely heard him. She was thinking about a day four years ago when her father had pulled a chair up for her next to his, behind his typewriter, and had done almost exactly what Francis was doing now. He'd created her college application essay, forcing her to sit quietly for eight hours while he formulated her incomprehensible, disorganized, and short autobiography. He'd said, "I put you kids in public school to keep you near me. You've got some advantage over the preppie shitheads, but they've got education over you."

It was completely illegal, but he didn't give a damn.

Francis was reading aloud. " 'My thesis will consist of a one-act play—the fruit of my studies in the exploration of the interrelationship of language, literature, and life.' "

She thought, they created me. They'd made up an image of her, and she'd gone ahead and fulfilled it. To make them happy, to make them proud. Francis had taken her on freshman year, he'd helped her with papers, picked the right teachers who would be understanding of her deficient education. Fate had brought her to Francis. Maybe fate would write the fucking play, too.

"Francis, I've never heard such a crock of shit in my life."

She wanted to tell him all this. That it was time to stop playing now.

"Francis, forget it, okay?"

He ripped the sheet from his typewriter and handed it to her, turning hard and cold as that coach he'd mentioned earlier.

"Out of here. Go fix this thing up. Add anything you want to it. I want a clean copy of it in my box Wednesday morning. And go sit in front of your typewriter for a few hours. The play's not going to write itself."

She walked out with her head hanging between her shoulders.

She diddled with dialogues and scenes that came off sounding self-important and full of chintzy tragedy. She began to hate herself. What saved her from complete despair was that she was practically ninety-nine percent sure the committee on University Majors would never buy Francis's idea.

But the committee did. And three weeks later, with not a word written, she was stuck with a full workload from her classes, and her entire play to write.

She stopped sleeping. She waited for the idea to come to her in all kinds of states—drunk, stoned, coked up, coked down—nothing. She cried to her old buddy Falcon, who tried to be understanding, though he told her he could not see *how* she'd gotten herself into this thing.

One night it came to her, while she tossed in her bed in a state between waking and sleeping. It was as though her subconscious had been lying in wait with a net for the idea to come.

She jumped out of bed, made a pot of coffee, and wrote. It was the set that came to her, not the actual lines. But as she wrote she realized that other scenes she'd written in Francis's last year's class would fit in.

She envisioned the set as though she were a spectator in the front row of an otherwise empty theater. The stage is dimly lit. Three feet stage right of center is a bed set at an angle facing stage left. The head of the bed is raised two feet so that she has a good view of the pale man lying in it. He's got a circle of yellow light around him, around the whole bed. Then on the other side of the stage there are two ugly orange waiting-room sofas, one facing straight out, one set diagonally so that it faces the bed and her, in the audience, as well.

On this side are the sick man's wife and two children, boy and girl around sixteen. The wife is drunk and still drinking. Scotch. The bottle of scotch and paper cups are the only props. There's a round-faced, portly man there who serves as arbitrator when the fights between the mother and daughter break out. There's also a French woman, beautiful in a Morgan Le Fay kind of way. She's the best friend, there to console, but she's jealous of the mother and make things much worse.

The sick man can hear them, but he can't respond to what they say. He can only talk when someone is inside his room, within the circle of light.

Francis analyzed it scene by scene, and then oversaw staged readings of the scenes in the old theater. Chloe was using dialogues she'd written the previous year, between brother and sister, mother and daughter, rewriting so that they fit within the context. There was new material as well. Francis was pleased but he never let up on her.

She took the first completed draft to Clark Smith from her last year's playwriting class. He read it and asked her to meet him for coffee in the student-center cafeteria.

He told her he wanted to direct it second semester, have a production of it in the student theater. Chloe said she wanted him to play the father. He said he'd direct it *and* play the father if she played the mother. She said no. She wouldn't play the mother for anything in the world.

Clark went over some of the scenes he thought needed the most work. They drank coffee till it began to affect them like speed. He said, "I didn't know you were such a sad person."

She told him she didn't think she was.

"Why did you quit acting?"

She'd been in the middle of a thought about a particular scene; his sudden interest in this personal stuff made her uneasy.

Automatically, she told him what she told everybody.

"I have this recurring nightmare that I'm standing on a stage in front of thousands of people and I can't remember a thing I'm supposed to say."

Clark laughed. It was actually more of a snort.

"You and eighteen million other actors. That's cliché, my dear. Every champion high diver belly flops some time."

"Yes, but when I used to high-dive, my father was there to catch me in the water."

He stared at her. She stared down at her Styrofoam cup. She wanted to pass over this quickly but did not know what to say. The last statement had not come from her consciousness, and she did not want to talk about it anymore.

"I think," Clark sighed, rubbing his eyes, "that you're afraid of being beautiful, that you'll get used. And maybe you think you're not all that good. What do you think?"

"I could have been very good," she said. Her tone was not defensive, but distant and cold.

He was reminding her of moments she'd tried desperately to forget. There had been that spring night when they'd taken her father away on a stretcher because he could not get his breath to climb down the stairs. *Daddy I'm not going to the hospital with you because there's the tryouts for "The Crucible" tonight . . . That's okay, honey.* But then there had been her mother to remind her: *You ungrateful child.* Chloe had tried out for the part of Abigail Williams, and she'd been perfect. Because she felt rotten and guilty and worried about her father she'd poured herself into the lines, giving the reading enormous range. Gilbert, founder of the Sandpiper Players, her mentor, her hero, called her back to read and then called her back to read again. Two days later he told her in a completely flat, insensitive tone that he'd given the lead to someone else. Then he offered her an inconsequential part, one of the chorus of possessed girls. Burning with fury and hurt pride, she'd turned it down. *My father's in the hospital,* she'd told Gilbert. *I don't have time to waste on a bullshit part.*

And then her father had died. Her courage fled. She became convinced, *I'm no good.*

Her father had told her, "There's always going to be someone trying to screw you in this business. Look at Marilyn Monroe. But don't worry, no one's going to try to screw you as long as I'm around."

He had been powerful and people were afraid of him.

But then there were the Professors of Theater at Cromwell who hadn't made the big time, who were angry as hell and paying back the world by playing shark in their tiny Cromwell pond. They weren't all like that, thank God, but there had been enough of them.

Chloe's head dropped between her crossed arms. Clark slid his chair around to her side of the table.

"Listen," he said, "I'm sorry I brought this up. It's none of my business."

But she told him everything. Later she did not remember much of the conversation, just that she was speaking to her own wet breath on the Formica table.

And then almost harshly Clark responded.

"Did you ever think that maybe that guy Gilbert was trying to prepare you in some way? Make you see it in small, you know, before you came here and got smacked down big? Most of the time with professional acting it's a question of taking the smaller part and shutting up about it, because you have to love the *art*, not just the glory. I mean there is no possible way the guy could have known that your father was going to die."

* * *

She had run around all morning dropping off the final, irrevocable draft of her play to her three readers. There was Ozerov in the Russian department (he'd wanted her to write her thesis on Tolstoy but finally gave in—he was reading the play as a favor); there was Al Mariaux for whom she'd TA'd; and there was Francis who knew the play by heart.

She sat on the steps outside Francis's office and relaxed, soaking in the greenness of spring. Now that it was out of her hands she didn't much care anymore. She knew she'd care tomorrow or the next day, but right now it felt good to be rid of it.

Just then Joe Gillan and his new girlfriend passed and waved. The new girlfriend always smiled nervously when her eyes met Chloe's. She was an athletic girl with long straight blonde hair, a round face, and the waddle of a tackle.

New was rather pejorative as it had been over a year since Joe had up and moved out of old Martie Stein's room and into her best friend's, directly across the hall. It had happened just weeks into last year's spring term, while Chloe and Annie had been away. Chloe thought (self-righteously, she admitted) that Joe had been shockingly cruel to poor Martie Stein. She was still trying to get over it. But the hell with you, Martie Stein, Chloe thought. You deserve it in my book.

Chloe wondered as she watched Joe and his new girlfriend walking happily together, What could possibly have constituted his staunch morality? It had been fed to him like a memory is fed into a computer. He was able to recite his principles on command, in self-defense. He had used them against Chloe as a fail-proof safety valve when she'd argued with him and he'd felt he was losing the upper hand. His character was entirely equivocal and she did not understand him.

Yet there had been something honest and powerful in their relationship. There had been the long winter nights when her radiator hissed parching heat into her tiny room, and he'd been moist and comforting beneath the covers. There had been his voice that had talked her through hours of the blackest depression. She had been ill, passing through so many phases of grief, without knowing it. And they'd danced together for entire nights; then she'd been able to forget herself completely. And she had needed a staunch disciplinarian to replace her lost figure of authority.

It was a terrible shame, she thought, that Joe was so convinced of his own stupidity. He did not consider himself intelligent, and refused to learn anything. But he read people in an almost psychic way. They were drawn to his charisma and charm. These things had reminded her strongly of her father.

She watched Joe's body and his girlfriend's sink below her line of vision, where the lawn began to slope toward York Street. They were probably heading back to his room at Kappa Phi. For a little afternoon delight, maybe? First their legs disappeared, then their

behinds. His girlfriend's head went before his. Chloe watched the
tip-top of his head, a black tuft of hair, and then nothing.

* * *

They lined up alphabetically at the top of the hill, around the
ivy-colored observatory. The day promised to be a hot one. By
eleven they would be sweating out their hangovers, listening to
their left-wing politician speaker. The sun would be beating down
full force, trapped between the green hill and the red brick buildings of the main campus.

Down there already the parents and relatives were milling
about in their bright summer suits, picking their seats.

Annie tried to zip up Chloe's gown. Chloe shooed her away. "It's
too hot already."

"But my dear, this is a serious occasion. It's indecent to show
your undergarments."

"It's a T-shirt, you jerk. Leave me alone." They giggled. Last
night they had drunk much too much French champagne, bought
with Jack's 100-dollar bank check. "Your father would be so
proud." Jack's note had said, "Go out and buy yourself something
nice. Now there are two Phi Betes in the *family:* You and me!"

"Un peu de décorum, children," Annie said. "Azzed's never
seen an American graduation."

"I bet he's thrilled," Chloe said, searching the swarm of red
gowns for Falcon.

"Have you seen Falcon up there by the D's?" she asked Annie.

"No, as usual he's late. If he's up, it'll be the first time he's awake
before noon since 1977. My dear, can you believe it? After this it's
the hard cold world." Annie had been saying this for three weeks
but did not seem entirely convinced herself.

"Maybe for you. I'm going back to school."

"You damn refugee of life," Annie said, and hugged Chloe
around the shoulders.

*"Francis," Chloe had said, "what's the best acting school in New
York?"* She'd burst into his office on a determined whim.

"What, in my opinion, or for you?"

"For me."

He couldn't believe it.

There had been no audition at the Neighborhood Playhouse

School. The charming fatherly man with bifocals like Francis's had asked her questions about her interest in acting. Not what she'd done, particularly, but what plays she liked, which actors interested her. He listened intently while she told him she'd been surrounded by actors and playwrights her entire life.

Finally he'd looked down at her application and asked, "Your father was John Raymond the playwright?"

"Yes," she said, thinking they might discriminate but I am what I am. Then she told him how she'd quit.

"Was it his death that caused your change of heart?"

"I had no change of heart," she said evenly. "Never. I completely lost my courage. But I would not have gone straight to acting school in any case; my father wanted me to go to a liberal arts college."

Her autodidactic father who had gone to college one year on the G.I. Bill and had quit because they told him there was no future in writing plays—journalism, they told him—had insisted that Chloe go to college.

The interviewer nodded slowly. She then got heated up and told him about the Sandpiper Players. She'd played the little Catholic nurse in their production of *One Flew Over the Cuckoo's Nest* six nights a week for an entire summer and when the play had finally closed, she'd felt completely without focus. The man smiled and said that his sister, who owned a summer house out in East Whitman, had actually seen the show and told him about it.

"She didn't mention *me*, did she?" Chloe had asked, laughing.

The French horns and trumpets announced the beginning of the procession. Chloe lifted her gown and ran up to the F's. The seniors were laughing and chattering in the double queue. She found Maggie Feinberg and yelled to her over the hubbub, "Where's Falcon?!"

Maggie's head turned from side to side, she threw her arms up and shrugged apologetically.

The queue began to move, and Chloe ran back to her place at the rear of the line.

The horns by the observatory were echoed by a fanfare at the bottom of the hill. Once, at a chateau in France, she'd heard the commencement of the hunt. The clear sharp blasts had promised excitement, but there had been a touch of sorrow to the longer sounds, as today.

She opened the crumpled program she'd been holding and found her name on the High Honors list. Check it out, Mr. and Mrs. Gillan. All at once the line moved, and she was pushed forward. Sherryl Ray, her alphabetical partner, grasped her arm and led her gently down the hill. "That Goddamn Falcon," she mumbled. "That fool will *never* get his shit together."

On this tremendous day Falcon's parents would be proudly watching for him down there, and he couldn't even get it together to give them *that!* My God, what she wouldn't give to see her own father just once, for one second, seeing her walk by in her red cap and gown. She was suddenly blinded by tears and the world sank in a whirl. "My God," she said to Sherryl Ray, "my daddy's not here."

She had almost expected him to appear, maybe over her right shoulder, like Zeus showing himself to one of his mortal children. She had expected to find him down below at the edge of the crowd. He would be in front, to get a better look at her.

The crowd split like the Red Sea to let the seniors pass. She saw nothing but blurry faces through her tears. In her mind she had to imagine him there. In his blue Saint Laurent summer suit, with a loud silk ascot tie around his neck. That ridiculous leather satchel that he kept his notebooks and billfolds in was slung over his shoulder (she could see Falcon saying, What is this guy, some kind of fag?). And his hair was longer than the other fathers', sandy-colored and greying at the tips.

She saw him open the program and stare at her name. Chloe Daphnis Raymond for his dead sister who had been named by his dead father. He did not crack a smile, but his thin lips twitched as she passed him.

Sherryl Ray squeezed her forearm. Sherryl was half Indian, and half daughter of a Methodist missionary. "I understand how you feel," she said gently. "My parents are in India and could not come today. They're here in spirit," she nodded. "Your father is too."

"Thank you," Chloe mumbled. What a crock of shit, she thought, but made an effort and wiped at her eyes with the sleeves of the gown. Last night's mascara stained the cuffs black.

I'll never get married, she thought. Fuck all these ceremonies.

She saw her mother in a pale Chanel suit standing two people back from the edge of the path. She had that crazy look, her rounded eyes concentrating on nothing and then flitting away so that she would not cry. Next to her mother was her friend, a handsome middle-aged man in a beige linen suit. He wore a red rose in his lapel and a Panama hat. His blank expression made Chloe feel foolish. Last night he'd told her that all his suit vests had lapels. What the fuck does that have to do with me? she thought. You jerk, how dare you come to my graduation. She had nothing against him, really. It was simply none of his business and she did not like for him to see her cry.

Then she found Eric standing beside her. He forced himself not to avert his eyes when he saw her twisted face. "I'm sorry," she mumbled. They did not break down in front of each other, it was their unspoken law. But today she could not help herself. Eric did a strange thing. He walked alongside her, in front of the crowd, and held her hand. Then he kissed her wet face and disappeared as though he'd never been there at all.

She sat in her folding chair facing the podium and watched the left-wing politician preparing to speak. She was gathering her wits, breathing deep, sleepy sighs after her torrential cry.

The speaker began: "Yesterday at Yale's commencement our dowdy Republican ambassador spoke for two hours and fifteen minutes while his audience roasted in the midday sun. I timed my speech last night, and am happy to inform you that it is exactly thirteen minutes, thirty-two seconds long."

Chloe laughed with the others. She thought, This isn't so bad. What's wrong with me?

The speaker informed the seniors that their baccalaureates were not death certificates. "As one Cromwell president put it, 'If at thirty you still consider your four college years the best years of your life, Cromwell has failed you.'"

Last night she'd thought Falcon had been serious. She felt betrayed. He was a good, trustworthy friend to the people he cared for, but that did not include himself.

There was something definitely romantic about annihilating yourself over grief. Grief is something people like to hold on to. Why? she thought.

She heard her name being called out. She heard vague clapping and her heart beating loudly as she climbed the stone steps to receive her degree. She saw Francis Morgan among the professors standing on the podium. He was dressed in his black and purple ceremonial gown. He'd tilted the flat cap at an angle, and she laughed because he looked like a self-important Sir Thomas More. But then he winked at her. Only his eyelid moved on his stony face. She blew him a kiss and he turned stoplight red. Her skin felt taut to crack from the crying, but she laughed and laughed on her way down the steps. The audience was clapping for the next recipient. Her heart felt like a day full of sunshowers. In France, on those days they say "the Devil is beating his wife." The wife is crying but the world is happy. Poor little Daddy, she murmured, you'll never know. All this time I thought I was doing my work for you.

But it must be for me.

He had told her that she would outgrow him. That his absence would make her strong. Having survived the lack of him, she was certain now that she would never crumble again.